Catherine Gavin was
academic life, politics
at the German surren
was later decorated
France and Germany
acclaimed novels as *Madeleine, Traitors' Gate, A Light Woman, The Glory Road* and *A Dawn of Splendour*.

By the same author

Fiction

A Dawn of Splendour
The Glory Road
A Light Woman
The Sunset Dream

THE FRENCH RESISTANCE

Traitors' Gate
None Dare Call it Treason
How Sleep the Brave

WORLD WAR ONE

The Devil in Harbour
The Snow Mountain
Give Me the Daggers
The House of War

THE SECOND EMPIRE QUARTET

The Fortress
The Moon into Blood
The Cactus and the Crown
Madeleine

Biography and Politics

Liberated France
Edward the Seventh
Britain and France
Louis Philippe

CATHERINE GAVIN

The French Fortune

Grafton

An Imprint of HarperCollins*Publishers*

Grafton
An Imprint of HarperCollins*Publishers*
77–85 Fulham Palace Road,
Hammersmith, London W6 8JB

Published by Grafton 1992
9 8 7 6 5 4 3 2 1

First published in Great Britain by
HarperCollins*Publishers* 1991

ISBN 0 586 20908 5

Set in Palatino

Printed in Great Britain by
HarperCollinsManufacturing Glasgow

To Helen Lillie

1

There was an ornamental clock on the bedside table, the property of a landlord who had fled from the French Revolution into Switzerland. The gilt clock face was supported by two painted china figures, a shepherd and a shepherdess, the former minus a head. Marie Latour disliked the clock, because it reminded her of the guillotine which still stood in the Place de la Révolution, and because it ran chronically slow. Now it said a quarter past nine, which meant it was nearer ten o'clock in the morning. Ten was the hour when Marie was expected at the soup kitchen on the Seine embankment, where for more than six months she had been responsible for a first aid post.

She had slept late after a harrowing day and a wakeful night. She had dozed to dream that her young husband lay beside her, and woke to realise that he was on duty in the dark Paris where the cannon of General Buonaparte had cleared the streets of rebels. Charles was one of the soldiers detailed to disarm the populace: he was still in the Sections and still in danger.

Marie had passed again and again through a half sleep and woke to the clatter of cavalry and the tramp of armed men. She had risen to wander through the chilly apartment from the bedroom to the salon to listen at the outer door for her husband's step, and back again to look across the Seine to the Tuileries. In the former palace of the Bourbons the Convention was still in all-night session, for the Tricolore was flying from the roof. She could see it by the light of the watch-fires which had burned for twenty-four hours.

The last time Marie fell asleep was the worst. In the dream she heard the groans of wounded men and saw the steps of the St Roch church running with blood, but at last the nightmare slid into oblivion, while daylight broke on the sixth of October, 1795.

Awake, she ran barefoot to the bedroom window. Outside, the Quai Voltaire was empty except for an armed sentry at the corner of the Pont Royal. He was standing guard on the staircase leading down to the lower embankment where Marie worked among the homeless and the destitute.

The sight of him awoke the guilt she had stifled during the desperate hospital hours of yesterday. By rising to that emergency she had abandoned her friends: Citizen Vincent, an elderly priest who had refused to take the civic oath, and three nuns turned out of their convent when the religious orders were abolished after the Revolution. They all went from shop to shop begging for rejected food and stale bread to make into food for the famished – food for the body instead of food for the soul.

The thought of their need roused all the vitality of Marie's twenty-one years. She washed in cold water, dressed in old clothes, and dragged a comb through her short fair hair. The fire in the salon grate was set, which proved that the battle of yesterday had not prevented the concierge's wife from coming up as usual to tidy the apartment. Marie herself had kept the stove in the kitchen alight during her sleepless roaming, and the water in the cauldron on top was warm. She added more wood and drank a cup of milk for breakfast. She was torn between the need to go to the soup kitchen and the desire to wait for her husband, whom duty might keep away from home for hours. They had been married for less than eight weeks.

Making up her mind, she pulled on last winter's over-

8

coat and started downstairs. On the next floor a door was opened and closed gently. It happened every day, and on the ground floor too. Marie had seldom encountered any of their neighbours, but she knew that she was watched and so was Charles, a conspicuous figure in his regimentals. The Latours were bound to be objects of suspicion to the quiet, elderly inhabitants of 17 Quai Voltaire. Perhaps some of them, like Marie Latour when she was Marie Fontaine, had been sent to prison by the Revolutionary Tribunal. Perhaps, like herself, they had escaped the guillotine only by a stroke of luck. However it was, to survivors of the Reign of Terror any new arrival, anybody young, was a threat to their uneasy peace.

After living through six years of Revolution, Marie knew better than to question the concierge's wife about the other tenants. Questions were not welcome in the Paris of 1795, although Citizeness Camille Bélard knew everything that went on in the house. She was on the alert now, tapping on the window of the *loge* as soon as Marie appeared in the yard. Throwing a shawl round her shoulders she came running out to seize the girl by the hand.

"Citizeness!" she cried, "I hardly expected to see you! After all you did at the hospital, you must be exhausted. Everyone is talking about you – "

"I did very little," said Marie, "and who's everyone? There's not a soul to be seen on the Quai Voltaire."

"Ah, but in the shops," said Camille. "I was at the baker's and the grocer's in the Rue des Saints Pères this morning before eight o'clock, and people were full of it. Isn't the citizen lieutenant proud of you?"

"I don't know," said Marie. "But if the shops are open, then martial law hasn't been proclaimed. We're free to come and go?"

"Yes, but where are you going, please?"

"I? To the soup kitchen as usual. When you go up to the apartment, will you brew a pot of coffee? Lieutenant Latour may be home quite soon."

"Of course, but wait, citizeness. Maybe you shouldn't go down to the embankment at all today."

"Why not?" Marie tried to draw away. Citizeness Bélard was a thin little woman, whose greying head came only to the tall girl's shoulder, but in her excitement she had tightened her grip on Marie's hand. It gave her a feeling of being restrained, which since her long imprisonment in the Carmes she could not endure.

"They say there's no one there this morning," said Camille. "Except a sentry on the *quai* and a patrol down below."

"What in the world for?"

There was the rusty sound of the ancient doorbell ringing, and the jerk of the wire as Citizen Bélard, inside his *loge*, released the mechanism of the lock. While both the women watched an elderly man stepped over the high doorsill and came towards them. He was hatless and wore a shabby black suit. Citizeness Bélard drew a breath of relief.

"Here's Citizen Vincent, he'll explain it all to you," she said. "I'd better go up to your place and get started."

Marie went to greet the newcomer. The unfrocked priest was distressed and angry, but in his vexation he recognised the candour in the pretty face of Marie Latour.

"Citizen Vincent, it's good to see you," she said affectionately. "I'm sorry about yesterday, but I'm on my way to the soup kitchen now."

"Don't be sorry," said the man. "I heard you did splendid service at the hospital yesterday. It was a remarkable achievement – for a woman."

"It was nothing," said Marie. "They had no medical orderlies and no bandages, and I – well, you know I've had a lot of bandage practice lately! I did what I could until some doctors and male nurses arrived from the Hôtel Dieu."

"General Buonaparte must have been greatly obliged to you," said Vincent dryly. "I didn't know until yesterday how much you were in his confidence."

"What do you mean?"

"Yesterday morning, as soon as we arrived at our place, a patrol of soldiers arrived and told us to clear out. 'No soup for *sans-culottes* today,' their sergeant said. I walked across to the Tuileries to protest to whoever might be in charge. I found it was General Napoleon Buonaparte, a little Corsican on a big horse. Oh, Madame Latour, why did you bring that man to the place where we were all working together for our poor people?"

"I didn't bring him. He came of his own accord."

"In civilian clothes, and under a false name. You told me he was an Italian doctor interested in our first aid work. I didn't know he was going to command the government troops yesterday or order our shelter closed for good today."

Marie had rallied from the shock, and replied with spirit, "Were you in sympathy with the rebels, Citizen Vincent?"

"You know me better than that."

"Well, then! The general really did want to see our first aid work – "

"Because of what you told him."

It was impossible to tell a non-juring priest, vowed to celibacy, that Napoleon Buonaparte had come walking alongside the Seine one summer day because he was attracted to a woman called Joséphine de Beauharnais. Marie Fontaine had shared her apartment since they were in prison together, and Joséphine was afraid she would bring home some infection from the sick and ragged women of the riverside. Her admirer hoped to set her mind at rest.

"He didn't come because of me," said Marie.

"But why the civilian clothes? Why the assumed name?" asked Vincent.

"If he had come in uniform, some of those violent men looking for food might have done him actual bodily harm."

"Did you warn him of that?"

"No, I did not!" said Marie, stung. "Be reasonable, citizen! You know there were two mob attacks on the Convention this year already. Yesterday's was by far the worst, and it was defeated. My husband has been out all night making sure that all weapons have been surrendered. It's only natural that the government should mount a guard on places like the Seine embankments, where so many poor wretches go to ground. But they shouldn't close the shelters for – for good and all . . ." Her voice broke, and Vincent was touched in spite of himself.

"Well, well," he said, "perhaps I blamed you unfairly. You've done some very good work; I'm sorry it had to end this way."

"But won't the work go on?" exclaimed Marie. "Can't we move the soup kitchen and the first aid post to another place? Can't we apply for one of the National Property houses and begin again above ground?"

"No hope of that," said Vincent. "Unless you exercise your blandishments on General Buonaparte. Our work is to be transferred to the Hôtel Dieu and carried on by a doctor and his orderlies. The day of the volunteer is over, Madame Latour! Paris is to be regimented now, and made to march to the sound of the drum."

She could think of nothing better to say than "You've been calling me Marie." Then the rusty bell sounded again, the machinery whirred, and a tall man in a dusty uniform stepped inside the yard. "It's my husband," said Marie.

Charles Latour's duty of disarming the two Sections of Paris assigned to his detachment had taken far longer than expected. The first area was the Le Peletier Section, where the insurrection had started under the leadership of an officer called Damican, dismissed from General Hoche's command in the West for suspected royalist sympathies. Damican had gathered around him a huge rabble – some said twenty thousand – of royalists, Chouans from the Vendée, renegade National Guards and *sans-culottes* or "breechless ones" who had been beaten off by Buonaparte's cannon, and were now in flight or in hiding. Their sympathisers came pouring out of the hovels and tenements of Le Peletier to spit and jeer at the military, making the horses rear and the soldiers swear, while they reluctantly obeyed orders to produce and stack their weapons. It was seven o'clock before the job was done, and the soldiers were marched down to the Comédie Française, where a *soupe* was served in the foyer. Half an hour was allowed for the meal before they moved on to their second Section, the Palais Royal, where the local prostitutes, after a day of noisy alarm, met the men with ribald laughter and jests as annoying as the curses of Le Peletier.

During the half-hour's interval, two or three of his brother officers had told Lieutenant Latour that his wife had acted like a heroine in caring for the wounded in the Tuileries hospital. He ought to be proud of her. He said of course he was. But was he? The more he thought about it the more he felt Marie had been too eager to impress the high command, and presume on her rudimentary medical knowledge to push herself into a man's world. He had said to Buonaparte that he had told her to stay at home, and at that some of the men standing round the general had laughed. Laughed at him, Latour, as a husband who couldn't keep his newly wedded wife in order!

Back at the Tuileries his temper improved when he found that even after the long delay at Le Peletier his contingent was not the last to return. The men ordered to disarm the Odéon Section were still absent. That, and the award of two hours' off duty, sent him off across the Pont Royal with a growing eagerness to see his beautiful bride. He pictured her resting in bed after the hospital day, soft and warm and welcoming, holding out her arms to him in the gesture he adored.

But when he reached the house on the Quai Voltaire there she was in the yard, not beautiful at all but pale and drawn, in a black dress he hated and her old green coat, and with a stranger who might have been one of her

13

vagrant protégés. He said "Marie!" sharply, and she said "It's you!" as if she hardly knew him.

The sight of Charles Latour, scowling and grimy, with a heavy stubble of beard, took Marie back two years to the October day when she saw him first. Then he was a sergeant in the National Guard, calling himself Vautour, "the Vulture", bullying his way into her uncle's pharmacy and setting off a chain of events she still hated to remember. Then they had been antagonists, now they were man and wife and very much in love, but when their eyes met across the yard the honeymoon was over.

Neither was aware of that moment of change. Latour went quickly to his wife and kissed her hand, calling her *chère amie* and saying she must be very tired. Then, with a disapproving glance at the shabby stranger, he asked whom "this individual" might be.

The former priest smiled. "I had the pleasure of being a guest at your wedding reception last August," he said. "But you had eyes only for your beautiful bride, *mon lieutenant*, and hardly noticed two old fellows like Citizen Carrichon and me."

"Darling," said Marie reproachfully, "You do know Citizen Vincent, who was in charge of the soup kitchen on the embankment?"

"Closed this morning by government order," said Vincent.

"Is it though?" said Latour. "I'm very glad to hear it. I never approved of my wife working among those Seine-side wastrels. It was too much for her."

"Not from what we hear of her activities yesterday," said Vincent. "Madame Latour – Marie – I mustn't detain you now. Let me thank you again for all you've done for us – "

"I wish it could have been more," she said sadly, and bowed her head in acknowledgment of his word of farewell. But Marie was not silent long, for as he crossed to the doorway he heard her say urgently, "Charles, have you been at the Tuileries? Did you see the general?"

14

He thought the little Corsican had bewitched them both. He could not see Latour's negative shake of the head, nor after the door closed hear Marie's still more anxious query:

"Did you hear anything about the wounded?"

"I even saw them, dear. I walked right into the ward as bold as brass – after all, it was my own *chambrée* when I was in the National Guard – and talked to one of the doctors. Ten of the casualties were taken to the hospital at the Hôtel Dieu, and the other fifty are all doing well."

"Oh, I'm so thankful!" They had started up the stairs with Charles's arm round his wife's shoulders, and both instinctively lowered their voices. "That makes up for the disappointment about the soup kitchen."

"Do you really mean the place won't open again?"

"Not on the embankment. It's going to reopen at the Hôtel Dieu, under medical supervision," Marie told him.

"Well, then, what's all the fuss about? It's a good solution. I'm glad Barras and company had the guts to close that den of sedition under the arches."

"It wasn't a den of sedition!" Marie retorted. "And I don't think Barras had anything to do with it. Father Vincent believes it was General Buonaparte, and says it was all my fault for drawing his attention to the place."

Latour whistled. "Buonaparte putting down armed rebellion and soup kitchens at the same time?" he said. "He's quite equal to it." He opened their front door. As soon as he heard the clatter of pots and pans in the kitchen he stopped in the dark little hall and took Marie in his arms in such a close embrace as always fired their passion and roused her body to an immediate response. After a long kiss he buried his face in her bright hair. He was amazed when Marie pulled away from him and said, "Oh don't! I'm sure my hair smells of the hospital. I'm going to wash it as soon as I can."

It was a rejection which Latour resented, and a spiteful impulse made him say, "Smells of the hospital, does it? That's the price you pay for being a heroine."

"I'm not a heroine."

"Everybody seems to think so."

"Yesterday's heroes were the men like you, who rode to fetch the cannon from Les Sablons."

"That was in the line of duty. It was you Napoleon praised."

All Marie said was "I'll see to the coffee," and escaped. Her husband hung his belt and pistol holster on a peg in the hall, and reached the salon in time to help Camille Bélard carry a ewer of hot water into the newly tidied bedroom. He answered a spate of questions good-naturedly until she hurried away to light the salon fire. As he began shaving he heard Marie telling the woman to go home now, she would set the table herself. This was followed by the fragrance of coffee and the pleasant clink of crockery.

The cups and saucers were made of Roanne earthenware from Marie's old home in the Rue St Honoré. The gay little painted figures of the pattern looked cheerful in the thin firelight and did something to brighten a room in which the window was now splashed with rain. Through the misted glass Marie could see a new sentry on duty at the river stairs. The first man had been tall and thin, this one was short and stocky and wore a rain cape. So a military routine had been established already, by order, she was sure, of a general for whom no detail was too small, no organisation too precise! Marie was still smarting under Citizen Vincent's implication that the soup kitchen had been closed because of her – what was she to call it? acquaintance, friendship, association? with Napoleon Buonaparte. She was worried about Vincent's own future and that of the former nuns. She had never known where they lived, and could only hope that Father Carrichon, the non-juring priest who had sent herself to Vincent, would have an eye to their welfare.

If Marie lingered on those doubts it was to keep her mind off her husband's cutting remarks about the price she must pay for "heroism" and the general's praise.

Buonaparte's praise had consisted of two brief words "Well done!" – were these enough to kindle what appeared to be the jealousy of one of his loyal subalterns? She dreaded more sarcasms, but Charles Latour was amiable enough when he came out of the bedroom shaved and brushed and grateful for a cup of steaming coffee. His only criticism was that the bread was stale.

"I'll get a fresh *baguette* after the second baking." And Marie produced a golden honeycomb, an exceptional treat in such hungry times.

"Where on earth did that come from?" asked Charles.

"I've been saving it up, dear. I got it last week at the Courbevoie market garden, when I went out with Teresa Tallien to see her little girl."

"H'm! Tallien himself was very much in evidence last night; I suppose Teresa was safe at home in their Luxembourg apartment. I'm not so sure about your friend Joséphine."

"What about Joséphine?" asked Marie, alarmed.

"That new house of hers in the Rue Chantereine is pretty close to the Le Peletier Section. Some of Damican's runaways may have slunk into her stables for shelter until the hue and cry dies down. Carrying the weapons they didn't turn in, of course."

"Oh Charles, how dreadful! Joséphine will be terrified."

"I dropped a hint to General Berthier this morning, when he was taking in reports at the Tuileries, and asked him to pass it on."

"Then Barras will have set a guard round the villa," said Marie, satisfied. "Go on, darling, tell me more," and listened intently while her husband launched into an account of the hostility of Le Peletier, the jeers of the Palais Royal, and the brief halt for a meal at the Comédie Française. She loved the way his face lit up when his enthusiasm was kindled. Charles Latour was twenty-four, and after six years of Revolution and army life looked a good deal older. Dark hair and dark eyes added up to handsome looks, but as time went by his looks were those which had belonged for centuries to the family of de la Tour de Vesle. He would have looked his best in the white powdered wig and lace ruffles of an age gone when the Bastille fell.

"But darling," she said when the spirited narrative ended, "if you went from the theatre to the Palais Royal you must have passed the church of St Roch. Have they – did you see – how did it look this morning?"

He knew that on the day before she had seen the steps of St Roch, her own parish church before the Revolution, running with the blood of the rebels. He knew too, that on the very day he saw her first, Marie Fontaine had stood on the steps of the church to watch the tumbril bearing Queen Marie Antoinette on the way to the guillotine.

"A labour squad worked by torchlight to clean the place up," he said gently. "There's no trace left of the cannonade."

"Oh, thank heaven for that!"

"One thing I forgot to tell you," said Charles, "about stacking the weapons surrendered in the Palais Royal. We piled them up in the arcade, just opposite the old National Workshop. Remember when you did your obligatory service there, sewing army shirts?"

"It was only two years ago," said Marie. "Before I went to prison, before you came back. Of course I haven't forgotten," and she sighed.

"Cheer up, my love," said Charles kindly. "You're down-hearted this morning, it's the reaction from yester-day. And you're still worried about that wretched Vincent place, aren't you?"

"I'm worried about the poor devils who came to the Vincent place, as you call it. I don't know how they'll respond to organised charity at the Hôtel Dieu."

Wisely, Charles Latour did not reply in words. He walked round the table and kissed his wife, standing behind her chair and cupping her head in his hands, pressing his lips on her forehead, her cheeks, her mouth.

18

"Darling," he said, "don't try to do too much today. I want to find you rested and lovely when I come back."

"Are you going to the Tuileries now?"

"No, to my boring old desk in Plans, but surely I'll know what the next move's going to be." He felt her rub her cheek against his right hand, and at last her lips were pressed against his palm. Ah! that was what she wanted to hear: the next move, for him and for his general! "My sweet," he coaxed, "wear one of your pretty dresses this evening. I don't like to see you in that old black thing."

When Charles Latour came home that evening, he found a pretty, smiling girl in a prune-coloured dress, ready with her greeting kiss. He also found a bright fire, an oil lamp with a rose-coloured shade, and a supper table set with sparkling crystal and silver and fresh flowers. Which meant that his first coherent remark was, "You went out in the rain."

"Only to the flower stand on the *quai* and then to the bakery. Before that I was busy all morning."

"Doing what?"

"Having a sponge bath, washing and curling my hair, polishing my nails, and useful things like that."

She looked like a woman of fashion, not a hospital drudge, with her curls restrained by a fillet of gold satin to match the sash tied beneath her breasts. Her hair, too dark for flaxen and too light for chestnut, had been compared by Sergeant Vautour, in a poetic moment, to poplar leaves in autumn.

"You're beautiful, Marie," said a man in love. "Ready to hear some good news?"

"Oh, what?"

"I've got my promotion."

"Darling! Captain Latour, how splendid! Congratulations!" She clapped her hands. "Was it because of your ride to bring back the cannon?"

"I think so, for Junot's a captain too, and Murat's promoted to major."

19

"And the general himself?"

"Brigadier Buonaparte is now Major-General, commanding the Army of the Interior."

"The Interior? He wanted the Army of Italy."

"He did. It's been a long day, Marie, and it's a long story."

"Tell me over supper. My poor dear, you must be hungry."

"Give me a glass of wine first, and while I get out of some of my heavy kit you can read this letter. It's as much for you as for me."

She poured the wine, and took the little cocked-hat of pink paper in her hand.

"Who's it from?"

"Your friend Joséphine."

While Charles was in the bedroom, taking off his high army cravat and heavy tunic, Marie read the letter from Madame de Beauharnais. It ran:

Dear Charles,

How sweet of you to think of me! My little household was not disturbed last night, and General Buonaparte has placed the villa under guard, so I feel quite safe. My only concern is that I may have to postpone my housewarming party, at which I hope to welcome you both. I hear dear Marie did wonders yesterday. Kiss her for me, and accept the thanks of

Joséphine Tascher de la Pagerie Beauharnais.

P.S. Lieutenant Lacombe is a charming boy.

Charles came back to the salon. He owned no civilian clothes, and was still wearing his army breeches and boots. But his shirt was open at the neck, and the lines of fatigue were gone from his face. He grinned at Marie's air of perplexity, and kissed her.

"Is that a kiss from Joséphine?"

"No, from me."

"But I don't understand," said Marie. "Did you write to Joséphine?" She knew there was no love lost between her friend and her husband. Joséphine thought Charles Latour contentious and opinionated, and he thought she was insincere.

"No, darling, I didn't write. But I thought I should make sure she hadn't been molested last night, and I didn't want to go to the Rue Chantereine myself in case Buonaparte sent for me."

"And did he?"

"No, he didn't come near Plans today. He's got a new office at the Tuileries, in the Pavillon de Flore. I sent one of our junior officers to enquire."

"Lieutenant Lacombe. Is he a charming boy?"

"No, he's a spotty little fellow, about nineteen years old. But all's grist that comes to Joséphine's mill, and he came back raving about her. What did you think of her letter?"

"Typical," said Marie. "Absolutely typical. The fortune of France was in the balance yesterday, and all she was thinking about was her housewarming party. But it was very sweet of you to think of her, darling, I'm sure she appreciated it. Now let's have supper." She went off to the kitchen, there to digest the fact that Paul Barras, who was Joséphine's lover, had not set the guard round Joséphine's new home, and Napoleon Buonaparte had. He was not her lover: at least, not yet.

Except on the tables of the speculators and the war profiteers, rationing was as strict at the end of 1795 as it was when Marie Fontaine kept house for her uncle Prosper. She had prepared a soup of potatoes and leeks, a staple dish in the earlier household, a few slices of cold ham, a lettuce salad, with bread and the depleted honeycomb as a dessert.

"If I'd known about your promotion we could have had something special to eat, and a bottle of champagne," said Marie, when they were seated at the table.

"We'll go to a restaurant tomorrow night, and celebrate."

"But will the restaurants be open?" Charles nodded. "That'll be lovely," smiled Marie. "But now do tell me why Buonaparte didn't get command of the Army of Italy."

"I don't know what happened today, but I can guess. The Convention ordered Barras to lead the troops against Damican's men, and he lost his nerve before the rebels even attacked, and Buonaparte took his place *on condition* that he was appointed to take the field in Italy. That much I know from Junot, and he was there."

"So then?"

"Today the other Directors said Barras had acted without authority, and refused to confirm the appointment."

"The other Directors! They aren't even installed in office yet."

"Nor would they be, if Napoleon had lost the battle yesterday."

"What do you think will happen?"

"Barras might be persuadable, if Joséphine speaks up for the general."

Marie's lips tightened. "I don't think Napoleon will ever have to rely on petticoat influence," she said.

"You being an authority on Napoleon, of course."

"We were boy and girl together, or almost," said Marie, and rose to clear the table. Her husband jumped up and took the tray from her hands. "Don't bother with that now," he said. "I've something important to tell you." He threw a big log on the fire, dusted his fingers on his handkerchief and held his hand out to Marie. "Come and sit on the couch," he coaxed, "and listen to my news."

What he called the couch was a day bed with a velvet cover, once red but now faded to a dull brown, set beside the fireplace beneath a darned wall hanging which imitated the Bayeux tapestry. Marie settled contentedly into her husband's arms.

"I had an unexpected visitor at the Bureau of Plans today," he began. "My father's attorney, Maître Vial."

"The man who once told you I'd been guillotined with my uncle?"

"Yes, he got that wrong, thank heaven, and apologised for it at our wedding reception. But there was no mistake this time. He brought a letter from my father in England."

The delivery of letters to and from the French in France and the émigrés in England was slow and uncertain. Neutral travellers could be persuaded, for a consideration, to act as postmen, but neutral travel to France had fallen off considerably during the Reign of Terror. Fishermen on both sides of the Channel took pay for the delivery of letters to the secluded coves known to smugglers, but the letters took a long time to reach the capital cities. It was two months since Charles had written to his parents to tell them of his marriage, and no wonder Marie sat upright and said in excitement, "Charles! A real letter? Not just a message like the one that told you of your brother's death?"

"A real letter addressed to the Comte de La Tour de Vesle, care of Maître Vial, etc. Nothing *ci-devant* about my father the marquis!"

"And it was a good letter, darling?"

Marie was afraid of asking the wrong questions. She had come to realise that the contradiction in her husband's nature came from the long breach with his family when he ran away from home at the outbreak of the Revolution rather than emigrate with them to England. Six years later his only brother, tired of life as a gentleman farmer in Wiltshire, joined the ill-fated expedition to Quiberon Bay in which seven thousand young Frenchmen, financed and armed by Britain, invaded France on behalf of the royalist cause. They were defeated by General Hoche, and seven hundred of them, wearing English uniforms, were shot as traitors. Among them was Edouard de la Tour.

It was Charles's grief and anger at his brother's death which had moved Marie Fontaine to yield to him in body and spirit before their marriage, and since that time she had learned not to break his painful silence where the parents and their dead son were concerned. Tonight, for once, he seemed eager to talk.

"Yes, it was a good letter, a very friendly letter, with congratulations on our marriage and best wishes for the future," said Charles, drawing freely on his imagination. "Father said he had made a new Will in my favour, since I was now the heir to his lands and titles, but he warned me that the lands didn't include the estate in Wiltshire, because they were selling it and going to live in London."

"Too many memories in Wiltshire, perhaps."

"That's it. My mother can't bear the place since Edouard's death."

"Did she write too?" Marie risked the question.

"No, she didn't, dear. My father says she's in poor health, suffers from migraines, that sort of thing; she doesn't feel up to writing."

"I'm very sorry." Marie wondered, not for the first time, what Madame la Marquise de la Tour, who had been a great heiress and a lady-in-waiting to Queen Marie Antoinette, had said when she learned that her second son was married to the niece of an apothecary, a girl who had sold medicines and cosmetics across the counter of his shop. She thought it was significant that Charles had not produced the actual letter, which was probably locked into his desk at the Bureau of Plans. He showed me Joséphine's letter, he didn't show me his father's – why? Because there were things in it which might have vexed me?

Charles Latour was not too self-absorbed to miss the tension in Marie. He lifted one of her hands to his lips, kissing the slim taut fingers until they relaxed before he went on:

"My family left France so fast, Marie, just after the Bastille fell, while the king was still on the throne and there were no restrictions on travel, that they were able to transfer their fortune to an English bank, take out jewels and most of the family silver, even some furniture and a

24

whole retinue of servants. I wonder what became of *them*. My father doesn't seem to realise that the house in Versailles and my mother's estate in the Ile de France were confiscated as National Property and sold to speculators, and that his own farms were destroyed by the Duke of Brunswick's troopers when the war began – "

"But the land remains," said Marie. "Land is indestructible."

"I hope you're right, Marie. Since the estate agent was guillotined for complicity with the enemy, Maître Vial has had no news from Vesle."

He thought that Marie was too fond of making sweeping statements like "Land is indestructible" (much she knew about it) but the word "guillotine", reminding her of her uncle's execution and her own narrow escape from the scaffold, always silenced her. Charles Latour went on with what he had to say.

"However, my father left some funds in Maître Vial's keeping, and now he writes that I may draw on them. Very generously, I may add; we shan't have to struggle along on a captain's pay, my dear."

Marie, with her cheek on his shoulder, murmured something appreciative. She knew he didn't mean to give her details of the generosity: her husband, like her uncle Prosper Fontaine, believed that a woman had no concern with money matters.

"I thought a lot about it after Vial left," Charles admitted. "At first I thought I ought to spend it on renting a better place than this. The Quai Voltaire was a home of sorts, at least it was when we got married, but it has its drawbacks. The kitchen is awful, and I hate to see you hauling those great cauldrons of water. We can't receive our friends decently – " He was interrupted by Marie's cry of protest:

"Oh, Charles! Not leave our first home yet! Where we've been so happy!"

"You sentimental little goose," said her husband fondly,

"don't you think we could be even happier in a place that's not so shabby?"

"It's home," she said obstinately, and could say no more. Her girlhood in the Reign of Terror, when an impulsive word could cost a life, and even more her four months in the Carmes prison, where her silent fortitude was the support of women under sentence of death, had made Marie Fontaine incapable of speaking her emotion. All she knew was that here she had been for the first time in her life the mistress of the place, and she valued it accordingly.

"Well, darling," said Charles, "if you can put up with it for a few months longer, we'll stay. I came to the conclusion today that we should stay. I'd like to leave a good round sum of money with Vial so that whatever happens to me you'd be looked after."

"Whatever happens . . . ?"

"You know that if Napoleon gets his wish and invades Italy, I'll be with him. When he was out of luck himself and posted to Plans, he took Junot and me with him, out of Nice and into a dead-end job in Paris, and now he's riding high he's bound to take us along. An Italian campaign will be a long one, and nobody can tell how it'll turn out: I'd go mad if I thought I'd left you penniless."

She thought rebelliously "I wouldn't be penniless!" but she said nothing; she buried her face in his bare throat instead. In the grate an old log broke in two across the fire-dogs Marie had improvised from bricks, and a shower of sparks flew up the wide old chimney. To the girl it seemed a fitting ending to the day she had thought would see a dawn of splendour. Instead it began in disappointment and disharmony. Yesterday's victory had yielded to argument and compromise, and two happy people were vaguely unhappy, uncertain of a future which depended on the rising Star of Napoleon Buonaparte.

2

Next morning Marie, refreshed and happy after a night in her husband's arms, was glad to welcome a visitor bringing good news. This was a woman twice her age, who had been a witness at her wedding, and whom she had known for many years before the Revolution. Marie-Josèphe Beauchet had been the personal maid of Adrienne de Noailles, Marquise de La Fayette, when that lady lived in the great Hôtel de Noailles next door to Prosper Fontaine's pharmacy in the Rue St Honoré, and often invited little Marie to come into the vast garden and play with her own boy and girls. Marie-Josèphe was married now to a minor functionary in the Court of Bankruptcy. He and she lived in lodgings in the Rue de Courty, staunch royalists and devoted to the survivors of the Noailles and de La Fayette families – a living proof of Prosper Fontaine's maxim that the surest way to escape the guillotine was to take no part in politics but to live quietly in the very eye of the storm. Fontaine had not lived up to his own beliefs, and having engaged in politics of a very senseless sort had died by the guillotine on a July day fifteen months before. The news which Marie-Josèphe brought was that at long last the guillotine had been removed from the Place de la Révolution, now to be renamed the Place de la Concorde.

"Dear Marie, it really is the end, isn't it," she babbled. "No more killing, no more imprisonment! The Revolution has really worked itself out at last! If this is a foretaste of

27

what the new Directory will bring us, maybe peace with Austria will come next, and my poor dear lady will bring her husband safely out of prison!"

Privately, Marie thought this was carrying euphoria too far. General the Marquis de La Fayette, sometimes called the Hero of Two Worlds, had fallen out with the Convention, deserted from his army command and crossed into Austrian territory, where instead of being welcomed he was promptly clapped into prison. His frail, devoted wife, still suffering from her own imprisonment, was on her way to Vienna to beg his freedom from the Emperor of Austria.

From what she knew of them, Marie doubted if any of the five Directors-elect would lift a finger to support her. But she kissed Madame Beauchet's round chubby face, so often anxious but beaming today, and smiled agreement with the fantasy. Then she made a pot of hot chocolate, and while they drank it enjoyed the luxury of a talk about old times, about the games in the Noailles garden, and especially about Prosper Fontaine, who had left all his worldly goods to his niece. It was restful to be with a friend who was not disturbed by the closing of the soup kitchen ("after all, Marie, I've heard you say yourself the government should organise shelters for the poor!") or at all interested in the ambitions of General Buonaparte. After two days of strain Marie was calmed and strengthened, and readily agreed to go back part of the way with Marie-Josèphe and see the miracle in the Place de la Révolution.

They walked together as far as the Seine bridge soon to be renamed the Pont de la Concorde, and looked across the wide square at the place where the guillotine had stood. There, where the king and queen had died, and with them the noble of blood, the noble of intellect, the brave, the rich, the cowardly and the poor, the survivors were walking, laughing and buying sweets and toys for their children from the stalls which seemed to have sprung up overnight. It was a *jour de fête*, a holiday, and when Marie-Josèphe said she must hurry home to cook her husband's dinner, Marie kissed her goodbye and set off homeward down the *quais* with something of the good woman's holiday spirit in her heart. Common sense told her that a guillotine was only a contraption of planks and a knife and the machinery to make it work, which could be reassembled in an hour if bad times came again, but what if better days were ahead for France? If not for the passers-by, most of them smiling too, Marie Latour could have laughed aloud and even danced down the Quai Voltaire. She had never been a boisterous child. Living in the pharmacy, she had constantly been warned to be quiet, and only on the Sundays when her cousin Michel came home from the botanical gardens could she count on a few gentle outdoor games, like battledore and shuttlecock, with that demure apprentice. Then Michel had fallen at Valmy, in that first of all the battles won by the young Republic, and the thought of his death, and his father's, brought Marie Latour soberly home to her own front door. At least the guillotine was gone.

Her next visitor, who arrived as dusk was falling, had never been known for her calming influence. A resounding double knock announced the arrival of Teresa Tallien, who entered with cries of "Darling!" and enveloped Marie in a cloud of musky scent. In the dark little hall it could be felt rather than seen that Teresa, known as the scantiest-dressed woman in the half naked "new society" of Paris, was warmly dressed in wool and fur. When she ushered her friend into the salon Marie thought, not for the first time, that Teresa's beauty had diminished since the days when she was hailed as Notre Dame de Thermidor, the woman whose influence had led to the overthrow of the tyrant Robespierre and thus to the end of the Terror.

Teresa was only twenty-two years old to Marie's twenty-one, but in spite of expert make-up she looked much older. After an early marriage, and an early divorce, followed by imprisonment as an aristocrat, Teresa had saved herself from the guillotine by yielding to Jean Tallien, then the commissioner of the Republic at Bordeaux, who set her free. Their wedding took place shortly before their child was born. These adventures had been the prelude to more than a year of over-indulgence in food and wine, of late nights and libertinage, which had left its mark on her vibrant Spanish beauty.

She had lost none of her self-assurance, however, and exclaimed as soon as she entered the salon:

"Marie, what on earth are you doing?"

The chairs were covered with what looked like evening dresses, while on the round table was a clutter of hair ornaments made of feathers and artificial flowers.

"I'm sorry the place is so untidy," said Marie. "I was looking through my last year's wardrobe to see if there was anything worth keeping." She laid the dresses on the day bed. "Do sit down, Teresa. That armchair's quite comfortable with a cushion at your back. What magnificent furs!"

The visitor was wearing a long sable cape, of a quality seldom seen in Paris since the days of the court at Versailles.

Citizeness Tallien put her finger to her lips. "Just one of Jean's little acquisitions," she said. "Are you interested? Would you like to have sables of your own?"

Marie evaded the question. "I'm more concerned about what to wear when Charles takes me out to dinner tonight," she said. "All last year's dresses look as if I'd danced them to rags."

"Going out to dinner? Are you emerging from your bridal solitude at last, or is it a celebration?"

"A celebration of Charles's captaincy."

"Not of your heroism at the emergency hospital?"

"My heroism!" Marie's voice was sharp. "I'm getting tired of that word. Are people at the Luxembourg talking about the hospital too?"

"I don't know about people. Napoleon told us about it when he dropped in with Paul Barras about ten o'clock last night. They were both singing your praises, dear, congratulations."

"Thank you." Marie turned towards the sideboard. "Do have a glass of madeira and let's talk about something else."

"I mustn't stay long, darling. It's going to rain, and Jean gets furious if the horses are kept standing in the wet . . . Oh well, just half a glass if you insist. Listen! Why don't you order some new clothes from Cécile and tell her to send the bill to your husband?"

"I don't want to do that," said Marie, and Teresa shrugged. She flung the magnificent sables off her shoulders and accepted the proffered madeira, while Marie sat down with half a glass of wine for herself. "Tell me about last night," she said. "Did your visitors drop in separately, or together?"

"Together, and apparently the best of friends." Teresa laughed. "Why? Does that surprise you?"

"I heard the general expected Barras to appoint him to the Army of Italy."

"Barras can't do that on his own, and Napoleon knows it. That's why they were together. Napoleon means to keep him to his promise, and won't let Barras out of his sight until he gets all the Directors to agree."

"Will he get Carnot to agree? Carnot wants the attack on Austria to be concentrated in the north, and not through Italy."

"Carnot *is* the difficulty. But don't worry, I mean to keep Barras up to the mark myself." She set down her glass with an air of ending the topic. "Why I called," said Teresa Tallien, "was to make sure you were none the worse for your experience, and to ask if you'd like to drive to Joséphine's with me."

"Oh, Teresa, I don't think I want to go as far as the Rue Chantereine today . . ."

"I had a note from her this morning about postponing the famous housewarming party, and I think she needs our moral support."

31

"But it's getting late, and I must tidy up and get dressed before Charles comes home."

"What a dutiful little wife!" said Teresa mockingly. "But seriously, Marie, are you and Joséphine quite as good friends as you used to be?"

"Of course we are! I spent hours with her last Monday, trying to arrange the furniture in her new reception rooms. Paul Barras has done so much, I wish he'd given her a few more chairs and tables."

"I think Paul feels he's done quite enough," said Teresa with an enigmatic smile. "It's not his fault that Alexandre de Beauharnais sold most of the furniture when he and Joséphine were divorced."

"I suppose not. But the rooms do look empty. She'll have to do as we do here – fill the gaps with flowers and books."

Citizeness Tallien looked critically round the shabby room. She had seen it bright with candles and firelight when she and Tallien paid their wedding call, and not, as now, barely warmed by a very small fire and darkened by the wet mist rising from the Seine.

"The Quai Voltaire's a good address, dear, and this place could be made really attractive if one spent money on it. But who wants to spend money on a short-term rental? Six months, isn't it?"

"Six months? It's only three, and they'll be up soon. I was talking to Charles last night about renewing the lease –"

"Marie, why? Surely you could requisition a better place than this."

"This isn't requisitioned." There was a slight edge to Marie's voice. "We pay the rent the owner asked."

"Count Laurent Ovize?"

"That's his name."

"I knew the mean old skinflint when I was married to de Fontenay. I bet he sold his decent furniture and left those gimcrack bits and pieces for the tenants."

"They're certainly not as solid as the good Breton furniture I rented to *my* tenants in the Rue St Honoré."

"Marie, do you ever – " Teresa stopped short. She had been going to say "Do you ever regret letting your uncle's house and pharmacy?" but realised in time that it would be like saying "Do you regret your marriage?"

"Do you ever think," she went on smoothly, "of moving into an apartment in the Luxembourg? Two or three are newly renovated and still vacant, and now would be a good time for you to make the change."

"To the Luxembourg? The Latours at the Luxembourg, hobnobbing with the new Directors and important legislators like Jean Tallien? A mere captain in the Bureau of Plans doesn't rate a lodging in a palace, even if it was a prison only a year ago."

"Even if the mere captain is also the future Marquis de la Tour de Vesle?"

"The *ci-devant* marquis, and his father is very much alive in England, Teresa."

"Well, never mind about the marquis, think about yourself. Jean could easily arrange a requisition order for you, and the Luxembourg is where you ought to be, among your friends. In closer touch with the people who're making plans for the French fortune – "

"I thought it was for their own fortunes."

"It's all part of the same thing – to put an end to the Revolution. We miss you, Marie, with your quick wits. We need you when we're discussing politics, from the soup kitchen to the new Constitution – "

"Ah!" said Marie. "The soup kitchen. Of course you know about that too."

"We know everything, I tell you, and you ought to be with us. Think what a help you'd be to Captain Latour's career. He's by way of being a protégé of Napoleon's, isn't he?"

"He fought under Napoleon at Dego," said Marie. "I know he wants to fight again."

Teresa saw her advantage. "But, darling, don't you see

that's the best of all reasons for you to be living among friends? If your husband goes to war you'll be all alone here, day after day and night after night, without anyone to turn to if you need help. What if you have a baby?"

Marie thought of the neglected little girl at Courbevoie. "It doesn't seem much of a world to bring a baby into," she said.

"Sometimes they don't wait to be invited," said Teresa. "Do think about it, Marie! Talk it over with your Charles. I'm sure he only wants you to be happy."

"I'll tell him about your kind proposal, Teresa dear."

When Charles Latour came home that evening the old dresses had been cleared away, and Marie was wearing the one he liked best of all: the blue she had worn on the night in that same room when he first became her lover. He was sentimental about the blue dress and she loved him for his sentiment: nearly half an hour was spent in kissing and caressing and whispering before he asked for the news of her day. When she told him about the proposal that they requisition an apartment in the Luxembourg he was vehement in his scorn.

"I wish Teresa would mind her own business," he said. "What makes her think we'd want to consort with that Luxembourg riff-raff? Crooked politicians and shady financiers – "

"They aren't all riff-raff, Charles. The de Monniers are nice people and you were pleased when they gave a dinner for us – "

"They're all right – "

"And you were more than pleased when Barras gave our wedding reception in his splendid apartment – "

"Yes, I appreciated that, but it was a special occasion, it wasn't like going to *live* there – "

"The five Directors will be living there after their installation."

"Does that impress you?"

"Teresa thinks it would do your career good, for you to

34

be closer to the great men. Above all to Napoleon. Is he going to live there too?"

"No, Junot says he means to stay on in that wretched little hotel on the Rue de la Huchette, where he can live for three francs a day."

Marie sighed. "He ought to be in a better place."

"Perhaps you think we should too. Eh, Marie? Does the Luxembourg tempt you after all? Grand staircases and big rooms furnished with the loot from pillaged houses – 'acquisitions', I've heard Jean Tallien call them."

"His latest 'acquisition' is a sable cape for Teresa – Versailles loot, I imagine. And as for the big rooms I remember that only last year those same rooms were crowded with prisoners on their way to the guillotine, my own uncle among them. Every time I visit there I think I see his ghost."

Charles drew her close to him. He saw tears in her eyes and kissed them away.

"Don't worry," he said. "We're not going to the Luxembourg; I was only teasing you. I went to Vial's office today and told him to arrange a further six months' lease, renewable, with Citizen Ovize's notary. So we'll be staying here at least until April. *Now* are you pleased?"

She was speechless with pleasure. He told her to dry her eyes, put powder on her pretty face and fetch her *sortie de bal*, because the cab would be at the door directly.

"But you haven't told me where we're going," she said in an effort at composure.

"A place called Nico's Murat told me about. It's in the Galerie de Valois, the most respectable side of the Palais Royal – which isn't saying much."

Marie's *sortie de bal*, or evening cloak, was part of her finery of the previous year, and was made of dark red velvet. When the high collar was pulled up against her cheeks it shed a little colour on a complexion as smooth and delicately pale as the petals of a tea rose. Charles kissed the nape of her neck as he settled the cloak round her shoulders, and suggested going on to dance at Frascati's after dinner. Marie was laughing, as they hurried downstairs, at the prospect of the evening's gaiety. She was a true child of her city, where eagerness for enjoyment had kept the theatres filled even while the Terror lasted. In prison Marie Fontaine, alone and in the shadow of death, had never lost heart, and now, with her handsome husband by her side and her pride in Napoleon's victory over the rebels, she was climbing towards the peak of enjoyment.

The Quai Voltaire was dark, but the rain had held off and the stars were shining, while the Place du Palais Royal, by contrast, was blazing with light. That square devoted to pleasure had regained its tainted beauty since the days when Marie did her national service in the manufactory where the conscripted women sewed shirts for a French army short of uniforms, boots and even weapons. The theatre built by the Duc d'Orleans was as lively as if the regicide had never gone to the guillotine as Philippe Egalité, and on the steps there was a constant trading in illegal currency. The central fountain had been cleared of rubbish and was playing; the grass parterres had been weeded and swept. The arcades were lit by lanterns swung on cords which in the early days of the Revolution had been used for summary executions, and now illuminated shops and cafés. There were also a few restaurants, opened by chefs whose former employers had been sent to the guillotine as *aristos*: Nico's, said Charles Latour, was one of those.

"I never heard of it," said Marie. Restaurant dining was newly popular. A year before, when they were released from prison, she and her friends fell victim to the dancing craze which swept the capital, and the music of a good orchestra meant more to them than a good dinner.

"Murat says the place has only been open for three weeks," said Charles. "Even so, you have to book a table. Well! If this is Nico's, it doesn't look too showy."

The cab had pulled up outside a former shop with a double front, the windows covered by thick white lace curtains, with the one word "Nico" in enamelled capital letters on the glass. Nico had once been "Monsieur Nicolas", the valued chef of the young Marquis de Saint Maur who, although Marie had never heard of him, had died by the guillotine on the same day as her uncle, in the Square of the Throne Overthrown. Since then the chef had taken every job that offered, from washing glasses in a slum café to waiting at table when the New People gave their vulgar banquets, until he had earned enough, added to a lifetime's savings, to open the restaurant where he now stood bowing at the door.

"Be the welcome guests, citizeness and citizen captain," he said. "Please to enter."

The discreet frontage of Nico's hid the luxury of a very small restaurant holding only fifteen tables with pink linen cloths and bowls of autumn roses, the walls covered with pink toile de Jouy, and the subtle lighting coming from silvery candles in girandoles on the walls. Marie's first exclamation, "Why, it's more like a bedroom than a restaurant!" seemed to please Nico, hovering attentively, for this was the effect he had tried to achieve. While she studied the other guests, some in uniform and all well dressed, Charles and Nico held a long serious conference on the menu and the wine list, satisfactory to them both. Marie smiled approval of the final selection.

She had very little experience of restaurants, and in fact it was only since Thermidor that women calling themselves respectable were seen eating in public. She had dined once at Le Grand Véfour, opened in the same locality long before the Revolution, and once with Joséphine de Beauharnais and a group of friends at Véry's, where in famished Paris the menu listed thirty fish dishes and thirty dishes of meat and game, a horrifying contrast to the soup kitchen fare. Nico offered only a few excellent choices, from which the Latours ate a grilled sole from the Channel, a *salmis* of partridge and a confection of quince jelly. Captain Latour's promotion was toasted in a noble chambertin. They sat long over the meal, delighted with each other and with the anonymity of the skilfully created atmosphere.

It was after ten o'clock and they were getting ready to leave when two officers entered the rosy room, to be greeted by Nico with regretful shakes of the head. "Murat and Junot, of all people!" said Charles. "And Nico's telling them he hasn't a table free. Shall we be generous and give them ours?"

"Oh, yes!" Like everyone else in the room Marie was intrigued by the sight of Major Murat, instantly recognisable by his handsome face and his cavalryman's swagger. He had been a Paris celebrity since he brought up the cannon for Napoleon on the day of the rebellion. Marie, who had not met him before, watched as he and Junot greeted Charles, smiled their gratitude, and came up to where she sat with salutes and a jingle of spurs.

"This is an honour, Madame Latour," said Murat, bowing over her hand as a waiter hurried to bring chairs and carry away shakos and army cloaks. "I've heard great things about you; it's a pleasure to meet you at last."

"Why didn't you take the good advice you gave to me, and book a table at Nico's?" asked Charles. "I didn't know you meant to come here tonight."

"Neither did we," said Junot, laughing his noisy laugh. He was a captain now, but he had hardly changed from the fighting sergeant who had saved Colonel Buonaparte's life when the British were driven out of Toulon.

"What happened?"

"Let me have a glass of wine, and I'll tell you all," said Murat. "I've been talking till my throat is dry."

"It's so late, you must want something to eat as well," said Marie. "Do please order."

"But aren't we crowding you unmercifully . . . You're very kind, madame. The truth is, we 'dined' at an hotel in the Rue de la Huchette, and we're famished."

"We dined off a platter of cheese a mouse would have turned up its nose at," said the irrepressible Junot. "Eaten at breakneck speed, of course. Waiter! A bottle of your best chambertin, quick as you please!"

"I can recommend it," said Charles Latour, and Marie looked at him nervously. Dinner in the Rue de la Huchette – that could only mean with General Buonaparte, a dinner from which Captain Latour had been excluded. Marie, who knew how jealous he was of Buonaparte's favour, could only hope that he would hide his feelings.

"Was this a social visit to the Rue de la Huchette?" asked Charles when the newcomers had food before them.

Secrecy and security were not important in the Paris of 1795, except to the English spies with whom the city was said to be infested, but Murat had had time to reflect that his promise to tell all could hardly be carried out in a small crowded room unless his words were cryptic and his voice low. He answered briefly:

"We were there to discuss a trip to the west country which our host has been ordered to take."

"Ordered by whom?" said Marie. "By the present Convention or the future Directors?"

Murat concealed his surprise. Pretty girls – and Latour's wife was a very pretty girl – were not supposed to understand the workings of politics.

"By the Convention at its last gasp, madame," he said. "Our host is expected to meet a distinguished colleague, and discuss a project dear to the Convention's heart."

"Are you going too?" asked Latour.

"We're both going," said Junot. "He wants his own witnesses to the conversations."

Marie saw the frown which too often disfigured her husband's good looks appear on his forehead, and sighed inwardly. It was easy to guess that the colleague Buonaparte was being sent to meet was General Hoche, commander of the Army of the West. Hoche was the man who had ordered the execution of Charles's brother, and other Frenchmen dressed in English uniforms, for their share in the invasion at Quiberon Bay. Would Charles have wanted to join a mission to Hoche, presumably to discuss the project of enlisting Irish help in an invasion of England? Yes, she thought, he would, if it meant being in Napoleon's confidence. And the odd thought crossed her mind that there was a fourth man at the table, in appearance so much inferior to the other three. Small, thin, sallow, insignificant as he was in physique, the personality of Napoleon Buonaparte dominated them all.

Charles was asking how long the expedition to the west would last, and was told about three weeks.

"Then you won't be back before the election," said Marie.

"Madame, the election's a foregone conclusion – now."

"I suppose it is." Marie, who was watching them both closely, saw Murat's eyelid flutter for an instant, and Junot's answering smile. She thought of a way, a not very convincing way, to bring the scene to an end.

"Major Murat," she said with a light laugh, "please don't think me rude, but we really were about to leave when you came in. You're so cramped at this little table, I'm sure you'd be more comfortable without us . . . and then, when you're back in Paris, you must come to dinner with us at home. You too, Andoche, you're always welcome."

Murat sprang up, protesting that he was driving them away, while Andoche Junot kissed Marie's hand and said familiarly, "I bet you just want to go dancing!"

She laughed outright (perhaps she was overdoing the hilarity?) and said "Something like that!" Then her cloak was brought, the bill paid, goodbyes and thanks spoken. Nico bowed them out and sent one of the urchins who haunted the Palais Royal running for a cab. Charles Latour's face was in darkness, turned away from the light of the corded lantern, when he said,

"You don't really want to go to Frascati's, do you?"

"Not if you don't."

"Perhaps we should go home."

It was not eleven o'clock when the cab set them down

on the Quai Voltaire, and upstairs the salon was still warm. Charles went to the fireplace and kicked the smouldering logs to a blaze. He stretched out his long arms on each side of the chimney-piece, and his face was still averted as he said,

"Funny way to end a celebration. Why did those two fellows have to turn up at Nico's?"

"Or why did we invite them to our table?"

"I – I didn't know where they'd been. Nor that they'd be so full of self-importance – "

"Oh Charles, why should you care because they're going to see Hoche with Buonaparte?"

Marie had dropped into her chair at the dining table, with the red cloak still around her shoulders. Something in his pose irritated her: that martyred pose, bowed beneath an unjust burden . . . but now he turned to face her.

"Hoche? You guessed that, then?"

"It wasn't very difficult. But I wonder how Napoleon will enjoy meeting Hoche, who was Joséphine's lover when we were all in prison."

"I never knew that before!"

"You were at Nice or Entrevaux, I don't know which."

Charles waved his whereabouts aside. "I understand, in a way, why those two were chosen," he said. "Murat's senior to me, and he's the man who brought the cannon from Les Sablons . . ."

"So did you."

" . . . and Junot saved Napoleon's life at Toulon."

"Perhaps you'll save his life some other day."

Something in Marie's light, half-amused tone exasperated her husband. His voice was loud and angry when he flung at her, "Don't pet and coax me as if I were a little boy!"

"Don't behave like one, then. Charles, try to remember that Buonaparte knows perfectly well that Hoche was the man who ordered your brother's execution. It was to

41

spare you the meeting that he didn't include you in his mission."

"Buonaparte can do no wrong in your eyes."

"I don't believe those two men tonight had any idea of the Hoche problem. They were only teasing you because they saw you were jealous. It was so obvious that they were beginning to laugh at you. I didn't like that. I tried to head them off."

"In what way, pray?"

"By putting the vital point to Murat – would they be back in Paris before the election."

"Why do you call that the vital point?"

"Good heavens, isn't it obvious? Barras regrets his rash promise to give Napoleon command of the Army of Italy. He sends him off to Hoche, at Nantes I suppose, to get him out of Paris and *keep* him out of Paris, until the Directors and the two new Chambers are firmly in place. Then they can come down on him with the full weight of the new Constitution, and he'll have to go on doing as he's told."

"That's quite an exposition, Marie," said the man ironically. "You've become politically acute since you went in for the heroism business."

She flushed as if he had slapped her face.

"I think I'll go to bed," she said.

"Sleep well."

He opened the bedroom door with elaborate courtesy. For the first time without a caress or even a word of love, they parted for the night. In bed they lay apart, while the clock of the headless shepherd ticked away the ending of another day which had failed to live up to its promise.

3

It was their first tiff – a quarrel he refused to call it – and
as he dressed next morning in the bedroom which his
wife had already left, Charles Latour's mood veered from
regret to self-justification. Marie had been so sweet at the
start of their celebration, that perhaps he should have
kept to the dancing plan, laughed and joked in the spirit
of the evening, certainly not jeered at her belief in Buonaparte. It was a hundred to one she was right, and that the
Corsican had not included him in the mission so as to
spare him a meeting with his brother's executioner. But –
devil take it! – she very often *was* right, and no man could
listen to her little homilies without standing up for himself. She ought not to have said that his two good friends
were laughing at him. Or he ought not to have given
them cause to laugh. In a turmoil of mixed feelings
Charles went to breakfast, which was bound to be an
awkward meal.

But Marie came in smiling from the kitchen with a letter
in her hand.

"See what came by messenger while we were out last
night!" she said. "Camille brought it up just now."

For one wild moment he believed it was a summons
from Buonaparte.

"Why didn't the woman come upstairs and push it
under the door?" he said. "Haven't you opened it?"

"Of course not, it's addressed to both of us. But I know
the handwriting; it's from Citizen Guiart."

Guiart. The name was like a stone falling on the sudden bloom of hope. He broke the seal of the letter and read aloud:

"Citizen Professor Louis Jacques Guiart presents his compliments to Captain and Madame Latour, and hopes it will be convenient for them to receive him on Thursday evening at nine o'clock."

"Thursday – why that's tonight!"

"As good as any other night," said Marie briskly. "He's only announcing his wedding call."

"In this formal way?"

"He was brought up to formality."

"Do you know him well?"

"I've known him all my life, he was a great friend of my uncle Prosper. But you know him too, Charles, you met him at our wedding party." Marie was smiling, but a delicate inflection in her voice reminded Charles that he had conspicuously failed to remember Citizen Vincent. "Of course I do," he said. "He was the apothecary who gave you medicines and stuff for your first aid work. I didn't know he was a professor."

"He was Professor of Botany at the Collège de France before the Revolution, and he's still Professor of Pharmacy at the Collège de Pharmacie. Oh, I'm so glad he's coming to see us! He'll be able to tell me what's become of Citizen Vincent, and the nuns – the women who were his helpers."

"You'll like that." What Charles liked was to look at Marie's glowing face, so different from what he had feared to see after last night's scene. Darling girl, whatever else she was, she wasn't a sulker! When she stood up and walked round the table to give him another cup of coffee, he put his arm round her waist and drew her close.

"Marie, I adore you. Can you forgive me for the wretched things I said last night?"

"Darling, you have quite as much to forgive as me. Let's not talk about it any more."

He laid his head against her breast, and they were

entwined for so long that it was only by a strong effort that Charles muttered "I'll be late for the damned Bureau!" and tore himself away. Marie waved goodbye from the front door with a happy laugh and a call of "Don't be late for the professor!" But as she turned back indoors Marie was by no means certain that Guiart's note announced a courtesy call. She hoped it had nothing to do with Louis Rocroi, the young apothecary whom he had sponsored as the tenant of her own house and pharmacy. She knew Charles hated to be reminded of her ownership of property.

Nine o'clock brought Professor Guiart, punctual and prosperous in a handsome black surtout and a beaver hat. He was more ingratiating than Marie had ever known him, praising the location of their new home, praising her good looks and her husband's promotion, and finally praising her courageous action at the field hospital.

"People make too much of that," said Marie.

"Your uncle would have been proud of his pupil," said Guiart gently.

"His pupil – I suppose I was. Certainly everything I learned from him was useful at the soup kitchen, like the medical supplies you gave us so generously. Oh! do you know anything about the new first aid post, or what became of Citizen Vincent and his helpers?"

"Not about them, at least not directly," and Marie saw the subject was taboo. "The post at the Hôtel Dieu will take a little while to become – acceptable. At least, there were very few outpatients there this morning, when I called at the hospital by invitation."

"I was afraid of that," said Marie. She sounded so dejected that her husband said bracingly, "A hospital's the right place for official charity. I've heard Marie say so more than once."

"Yes, of course." Guiart's eloquence seemed to have run down. He twirled the stem of his glass in silence, started to say "Marie!" and then apologised to her husband.

"You must excuse the informality, Captain Latour," he said. "I've known madame your wife since she was a little girl."

"So she tells me."

"Marie, do you remember the day I came to call on you accompanied by your lawyer, when you were the guest of the *ci-devant* Vicomtesse de Beauharnais?"

"In the Rue de l'Université." It would have been impertinent to correct him: to point out that she was not a guest, since her uncle's legacy enabled her to share all the expenses of the flat with Joséphine de Beauharnais. In any case, it was none of his business.

"I came to you on behalf of the young man who is now your tenant in the Rue St Honoré."

Oh heavens, thought Marie despairingly, here we are at Louis Rocroi and his wife, and Charles won't be pleased. Guiart went on:

"You named a rent for your premises which I thought excessive – "

"But which was eventually accepted," said Marie.

"You offered to reduce the rent on certain conditions – remember?"

"To reduce it if you would take me into your own laboratory and give me instruction in pharmacology – I mean pharmacy. You refused, saying you had no time to teach young women, and your research assistants would object to sharing the laboratory with a girl."

"You never told me that, Marie," said Charles Latour.

"So I took Monsieur Guiart's advice," smiled Marie. "He said there would be no women apothecaries for a hundred years, and what I needed was a husband and a home. And now I've got them both!"

"Marie – my dear girl – " protested Guiart, "all that was two years ago, and since then you've more than proved yourself. I've come to offer my apologies, my instruction and a place in my private laboratory – unless marriage has stifled your ambition."

"Good God!" Charles Latour's oath was as fervent as a

prayer. "You can't be serious, monsieur. You can't suppose my wife really wants to be an *apothecary*?"

"Let her tell me herself," said Guiart.

Not looking at her husband Marie said slowly, "No, marriage hasn't stifled my ambition. But it has put some bounds to it. My uncle used to tell me that a boy had to study from three to six years before he could receive the certificate of the Society of Apothecaries. I don't think I could commit myself for three years, even if the Society would accept me as a candidate. But if I could study with you, even if it were only for a few months, I would – it would be wonderful."

Her voice failed, and Latour said roughly, "Nonsense! Do you think I could agree to your spending your days in a workroom with – how many young men? Ten? twenty? Teased and made fun of, maybe worse?"

"I spent my days with prostitutes when I was sewing shirts in the Palais Royal," said Marie. "I've a right to work at a decent job if I'm offered one."

Charles, almost speechless, managed to say, "That's sheer feminism! You – you've been reading Madame de Staël!"

Guiart, whom they had both forgotten, said firmly, "I'm afraid you're up against the spirit of the Revolution, Captain Latour. There are new women among us, believing in their own rights as well as in the Declaration of the Rights of Man. It may help you to know that my apprentices, all fifteen of them, work in my new commercial laboratory in the Rue du Louvre. In the old labo Marie would only be with Monsieur Robert, old enough to be her grandfather, and his juvenile assistant. Far more important, the skills her uncle taught her would be of use from the very first day. Did you know the former convent of Val de Grâce had been reopened as a military hospital?"

"Yes I did," said Charles sullenly.

"I've undertaken to provide a stock of medicines, pills, potions, cataplasms and so on, for the use of the medical staff. Marie has had experience of that work and could help at once, if you consent."

"Consent?" said Marie.

"Your husband's consent would be required, my dear."

"I'll consent to nothing until I hear more details. What are the working conditions in your labo, as you call it?"

"The men have one day off in every ten, like all citizens."

"I won't agree to my wife working nine days out of ten, not for all the doctors in Val de Grâce. She ought to be paid for it, and I won't agree to that either. The Comtesse de la Tour de Vesle is not obliged to work for pay."

Ignoring the gaucherie, Marie put in, "No, never mind the payment. I only hope Monsieur Guiart's offer doesn't include a reduction in the Rocrois' rent."

"There speaks the business woman, standing up for her rights," said Charles sarcastically.

"My proposal has nothing to do with the young Rocrois," said the apothecary. "Nor does it mean that Madame Latour would be expected to work the hours of an artisan. It would be easy to make a suitable arrangement." He rose to go. A man who knew them both had told him not to be too insistent. "Latour's an able fellow with a stubborn temper," he had said. "If you goad him into making too many objections he'll never give his consent. Don't set them to quarrelling with each other, citizen." In obedience to that man, Guiart said mildly, "I'm sure all this has been a surprise to you. Why don't you take a week, I mean a *décade*, to think it over and talk it over, before you decide? Captain Latour, I'd be delighted to see you at either of my workshops, and Marie, why don't you refresh your memories of the old labo before you come to work there? You'll find me in the Rue St Honoré every morning between ten and eleven. Now, let me say thank you for your hospitality, and *au revoir*."

He could tell by her eager face, as she curtsied to him at the front door, what Marie's decision would be. But it didn't depend on her, and her husband's goodnight was polite but entirely noncommittal. Charles waited until the sound of Monsieur Guiart's footsteps had died away before he said, with his arm round Marie's shoulders, "That was quite an unusual wedding call!"

She did not reply directly, but leading the way back to the salon asked why he had never told her about the conversion of Val de Grâce.

"Why? I didn't think you'd be interested in a former convent reopened as a hospital."

"Why not? I spent four months in a Carmelite convent reopened as a prison. Since you knew about the place, you must know where the patients are to come from. But then you never tell me anything about your work."

It was true enough, but not for reasons of security. Captain Latour honestly believed that the female mind was incapable of understanding the minute details of army organisation, but in this case she deserved to know.

"There are only fifty patients in Val de Grâce at present," he said. "They're the men wounded in the cannonade a few days ago. You cared for some of them. All of them wore your bandages in the field hospital, for the first night at any rate."

Marie's face was white. "Those poor fellows were moved from the Tuileries?"

"They couldn't be kept there indefinitely. The Tuileries is the seat of the Convention, not an emergency ward. Don't look so dismayed, Marie. They're getting professional attention now."

"I wish I could help to care for them still."

"Oh no! You've done your part. You mustn't get involved any further."

"You think the right place for me is sewing army shirts?"

"I think the right place for you is in our home," said Charles, and gathered her in his arms. "Darling, only the other day you told me how happy you were here, how you didn't want to leave the Quai Voltaire, and so on.

49

Now you seem to want to spend hours – days – weeks – grubbing in an apothecary's den. Can't you really be happy here with me?"

"I *am* happy," said Marie. She lifted her lovely face, softened by emotion, for his kiss. There was nothing soft in the voice which said,

"But I want the apothecary's den too!"

Very little more was said about Professor Guiart's proposal. Charles and Marie were both under strain, and went without delay to bed, where they found a happy solution to their problems. Charles awoke feeling that the preparation of medicines for an army hospital gave point to Marie's laboratory work and would look well on his own record, and that when he was satisfied on certain details he might gradually withdraw his opposition. He said nothing of this to Marie, and she said nothing to him about another visitor she expected that day. They were passionate lovers still, but now there was less confidence between them.

Marie's visitor was an elderly man, the clerk of her lawyer, Etienne Favart. Maître Favart had twice asked her to marry him, and had taken her refusal with good grace, but he had protested angrily when she promised to marry a soldier without a franc to settle upon her. They had not met since Marie's wedding, and it was the clerk who brought the rent paid quarterly by the Rocrois, and obtained her receipt.

"Madame Rocroi brought the rent to our office herself this time," volunteered the clerk. "Her husband is deeply engaged in some research."

"Indeed!"

"The young lady asked particularly for you," the clerk continued. "She seems to regret that you've never been to call on them."

"They were guests at our wedding party," said Marie, "and I never meant to be an intrusive landlady."

"Quite so," said the man, and took his discreet departure. Marie locked the substantial sum he had brought into a small safe which once belonged to her uncle, put on her old green coat, which Camille Bélard had brushed and sponged with ammonia, and set off across the Tuileries garden to the Rue Royale.

Two hours later Charles found her studying some swatches of soft woollen material spread out on the dining table.

"What have you got there?" he asked.

"Maître Favart's clerk was here," she said casually, "so I'm in funds again. I went to Madame Cécile to order a winter dress and coat, and these are samples for you to choose the colours you like best."

"You're very sweet, Marie, but before you go any further let's be clear on one thing: I'm in funds too, you know, and whatever you order, I'm paying the bill. I haven't bought you so much as a pair of gloves since we were married. So now's the time to begin."

"Dear Charles!" Marie thought, as she kissed him, how much pleasanter it was to receive his generosity than do as Teresa Tallien had suggested – "tell your dressmaker to send the bill to your husband." It was pleasant, too, to discuss styles and shades with him, and hear his definite opinion that blue was her colour. She should get a darker blue than the dress he liked so much, and also, what do you call it, something thicker than the flimsy stuff the girls were wearing last winter which started enough cases of pneumonia to fill every bed in Val de Grâce. Whereupon Marie produced one purchase brought home with her, a cap made of fox fur from the Auvergne, a sure protection against cold in the head.

"It suits you, Marie. Better than the red cap of liberty."

"My only headgear when I knew you first." It was good to be able to make jokes about the hardships of times past, and they both enjoyed an evening when war and politics were ignored. It was nearly over when Charles Latour said confidently:

"I thought you'd go posting off to Guiart's laboratory today, instead of your dressmaker's!"

"Oh, there's no hurry. I thought the day after tomorrow would be time enough. I *would* like to see the old place, though. Sure you won't come with me? He invited us both, you know."

"It isn't in my line, Marie. But you go and then you can tell me all about it. Where exactly is his place in the Rue St Honoré?"

"At the far end – near the Rue du Pont Neuf."

"That's too far for you to walk. I'll get you a cab from the new livery on the Rue de Bourbon."

All this was much better than Marie had expected, and she was in high spirits two mornings later, when she set out in the hired cab through less familiar streets. Down the Quai de Conti, past the house where Marie and Charles had met after their separation of nearly two years, and across the Pont Neuf went the cab, and north to the Rue St Honoré and what she had been accustomed to call "Monsieur Guiart's *officine*." The people in the streets seemed quieter, and perhaps because there were more troops on patrol, there were far fewer beggars, and no speechifying at the street corners. Nobody could have told that this was the first day of the ballot for the Constitution of the Year Three, that controversial issue which only a week earlier had led to the armed rebellion defeated by General Buonaparte. Voting was to go on for nine days, and would be the privilege of only 30,000 electors in the whole of France. If the Constitution passed, it would bring in a new era of property and liberty, and the days of the Terror and the *sans-culottes* would indeed be over.

All seemed set fair for the future. But to a child of the Revolution the calm could be deceptive. Paris was like a volcano, with the lava of unrest always seething under the thin crust of conformity.

When the cab set her down Marie stood still for a moment, looking westward up the street she knew so well. Her own pharmacy, now occupied by the young Rocrois, was too far away to be seen, but she could look beyond the gates of the Palais Royal to the church of St Roch. Where a week ago she had seen the steps drenched with the blood of the wounded and dying rebels, and where two years earlier, almost to the day, she had seen Queen Marie Antoinette in her bloodstained dress in the tumbril carrying her to the guillotine. Images of blood everywhere! With a shudder Marie opened the door of the old *officine* and stepped into the atmosphere of the peaceful past.

It was a tangible atmosphere, compounded of peppermint, lavender, ammonia and camphor, flavoured with wood smoke from a low hearth on which an extract kettle was simmering, presided over by a shock-headed boy. On the long counter stood an iron mortar in which the pestle was being wielded by an elderly man with a long grey beard, who stopped work immediately and held out both hands to the visitor.

"Mademoiselle Marie! Or should I say, madame, for you're a married lady now! Be the welcome guest! The *patron* told us you might honour us with a visit one of these days."

"And here I am," said Marie. "Citizen Robert, it's good to see you. It's been a long time since we met."

"A long time since you were a little girl bringing a basketful of medicines prepared by your good uncle. Ah, dear me, that poor Citizen Fontaine! What a death to die – what awful times we've lived in!"

"But we've survived them, we must think of that," said Marie. "Where is Monsieur Guiart? He told me he was always here by ten."

"*Le patron's* very punctual. You know that, madame, but he may have been detained at the Rue du Louvre. Did he tell you we'd gone commercial now? No more retail trade! Everything's under government contract here."

"So I understand." Marie's experienced eyes, taking in the equipment of "the old labo", had noted the sink and the litre measures, which were fixtures, and how few majolica pots remained on the wooden shelves, half obscured by something which was new. The tricolore cockade, of course had hung there for years, but Guiart had added the device borne by the Society of Apothecaries since 1629, a pharmacist's balance and two galleons, representing the ships which brought drugs to Spain from distant lands. It was as good a testimonial to respectability as any inquisitive revolutionary could expect to see.

"Bonjour, Marie!" Citizen Guiart was there, smiling and shaking hands, opening a door behind the counter and ushering Marie into his private room, and pausing for a moment to say "Jean-Claude! Run round to the Rue du Louvre and bring back the package I left there!" Marie's guess was that the shock-headed youth was not so much a laboratory assistant as a general messenger.

In the inner sanctum nothing had changed. Marie had seen, though only once before, the table-desk and the two mahogany chairs, the dun-coloured carpet and the walls lined with books. Motioning her to a seat, Guiart said at once:

"Well, my dear, what news have you brought? Has your husband given his consent to your studies?"

"Not yet, monsieur." Was she mistaken, or was there a shade of relief in the man's grimace? "But I think he will give it if I don't badger him."

"Captain Latour isn't a man I should care to badger," said Guiart. "His attitude was hostile two days ago. What makes you think he's changed his mind?"

"The last thing he said to me this morning was, 'Better go and find out what you're letting yourself in for.' That sounded positive, don't you think?"

"I do. And you, Marie? Are you positive that you want to commit yourself to a course of higher study?"

"Study?"

"Instruction from me will involve book work, you

54

know, as well as the preparation of medicines for the Val de Grâce hospital."

"What you said about Val de Grâce was what had a real effect upon Charles."

"I thought it might. But you must understand this, Marie: I know exactly how your uncle taught you, when you had to take his poor son's place. He taught you by example. You have neat fingers and you copied him exactly. It takes more than that to make a good apprentice apothecary." Marie nodded. "Fontaine had an excellent pharmaceutical library. Did you keep it?"

"I have all his books. Baumé, Sage, Macquier, Lavoisier, Gérard. I'm afraid I haven't read any of them. I've tried Voltaire and Diderot, but . . ."

"I didn't like to tell him I preferred to read romances," Marie told her husband much later in the day.

"I haven't seen any romantic novels in this house."

"Because I've been living my romance," she said with a smile that touched him to the heart.

"So what exactly does he propose for you?"

"Theoretical work in the mornings, practical in the afternoons."

"It's too much!" said Charles violently. "You'll make yourself ill."

"No, I won't. Please, Charles, do agree to my giving it a trial. Think, if you go to war I shall be all alone and the people at the labo will be company for me – "

"Fine company! Two old men and an errand boy, and you cooped up for hours in a smelly – "

"Den," said his wife.

"Yes, a den, the way you describe it. I swear I don't understand you, Marie, you're not like any girl I ever knew – "

"Isn't that why you married me?"

"I suppose it is." He took her in his arms. "Tell me the truth, Marie. *Why* do you want to work with Citizen Guiart? I can see it means a lot to you, but why?"

Marie realised that her husband's reactions were natural

to a man whose only idea of women's work had been his mother's graceful performance as a lady-in-waiting to Queen Marie Antoinette. She searched in her memory for any argument which should convince him.

"Charles, do you remember the night you got your father's letter, you told me you'd been worrying about going to war in Italy and leaving me penniless?"

"Yes, I remember, but thank heaven there's no question of that now – "

"No, but money wouldn't save me from being all alone here, and at the labo there'd be company."

She felt rather than heard him sigh. He had hoped, in the third month of their marriage, that Marie would have happy news for him, and that the prospect of a child would assure her of the best company of all. The thought of becoming a father had increasingly appealed to him since he knew he would inherit his father's title. The Revolution had made it an empty title, but it might not always be so. There might be a reversal of the French fortune, and yet another Constitution might restore the old nobility.

He could say nothing of all this to Marie, nor wish her to be left alone with his child if by ill luck he fell in battle. All he said was, "That's not a good enough reason, Marie. Tell me the truth!"

"Well then!" she said, and raised her dark blue eyes to his, "It would be my way of going to war."

4

General Buonaparte was not a man to be manipulated. He was quite aware that his mission to General Hoche had been arranged to get him away from Barras, who had rashly promised him the Army of Italy, and he was also aware that many Deputies wished him to remain in Paris if another riot should break out on the final election day. He had no intention of going as far from the capital as Nantes, and sent couriers ahead to invite Hoche to meet him in Tours.

When they returned to Paris Major Murat told an interested circle of officers that "our general" had come down hard on both the government proposals: to harass England by creating a revolution inside Ireland, or to invade England across the Channel. "He warned Hoche in so many words that 'wherever there is water to float a ship we are sure to find the English in our way'," said Murat, and heard a groan of "Defeatism!"

"Not a bit of it," retorted Murat. "Hoche himself isn't keen on a joint operation with the navy. 'Haughty ignorance and foolish vanity, that's the French Navy for you,' said Hoche."

"So the two were more or less of one mind?"

"Rather less than more after Napoleon kindly advised Hoche to show more clemency to the wretched peasants he's been smashing in the west."

"Napoleon being a model of forbearance himself," said someone, and there was a general laugh from men who had all come under the lash of the Corsican's sarcasms. But there was also a general feeling that now the elections would end without civil strife, and two days later the controversial Constitution of the Year III passed into law. France now had a two-Chamber parliament and an executive Directory of five.

Soon after that the Latours were surprised to receive a stiff card printed in gilt in the style of the old régime, in which Citizeness Lapagerie de Beauharnais invited them to a soirée at 6 Rue Chantereine "to meet His Excellency the American Minister, the Honorable James Monroe".

"Good heavens, that party has been postponed so often," said Marie, "I've been thinking of it as 'Joséphine's housewarming'. I'd forgotten all about the Americans. But she was talking about 'Barras's party for the Minister' as long ago as last June." She remembered that Joséphine had wheedled the villa from her lover on the grounds that she couldn't entertain his important guests in a rented apartment.

"The Americans were lying low until the elections were over," said Charles. "You never hear of Monroe at the Luxembourg."

"She wants us to come early, so let's do that," said Marie. A pathetic note had been enclosed with the invitation. Madame de Beauharnais claimed that Marie had neglected her since her own marriage and hadn't been to see the new house for weeks. She would find it much improved.

She must have coaxed more furniture from Barras, Marie thought, and made sure they arrived at the Rue Chantereine a good half hour before the appointed time. It was a wet November night and the roads were muddy, so was the private avenue leading between trees and empty flowerbeds to Joséphine's pretty villa. It ended in a gravel sweep from which a flight of steps, lit by flambeaux and protected by a red carpet, led to the front door. Charles Latour, saying "Mind those satin slippers!" lifted his wife from their hired cab and carried her laughing into the lobby.

Marie was wearing her wedding dress, for only the second time, and under her red cloak the lace and peau de soie glimmered like moonbeams. Charles, watching critically while a new maid removed the cloak, thought something was missing from the bridal finery, and realised that Marie was wearing a gilt fillet in her curls instead of the white rosebuds of their wedding day. Too bad she hadn't reminded him to buy her some, if roses could be bought in Paris in November! But Marie was lovely enough without flowers in her hair. And here came Joséphine, slender and graceful in lilac velvet, flattering and kissing them both, and he was kissing her hand.

"My dears, you're sweet to come early," she said. "And here's my boy Eugène, on holiday from school. Almost a man now, can you believe it?"

Marie had too much regard for the schoolboy who made his bow to exclaim, "Why, Eugène, how you've grown!" She knew he was only fourteen, but Eugène de Beauharnais was so tall for his age that he looked very well in a tail coat, and his fair hair had been cut in the new "Titus" style which was part of the current passion for classical antiquity. A few months as a junior ADC with General Hoche in the Vendée had helped him to cope with most situations, and he now invited Captain Latour to "come and see our new house before all the people come crowding in." Joséphine led Marie up the spiral staircase to her own bedroom.

It was very like her bedroom in the apartment they had shared. The fourposter bed, with fresh hangings of silvery gauze, stood against one wall, and in the fireplace logs of applewood were burning. The vast dressing table, laden with lighted candles, pots of rouge, crystal jars of scent, and even miniatures in silver frames, stood opposite. The carpet and curtains were worn and mended but richly coloured, and the whole room was impregnated with the essence of Joséphine, which was femininity triumphant.

The only difference from the old setting was in the ceiling, which the previous occupant of the villa, the notorious Julie Talma, had caused to be covered with mirror glass. It extended, Marie knew, to the walls as well as the ceiling of the adjoining dressing room.

By candlelight Madame de Beauharnais was beautiful. The dark ringlets brushed over her forehead and ears gave an illusion of careless youth, and the only flaw in her charming profile was the tightly closed lips which hid defective teeth. They parted in a smile as she surveyed Marie.

"Darling, how sweet of you to wear your wedding dress," she said. "You look adorable in it, just as you did last August. Lucky girl!"

"You're lucky too," said Marie. "Aren't you enjoying your new home?"

"Of course I am! It's twenty times better than the Rue de l'Université, don't you think?"

"You've done wonders with it, I'm sure. But won't some of your older ladies have trouble with that spiral staircase?"

"*All* the ladies, old and young, will give their wraps to the maids," said Joséphine with decision. "No one but you will be coming up to my own room."

"You think some of them might be shocked by the mirrored ceiling?"

"Oh, Marie, how you love to tease me! You know it would cost far too much to take the mirrors down. But never mind that now. I brought you upstairs for a private word. What's this I hear about your starting to study pharmacy?"

"Who told you about that?" Marie turned to the dressing table and studied her reflection in the glass.

"I don't remember, and I want you to tell me yourself. Is it true?"

"Quite true."

"What does Charles say?"

"Charles has been wonderful. He was shocked at first,

but when he realised it meant a lot to me he agreed to let me try . . . for no longer than six months and no more than three days in each *décade*. Then I go to Monsieur Guiart from ten o'clock till four. And I'm enjoying it!"

"You're a strange girl, Marie." Joséphine sat down on the side of her bed and picked at the embroidered quilt. "Isn't Guiart's place quite a long way from the Quai Voltaire?"

"Charles has arranged with a livery stable for me to go there by cab."

"Very generous."

"Isn't it?" said Marie, glowing.

"I don't mean generous to pay for the cab, that's nothing to a man in his position, but generous to allow you so much freedom. Most men expect their precious selves and their homes to be looked after as their wives' first preoccupation – "

"I'm sure you know all about that. But we have a *femme de ménage* now, who comes in every day and does all the shopping and the cooking, and Charles seems quite happy with the way things are run. He's very sweet to me, Joséphine."

"Marie, for a clever girl, you really are a fool," said Madame de Beauharnais. "Your Charles is sweet to you now, of course. But he's a handsome man, and many women would think him attractive. Be careful you don't lose him to one of them, or more than one, while you're stewing over your gallipots and trying to study a science that was never meant for women."

Marie reacted in a way intended to provoke. She bent over to give Joséphine a light kiss on the cheek, and laughed.

"Don't let's quarrel about it," she said, "and come along downstairs. I hear carriage wheels outside, and you ought to be standing on the doorstep, you know, to greet the American Minister."

* * *

Charles, with a half empty glass of champagne in his hand, was alone in the dining room, for which the new furniture had been provided by Barras. The dining table had been removed, the fashionable horse hair upholstered chairs remained. Vases in wall brackets were filled with roses, a reminder that these were on sale in Paris in November.

"Where's Eugène?" asked Marie.

"Outside, trying to sort out the carriage traffic. There's not much room for turning, and Joséphine's coachman doesn't seem able to handle it. That Eugène's a good boy, Marie."

"I know he is. Are the Americans in the traffic tangle?"

"I don't know, but I hear Teresa Tallien screeching somewhere."

The Talliens were the first to arrive, Teresa exuberant in a dress of the barbaric colours which suited her so well, copied in the feathers of her headdress, while her husband, with his hangdog look, lurked at her heels as usual. Marie, while she kissed Teresa, expected to see Ouvrard the banker in attendance, for Ouvrard was credited with being Madame Tallien's new lover, but the next to appear was Paul Barras, in all the glory of his costume as a Director. It had been designed by the artist David as an adaptation of what he imagined a Roman senator might have worn, and as a return to the elegance of the old régime. Barras had left his plumed hat in the lobby, but retained the mantle attached by golden loops to his long red coat with its lace collar and embroidered hem. With a silk shirt and silk knee breeches he wore a broad silk sash, through the knot of which was thrust a short or "Roman" sword. His good looks had survived years of debauchery, and he looked well in his fantastic garb. Charles Latour whispered in his wife's ear that the old boy must have thought he was coming to a fancy dress ball.

Marie kept a straight face while Barras greeted them both – perfunctorily, for Joséphine had ushered in three Americans, the Minister and two of his counsellors. Their faces were solemn and their French was deficient, but they made an effort to be agreeable, and as the rooms filled up Mr Monroe moved among a company more disposed to stare than fraternise with him.

Barras kept close to the guest of honour and made the introductions. Whenever he could he came back to Teresa and exchanged a few whispered words with her, and Marie, who had expected Joséphine's lover (but was he still her lover?) to play the host in what was in fact his own house, was amused to see how the part was taken over by young Eugène, who never left his mother's side.

Marie herself knew what she was expected to do. She had to move about and keep others moving; she had to talk and laugh and pass refreshments. There was no need for the last task tonight, since four hired waiters kept the champagne flowing and handed salvers laden with tempting food. But somehow the party never began to bubble with good cheer. Fifty guests were too many for the suite of small rooms, especially when they all crowded into the drawing room, which was enlarged by a bay window. The financial company (minus Ouvrard) did not mix well with the Luxembourg set, and Joséphine whispered to Marie in passing, "It isn't going well? The Americans are all so stiff, and Buonaparte has let me down! He ought to have been here an hour ago."

"I didn't know you were expecting him." Though I might have known it, Marie told herself.

"He came to see me the moment he was back from Tours, and swore he would be here tonight. Oh, and listen to that! Some fool has let Fortuné out of the back kitchen!" The distant barking of a spoiled pug dog was heard.

"Don't worry, maman, I'll make sure they put him on his lead," said Eugène, and hurried away.

"I'll go and talk to the other Directors, they aren't doing much to help," said Marie. Citizens Reubell and La Revellier, the only Directors to accompany Barras, were not attired as Roman senators but in plain tail coats. They were standing a little apart and looked as glum as the Americans. Marie had a soft spot for Director Reubell, the first partner to teach her that she had a natural gift for dancing. But she was intercepted by Teresa Tallien, who pulled her aside to ask roundly if she didn't think this soirée a wretched affair.

"It's not as lively as one of your own parties," said Marie.

"Joséphine should have hired musicians, I told her so. But she never listens to me – "

"An orchestra costs money, Teresa."

"She's in funds just now. Her poor old mother in Martinique sent her a banker's draft, that's how she was able to buy that sideboard and the two console tables in the small salon."

"Oh? I thought perhaps Paul Barras – "

"Paul's *through*, Marie," said Teresa with enjoyment. "He sent in the champagne and the roses and paid for the waiters, and that's *all*. She bought the new stuff from Julie Talma, who's feeling the pinch now she and Talma are divorcing. Lucky for Joséphine!"

"I suppose so. Teresa, why don't you go and cheer up the American Minister? He looks completely miserable."

"I can't understand a word he says."

James Monroe looked no more miserable than he felt. He knew, from private information received from Philadelphia, that his letters of recall were already on the high seas. President George Washington was not satisfied with his performance in France. A special relationship had existed between the two countries since the French fought side by side with the Americans in their War of Independence against Britain, the common enemy – La Fayette doing the posturing and Rochambeau doing the fighting. That relationship had been at risk since John Jay, Chief Justice of the American Supreme Court, negotiated a treaty between his country and Britain, which the French thought gave Britain too many trading advantages. Mr Monroe had had the mortification of hearing the United

States described in Paris as a British satellite. He didn't know how to deal with the situation. He didn't trust Barras and company, who were all in it for the money, and he wasn't impressed by the style of this wretched reception, which looked to him like a scene at a badly produced play. Barras, with his imitation sword, and Tallien, as usual making a meal off his fingernails, were for the downright American merely the rejects of the Revolution.

In a way he was glad to be going home, for he had presidential ambitions of his own which could only be fulfilled in the land of the free. It had done him no good to be sidetracked into an embassy to an unreliable ally. But going home a failure would be a black mark against him, even when Washington's mandate had expired.

Monroe's thoughts were running in such a familiar groove that he failed to notice the silence that had fallen, one of the many to fall on the dull company. Into that silence came the unexpected sound, not of carriage wheels, but of a horse being ridden rapidly up the avenue. There were voices in the yard, and Joséphine de Beauharnais, all smiles, motioned her son towards the front door.

"A late arrival, I presume," said Mr Monroe to one of his aides.

Eugène, anticipating the servants, ushered the late arrival into the salon, and the curious guests heard him announce deferentially:

"General Buonaparte."

The young general stepped forward to kiss the hand of his hostess. He was not wearing the gold-laced uniform which the occasion might have called for, but army blue with heavy gilt epaulettes and no insignia. His greatcoat, left in the lobby, had kept the worst of the mud splashes off his breeches, but his riding boots were spattered with the dirt of the wet roads. His hair hung in untidy dark locks to his shoulders.

"Forgive me, *chère madame*," he said. "I'm truly sorry to

be so late. I was detained by an inspection at Fort Vincennes."

"You work too hard, my dear general," said Joséphine in her sweetest voice, the Créole drawl she had brought from her old home in Martinique, and she allowed her fingers to remain in Buonaparte's while he spoke to her in lowered tones. It was a tableau easy to understand, and it was broken by Eugène, who said clearly "Allow me to present you to the American Minister, citizen general," and Barras moved to the boy's side to assist in the introduction. A hum of conversation broke out, as guests who had been torpid became animated and turned to their neighbours with new enthusiasm. Napoleon Buonaparte was not popular with, or personally known to, all the company: for most of them he was simply the little Corsican officer who had delivered Toulon from the British, and put down armed rebellion in Paris only a few weeks ago, but all of them felt the controlled energy in his body and the magnetism of his personality. Mr Monroe, when he saw the two men and the boy coming towards him, thought the salon had ceased to be a stage set with lifeless figures. The leading man had appeared on the scene.

After compliments had been exchanged as far as possible, the general began to chat with those guests whom he already knew. Napoleon was not a skilled conversationalist. His idea of a chat was an exchange of questions and answers, his questions being as probing as politeness allowed and the expected answers concise and informative. He moved on quickly and unsmilingly until he reached the two Latours.

"Our bride!" he said, kissing Marie's hand, "and in great beauty. None the worse for your hospital experience, I'm glad to see."

"Are *you* quite well, citizen general?" said Marie composedly.

"Yes indeed, I thank you. And you, Captain Latour? Murat has been talking about you to me."

"Favourably, I hope, sir?" said Charles.

"Quite," the general replied. 'But you, Marie? Does Guiart think you've made a good start to your studies in pharmacy?"

"How – how did you know about that?" she asked.

"Because I asked him to take you into his laboratory. Didn't he tell you so?"

As a young girl Marie had been given to blushing. Her delicate complexion had often been stained as red as the blood on the cobbles when she saw the tumbrils of the Terror pass. But the months in prison had hardened her, and so had her year in the New Society, amoral and profligate. Now, at Napoleon's words, she knew her face was crimson.

"No, citizen general," she said, trying to smile, "I didn't know it was you I had to thank. Monsieur Guiart let me understand he wanted to compensate for the closing of the first aid post."

"Yes, well, I knew that would be a disappointment, and so I sent for Guiart and told him what to do. But remember I was your sponsor, Marie. I expect you to do me credit."

"I'll try, *mon général.*" Marie curtseyed as Napoleon smiled and turned away. She was smiling herself, happy and excited, until Charles muttered, "I wonder you didn't kiss his hand."

She gave him one reproachful look and left him. In the dining room there were far fewer people, and there Marie stood exchanging meaningless pleasantries with her friends the de Monniers. *Kiss his hand!* Marie had kissed Napoleon's hand in her husband's presence on the day he broke the rebellion. It was an act of homage to the man Napoleon had it in him to become. Had Charles thought she was being flirtatious? Had Napoleon?

In her distress Marie had no idea how long she remained with the de Monniers. It might have been ten minutes, it might have been half an hour, before another bout of furious barking and an outburst of raised voices indicated that Fortuné had slipped his lead and, this time, had created havoc in the salon. He had bitten someone. But who was the victim? Was the animal dangerous? Rabid? People crowded towards the grand salon to enjoy whatever disaster might have taken place. It was Teresa Tallien who stopped the rush with a breezy "There's nothing to worry about! Fortuné bit General Buonaparte's ankle, but his riding boot saved his skin!" She added with a laugh, "The jealous brute!"

The party broke up soon after Fortuné was carried away by the horrified servants. Napoleon calmed Joséphine's distress, and informed all kind enquirers that no harm had been done, but he knew by the covert smiles that the victor of Toulon had not appeared to the best advantage while kicking out to rid one leg of a growling dog. The Americans left almost at once, feeling that such a farce would never be played out in the parlours of Philadelphia, and Barras, who had kept his finery well out of Fortuné's reach, was free to devote himself to Teresa Tallien.

Teresa's cry of "The jealous brute!" was meant for the little dog whose instinct had led him to attack the one person in the room who might take his place in his mistress's favour, but it applied equally to Charles Latour. His familiar devil, jealousy, had him by the throat. It was bad enough that Napoleon had interfered in their married life by starting Marie on the studies he disliked, but it was the Marie Fontaine of old days and not that aspiring officer, Captain Latour, who held his interest. He, Latour, could be dismissed with a word – "Quite" – (and what had Murat actually said about him?) while Marie was a woman who was not, in Napoleon's scoffing phrase, *"le repos du guerrier"*, the warrior's rest, but someone he expected to do him credit. It was humiliating! Seeing the move towards departure, Charles drank off another glass of champagne and went to find his wife.

There was a long wait, after all the thanks and good nights had been spoken, before their cab appeared, and during that wait Charles so far regained control of himself as to whisper to Marie, "Forgive me, dear. That was a wretched thing I said to you."

"What wretched thing?" she said, and took the initiative away from him.

"About – kissing his hand – "

"Oh, *that*? It didn't matter. I knew you'd been drinking a good deal."

He let her precede him down the steps and across the wet gravel (be damned to her satin slippers) and handed her into the cab without a word. So now she was implying he was drunk, was she? Insulting a man who never drank to excess! He'd seen enough that night to make him take an extra glass. Marie's blush! A tell-tale wave of crimson which, he wanted to believe, betrayed the secret passion which bound her to Napoleon.

Charles Latour was as sure as a man could be that he was Marie Fontaine's first lover, but who knew what sweethearting games she'd played with the connivance of her uncle Prosper? He'd seen her smirking at the young Buonaparte, with Prosper present, over a supper table at the Café de la Régence in the days when she claimed they'd been "boy and girl together". A likely story! Marie must have been eighteen then and Napoleon twenty-three, and both of them ripe for mischief. As the cab rumbled through the dark streets Charles almost succeeded in persuading himself that Napoleon's obvious infatuation with Madame de Beauharnais was a blind, and Marie's visits to the famous "labo" her cover story for secret assignations with the general.

He intended to charge her with it as soon as they reached home. Then he would assert his rights and possess her punishingly, brutally as he had never done before. Charles had reached this point of folly when he heard the sound of even breathing. Warm in the cloak which covered her wedding dress, the Comtesse de la Tour de Vesle had fallen asleep.

* * *

It was not on that evening, nor for several days more, that General Buonaparte became the lover of the woman he had desired since he first saw her. An impatient man, he had been patient from June till November while her affair with Barras ran its course. It was on a night near the end of November that he dined alone with her in the Rue Chantereine (Fortuné being securely tied up in the cellar) and when the servants were dismissed she sat pensively twirling the stem of her wine glass while he poured out, with a boy's fervour, the story of his devotion and his longing for its fulfilment.

He was six years younger than she was, but Joséphine de Beauharnais, a year after her marriage at sixteen, knew more about men and sex than Napoleon knew about women at twenty-six. She had enjoyed flirting with him, she thought he was amusing, and that was all. His ardour was more than her shallow nature could support, but people said he was the coming man, and he could give her back the position in the New Society which she had lost when Barras left her for Teresa Tallien. Barras was her last lover, but there had been others before him in the ten years since her divorce, even in the turmoil of the Revolution, but never one like this. Napoleon had risen from the dinner table and was kneeling before her, his eyes – were they blue or were they grey? – brilliant with pleading. Perhaps the time had come to yield. "Well then, my poor friend!" she said, and laid her hands in his.

Napoleon followed her up the spiral staircase to the bedroom where fragrance and candlelight made a new assault on his senses. His Spartan life in barracks and cheap hotels had not prepared him for the flowers, the fire, the glittering dressing table on which Joséphine laid a diamond necklace, fortunately redeemed from the pawnbroker. He had often kissed her neck and bare shoulders. Now she let him take off her muslin dress and something filmy she wore beneath, and undo her pale silk stockings. At last he strained her naked to his body, so that his epaulettes left marks upon her breasts. *"Chéri,*

70

you're hurting me," he heard her whisper, and tore off his uniform coat before he kissed the marks away.

The man who called himself the son of the Revolution was susceptible to luxury. His dead father had claimed the titles of nobility, and Napoleon, the former Jacobin, felt an extra thrill when he embraced Joséphine because an *aristo*, a *ci-devant* vicomtesse, was giving herself to him. He had had two or three romantic attachments in his life, and as a disciple of Rousseau he had treated the girls with respect. Other encounters had lasted for an hour, or at most two. The women he paid never commented on his virility or his lack of interest in the sex they purveyed. If those ladies of the town had compared notes they would have agreed that Lieutenant, or Captain, or Major Buonaparte's lovemaking (not that he ever called it that) was of the familiar garrison type – rough and rapid, and in his case more unsatisfactory than most. But in Joséphine's bed he was lying with an expert, who had been taught the arts of seduction by a "wise woman" at her old home – the same Euphemia David who predicted that some day she would be Queen of France – and by certain of the female slaves who caressed her during the long siestas of Martinique. The mirrored ceiling witnessed her clinging limbs, which restrained the man between them until he and she had reached the knife-point of ecstasy; witnessed the languors of rest while she whispered erotic words until he was ready for fresh transports; witnessed her easy tears.

The clock on her dressing table chimed four when he left her, and descended the spiral staircase to toss a coin to the yawning coachman who led his horse out of the stable. In a dream he rode back to the Tuileries, where he showed an impassive face to the sentries who turned out to salute him. He was mentally forming the opening sentences in his first love letter to the woman who had taught him how to make love.

5

He was with her that night and the night after, and by the third night their liaison was common knowledge. The coachman who looked after the general's horse told about being roused from his room above the stable. The new maid, Louise Compoint, who looked after the lady, talked about her disordered bed. The servants' hall at 6 Rue Chantereine, which Madame de Beauharnais had over-staffed, was the source of her new notoriety, discussed at the dinner tables of the New Society and in the press room of every scandal sheet.

It was not even mentioned in the apartment on the Quai Voltaire, where Charles and Marie Latour were busily papering over the cracks beginning to appear in their marriage. The only references they made to the unsuccessful reception for the American Minister had to do with the episode of the general and the dog, and they eagerly agreed with each other that Joséphine was perfectly foolish about that wretched little pug. The presence of a daily servant obliged them to talk impersonally while she served their breakfast and dinner. Citizeness Armande was a war widow, recruited by the concierge's wife from a garret in the Rue de Bourbon, only ten minutes' walk away. Her husband had fallen at Valmy like Marie's cousin Michel, which of course assured her of Marie's sympathy, but she was quiet by nature, and too thankful for regular employment to talk about herself to her new employers. Armande's silent presence was a

72

constant reminder to Marie of how much she owed to Charles's generosity in setting her free to go to the labo. I must think of him and nobody but him, she told herself over and over again.

After the revolutionary years of the clubs, the Committee of Public Safety and the stormy sessions of the Convention, the first days of the Directory passed peaceably while the new institutions were settled into their places. The Directors worked at the Luxembourg, where they lived, and the lower chamber met in the Palais Bourbon, fated to remain the only place of a French national assembly. The upper Chamber still met in the Tuileries, where General Buonaparte had his office, and where a message from Director Carnot gave him the news which fell like a thunderclap on the new government.

Received from Nice by Chappe telegraph, it informed Carnot that for the first time since the battle of Dego more than a year before, the Army of Italy had been in action. Under General Schérer it had defeated an Austro-Sardinian army on 25 November at the battle of Loano, in spite of Carnot's order, after Dego, that it was to remain inactive. Schérer appeared to be a disciple of Carnot, for no sooner was Loano won than he ordered his army into winter quarters, but at last a victory had been won against the Austrians, the bitterest and most dangerous of France's enemies. From that victory others might follow, and when the Bureau of Plans opened on the following morning Captain Latour was elated to receive a direct order from General Buonaparte to send him an appreciation of the strength and dispositions of the French Army of Italy.

Any junior officer in Plans could have told him that the army, in winter quarters, was at half strength, but Captain Latour could do better than that. Ever since Napoleon had found him at Entrevaux, in a mountain garrison high above the river Var, he had been close to the general's thinking on Italian strategy. He had done a reconnaissance from Mentone to the Sardinian border; he had

fought at Dego, and he knew the terrain. He knew that
Buonaparte had established three French divisions on the
mountain line between the Maritime Alps and the Apennines, and that desertions had been heaviest in the
mountains during the stalemate after Dego. Charles ransacked the Bureau's files for the details; he enumerated
the regiments still in place on the littoral and the shortages
of cavalry and artillery; he illustrated his "appreciation"
by well-drawn maps.

By working all day he was able to turn it in at the
Pavillon de Flore at five o'clock. It was received in Buonaparte's outer office by a very young man who introduced
himself as the general's aide-de-camp, Captain Le Marois.
Charles was too tired to be jealous, and all he wanted was
to get home and tell Marie about the developments of the
day. But he was detained by one man after another, all
anxious for the latest scrap of news, and when he reached
his apartment Citizeness Armande was already there,
moving between the kitchen and the salon and setting the
table for dinner. While she was there the conversation
was impersonal, but at least he had time to put his
thoughts together. So had Marie, as he could tell by her
absorbed face, but no sooner had the woman left for the
place she called home in the Rue de Bourbon than Charles
turned their chairs round to the fire and began to answer
Marie's questions.

"You've done a great job, darling," she said at last. "A
job that only you could do. I'm sure the general will be
pleased."

"I think he will."

"What do you hope to get out of it for yourself?"

"A chance to speak to General Buonaparte."

"Saying what?"

"That I want to get out of Plans and transfer to the
cavalry."

"The cavalry? Not back to the 4th Artillery?"

"I'm not a gunner, Marie. Not by training, at least."

"You've talked about this to Murat, haven't you?" she said.

"Yes I have."

"And Murat talked to the general?"

"I believe so." He wanted to make her look at him. She was sitting with her eyes fixed on the fire. "Listen, darling," he said urgently, "you've known that sooner or later I would go to fight, and now it looks rather like sooner than later. You have to understand – you told me yourself that helping out at Val de Grâce was your way of going to war. Well, this is mine."

"Yours is the soldier's way," she said, "and mine is only a woman's . . . Remember, this particular woman is very glad to have the chance."

Another silence fell, which Marie broke.

"You said, or you implied, that you didn't have a thorough artillery training. What about a cavalry training? Don't you have to learn to ride in formation, or whatever they call it? Didn't Murat say anything about that?"

"Something or other, I suppose," said Charles reluctantly.

"Where?"

"Fort Vincennes, or Grenelle, or the Champ de Mars. I wouldn't be going outside Paris, dear."

"Not until you go for good. Oh Charles!"

Suddenly she sobbed aloud. Neither her husband's jealousy nor his sarcasms could make Marie shed a tear, but at the thought of the parting, so much nearer today than yesterday, she wept.

Charles Latour lifted her into his arms and told her he adored her.

Forty-eight hours passed before Charles was summoned to the Pavillon de Flore. Young Captain Le Marois was not on duty. The ADC was his good friend Captain Junot, who greeted him with a grin and a whisper, "You're in high favour, *mon vieux*. Ask and it shall be given unto you."

With which cryptic remark he ushered Charles into Buonaparte's presence. The general was seated at a laden desk and greeted him with a nod.

"Sit down, Latour," he said. "I wanted to tell you myself that I found your appreciation helpful. Very full and very clear."

"Thank you, citizen general."

"It made me realise that Plans is the right place for you. What makes you want to exchange into the 21st Chasseurs?"

Under those cold, appraising eyes Charles said with difficulty:

"I think I could do better work there . . . than I can in Plans."

"On the strength of *one* reconnaissance up the High Valley of the Roya? *One* ride to bring cannon from Les Sablons?"

"I'm a pretty good horseman, sir."

"How much riding have you done in recent years?"

"Very little, sir. But one doesn't forget."

"I don't know about that, because I never learned to ride."

"Never?" It occurred to Charles that he had only seen the general on horseback recently, reviewing troops outside the Tuileries.

"My father's sister Geltruda tried to teach my brother and me when we were little boys. Knot your fingers in the pony's mane and hang on bareback! You, I suppose, were properly taught?"

"My brother and I had lessons in the *manège* at Versailles, citizen general."

"Quite so," said Napoleon. "Well, that's beside the point, Latour. When we met at Entrevaux, I was impressed by the maps you'd made in the mountains, and by your grasp of mountain problems. Your colonel speaks very highly of the work you do in Plans. What's at the bottom of this desire to exchange into the cavalry?"

"I want to be where the action is, sir."

"Ah!" said Napoleon, "that I understand. What I don't understand is why a newly-married man should volunteer to leave his wife for life in barracks. Have you talked this over with Marie?"

"I've told her about it," said Charles stiffly. "Naturally, she approves."

"Naturally?"

"Marie is too absorbed in pharmacy to object."

"She's a remarkable woman, Latour. I wish – " He checked himself. "Well, let's leave it at that. We shan't be leaving for Italy tomorrow, or the day after. Meantime I'll have a word with Murat; that comes first."

Napoleon nodded dismissal, and Captain Latour saluted and went out. When he had gone the general mentally completed the sentence begun with the words "I wish – " I wish I had not to face leaving the woman I love behind me when I go to war. His passion was so new, so strange, so devouring, that he could not contemplate its end. Before his eyes rose the seductive body he already knew by heart, the arms that clasped, the heart that beat for him – he drove the image from his mind as duty and ambition told him that work was waiting to be done.

He took up Latour's appreciation from his desk. He had already copied it in his atrocious handwriting, and the original, with his own notes, must now be sent to Carnot. Carnot, the military member of the Directory, as he had been since the battle of Valmy the military member of the Committee of Public Safety, was the man on whom his own command of the Army of Italy really depended. When that was confirmed, could he also persuade Carnot to divert troops from the Austrian Netherlands to increase opposition to the Austrians in the south? If not the odds against the French might be too great. Especially since the British, confound them, were reported to be subsidising the Austrian Emperor to put 200,000 men in the field. Well, he must start the whole thing going. He put the report in a sealed cover and shouted for Junot.

* * *

77

In those uncertain days (and was there never to be certainty in France?) Marie Latour spent her most contented hours in Monsieur Guiart's laboratory. Although she told Joséphine that she was enjoying it, her first two *décades* at the labo had not been particularly enjoyable. The professor, accustomed to lecturing to undergraduates, pitched his instructions above her head. As he began at the beginning of the history of pharmacy, Marie had to struggle with unfamiliar names like Asclepius, god of the healing art, and the beautiful Hygieia, who compounded his medicines, until they reached the Christian era and Galen. Her uncle had never mentioned these worthies, not even Paracelsus, but then Prosper Fontaine had been a sceptic, and not sentimental about his profession, though it had been his father's before him. It was only by the edict of King Louis XVI, later guillotined, that the apothecaries of France had been rated separately from the grocers.

The lectures only lasted for an hour, when Monsieur Guiart went back to the Rue du Louvre and Marie did practical work, much more successfully. The first thing needed at Val de Grâce was bandages and more bandages, and these she had been making for years, threaded on the back of a chair. Now she made them – roller bandages, double and single, many-tailed and so on – with Jean-Claude to hold the strips of calico taut. Citizen Robert sulked when *le patron* told his assistant to work with madame: he had been markedly less friendly to Marie since she ceased to be a visitor and became a pupil. When she didn't put on airs and graces, but shared their midday *soupe* with a crust of bread, he told Jean-Claude after she had gone home that they would make something of her yet.

That was about the time when Monsieur Guiart lent her his prized copy of Nicholas Culpeper's *Herbal* in translation. She wondered if he thought a girl baffled by Paracelsus was just capable of enjoying the herbalist-astrologer's pretty pictures of flowers.

One morning in early December there was an item in the *Moniteur* which Charles showed to Marie with a self-conscious smile. It ran:

Captain Charles Latour. Exchange from the 4th Artillery to the 21st Chasseurs, effective 15 January.

"Darling! You've got what you wanted! Are you pleased?"

He was very pleased indeed, she could see, and Marie reproached him with not telling her it was going to happen. "You must have known yesterday," she said.

"I wanted you to see it in cold print first. I trusted Murat, but one never knows."

"Why does the paper say you were in the 4th Artillery and doesn't mention Plans?"

"Plans never appears in the newspapers. To think I'll have to spend three more weeks in Plans."

"And three weeks more at home."

"Let's make the most of them."

There was plenty to keep Captain Latour's mind occupied in Plans, for on 19 December the two French generals commanding in the Austrian Netherlands concluded an armistice with the enemy, and transport had to be arranged to bring certain regiments back to Paris. The transport had to include the vehicles which did duty for field ambulances, for many wounded had to be taken on the long journey to the new hospital at Val de Grâce. Marie was kept busy too. She had been promoted to the branch of pharmacy she understood and liked best, the preparation of lotions and salves, in this case for the subsidiary ailments of men brought on a long journey in winter weather. Citizen Robert approved of the neat fingers which filled pots with balsam of Peru, for application on gauze to wounds and ulcers, and Monsieur Guiart supervised her preparation of arnica montant, for bruises, and of a powder called cinchona or quinine, the active principle of Peruvian bark.

Busy though they were, the Latours were determined to make the most of their three weeks' grace, and devoted their evenings to entertainment. This was all the pleasanter since Charles was so elated by his new prospects that he forgot to be jealous – not even of Buonaparte's young aide-de-camp, Captain Le Marois, forgot to be sarcastic at Marie's expense, not even to be critical of the food she set on the table. He took her to dine in the Palais Royal, to dance at Frascati's, and to the drama and the vaudeville. Once they saw Napoleon and Joséphine in a box at the Comédie Française, where Voltaire's tragedy of *Titus* was being performed. Talma, the former husband of the lady of the mirrored ceiling, was playing the lead, and Talma was the general's favourite actor. Joséphine was all smiles, and held a bouquet in her lap like a young girl.

Being a religious festival Christmas was not celebrated in a Paris where all church doors were locked and barred, but it was the season for parties, and the Latours gave three. The guests were young men who would be Charles's brother officers in the 21st Cavalry, and the young women they brought with them, who were at least introduced as their wives. Then there was a quiet party at the de Monniers' and a noisy one at the Talliens', with Teresa vociferous, Tallien more hangdog than ever, and Paul Barras very much in evidence. The New Year was the season for gifts and good wishes, and Marie sent presents to Eugène and Hortense de Beauharnais at the Rue Chantereine, along with an affectionate message to their mother.

Joséphine was nervous and tearful over the holiday season, though she tried to seem happy when the children were home from school. She was faced with a great decision. Napoleon had asked her to marry him, and was incapable of taking No for an answer. She had fallen into the hands of an ardent and impetuous lover, a man to whom she had given the first real physical satisfaction of his life, and he wanted to make sure of her before he went to war. She was a little afraid of his devouring passion, and she never knew how often, when they lay embraced under the mirrored ceiling, Napoleon's thoughts strayed to the problems he should have left at the Pavillon de Flore. Those troops from the Netherlands, now? Carnot was weakening, he was ready to approve all of the general's plan of attack in Italy, but how many reinforcements would he spare?

By the candle light Napoleon looked at Joséphine's dark head on the pillow. Her face was in shadow, but he knew there were tears on her cheeks. She had wept when he told her, earlier in the night, that he hoped to "snatch the laurel crown of victory or die on the field of battle". Poor darling! She shed tears at the thought of his death and cared nothing for his glory. A true woman! He remembered long ago saying much the same thing (for the words were seldom out of his mind) to a girl who had not wept. Serious blue eyes had been fixed upon his own, a young breast had lifted in a sigh of comprehension. He thought that the girl was Marie Fontaine.

6

On 20 February 1796 the appointment of General Napoleon Buonaparte to the command of the Army of Italy was announced in the *Moniteur*, and a thrill of excitement went through all the army establishments in Paris, especially where there were men who had served along with the general on the Mediterranean littoral. Captain Junot was one of these, but as an ADC Junot was at the Pavillon de Flore and not available for comment, and Captain Latour was in the Grenelle barracks with the 21st Chasseurs. Both of these men knew better than most Napoleon's long struggle for recognition, especially the two frustrating years – nearly three – which followed his early success at Toulon, the short imprisonment as a Jacobin which came after Thermidor, the months on "sick leave" in Paris after his refusal to take command in the civil war in the Vendée. They rejoiced that Carnot, once a captain of engineers, had been practical enough to keep the promise of a command which Barras had refused to honour.

It was not a laboratory day, and Marie was alone in the flat. Armande had served what passed for luncheon and eaten her own in the kitchen before going back to the Rue de Bourbon for the afternoon. Marie hoped that Charles would get an hour's leave from barracks as he sometimes did in the early evening. His colonel was good about leave, for the colonel of the Twenty-First was now Murat himself, and the brash young cavalryman had taken advantage of his swift promotion in the Army of the

Interior to ask for the post of ADC to the general of the Army of Italy.

Marie was lonely. Charles was dearer to her since the sword of separation hung over both their heads. She knew now that she had married in too great haste, swept away on a tide of sexuality as much as on the rebound from her youthful fancy: she knew now that when she told Charles "we don't know enough about each other" she had only meant that she didn't know the secret of her suitor's parentage, and he had to be told what her uncle had to do with the royalist plot which led to the death of Edouard de la Tour. But the emigration of the de la Tours and the tragedy of Quiberon Bay were tangible facts which two young and loving people could assimilate. The differences of character, the jealousy on his side and the obstinacy on hers, were what had made their first months of marriage difficult.

But here was a new year and a new war. She wanted him to come home and caress her, to tell her what orders had arrived from the new head-quarters for the movement of the Twenty-First towards the south. She knew that Charles had adapted himself easily to the new discipline, to the cavalry drill after the years spent in the National Guard, the infantry at Digne and Entrevaux, the time with Napoleon at Nice. She wanted him to be with her now for love and reassurance.

When the knock fell on the front door she was sure it was he, playing a joke on her, making her come and open. Instead it was Joséphine de Beauharnais who stood there smiling, beautifully dressed as usual, in a warm cloak and carrying a sable muff, but – as could be seen in the light of the salon – with something pinched about her face and nervous about the hands which clasped Marie's shoulders.

"Darling, what a nice surprise!" said Marie. They had seen each other very seldom in the previous weeks. "Sit down and tell me how you've been, and where you've been . . . and what you think about the news from Italy."

"I've been fairly well," said Joséphine. "At least I escaped the sore throat and cough that's been going around." She laid aside her muff and settled in an armchair, not lying back but sitting upright with her hands pressed between her knees like a child. It was one of her most appealing attitudes. "As for the news from Italy, or rather from Carnot, well – it was expected. I suppose Charles will soon be on the move?"

"Yes, but I don't know any of the details yet."

"Poor Marie. I saw you both at the theatre, looking magnificent."

"Oh – the night of *Titus*."

They were making conversation like two strangers. Joséphine began to say something about Marie's lovely presents to the children, and then broke off.

"Are the children all right, dear?" said Marie uneasily.

"Oh yes . . . well, the fact is, I have a piece of news for them . . . and for you. General Buonaparte has asked me to marry him, and I've said Yes."

"Darling! I hope you'll both be very happy." Marie rose from her own chair and pressed her lips to the cheek of Napoleon's promised wife. "I think that news was expected too," she said, and achieved a smile. "Is the general delighted now?"

Joséphine pouted. "He says he is. But he's a funny man, Marie! He gave me no peace until he had my promise, and now he thinks of nothing but beating the Austrians."

"I expect he means his victory to be a wedding present to you. He'll offer you a laurel crown instead of myrtle . . ."

"He wants us to be married before he leaves Paris. In about two or three weeks."

"You mean you're making wedding plans already?"

"We're planning to make the wedding as quiet as possible. After all, this is my second marriage, so there'll only be ourselves and the witnesses and the officials of the Second section – the Rue Chantereine is in the Second

84

section, did you know? . . . Marie dear, don't look so – so I don't know what . . . of course I would have loved you to be there, it was you who presented him to me at that crazy 'Victims Ball' . . . I sometimes wonder if it's I who'll be the victim . . . if I marry Buonaparte . . ." And Madame de Beauharnais burst into tears.

"Joséphine! My dear!" Marie took the woman in her strong young arms and rocked her as she had been accustomed to do when her friend had toothache. "You should be happy and smiling now. Napoleon loves you, everybody sees it, and you love him – don't you?"

"I suppose so," doubtfully, "but he's not like other men. So intense, he sometimes frightens me. And then I'm older than he is – "

"You don't look a day older."

"And he wants to have a child. Marie, I can't begin that nonsense all over again. I have two children of my own – "

"Yes!" said Marie, suddenly stern, "and what are they going to say to – a stepfather?"

"Darling, this is what I've come to ask you to do. A great favour and a great service. I want you to come back with me to the Rue Chantereine in the carriage, and then drive on alone to the children's schools at St Germain. Ask to see them, separately, and tell them Buonaparte and I are going to be married soon."

"Oh Joséphine," said Marie, aghast, "I couldn't possibly do that!"

"Why not?"

"I couldn't burst into a boys' school on such an errand. Eugène would be affronted . . . and how could I possibly explain myself to his headmaster?"

"I'm not so worried about Eugène. He isn't a jealous boy, and since he wants to make the army his career he's able to appreciate Buonaparte. You know how sentimental he is about his own papa? Well, Buonaparte is a general like poor Alexandre, and Eugène knows how a general can help him to get on."

"You've discussed your marriage with Eugène already, have you?"

"Not in so many words, no. But Eugène's very reasonable, he doesn't have Hortense's hysterical idea that I'll stop loving them both if I marry again. I've had one scene with her already, and I can't risk having another, perhaps in front of Buonaparte, Marie, do please help me!"

"No, Joséphine, this time you must help yourself. I really can't intrude in such a delicate, such a family matter."

"You were one of the family when you lived with us! Hortense knows you, she's really fond of you, it wouldn't be an intrusion at all!"

"Explaining to Madame Campan – and I've never even met her, would be as bad as explaining at Eugène's school," insisted Marie.

"No, because she respects Buonaparte. He sent one of his sisters to school at St Cyr."

"I remember, the eldest. He took her back to Corsica in '92."

"How do you know that?" demanded Joséphine, instantly suspicious.

"He came a few times to my uncle's house that summer, before he was reinstated in the army. It seems much longer than four years ago."

"He's already told Madame Campan that he wants to send her his two younger sisters so she won't want to do anything to embarrass him. He told Hortense about it, and she was quite impertinent. She seems to think the Buonapartes are nothing but Corsican peasants. Of course they're island nobility."

"Then here's an idea. Why not get Madame Campan to talk to Hortense? I'm sure she's a clever woman, and she must understand young girls. You should go straight home and write her one of your nice little letters explaining the situation, and have your man go out with it to St Germain today. Madame Campan will be thrilled to have the first news of your – your engagement."

"Writing about it will make it seem so true," sighed Joséphine.

"Doesn't *he* deserve the truth?" said Marie.

"Of course he does. I believe you're right, Marie. You're a clever woman yourself. You've always done me good, ever since we were together in the Carmes prison, and I'll do exactly as you say. I'll write at once to Madame Campan, and I'm sure she'll make Hortense see reason. And keep her at school until the wedding's safely over."

"Now," said Marie, "you only have to get the consent of Fortuné."

When Charles came home for an hour that evening Marie greeted him with a burst of tears which relieved her overcharged feelings, and which he believed to be prompted by the news of the change of command in Italy. His heart smote him, as he soothed her and caressed her, at the thought of leaving this frail young creature alone in Paris, and he despised himself for loving her better when she was weak and showed her dependence on him. But he was too anxious to tell his story to spend time on love-making: yes, the 21st Chasseurs had their orders, like other regiments based in Paris, and they were to begin the journey south on the twenty-seventh.

"To Nice?" said Marie incredulously.

"Not in one stretch, it's too far. No, we're to go as far as Lyon, commandeer fresh horses there, and show an army presence in the city, where the royalists have been giving trouble lately. Buonaparte wants his whole command to be assembled in Nice by the middle of March. He planned it all weeks ago with General Berthier, who's to be his Chief of Staff. Those damned Austrians have got a big shock coming before long!"

He was in high spirits, leaping from subject to subject, telling her his attorney, Maître Vial, would visit her next day and tell her about the financial arrangements. Vial would pay the rent of the apartment and make her a monthly allowance. She wanted to go on with Guiart – all right, but she had agreed to stop going to the labo in

April, was she sure it wasn't too much for her? Sometimes she looked rather tired. But she must promise him one thing – not, however lonely she was, to set up house again with Madame de Beauharnais.

"Joséphine won't invite me," said Marie. "She doesn't need a woman friend to share her home. She's going to be married."

"Married?" he said. "Not to Napoleon?"

"Yes. And very soon."

He held her a little away from him and studied her face. It was as calm as usual, but there were tearstains on her cheeks. With an unusual flash of perception he wondered if this was what the crying was all about? Not his own going to war but her hero's marriage to an "unsuitable" woman? He knew it would be wiser not to force the issue.

"H'm!" he said. "Going to make an honest woman of her, is he? Napoleon will have his work cut out."

Charles Latour had to leave Paris before General Buonaparte's wedding, but from the stories which reached his troop on the way to Lyon he heard of it as a hasty, hole-and-corner business, with a bride in tears, an unpunctual bridegroom and a registrar who grew tired of waiting for him and went home. He learned that the general left for his command two days after the civil ceremony, and guessed that he was thinking more of the battle front than of the woman he left behind him. What General Barthélemy Schérer thought Charles could not presume to guess.

On 26 March General Schérer was in a black mood, as he had been ever since the order of recall reached Nice. He was the victor of Loano, but much good his victory had done him, since he was to be superseded in the command by a boy of twenty-six who apparently knew more about playing politics with the Directory than the art of waging conventional war. Toulon – that was a flash in the pan two years ago, and a whiff of grapeshot to subdue a mob in a Paris street could hardly compare with the experience of General Schérer, who had served first in the royal and then in the republican army, attaining the ripe old age of sixty-one.

Well! He was ready to go. His bedroom and study in the private suite at GHQ had been cleared and his portmanteau was packed. He sat for the last time behind the big desk in the general's office, listening for the sound of his supplanter's carriage wheels and hardly aware of the three men who shared the room with him. They were his three divisional commanders, and the only one who dared to break the almost funereal silence was Sérurier, a veteran like himself. Sérurier had served in the royal army from 1755 until the Revolution and was thinking of retiring now. He too objected to serving under a boy.

He said, "The officers from Paris should be here at any moment now, *mon général*?"

"The vedettes reported that their carriage crossed the Var river at midday, so – yes, they'll soon be here," said Schérer. "I hope the orderlies have the refreshments ready."

"I'll look into it, sir." Sérurier left the room at a slightly rheumatic pace, and the general thought one of the younger men should have volunteered. Confound them! They were probably looking forward to the change. They were a couple of rough diamonds, typical of the new army. They were young, but not as young as the Corsican, and unlike him they were not graduates of Brienne and the Ecole Militaire. Augureau had begun life in the Paris gutters, found employment as a waiter and a footman, and then branched out as a soldier of fortune in Russia and in Prussia before returning to fight for his native land. He was smoking a filthy black cigar which made General Schérer cough.

Masséna was a local man, with a background even more picturesque than Augureau's. He had sold groceries from a stall in the market down by the seashore, he had run contraband across the mountains into Monaco, and he had been a sergeant-major in the Royal Italian Regiment. Training and discipline had made him a first rate soldier.

"You know General Buonaparte personally, Masséna?" said Schérer. He knew the answer, of course; every detail of the new command had been discussed in the previous two weeks, but he wanted to break the silence – else those two might think he was nursing vain regrets.

"He and I served together in this very headquarters when General Dumerbion had the command," said Masséna, and wondered if the old boy was entering his dotage.

"He is – ahem – rather small of stature, I understand?" Schérer had known the days when French soldiers were expected to be of a certain height, and spruce in their uniforms; fine-looking men, like himself.

"He certainly isn't tall," said Masséna, "but when he puts on his general's hat he looks two feet taller. I hope no officer in Nice will underestimate him, sir. I fought with him at the battle of Dego, and I know his worth."

"I hope he appreciates your loyalty – " General Schérer began stiffly, when there was a sudden clatter of wheels in the courtyard, and Augureau, who was sitting beside the window, exclaimed "Here they are!" He stubbed out his vile cigar and added with a grin, "Your vedettes are forming a guard of honour for the new man, general."

Disrespectful dogs, the pair of them! It was a relief to see Sérurier's honest face again, even though he only appeared in the doorway to stand aside and announce General Buonaparte. The Corsican came in and saluted, they shook hands. He was short and slight, certainly, but quite as spruce as any king's officer, and much more so than any other man would be who had driven nearly one thousand kilometres along the length of France. He was closely shaved, but when he took off his cocked hat (admired by Masséna) the lank black hair hanging to his shoulders made him look to Schérer like a *gamin* from the Paris streets. He presented his companion, General Berthier, "my chief of staff".

"General Berthier is known to me by reputation," said Schérer, with his first smile. Louis Berthier had been in the royal army like himself, and had fought in the War of American Independence, one of the contingent led by Rochambeau. An older man, he would be a valuable chief of staff to this little whipper-snapper . . . "I believe you know my divisional commander, Masséna?" he said, and witnessed a warm handshaking, while Augureau greeted his new commander with something like a conspiratorial smile. Two orderlies came in with laden trays.

"This is a modest repast, citizen general," said Schérer. "Nothing more than a *casse-croute*, the time of your arrival being uncertain. But a more substantial dinner is planned for seven o'clock. In the mess, so that you can meet as many of your field officers as possible."

"I hope to meet as many as possible *before* dinner," said Napoleon. "These refreshments are very welcome. But first let me give you this letter, which I was instructed to deliver directly to yourself." He took a letter in a sealed square cover from an inner pocket, and handed it to Schérer with a bow. "It is signed by all the Directors, and contains their congratulations, to which I add my own, on your important victory at Loano."

"Thank you, General Buonaparte. May I, in turn, congratulate you on your marriage? Will you take a glass of wine with me?"

Augureau looked sceptical of what he would have called "bowing and scraping", but the deposed general was pleased: the awkward meeting had passed off according to all the rules of military courtesy, and as the orderlies poured the wine he felt that the ice was broken. Napoleon praised the dry local *rosé*, ate some bread and goat's milk cheese with a few black olives, and broke off in a chat about old friends with Masséna to ask after his ADCs. "I left them to look after the baggage," he explained.

"Colonel Leclerc is looking after them," said Sérurier.

"Very good. Berthier, find Murat and Junot and tell them to report to me, with riding horses for the four of us, in two hours' time. I have some correspondence to attend to before we start on our tour of inspection."

"You will find writing materials in your own apartment, citizen general," said Schérer.

"Excellent! And as regards yourself, can you conveniently meet me in this room in one hour from now to show me the disposition of troops between Nice and the Italian border?"

"I am at your service, sir."

"I'll see the divisional commanders at eight tomorrow morning."

"You don't give yourself much rest, citizen general." It was Augureau who was bold enough to speak: all the others seemed stunned by the energy of the new commander. Who said, "Rest? The essence of my plan of attack is Speed, and there's a great deal to be done if we're to attack next week." He had decided to snub Augureau. "Now I must deal with my letters."

General Schérer led him in silence through a door behind the big desk, which led directly into a small study with a bookcase and a writing desk and chair. A door in the study wall opened on a comfortable little bedroom, where an orderly was waiting with a ewer of hot water.

"You weren't housed inside GHQ on your last tour of duty in Nice, I believe?" said Schérer.

"I had a wretched billet in the Rue de Villefranche," Buonaparte replied. "From which I was led out to fortress arrest one day eighteen months ago, on the charge of complicity with the Robespierre brothers . . . after they had both been guillotined."

"After Thermidor. Those were dangerous times, general, but your imprisonment lasted only for two weeks, I understand . . . We meet in an hour, then?"

"In one hour's time."

Left to himself, Buonaparte discarded his heavy uniform coat and cravat and washed his face and hands. He hoped to organise a tub bath before bedtime, for his mother had brought up all her children to take daily baths, and although these too often had to be shared Napoleon was as neat as a cat in his ablutions. Greatly refreshed, he dismissed the orderly and opened the window wide. The *Quartier-Général* lay in a town site, with no view beyond its courtyard and stables except the campanile of an ancient church, but he could hear not far away the surge and suck of the Mediterranean on the pebble beach and smell the flowers in some hidden garden. It was a balmy afternoon, such as often shines on that coast at the end of March, and for the first time since he tore himself away from his bride, and on the very threshold of war, the general felt a kind of peace. Across that sea lay Corsica, which he had left defeated, on this familiar shore he would emerge victorious.

In the anonymous little room with the writing desk he found a tray with quill pens, an inkstand in a tortoiseshell case and an ample supply of papers and covers. He had only one letter to write, and before beginning it he rested his head in his hands in what looked like an attitude of prayer. Napoleon had long been a stranger to prayer, and this moment was one of deliberately invoking other moments when he bent over a beloved body in a room with a mirrored ceiling. Drawing a long breath, in which his whole being expressed desire, he began to write.

My unique Joséphine,

Far from you there is no gaiety, far from you the world is a desert where I wander alone. You are more than my soul, you are the unique thought of my life . . .

7

Professor Guiart's laboratory was Marie's salvation before her husband's departure to Nice and those days preceding Joséphine's wedding. In the labo she found sympathetic companionship and the extension of her mental powers, because she found the work much more difficult than she had expected. Guiart had been quite right about her uncle. Prosper Fontaine had taught her the rudiments of pharmacy by example and not by precept, the "how" and not the "why" of the work, and she had copied him by the use of neat fingers and a quick natural intelligence. She had never read a prescription, much less written one; Fontaine himself had told her what to use for the bitters, carminatives and cathartics he sold across the counter of his shop.

Guiart made new demands on her. When he had taken her through the history of pharmacy from Galen to the (very recent) appointment of the first Apothecary-General to the French Army, he made her commit to memory a list of drugs under the headings of stimulants and depressives, some of which she had never heard, some of which Fontaine kept under lock and key. He had never burdened the girl with a name like antihelmentics, which meant quassia for threadworm and calomel for hookworm, nor had he explained the nature of ergot, made from the black fungus on rye, although that abortifacient had a big sale among the women of the *quartier*.

Marie was made to write prescriptions for the salves

and ointments she already knew how to make, prescriptions which each began with the symbol meaning "Take thou." This was the symbol of Jupiter, a survival of the days when all prescriptions began with a prayer to the god. This task, and the interpretation of prescriptions already printed in her tutor's handbooks of materia medica, required a knowledge of what he called the Apothecaries' System, the tables of weight for solids and the table of volume for fluids. For a girl with a retentive memory this was as easy as learning the list of drugs, and Marie could soon recite the list beginning "twenty grains equals one scruple" and "sixty minims equals one fluid dram" with the glibness of a pretty parrot.

But when it came to solutions, the solute and the solvent becoming one saturated fluid, a knowledge of arithmetic was required, and arithmetic had never been studied by Marie. Charles was quite right in saying that she looked tired when he came home to find her struggling with the professor's written questions, which included such posers as How Much Powder must be used

1. To prepare 2 quarts of a 2% boric acid solution
2. To prepare 1½ quarts of a silver nitrate solution.

Charles leant over her shoulder, asked one or two questions about silver nitrate, and then told her the answers by mental arithmetic, while she protested that her teacher expected her to show the working.

"They didn't expect us to do that at the Lycée Louis-le-Grand."

"You've been educated," she sighed. "I wish I'd gone to school!"

"Never mind, darling," said Charles, "You write a beautiful clear hand, far better than I do."

"I'm beginning to think it's my one accomplishment."

His answer to that was to give her, as a farewell present, a beautiful little Bréguet watch in the form of a brooch "to time your important experiments". The watch came with a little velvet stand, and took its place on Marie's bedside table, the clock of the headless shepherd being hidden in the kitchen cupboard. Marie loved to see it there when she woke up on the first lonely mornings.

She read a brief announcement of the Buonaparte-de Beauharnais marriage in the *Moniteur*, and two days later a report of the general's departure for Nice. She had heard nothing of Joséphine since her last visit, but after two days more had passed her coachman appeared at the flat with a verbal and urgent request for Marie's presence in the Rue Chantereine.

"Madame didn't write to me?" hesitated Marie.

"*Madame Buonaparte est souffrante*," said the man stolidly.

"Suffering from what?"

"Her maid will explain it all to madame."

The maid who greeted Marie at the villa was not the new woman, Louise Compoint, but Marie's old friend Agathe Rible, with whom she had shared many of the attentions required by Joséphine's frequent indispositions. To Agathe it was only necessary to say, when they met in the dining room, "I hope it's nothing serious, Agathe? What is it this time, bronchitis or toothache?"

"Bronchitis. Don't worry, she's getting over it now."

"How did she get it? The weather's been quite mild."

"*Madame veut trop faire la jeune fille*," said Agathe with a grin. "She *would* dress like a chit of eighteen for the wedding, and that's when she caught cold. Then next day *he* trailed her off to St Germain, said he wanted to see the kids himself. Hortense cried, and that upset madame and made her worse – "

"I'd better go right upstairs. Don't you come, Agathe, I know the way."

Joséphine might well have wished to "play the young girl" at her wedding (and the wedding dress she showed later to Marie was a girlish dress of spots and stripes with a net filling of the décolleté bodice) but she looked her age and ten years added when Marie entered her seductive bedroom. The fire burned high, but she wore a flannel nightgown with a camphor pad on her chest and the room reeked of herbal remedies. She held out her arms to Marie with a cry.

"Oh darling, it's all been so awful!"

"My poor dear, what went wrong?" Marie pulled up a chair to the side of the bed and took Joséphine's hot hand.

"Buonaparte was late for the wedding. Barras and Tallien and I were at the registry of the Second Section in good time, and so were the Public Officers – "

"*Barras* was there?" That her former lover should attend the wedding of his discarded mistress was too much for Marie to believe.

"Yes, he was one of Buonaparte's witnesses. And I must say he kept very calm. When I began to cry, I was so humiliated, he kept saying the general had such a lot to do, getting ready to go, but he was sure to turn up – "

"And of course he did," said Marie.

"Yes, but the senior Public Officer refused to wait for him, he said 'I don't care if the man's a general, he's not going to play tricks with the law,' and he went off home."

"So who married you?"

"His deputy, a little man called Leclercq. He had a wooden leg," said Joséphine drearily. 'But the worst of it was, he let the fire die down, so the room grew icy, and that's how I caught cold. We had to wait hours for the bridegroom, until he arrived with his ADC, Captain Le Marois. I thought he was too young to be a witness. I think the Public Officer thought so too, but he obviously wanted to be done with the whole thing, and lock up." She broke off in a fit of coughing and Marie handed her a lemon drink. "Oh, darling, I wish I'd had you for my witness! Everything would have gone well if you'd been there."

Marie seriously doubted her ability to produce General Buonaparte if duty called him to be elsewhere, but she only asked who the real witnesses were.

"For myself? Tallien and Calmelet. You know, Marie, last time I was married in church, and I'd no idea a civic ceremony was over so soon."

"I remember – about five minutes," said Marie. "So after that you came straight back here?"

"Yes, and that was awful too. Oh how cold the wind was in the street, I shivered all the way home. The servants had a nice little supper waiting for us, and I was thankful for a hot drink, but Buonaparte said he wasn't hungry, he wanted to go to bed. And then – oh, Marie!"

Marie sat silently waiting.

"You know Fortuné likes to sleep with me?" continued the bride. "Well, the bedroom door can't have been fastened properly, for he slipped in and we didn't know it until he was under the bedclothes and biting Buonaparte in the leg. He lost his temper and struck poor little Fortuné, and swore horribly, and I had to get up and find a bandage . . . and that – that was our wedding night, Marie."

The brilliant soldier had been wounded in action.

Nice was not a French city in 1796. As Nizza la Superba it had belonged to Piedmont, and Piedmont-Sardinia was the ally of Austria. The French Army of Italy was in Nice as an army of occupation. The Niçois accepted the situation, but there were disaffected persons among them willing to take the secret paths across the mountains and report on French troop movements to the Piedmontese, who would pass on the news to the Austrians on the plain of Lombardy.

Nice, where Schérer's army had gone into winter quarters after the battle of Loano, had seen a great influx of French troops during the month of March. Men from Paris, from the Armies of the Sambre et Meuse and of the Rhine, and from every army base where the Directors could be persuaded to release reinforcements for General Buonaparte poured into the city, until the Army of Italy numbered 40,000 men. At every conference with his divisional commanders the young general insisted that speed was crucial to their campaign. At every meeting with even junior officers as he quartered the city from daylight till dusk he repeated the same maxims: operate on interior lines, operate on enemy communications without exposing your own, advance in column by furious marching with skirmishers in front, and remember, speed will give us victory over an enemy stronger than ourselves.

After darkness fell he worked with his chief of staff, using mathematical instruments to calculate the distances between the three Austrian armies, each one of which was numerically superior to his own. He could see the mistakes their generals were making in allowing their divisions to be separated by lakes and rivers, but he did not for a moment underestimate them. Austria, the birthplace of the guillotined Queen Marie Antoinette, had been France's declared enemy since 1791 and was heavily subsidised by Britain. Napoleon noted, however, that the Austrian generals arrayed against him were elderly men. Marshal Wurmser was 72, Clairfayt 63, Alvinczy 62, and all were hidebound in the military traditions of fifty years earlier. He thought the endless drama of Youth versus Age might be played again.

When Berthier had leave to withdraw and the general was alone, there began the cherished hour of each day when he wrote to Joséphine.

I cannot pass a day without loving you. I cannot even drink a cup of tea without cursing the glory and the ambition which keep me apart from the soul of my existence . . . Joséphine! Joséphine! Do you remember?

Thus he poured out his heart in a flood of passionate words and erotic images, which gave him solace. At that time of his life, perhaps his happiest and best, Napoleon was living life on two levels, as the general who thought of everything in public and the husband thinking only of his adored wife in solitude.

Twenty-four hours before he gave the order to march the general held a review of the troops. As many men as possible were mustered on a space of waste ground beyond the Paillon river which would one day be named after the local hero, former stall-keeper and smuggler, Masséna. It was a warm April morning, full of the smell and sound of the sea, when Napoleon rode on to the dusty ground, followed by his staff, to the music of an army band. He came under the scrutiny of a thousand eyes, while flags were dipped and bayonets flashed in the sun.

Flags and glitter could not disguise tattered uniforms, battered hats and feet in any footgear but the regulation boots of the Army of Italy. Napoleon, as he surveyed them, thought that probably not since the first Revolutionary victory at Valmy had such a band of *sans-culottes* stood up to face the enemy. Somehow he must find words to inspire them with a belief in victory.

Charles Latour, on horseback, remembered the admission Buonaparte had made about his own horsemanship, and noted that the man was sitting straight in the saddle and certainly not holding on to his horse's mane. He had seen the general only once since the belated arrival of the 21st Chasseurs at Nice, and when he began to address the troops Charles was amazed. Twice before he had heard the general speaking in the open air, after Napoleon had brought "Sergeant Vautour" out of a blind-alley posting at Entrevaux and made him take back his family name and with it a commission, here in this very city of Nice. Then inexperience had masked Napoleon's dominating personality. Now he had found himself. The self-confidence was there, the voice was correctly placed and audible from all sides of the crowded square, and the words were astonishing.

"Soldiers!" said Napoleon, "you are naked and ill-nourished. The government owes you much but can do nothing for you . . . I will lead you into the most fertile plains in the world, where you will find great towns and rich provinces. Within your grasp will be glory, honour, riches! Soldiers of Italy! Shall you be found wanting in constancy, in courage?"

A cheer assured him that he had touched a chord in the heart of his ragged army, as much by his implied criticism of the government as by his promise of rewards to come. With a roll of drums the band began to play the *Marseillaise*, which since the last Bastille Day had replaced the *Reveil du Peuple* as the national anthem. Charles Latour, always reminded by that music of the day when a drunken rabble bawling the words gave him an excuse to kiss Marie Fontaine for the first time, felt his old admiration for the general revive as Buonaparte, saluting, rode off the field.

Next morning the army began to move by divisions along the Corniche road through Monaco and the Free City of Mentone, where the commissary wagons had been sent to meet them with the first meal of the journey. The cavalry was riding rearguard, and Latour was flattered when Napoleon, himself riding among the troops, came up with the 21st, singled him out, tweaked his ear and asked if he would remember, when they crossed the Carei stream, his own reconnaissance of nearly two years before. "The men your maps helped to post on the Piedmont frontier at Cuneo are on their way to join us in Mentone," he said. "See what you think of them."

What the general thought of them was revealed only to Berthier. The guardians of the frontier were in as poor shape as the men from the Apennines, and the speed of forced marches could not be expected from them. They were ordered to hold on to the stirrups of the cavalry to help themselves along. The Chasseurs gave them tobacco and furtive sips of brandy, and Napoleon rode to the rear several times to watch their progress.

Remembering the total inadequacy of the bridge over the gorge between France and Italy, the general had sent sappers ahead to reinforce the planking and stonework of what Masséna might have recognised as a smuggler's bridge. They could not enlarge it, and the army's progress was slowed up. Augureau's division was the only one across to eat the evening *soupe* on Italian soil. Buonaparte watched the troop movements for some time after he had eaten, and before he wrapped his old grey coat around him for the first night's bivouac he strolled down among what the natives called the Red Rocks for a glimpse of the familiar sea. The moon was rising, and by its pale light he saw, like an unlucky omen, the white sails of a British squadron on its way west from the Gulf of Genoa.

The Italy of that time was merely a geographical expression, a conglomerate of several states all more or less under the authority of the ancient and Holy Roman Empire. Napoleon's plan was to tackle the satellite states one by one, and to reduce the Holy Roman Empire to the modern and manageable imperium of Austria, and he began by driving a wedge between Piedmont, with its capital at Turin, and its Austrian ally.

He achieved this in less than three weeks after leaving France.

He defeated the Piedmontese-Sardinian army under an Austrian general at Montenotte on 12 April, Millesimo on the thirteenth and at the second battle of Dego on 16 April and Mondovi on 22 April. The end of this whirlwind campaign was that the enemy sued for peace, surrendering three key fortresses and all their artillery to Buonaparte, and the city of Nice, with the province of Savoy, to France.

Napoleon had promised his men to lead them into the most fertile plains in the world, and in the months of April and May he kept his promise. In a land of lakes and waters, fruit orchards and vineyards, vegetable fields and gardens, the famished Frenchmen feasted on fowls, eggs and cheese, trout, polenta, green vegetables and wine, so that every day's *soupe* became a banquet. They were living on the country, but not as conquerors, for the general threatened severe punishment for looting, and the peasants were spared thieving and violence. They parted with their best to the liberators of Lombardy. They cheered the man who had beaten the Austrian oppressor when they saw him go by, his inconspicuous height diminished by his enormous sabre.

General Buonaparte had captured forty cannon, a welcome addition to the twenty-four with which he had entered Italy, but he had no siege artillery and no pontoon bridges, for which he importuned the Directors by every one of his daily couriers to Paris. Lombardy was a land of rivers: the Po, flowing through Turin to the Gulf of Venice, its tributary the Mincio, the Ticino along the Piedmontese frontier, the Adda, the Lecco and the Adige. Marshal Wurmser's three Corps were divided between the Mincio, the Adige and Lake Garda, but the time to deal with Wurmser was not yet.

Napoleon was still fighting Beaulieu, who was fumbling round the rivers with his troops strung out in the old-style line of battle. He had seen the Corsican's tactics of attacking in column during the Piedmontese debâcle and should have been able to counter them, but he trusted in his big battalions and was bewildered by the French speed and their ability to surprise. Hidebound by his belief in the art of war outdated fifty years before, he was quite unprepared for Napoleon's attack at Lodi Bridge on 6 May. He expected a frontal attack, if one should come at all, when he crossed the Adda, instead of which Napoleon took 3,500 men from his cavalry and grenadiers, and armed with cannon fell upon the Austrian rearguard, 12,000 strong. He had his personal artillery tactics of using a massed concentration of guns to blast a selected spot, and when his cannon had cleared the way he seized a flag and led the cavalry across the bridge. Charles Latour, carried away by his leadership, followed close behind the flying figure who, without any niceties of horsemanship, was the first man in the charge.

When the battle of Lodi Bridge was over there came the aftermath. Beaulieu's troopers, in full retreat, took their wounded with them. Their dead they left on the banks of the Adda or in the river. Medical orderlies were tending the French wounded under the direction of a young doctor called Legendre, who had frequently complained to Napoleon about the inadequacy of his *Service de Santé*. A few hastily erected tents represented a field hospital, and a grave-digging detail had started work. Charles Latour, who had received a blow from the flat of an Austrian sabre on his left elbow, which was throbbing painfully, was ordered by Colonel Murat to supervise the farrier-sergeants at their grim task of putting out of their misery the injured horses of the 21st Chasseurs. The Adda was running red, and on its further bank Napoleon sat on a big drum, oblivious to the sights, the sounds and the smells of carnage. There had been sweat on his hands, now stained by the leather of his reins, and sweat on his face, grey with dust and grime, but he was dictating as calmly as if he were in army headquarters at Nice. Half a dozen men, officers and secretaries, stood around him, writing down his commands. He had already dictated his own report of the action for the Directory (copy to Nice) and had passed on to the purchase of remounts from neighbouring farmers, and an order to all company commanders to compile and submit lists of their dead and wounded men. As Latour came abreast of the group the dictation had evidently come to an end, for Napoleon rose to his feet, and as the young man passed him with a mechanical salute he heard the general say,

"Now, citizen soldiers, the road lies forward to Milan."

8

On the first of May, a few days before the battle of Lodi Bridge was fought, Marie returned home tired and discouraged. It had been a difficult day. Monsieur Guiart had brought in a young man named Bernard Curtois, a former apprentice who was about to enter the army's *Service de Santé*, and of whom he was obviously proud. "Only nineteen, Marie, and given a lieutenant's commission immediately!" he said. Marie congratulated Lieutenant Curtois sincerely, and he repaid her with jests about "pretty girl apothecaries" and the "love potions" he presumed she was compounding. Jean-Claude sniggered, Citizen Robert smiled grimly, and their master had the sense to take his effervescent protégé off to the Rue du Louvre. Marie was vexed enough to make a mistake in the preparation of a febrifuge, which earned her a reprimand from Citizen Robert.

She walked home thinking of her husband. His letters from the south were few and far between, and the regular military post was slow, but they were always cheerful, and referred to the early battles as trifling affairs. The big battles, according to Captain Latour at the end of April, were still to come. It was not a reassuring thought. It was still in Marie's mind when she crossed the Pont Royal and saw Eugène de Beauharnais standing outside the great wooden door of number 17.

"Why, Eugène, have you been waiting for me?" she exclaimed, hurrying up as he took off his hat and bowed.

A visit from Joséphine's son was totally unexpected. He had never come to her home before.

"I hope you don't mind, madame," the boy said, blushing. "Your concierge said you were at a laboratory, but you would be back about five, so I waited."

"Have you been waiting long?"

"Since four o'clock,' Eugène confessed.

"My dear! Come in at once and have some hot chocolate." The hand he put in hers was very cold. May had come in windy and chill.

In the courtyard, struck by his patience and pallor, Marie asked if everything was quite all right at home. "Is your mamma well?" she asked. "Hortense?"

"They're both well, thank you. Have you good news of Captain Latour, madame?"

"He seems to be enjoying the campaign."

"Lucky man!"

On the stair Marie said lightly, "I needn't ask if you have good news of General Buonaparte. All Paris is praising his victories."

"He writes to mother every day. I hope they'll let me go to join him soon."

Once inside the flat Marie left the visitor in the salon and went to the kitchen to make a jugful of chocolate. When she returned Eugène jumped up and took the tray from her hands.

"I'm sorry to put you to so much trouble, madame. Forgive the question, but have you no maids to wait on you?"

"I have a part-time maid, but she goes home in the afternoons . . . But why are you calling me madame, Eugène? It was Marie when we all lived together in the Rue de l'Université."

"That's just it!" cried the boy. "Madame – Marie – you never come to the Rue Chantereine now!"

Not quite sure where the conversation was to lead, Marie said the Rue Chantereine was a long way from her present home, but she had been at the villa several times while he was away at school. "Is that what you came to tell me, Eugène? That I should be with your mother more? Because I see her often in other people's houses – last week at a party at Madame Tallien's."

"Was anybody with her?"

"What do you mean by anybody? There were seventy people there. I've no idea who was with whom." In fact Marie had been struck by the affability Joséphine showed to her former lover, Paul Barras.

"She goes out every evening, and sometimes at noon as well."

"She's the wife of General Buonaparte, so everyone wants to meet her. Is something wrong, Eugène?"

"I've been so worried – Marie, I hate discussing her, it seems so disloyal – but anyway . . ." He was stammering in his embarrassment. "I asked for a holiday today and came in from St Germain to see her . . . She'd gone to a luncheon party at Madame Gohier's. Do you know the Gohiers?"

"Certainly I do. They say he'll be a member of the next Directory. There's no harm in a party at their house, my dear!"

"It depends on who was there. She sees some very queer people – one in particular. I – I can't say any more about that."

She can't be such a fool as to have taken up with Barras again! So Marie thought, but she sat silent until Eugène de Beauharnais, making a great effort, begged her to share his mother's home again. She told him it was impossible.

"I'm sorry, Eugène, but things have changed. Your mother has remarried, and I'm married too. We can't put the clock back to the Rue de l'Université time. Now I go to the labo three days in every *décade* – "

"I don't understand about the laboratory. What exactly do you do there?"

"Study pharmacy, like my grandfather and my uncle before me."

"Isn't it very difficult?"

"Sometimes. Do you learn chemistry at school?"

"Oh no. Latin and Greek mostly. French and mathematics too."

"I never even learned arithmetic."

"Maman says you're very clever."

"Not as clever as she is."

"She has a great respect for you. She's told Hortense and me a hundred times how brave you were in prison. She says, 'Marie kept us all together. She kept us from despair.' Oh, Marie, won't you please help us to keep her now? I know it's an impertinence to ask you, but won't you come and live at the villa? I'm sure she'll do everything you say."

"It isn't an impertinence, but it is impossible. This is my home. This is where my husband writes to me, and this is where he expects to find me when he comes back. Do you understand?"

"I think I do,' said Joséphine's son, "but there's something more. My – my stepfather's brother's in Paris now."

"Monsieur Joseph Buonaparte?"

"Yes, with his wife, I've got to call her Aunt Julie. She seems all right. But *he* – he's always at the villa, nagging my mother about extravagance, and he watches her like a cat with a mouse. I'm so afraid he'll carry stories to the general."

So there are stories to carry, thought Marie. Oh, Joséphine, what a fool you are!

"Is money part of the trouble, Eugène?" she asked.

"Well – yes. She goes out so much, she needs a lot of dresses, and she hasn't had a remittance from Martinique for a long time."

The boy's eyes were fixed on Marie's in hope. She said, "Your mother is still too young and pretty and – lively, to live alone at the villa. How about inviting Hortense's old governess, Mademoiselle de Lannoy, to come back and take over the running of the household? She was doing that very economically when I knew you first in the Rue St Dominique."

"Mother could twist poor old mademoiselle round her little finger. You must have seen that yourself!"

"I suppose she could . . . Well then, there's nothing else for it, I must talk to her myself. You're going back to the villa to dine and sleep?"

"I told Louise I would be back."

"And you didn't say you were coming to see me?"

"I didn't think of it till later."

"Then you must tell your mother as soon as you get home."

"Oh Marie, must I? Wouldn't it be better to say nothing?"

"You mustn't begin by being underhanded." To a boy just learning to appraise women critically, she was not quite the pretty Marie Fontaine of a year ago. She looked weary and jaded after her day's work, with her fair curls tumbled and her dress not very fresh, but somehow she seemed to have taken on a new authority. He nodded acquiescence.

"Give her my love," she went on, "and tell her I'll come to see her – not tomorrow but the day after – say the third of May, in the afternoon. Then I'll try to find out what the trouble is."

"Oh Marie, thank you!" Eugène smiled for the first time, a boy's smile, lively and carefree, as if the responsibility for a beloved but wayward mother had been lifted from his shoulders.

"Tell her that when she was out you had a fancy to come and see me and ask after Charles."

"I will."

"And now I think you ought to go. The Gohier luncheon was over long ago, and you mustn't keep your mother wondering where you are." She rose to her feet and the boy got up too. Eugène took her hand and kissed it in farewell. "Madame, I don't know how to thank you," he said, and turned to go.

"Stop a minute," she said before he reached the door. "You'll be late for dinner if you walk all the way. There's a livery we use on the Rue de Bourbon, near the Rue du Bac, where you can get a cab."

Eugène came back to her with a laugh. Greatly daring, he kissed her on the cheek and said teasingly, "Dear Marie, always so practical!"

Marie laughed too. "It's not a bad thing to be," she said.

When her cab took Marie up the avenue which led from the Rue Chantereine to the villa, she had time to note that the borders had been planted with rose bushes covered with tight green buds. It was a warm day at last, almost too warm for Marie in her blue overcoat, and the windows of the villa were wide open, their white muslin curtains moving in the breeze. The maid Louise, with her hands in the pockets of her white lace apron, was waiting on the steps, and greeted Marie in her too-familiar way.

"Madame's waiting for you in the little salon," she said. "She's doing her accounts. And they take some doing, if you ask me."

"I don't ask you," said Marie. "That will do, Louise, don't trouble to announce me." Slipping off her coat, she gave it to the woman and went alone through the reception rooms until she reached the little salon where Joséphine, sitting at an escritoire which was one of the few possessions she had brought from the apartment, sprang up with the usual effusive greeting. She was looking charmingly pretty in a dress of pale lilac muslin, the hem embroidered with violets, and her black hair, free of the usual fillet, coiled in a chignon on her neck.

"You're an angel to come to me, Marie!"

"But you're very busy. I'm interrupting you," said Marie, indicating the bundles of paper, tied and docketed, which looked out of place on the dainty desk. Joséphine pouted.

"Eugène told you my dear brother-in-law has come to town. He insists on seeing my household accounts, and my attorney – you remember Maître Raguideau? – says

I'd better show them, if only to keep the peace. As if it were any of Monsieur Joseph's concern! There!" She gathered up the bundles and threw them into an empty drawer of the escritoire.

"What has the way you run your house got to do with this Joseph? What does *he* do?"

"He's some sort of a merchant in Marseille. He had the impertinence to tell me he was in Paris to look after his brother's interests."

"I thought the Directory was doing that."

"Well . . . you see . . ." for the first time Joséphine seemed to hesitate. "My poor Bonaparte promised to settle eighteen thousand francs a year on me when we married . . . and as I tell Joseph, that would hardly keep me in clothes."

Marie was nonplussed. Eighteen thousand, promised by a soldier who hardly had eighteen hundred to his name! "Why do you call him Bonaparte?" she asked. "That's not how he spells his surname."

"It is now," said Joséphine. "He thinks Buonaparte's too Italian. He told the Directors he would change it when he invaded Italy."

"I see," said Marie. "And that's what you call him – Bonaparte?"

"Napoleon's such a ridiculous name. His mother told him he was called after some Greek saint, which I don't believe, and he says himself it means 'lion of the desert'. How would he like it if I called him Lion?"

"He's making his name famous," said Marie, "and yours too. Is that what he puts on his letters – Madame Napoleon Bonaparte?"

"Oh, don't talk to me about his letters, he never stops writing. I thought the Army of Italy was short of men, it certainly isn't short of couriers. Look at this!" She pulled open another drawer, so crammed with letters that half a dozen fell out upon the desk. Marie saw that three of these were sealed.

"You haven't opened some of them!"

Joséphine looked slightly ashamed. "Sometimes I really can't read them, his handwriting's so bad. Look at *this*!" The open sheet she held out to Marie did look as if a demented spider had been trying to climb out of the inkwell. Marie, with difficulty, deciphered a few lines.

You know very well [Napoleon wrote] that I cannot forget our little visits. You know – the little black forest. I give it a thousand kisses and I am waiting impatiently until I can get there.

For a moment the words made no sense to Marie, and then she understood what the writer meant by the little black forest, and threw down the page as if it burned her hand. "You ought not to show this letter to anyone," she said, "and I hope you keep your escritoire locked up."

"Oh, I do, I do!" protested Joséphine, and her husband's letters, like her household accounts, were put under lock and key directly. "Don't worry, darling. That was a silly letter, and it was silly of me to let you see it, but Bonaparte doesn't always write such nonsense. When he went to Nice he kept pestering me to join him there. As if I could!"

"Why couldn't you?"

"Go on such a long journey, a dangerous journey, through such an unsettled countryside? It was out of the question, but he kept on and on about it until I found a way to shut him up. I gave him to understand that I was expecting a child."

In a voice so harsh that Joséphine raised her eyebrows, Marie said, "What do you mean by 'gave him to understand'? You told him you were pregnant by him, is that it?"

"Well, yes, but not point-blank in the way you mean. Very, very delicately indeed."

"But it wasn't true?"

"No, of course it wasn't true. It was a kind of self-defence, such as we poor women sometimes have to use."

"And when you do meet again, and there's – nothing, what'll you do then?"

Joséphine laughed, a high tinkling sound. "Tell him I miscarried, of course."

Marie looked around her at the pretty room, the furniture bought from Madame Talma, the graceful escritoire, the harp bought for Hortense, and it seemed to her that the bleak, overcrowded cell in the Carmes prison where she met Joséphine first, was preferable to this. She had always known Joséphine was a wheedler and she had been fond of the wheedler; now she knew the wife of Napoleon Bonaparte was a heartless liar.

"Don't look so serious, darling." The seductive Creole voice came to Marie from a distance. "You're nearest the bell-rope, so ring, please, and let's have tea, and enjoy it, before dear Joseph comes nosing his way in. That man can scent food from afar – he's nothing but a glutton."

Marie rose mechanically to obey. Her hand was on the embroidered bell-rope when the door of the salon opened halfway, and at the level of her own face she saw an unnerving sight – not another head, but a pair of feet in glossy riding boots.

"Joséphine, look!"

A young man, dressed in uniform but bare-headed, entered the little salon walking on his hands. As soon as he saw Marie he turned a somersault, stood right way up and bowed. "Forgive me, *chère madame*," he said to Joséphine, "I didn't know you had a guest."

Madame Bonaparte, all smiles, gave him her hand to kiss. "I told you not to come today," she said.

"I didn't think you meant it."

"You are naughty," she told the newcomer. "Madame Latour, may I present Captain Hippolyte Charles, of the Hussars?"

They assured each other that they were enchanted to meet. Captain Charles was slight and dapper, very well-groomed (not a hair had been ruffled by his being upside

113

down) and sporting a pencilling of the moustache which was just coming into fashion among the officer class.

"Madame Latour's husband is in the Twenty-first Chasseurs," said Joséphine.

"Serving at the front in the Army of Italy," said Marie. She had got over her first surprise and was asking herself, Who is this little mountebank, and what is he doing here? "What hussar regiment are you in, Captain Charles?"

"I've been detached from the Hussars, madame," the man replied with an ingratiating smile. "Alas, I wasn't posted to the front. My military duties are now on the administrative side."

"If you please," said Louise, entering with a smile of complicity which seemed to embrace them all, *"Madame est servie!"* With a sigh of relief Joséphine led the way to what was rather ostentatiously called the grand salon, thus putting an end to any further questions by Marie. The salon was the room with the bay window, in which now stood an *étagere* filled with flowering plants, exotic and scented, such as Joséphine loved to have around her. It also contained a piano which nobody could play and some rather flimsy chairs and sofas, and in the centre of the room a tea table and two occasional tables, each holding a silver tray with little cakes.

Captain Charles gallantly seated the ladies and handed the silver teapot to his hostess. He had been crestfallen at the first sight of Marie but was regaining his spirits rapidly. He had great faith in his charms for the female sex, and this pretty, fair (but inquisitive) girl was exactly the sort of object with whom, under other circumstances, he would at once have engaged in flirtation. As it was he launched a stream of chatter at Joséphine: gossip of the boulevards, of behind-the-scenes at the theatres and the latest emigré scandal; the whole performance laced with rhyming jokes and puns, at which he was an adept. Joséphine laughed heartily, and even Marie, whom his white-toothed smiles included in the gaiety, laughed more than once at his sallies. Basking in feminine approbation, the former Hussar went so far as to take the fine linen cloth from under one of the cake trays, tie it round his head turban-fashion and announce an impersonation of "a Negro mammy from Martinique." His imitation of Joséphine's Créole drawl made Marie gasp, but the lady herself cried "Bravo!" and declared she might have thought herself back again in the sugar fields of Trois Islets.

Perhaps it was lucky that the impersonation was over and the cloth replaced under the cake tray before Louise opened the door to announce Citizen Joseph Bonaparte, for the first words of Napoleon's brother, after bowing to the ladies, were "Ah, Captain Charles! You here again? Your military duties don't appear to take up much of your time."

"Madame Bonaparte entrusted me with a small commission, sir, – a purchase I handed over to the gardener," said Captain Charles readily. "I've been rewarded with a cup of tea."

The newcomer scowled. "A purchase, eh? What have you been buying this time, Joséphine?"

"Only a new kind of fertiliser for my roses," she answered meekly. "They're not doing well in city soil. I tell your brother we must look for a place in the country some day soon. Let me present you to Madame Latour – Monsieur Joseph Bonaparte, Marie – and sit down; you'll enjoy a cup of tea."

When he had bowed to Marie, and seated himself heavily, when she filled his teacup, Joséphine went on. "You must treat Madame Latour with great respect, Joseph. Her husband is in Italy with the general, a captain of cavalry, and she's a learned lady in her own right, a student of pharmacy. And a very old friend of my Bonaparte."

"Really?" said Joseph with a smile. "Where did you know my brother, Madame Latour?"

"In Paris, sir, four years ago. My uncle was his friend."

"Four years ago! Ah, those were difficult days for France

– and for Corsica." Selecting a cream cake, Monsieur Bonaparte seemed disposed to let the subject drop. From under lowered eyelids, Marie studied him with great interest. She knew that he was only a year older than Napoleon, which made him twenty-seven, but he looked like a man of forty. There was a certain family resemblance to his junior, but the whippet slimness and alertness of the soldier had been overlaid, in the civilian, by a coating of fat, and his fashionably short hair was already sparse. Remembering Napoleon's confidences of long ago, she knew that the brothers had started out equal at ten and nine years old, with royal scholarships to the school at Autun where they learned to speak French, and that after their father's early death Joseph had forged ahead as the *chef de famille*. But in spite of what the law said that family, consisting of the widowed mother, three growing boys and three young girls, had become the charge of the second brother, and the effective head of the family was Napoleon. All his pathetic economies were made for them, while Joseph married a rich merchant's daughter and embarked on a commercial career. Napoleon make a marriage settlement of eighteen thousand francs a year! It isn't possible, thought Marie.

Guiltily she realised that she had been dreaming, hypnotised by the sight of Monsieur Bonaparte forking his way through two *madeleines* and three *babas au rhum*, and yet they had been talking about the war in Italy, the subject which engrossed her heart. Or rather, the brother-and sister-in-law were talking, the former Hussar seemed to have nothing to add to a discussion which began with the one saying "Have you had your daily letter, *ma belle-soeur*? Everything going well?" and the other replying, "Yes, oh yes! The general says he'll have another victory to report very soon!" It continued in a totally uninformed discussion of the rivers of Lombardy, which Monsieur Bonaparte conducted with his shoulder turned on Captain Charles. Who took advantage of Louise's entry with fresh hot water to get up and say politely, "Alas, madame, I must return to duty. If I can do anything more for you at the market garden, you have only to command me."

"You must come again soon," said Joséphine, and gave him her hand to kiss. There were no expressive glances, no lingering clasp of the fingers; Captain Charles's adieux to the whole party were eminently correct, and presently they saw him riding down the avenue on a skittish horse whose paces suited his own jaunty style.

"Where does that fellow's military duty lie, I wonder?" said Joseph Bonaparte.

"He's something to do with the Purchasing Commission, I believe," said Joséphine. "Another cake?"

"No thanks . . . Do you know, I think I'll follow his example and take myself off. We've been neglecting your charming friend – and those accounts can wait until tomorrow."

"I'm afraid I've interrupted your business," said Marie.

"You mean you want to come back tomorrow?" said Joséphine suppressing a sigh. "Then come to luncheon. Bring Julie."

"Thank you, but Julie doesn't wish to be involved in business matters." Turning to Marie, the man said, "I should like you to know my wife, madame. May she send you our cards? Will you give me your address?"

She told him, and asked if he and his wife had found a house or an apartment to please them.

"Our stay in Paris depends on my brother," he said, "we've found a comfortable hotel not far from the Rue Chantereine. Till tomorrow, Joséphine – at luncheon, eh? *Mes hommages, mesdames.*"

"Come into the little salon, darling," said Joséphine, as soon as he had gone. Her lips were tight with temper, and as soon as the door was shut she burst out: "Now that you've seen that sample, do you wonder I'm not anxious to know more of the Bonaparte family? *Quel gros bourgeois! Quel lourdaud!*"

"Bourgeois he may be, but he isn't a lout," protested

Marie. "And what have you against the family? You told me their mother wrote you a very nice letter."

"I've a feeling Bonaparte dictated it."

"I know he's annoying you about money, but I rather liked Monsieur Bonaparte. He wasn't as interesting as Captain Charles, though."

"Oh, isn't he fun? I knew you'd like him, everybody does. He's so amusing! Everyone wants him at their parties."

"I'm sure they do. He's a very good mimic . . . Where did you meet him, Joséphine?"

"Oh, we met – now let me think. We met at one of Paul's parties, not long after I was married."

"Paul Barras? And he's the civilian member of the Purchasing Commission, isn't he?"

"I believe so. And he's one of the Directors too, let me remind you."

"Of course, a most important man. But was Captain Charles known to any of your other friends? People who could vouch for him, like the Talliens or the de Monniers?"

"They know him now, at any rate. Marie, why are you asking such a lot of silly questions?"

"Because I'm worried about you, Joséphine."

"But why? Did Eugène say anything about Hippolyte? My children are so jealous of my friends!"

"Eugène would never betray your confidence." Nor did he; Eugène only said there was one in particular among her queer friends that he feared, and after the antics of the afternoon Marie was sure that the "one in particular" was Captain Hippolyte Charles.

"I don't know about Eugène," said Eugène's mother, fiddling with the keys of the escritoire. "He was very sulky before he went back to St Germain, just because I teased him about you."

"About *me*?"

"It was the most harmless teasing – about going off on his own to pay his addresses to a married lady. 'You're beginning early,' was what I said."

"After all, Eugène is only seven years younger than me," said Marie with a smile.

"Thank you, my dear! Is that intended to be a kind reminder that my husband is six years younger than I am? Not on our marriage certificate! I took four years off my age and Bonaparte added two to his, so we're both registered as twenty-eight!"

"Was that your idea or the general's?"

"It was Bonaparte's."

"Then it was a very kind and chivalrous idea." Marie saw the other woman's lips begin to tremble, and said gently, "Darling, why are you so unhappy?"

"I – I'm not unhappy!"

"I think you must be, when you think of your husband, so far away and fighting for France. Joséphine! have I ever criticised your private life? I knew about your affair with General Hoche in prison. I knew when you started another with Paul Barras. It was nothing to do with me, and I didn't interfere. But Joseph Bonaparte might. What will you do if he tells your husband that within a week of your wedding you'd begun an – an intimate friendship with a – a little imp of a man who looks even younger than the general himself? Joséphine, I implore you, put an end to it now!"

Joséphine was sobbing before she ended her appeal, but it was her habit to escape from reality in tears. Marie, as so often before, kissed her averted cheek and chafed her hands, listening to the muffled whimpers of "I can't – I can't – it'll all end in trouble – oh, what shall I do?" But when the sobs became hysteria and turned into screams she rang the bell for help, and the faithful Agathe – thank heaven it wasn't Louise – came in so quickly that she might have been listening at the door.

Agathe knew where the valerian was kept in madame's dressing-room; Agathe would take her upstairs, put her to bed and administer a dose of the nerve drops. "This is her third attack of hysterics in ten days," said the maid.

"Oh Agathe, what's the matter?"

119

"Those two men excite her – Monsieur Bonaparte and that little – " Agathe's expression supplied a descriptive word. "I wish General Bonaparte would come home."

"Oh, so do I."

"Or that you would come and live with us again, Madame Marie. Do you want to go up and sit beside her now?"

"I'd better go back to the Quai Voltaire, Agathe. I seem to do more harm than good."

"If you really mean it I'll tell that idle fellow to put his horses in the carriage and take you home."

Marie insisted on walking, and she had her way. As she went down the avenue she noticed that the roses seemed to be thriving well in city soil, for the green sepals were beginning to unfold on the first gleams of colour, and the afternoon sunshine fell softly on the happy Bonaparte home.

9

The road lay forward to Milan, but the journey took longer than Bonaparte had expected, because Beaulieu's army made an attempt to bar his progress, sustained another defeat at Borghetto, and fled into the Tirol. Then there were only the Austrian stragglers round Milan to pursue, and on 16 May Napoleon entered the Lombard capital.

The 21st Chasseurs distinguished themselves at Borghetto. Murat led the charge, and Charles Latour would have been close behind him but for the bruising and swelling of his elbow which hampered him in the control of a remount which had never stood fire before. He was feeling better by the time of the entry into Milan, and his modest share in a triumph such as he had never known.

Neither had Napoleon. For the first time church bells rang *for him*, flowers were strewn in the road *for him*, and the Mayor and councillors, waiting in front of the Duomo, offered a civic welcome *to him alone*. The Austrian hand had weighed heavily on Lombardy, and the Milanese went wild over their deliverer.

A palace was placed at his disposal by the Duca di Serbelloni, and as his host led him up a splendid staircase, lined with statues and ancestral portraits, Napoleon resolved that though this was his first palace it should certainly not be his last.

"I hope you will make my home your own for as long

as you please, General," said Serbelloni. "Is there anything my people can bring you?"

"My orderly was told to follow us, he's probably in your kitchens now. If he could fetch me some hot water?"

"The footmen will see to that. Now here is the guest apartment prepared for you in haste this morning. I hope nothing has been forgotten . . . Open the shutters, Marco,' he said to a lackey who had come, soft-footed, up behind them. Bars of sunlight fell in order across a handsomely furnished library.

"*Ecco!*" said the gracious host, "I'll leave you to get some rest. The civic luncheon begins at half past one, so you have nearly an hour and a half in hand."

"I'm deeply grateful for your consideration, Duke. I've ordered a day's rest for all troops; they'll want to celebrate with the citizens of Milan."

"Enjoy a siesta this afternoon, General." Serbelloni hesitated. "If you'll forgive my saying so, you're looking tired."

Bonaparte shrugged, and when the duke had gone he smiled. The idea of a siesta was ludicrous. It was a rest day for the troops, but not for the general and his chief of staff, who would meet for work as soon as the luncheon was over. Marshal Wurmser and three Austrian corps were somewhere in the hills above Lake Garda, and shock tactics must be prepared for them.

The lackey coughed discreetly. "Pardon, *Eccellenza*, the bedroom is this way, and the bathroom through that door over there."

"Thank you." He followed the man into a state bedroom which, as he had expected (knowing the Italian – and Corsican – fear of the midday sun) was wrapped in darkness, and asked him to open the shutters there too. He took off his belt and heavy blue tunic, and said he wanted to write some letters. He had noticed that the desk in the library, however hastily prepared, was well furnished with writing paper, ink and sealing wax.

There was only one letter Napoleon wanted to write –

to Joséphine; the Directory had been informed on the previous day (by courier to Nice, by Chappe telegraph to Paris) that he was about to enter Milan. It was the condition Carnot himself had imposed on the issue of an exit permit to Madame Bonaparte – that her husband should be in Milan before she joined him, for the prudes in the Directory evidently thought he would spend all his time in bed with her and neglect his duty. Dipping his pen in the inkwell and remembering the great bed he had just seen, Napoleon imagined a siesta with Joséphine in that darkened room, and could hardly command himself to trace the opening words, *mi dolce amor*. Then, annoyingly, the lackey was there again.

"*Eccellenza*, you expressed a wish for hot water. Would it please you to take a bath now, or later in the day?"

A bath! After a month when his ablutions meant having a bucketful of cold water flung over his naked torso, *a bath*! "Now, if you please," the general said, and was told that his orderly was here. "Let him come in," and the man appeared, a real *sans-culotte*, dropping Napoleon's campaign valise on the Oriental carpet, exuding a powerful odour of garlic and red wine, and startled to hear that his officer was about to take the dangerous step of bathing.

The bathroom, at first glance, was the brightest room in the guest apartment, for the shutters had already been flung back and the sunlight was streaming through a window covered only by net. The floor was tiled with white marble, sloping slightly to a gutter in the middle, over which the tub was placed. It had been filled by two men in sacking aprons, strong enough to have carried brimming buckets of boiling and cold water up the back stairs. They escaped by that way now, after bowing to the French general when he entered, unimpressive in a white robe brought him by the lackey. No epaulettes, no sabre, no nothing! They reported in the servants' hall that he knew enough Italian to say *grazie*.

Napoleon looked round him appreciatively. The room

reminded him of his childhood home (though the Ajaccio bathroom had had a stone floor) even to the final detail of a live gecko lizard, sitting in a corner like a little dragon and poised to catch flies. He had asked for warm water in order to shave, and there were two china basins on a marble shelf which ran all down one side of the room, and was surmounted by a mirror. He had shaved at five o'clock that morning, with a blunt blade and peering into a little glass held up by his orderly, but with his dark jowl he must shave again if he was to make the *bella figura* by which Italians set such store at the civic luncheon.

At twenty-six Napoleon Bonaparte was not vain, and when he had used the second basin to wash the long black locks which Joséphine was always teasing him to have cut, he thought his reflection in the mirror was quite creditable. Eyes reddened and cheeks drawn, perhaps, but tired – no!

In the Serbelloni household they thought of everything. There had been razors and a bowl of shaving soap on the marble shelf, and here were sponges and soaps on a china holder laid across the tub. As he lowered his meagre body into the warm water, to which a few drops of herbal oil had been added, Napoleon remembered Joséphine's telling him that the best thing after her release from prison had been having a tub bath in her own home. Was waging war a kind of prison from which he had escaped for a day?

He thought of Joséphine while he soaped and soaked in the tub, and while the water lapped his body Napoleon's thoughts grew more and more sensual. He and she had never bathed together. That was a joy in store, and this Italian bath was big enough for two. It might hold them both if she came quickly enough to Milan. He determined to tell her so when he finished the letter beginning "My sweet love". He knew Joséphine had an erotic imagination to match his own, and this image would fire it.

She didn't write to him as often as he would have liked,

and he believed she was afraid of the long journey from France just emerging from Revolution into war-torn Italy. He had assured her that the Directory would give his wife a military escort and do everything to ensure her safety, but if there really was a baby on the way (she seemed rather doubtful about that, much as he was hoping it was true) she ought to have a woman friend with her as well as a maid. What a pity not one of his sisters was available. At such a time he wanted to knot closer and closer the family ties which meant so much to him.

There were no ladies at the civic luncheon, but the belles of Milan were out in force at the gala performance in La Scala. The hero of the day sat alone with the Prefect in the box of state. He was not particularly interested in the performance of a new opera by Cherubini, for Napoleon cared little for music, and sometimes liked to shock by saying his favourite instrument was the drum, which replicated the sound of cannon fire. But he enjoyed the applause his presence caused, and the whispers of the beautifully dressed and jewelled women who never took their eyes from his box.

"Not handsome, no, but he has a certain style," some of them were saying, and others, "How young he looks – a mere boy!" All hoped he would stay on in Milan, while some wondered what his wife was like. "A Créole, they say she is – d'you suppose that means she's black?" One beautiful blonde woman, sitting in the box just opposite with a much older man, never took her mother-of-pearl opera glasses from his face during the whole of the first act. The conductor waved his baton not at his orchestra but at General Bonaparte. The soprano ogled him during her every aria, the tenor struck attitudes at him and the ballet girls danced at him, and all the time Napoleon was thinking that if his wife were there she would be the queen of the festivities.

Napoleon was trying to fall asleep that night and still thinking about the problem of getting Joséphine to Milan, when it occurred to him that the ideal companion on her difficult journey would be the girl he still thought of as Marie Fontaine.

When Marie returned to the Quai Voltaire after her troubled visit to Madame Bonaparte, the concierge tapped on the glass of the *loge* to attract her attention and came out carrying a letter. "Your friend Citizeness Beauchet called while you were out," he said in his gruff way. "She was sorry to miss you. She left this letter."

"Thank you, Citizen Bélard." Marie, too, was sorry to have missed Madame Beauchet, for she felt guilty about her neglect of that good old friend. She had taken baskets of fruit and whatever invalid delicacies she could find to the Rue de Courty in February, when Marie-Josèphe was nursing her husband through a bronchial attack which threatened to become pneumonia, but then the business of getting Charles's belongings ready for the campaign in Italy, added to the labo days and the increasing difficulty of her studies, took up most of her time. And now there was this business of the de Beauharnais children and their mother! She opened the letter when she was in the apartment, undisturbed except for the sounds of Armande preparing supper. It was heavily sealed, and when spread wide very short, without a salutation or a complete signature.

Will you come with me next *décadi* [it ran] to see the ground the Princess von Hohenzollern has bought at Picpus? An old friend hopes to meet us there. M.-J. B.

The wording was an attempt at secrecy, natural in a woman who had lived through the Terror, but it was unnecessarily cryptic. Picpus was the Golgotha where 1,306 victims of the guillotine, half of them people of the working class, had been flung into a common grave during a few summer weeks in 1794, and the Princess von Hohenzollern's purchase of the site for conversion into a respectable graveyard had already been mentioned in the newspapers as one more example of the Directory's wish to bury the memories of the past. The guillotine had stood in the Square of the Throne Overthrown, as the wags called it, and Marie's uncle had died there, along with Joséphine's first husband and the Princess von Hohenzollern's brother the Prince von Salm on the day the public executioner, Sanson, broke his own record by chopping off fifty-four heads in twenty-four minutes. Marie shivered at the recollection. But – "I must go," she said to herself, "out of respect for Uncle Prosper's memory, and the memory of the Noailles ladies who died with him and who were always good to me, and to support poor Marie-Josèphe, who will feel it dreadfully, because of poor Madame Adrienne in her Austrian dungeon."

Next morning, as she was about to step into the cab which took her to the labo, Marie received another letter, delivered by a coachman who sprang off the seat of his carriage to hand it to her. She recognised the two black horses and thought it might be the promised message from Agathe Rible, but then she saw the familiar pink cocked-hat of Joséphine's correspondence, tied to a tight little bunch of pink rosebuds.

> Darling Marie [the dainty note began]. Forgive me for being so naughty yesterday [naughty was a favourite word of Joséphine's] and spoiling your visit. Agathe insisted on sending for the doctor, who gave me a sedative and told me to stay in bed for a couple of days. Come again soon to your loving Joséphine.

"Thank you," Marie said to the man. "Tell your mistress I will write." She stood on the pavement after he had moved off, heedless of her own driver's impatience to be gone, thinking how typical of Joséphine was the bed rest, which might save her from her brother-in-law's investigations for two days at the most, and the wheedling letter. Marie had been shocked and angry yesterday, and had told herself she never wanted to see the woman again, but as the faintest scent from the rosebuds disengaged itself in her warm hand she told herself that she would have to give *la câline*, the wheedler, one more chance.

Monsieur Guiart brought another visitor to talk to her that morning, who made a happier impression than young Bernard Courtois. He was Dr Claude Berthollet, a distinguished chemist who had sometimes called on her uncle, and who perhaps for his sake took Marie seriously. He watched attentively while she prepared spirits of ammonia, and even took up the page on which she had scribbled her calculations from the Table of Volumes of the quantities of oils of lemon, lavender and nutmeg she should add to 4% of ammonium carbonate. His comment, "You have neat fingers, Madame Latour. Your uncle would be proud of you," although it was no more than Monsieur Guiart had said before, went a long way to increasing her self-respect.

During the next few days Marie's anxiety increased. There was no news of Charles, or of any advance in Italy, and though this may have worried their Directory there was no sign of worry among the people of Paris, preoccupied as ever by rising prices and scanty rations. France had been at war with one or more of her neighbours for five years and had fallen into a state of apathy in which war was the norm, as the guillotine once had been.

On the *décadi*, or Tenth Day which in Revolutionary France had replaced the Christian Sunday as the day of rest, Marie went to the Rue de Courty in a cab (decidedly the Latours' livery stable bill was going to be higher than usual in this month of Floréal, Year IV) and picked up Marie-Josèphe, who had been warned in advance. She had expected a tearful greeting, for of the three Noailles ladies who had gone to the guillotine one was the sister, one the mother, and one the grandmother of her beloved Adrienne de La Fayette. She had had no news of Madame Adrienne since the previous October, when the American consul at Hamburg, who had done what he could to dissuade the headstrong woman, wrote to tell her that Adrienne had failed in her appeal to the Austrian Emperor, and gone with her two young daughters to share her husband's prison at Olmütz. But, unexpectedly, Madame Beauchet was optimistic.

"General Buonaparte – I forgot, we're supposed to call him Bonaparte now – is doing so well, he'll soon be in Vienna, and *force* the Austrians to release the Marquis de La Fayette!"

"I hope you're right, my dear, but our troops are still a long way from Vienna."

"Poor Marie!" Madame Beauchet patted her hand. "Are you thinking it'll be a long time before your Charles reaches Vienna?"

"I worry about him all the time," Marie confessed, and her friend murmured some consoling words. For the rest of the way they talked only of Captain Latour. Marie-Josèphe was following her own rules of security: there could be no safer topic than a soldier of the Republic when one was sitting behind a strange cabdriver. For security's sake, too, she suggested that they ask to be set down at the place where the Bastille had stood. It was not far from their actual destination, and it might be imprudent to be driven up to the Rue de Picpus in style.

Grass was growing over the site of the Bastille, where five or six years earlier the *sans-culottes* and their women had danced the *carmagnole*, and while they paused to survey the scene Marie asked Madame Beauchet if the old friend they were to meet was Father Carrichon, who had been with her uncle and the Noailles ladies in the last hour of their lives.

"You've guessed it, Marie. The good father wants so much to see you again."

"I'm so glad. I haven't seen him since just after our wedding day, when he came to the Quai Voltaire to give us the blessing we were denied. Perhaps he'll be able to tell me what became of Father Vincent and the women who helped at the soup kitchen."

"Perhaps he will . . . He's going to meet us at the – the place. You've been there before, haven't you?"

"Once," said Marie, "just after I came out of prison. It

was horrible." She remembered the bare, unequal surface of the hastily-covered pits where the poor bodies had been flung.

It was not horrible now. The victims of Fouquier-Tinville – for it was he, the terrible Public Prosecutor, who had condemned every one of them to die, only to die by the guillotine himself – had been lifted up by night and laid down again in a seemly fashion, to be covered over with levelled earth and squares of green grass which seemed already to be growing together. Father Carrichon was waiting for them, still the same gentle priest who had heard Marie's catechism when St Roch was her parish church and not a place of awful memories. In the days of the Terror, when he risked his life as a priest who had refused to take the civic oath, he had assumed some strange disguises, as a mason, a carpenter or some other artisan, but now he appeared in the role that suited him best, as a middle-aged school teacher, with a wallet full of his "pupils'" essays under his arm.

The three walked slowly round the ground "consecrated already by the prayers of the passersby," Father Carrichon told them, and Marie whispered that someone said a chapel would be erected here.

"Not yet, my child, that cannot be; but when France, her eldest daughter, returns to the arms of Mother Church, there will be perpetual worship at the graves of the martyrs."

Marie walked on in silence, while the priest, in an undertone, told Madame Beauchet again about the last moments of "my ladies", as she called them, and she was soon wiping away the tears. She was not the only one: there were other women in the silent groups they passed who had their handkerchiefs at their eyes, but by common consent none of the mourners, from whom the shadow of the Great Fear had not yet lifted, lingered long at that tragic ground.

As they walked back a short distance to the place of execution, Marie asked Father Carrichon if he could tell her what became of Citizen Vincent and his helpers after their work among the homeless was transferred to the Hotel Dieu.

"I can tell you all you need to know," said Father Carrichon with a smile. "They are all safe. I hope you never heard of a so-called clinic, far away on the outskirts of Paris, where the exiles are cared for, the royalists, the returned émigrés, the priests in hiding, and that is where our friends have found a refuge. The nuns care for the sick bodies, and Father Vincent brings them the Bread of Heaven."

"And do you go there too, Father Carrichon?"

"Fairly often."

"Then please give them my love, and ask their prayers for my husband."

"I will, my child – " and then Madame Beauchet interrupted to ask fearfully if they were quite safe in this wild place.

The Square of the Throne Overthrown was not wild, but merely convivial with the gaiety of half a hundred working-class families come out to enjoy a warm May *décadi* at the Punch and Judy shows, the shooting galleries where the prize was gingerbread, the roundabouts and the swings. While the band played a deafening tune Father Carrichon told Marie where the guillotine had stood – "on the far side, close to the Barrier of the Throne" – and how he had been close enough, among the gloating spectators, to see the composure on her uncle's face as he mounted the steps to the scaffold.

"And where did you give them your blessing, Father?" said Marie, forcing herself to calm.

"I was standing on the corner when the tumbrils came up, where that boy is singing now – "

But Marie's hearing was better than the priest's.

"He isn't singing, Father," she said sharply. "That's a newsboy from the *Moniteur*. Can't you see his bag of papers? Listen! He's calling an extra."

Piercing the clamour of the square came the boy's treble:

"Great Victory in Italy! Bonaparte victorious at Lodi Bridge!"

10

Two months after Napoleon entered Milan, Marie Latour arrived in the Lombard capital, in what capacity she was not quite sure. As Charles Latour's wife? Certainly; that had been the bait offered by Joseph Bonaparte and Joachim Murat when that ill-assorted pair arrived at the Quai Voltaire to persuade her to undertake the journey. As companion or chaperone to Joséphine? Equally certainly; that was the reason for her presence in the great travelling coach which jolted its way over rough roads and mountain tracks from Paris into northern Italy. Napoleon, his brother said, wanted his wife to be accompanied by a "lady" as well as attended by a maid, for under the Directory people were beginning to talk about "ladies" as they did under the old régime.

Marie temporised. She could not accept the invitation, she said, until she knew her husband approved of the scheme. In vain did Murat, whose chief mission to Paris was to start the reluctant Madame Bonaparte on her way, take it upon himself to answer for Major Latour's approval. Injured at Lodi, the sight of his wife would compensate for his suffering, etc, etc. But Marie waited for a word from Charles, and when it came it was quite definite. It said nothing about his health or his battlefield promotion at Borghetto, but showed his longing to see her in Milan.

I know my brave girl will make light of the long journey. [the letter ended.]

Come, oh! come to me if you can!

Then Marie went to see Joséphine, who with her sweet ability to sweep all disagreeables under the carpet said nothing about their last strained meeting but welcomed her with open arms. With her usual luck she had received a remittance from her mother's bankers, so that Joseph Bonaparte admitted her finances were in good order, and he was preparing to escort her to Milan. Joséphine, however, was still unwilling to set out. She had a new scare about the brigands they might meet on the way. One gang called the Company of Jehu, of royalist sympathies, was a menace to travellers in the south, while an apolitical group, even more picturesquely named Hot Feet, was pillaging lonely farms in central France.

"We won't be going near any lonely farms, and Murat says the Directory will give us a cavalry escort," said Marie. She knew that danger was only one more excuse for her friend's reluctance to leave the gaieties of Paris. Parties at the Luxembourg, parties in the Palais Royal, parties to which she was too often escorted by Captain Hippolyte Charles, were for Joséphine far more glamorous than what she called "the life of a camp follower". Marie went to no parties, except one called a farewell party, prematurely and exuberantly given by Teresa Tallien, but went quietly ahead with her preparations. She was in funds, for she had the whole of her tenants' April rent in hand, plus a substantial sum produced by Maître Vial, and she bought a new dress from Madame Cécile, with a leather portmanteau to pack her clothes in. She had long talks with Monsieur Guiart and Dr Claude Berthollet, and just as she was beginning to chafe at the delay, several still longer talks with Colonel Andoche Junot.

Junot, who had been sent to Paris to replace Murat and to fetch Joséphine to Milan, told Marie much that she wanted to know. About Charles: "Don't worry your pretty head about Charles, Marie. He's all right. One of our doctors, a fellow called Legendre, who's always predicting disaster, says he'll probably have rheumatism in his elbow when he's an elderly man, but not this year."

"He's only twenty-five this year," laughed Marie. "Is he still in Milan?"

"No, but he'll get special leave when you get there. He's wild about seeing you."

"If we ever get started . . . Andoche, what's General Bonaparte doing? Why has there been no major action since Lodi Bridge?"

"Well, for one thing, old Wurmser's still holed up behind Lake Garda; the Staff thinks he's waiting for the new levies the British are paying for. And for another, the general's been on tour for three weeks, doing some odd jobs for the Directory."

"What sort of odd jobs?"

"I don't really know," said Junot evasively. "Political stuff, not the sort of thing the fellows discuss with me. Now he's gone to supervise the siege of Mantua."

"I should think a siege would be too slow for him," said Marie. "Oh, Andoche, do make Joséphine get a move on! We should have left a month ago."

"I'm under orders to do just that," said Junot. "And so is she."

There were no more delays. The date of departure was fixed for 28 June, or 10 Messidor, and next time Marie went to the Rue Chantereine she was horrified to learn that Captain Charles would be of the party.

"Oh, Joséphine! Do you think that's wise?"

"Yes, why not? He's only coming with us as far as Lyon, where he has some business . . . and you know how I love to help my friends."

"Purchasing Commission business?"

"I expect so. I don't understand these things."

"But do you think your husband would approve?"

"His precious brother hasn't objected, and Joseph's really in charge of the party, isn't he? Don't look like that, Marie. I don't know why you disapprove of poor

134

Hippolyte, but he won't get in your way. He'll ride in the second coach with Junot and Louise."

"As far as Lyon."

On a fine June morning, after six weeks delay, an imposing procession started from the Rue Chantereine, while Madame Julie Bonaparte, Eugène and Hortense waved goodbye from the garden. Agathe Rible, who was to look after the villa from which most of the servants had been dismissed, had said a tearful farewell indoors. Joséphine and Marie were in the first coach with the dog Fortuné between them, while Joseph sat opposite "like a prison warder" as his sister-in-law said resentfully. Hippolyte Charles, the maid Louise and Junot were in the second coach, the cheerful Junot not affronted at being paired off with a servant, especially a pretty one, and the third vehicle was a *fourgon* piled with baggage. The cavalry escort was commanded by a young officer called Marmont, who rode ahead at intervals to order meals and beds for the travellers.

For the first hundred kilometres Marie enjoyed the journey. While Joséphine dozed elegantly and her brother-in-law snored, the girl was wide awake, watching everything that passed. All was novelty: the towns, the villages, the countryside, and in the waits at the post-houses, where fresh horses were backed between the shafts, she saw new faces, heard new dialects and came to a new understanding of her country.

Captain Hippolyte Charles behaved very well. The only privilege he claimed was giving his arm to Joséphine when, to spare the horses, the passengers had to get out and walk up the stony hill tracks, and his quips and jokes enlivened the meals eaten in mediocre hostelries. He behaved better than the maid Louise, who was increasingly pert to her mistress, and he only once fell into disgrace with Junot, the victim of one of his practical jokes. The former Hussar left them all as soon as they reached Lyon, where they saw none of the predicted unrest, just as they never met a Jehu or a Hot Foot on the road.

On the next long stage from Lyon to Turin, the capital of conquered Piedmont, they were all growing tired and perhaps apprehensive, but the name of Bonaparte worked wonders, and a suite of rooms was placed at their disposal in the Palazzo Madama. On the way across the mountains to Milan the army presence became very evident, not only in the movements of French infantry, but in the awkward encounters with convoys of wagons and drays, closely covered and heavily guarded. The officers in command of the convoys interrogated young Marmont sharply, but refused to answer his or Junot's questions.

At last the day came when they reached a hamlet within an hour's drive of Milan, and Marmont rode ahead to announce their immediate arrival. The travellers sat in the unkempt garden of a shabby inn which could produce nothing but bread and goat's milk cheese, while the troopers of the escort, before they fed, unsaddled and watered their horses at the fountain. Junot, in good spirits as usual, tried to keep a conversation going: the civilians were almost too tired to talk. Marie was nervous. As the hot afternoon hours wore on she began to fear that something had gone wrong. Marmont was away too long, and when he appeared at last the sight of his face confirmed her fears.

"Bad news, madame," he said to Joséphine. "The general is not in Milan."

"Not in Milan?" cried Joséphine. "Where is he? Is there a battle? Are we in danger? Where has he gone to, when he was expecting me?" She burst into tears, and hardly listened to the young man's explanations that General Bonaparte was on his way back from Mantua, where he had gone to supervise the siege operations, and the duty officer at headquarters had at once despatched couriers to inform him of madame's arrival.

"By headquarters I suppose you mean the Palazzo

Serbelloni," said Joseph Bonaparte, " – Joséphine, control yourself – did you see the duke himself?"

"The Duca di Serbelloni is on his way to Nice, sir, and goes on to Paris," Marmont replied. 'He left orders for your every comfort. I suggest we go on to the city as fast as possible . . . Saddle up, you men!"

"Napoleon ought never to have gone away!" sobbed Joséphine. "After entreating me to join him – after *imploring* me for weeks – he should have waited for me!"

"Come on, Joséphine, cheer up," said Junot. "He may be back tomorrow. He's a fast mover, don't you know that yet?"

Andoche Junot's bluff words annoyed Joséphine, but they did her more good than Marie's coaxing or Louise's smelling salts. She was irritated enough to get back into the carriage without more ado, and as the summer dusk was falling they arrived in front of the great granite façade and the Ionic columns of the Palazzo Serbelloni. She was able to reply graciously to a little speech of welcome made in creditable French by the duke's major domo, who assured her that His Excellency the general was hastening to her side, and she even smiled when the man begged leave to tell Marie that her husband, *il signor conte* de la Tour de Vesle, was in good health.

Madame Bonaparte was led upstairs by a retinue of Italian domestics, and Marie was attended by a pretty little maid who said her name was Rita. A room was ready for her on the *piano nobile*, a compliment due to the *contessa*, a title repeatedly used by Rita and by another maid called Barbara, who was preparing the hip bath standing in an alcove of the restful room. The walls were covered in green moiré silk like the chairs and sofa, and the bed hangings were of striped silk in green and cream. It was also a room of contradictions. A crucifix of olive wood hung on one wall with a *prie-dieu* beneath it, while above the dressing table, on which a bowl of white roses had been placed, was an engraving of the Raphael

Madonna. Yet on a wide shelf behind the bed stood the marble bust of a naked woman, holding aloft an oil lamp which shed a subdued light on a voluptuous nest of lace and white bed linen. The woman's breasts were lifted proudly and her lips curved in a smile of complicity which reminded Marie of the maid Louise – of Louise, and a drawer in Joséphine's escritoire which was not always kept locked.

The thought was fleeting. The warm bath and a dainty supper tray brought other memories, of the night when Marie Fontaine was released from the Carmes prison, and received just such care and cossetting in the home of Joséphine de Beauharnais, who had said so truly that she loved to help her friends. "I must never forget how she helped me!" was Marie's last waking thought. She was asleep before Rita came to turn out the lamp and take away the tray.

Before noon next day the couriers came back, having ridden hard with the good news that they had intercepted General Bonaparte on his way to Brescia. He was assembling his escort and expected to reach the palazzo about three o'clock: his brother and Colonel Junot had ridden out to meet him. Marie thought about that meeting as she explored the splendid empty rooms of the Palazzo Serbelloni, and prayed that Joseph might say or do nothing to spoil the reunion of the husband and wife. Joséphine was in the hands of two Italian women, summoned in haste from the leading *salon de beauté* of Milan, who were giving her a manicure, a pedicure, a shampoo and a facial massage.

"Joséphine, you do look wonderful!"

Marie was sincere in her praise. Madame Bonaparte, as she descended the grand staircase and came slowly across the hall to where Marie stood near the front door, looked ten years younger. Cosmetics, skilfully applied, had erased the little fans of wrinkles at the corners of her eyes, and lip rouge made the mouth which was usually too tightly compressed seem wide and generous. She wore a simple white muslin gown, with no jewels, and her unbound hair was gathered in a knot at the nape of her neck. The whole effect was dewy: Joséphine looked not so much like a bride as like an ingénue.

She smiled and took Marie's hand. "So do you, darling."

"This is the great day," Marie insisted. "Aren't you excited?"

"Of course," said the general's lady. "And so are you – bubbling over. What it is to be twenty-one!"

"Twenty-two," said Marie with a laugh. "Remember, I had a birthday on the journey."

"So did I," said Joséphine with a sigh. "Poor birthdays, with no celebrations!"

"We'll celebrate tonight."

"*You* don't look very festive," said Joséphine with a sharp look. "You've had that blue dress for a year."

"It's Charles's favourite. I'll wear something new tonight."

"To look nice for the general, eh?"

It was the kind of little feline touch which chilled Marie. But she was forgiving, she knew her friend was very nervous, because the hand in hers was cold and damp. She doesn't know what she's saying, Marie thought, and then aloud, "Listen! He must be coming! I hear cheering in the street." She gave Joséphine a little push. "Go and stand at the top of the steps and let him see you first – alone."

Now the cheering spread to the courtyard, as the staff officers housed in a separate wing of the palace hurried out and caught sight of the graceful lady dressed in white, and the great gates were pulled open and Napoleon Bonaparte rode in alone. His cavalry escort came clattering over the cobbles behind him, with plumes, bugles and guidons mingled in a splendour eclipsed by the general himself. Instead of the familiar grey overcoat and cocked hat Napoleon wore a new uniform, as brilliant in its own way as the fancy dress sported by the Directors. The tunic, fastening with gold lace, was black like the breeches, with two lines of white and scarlet replacing a cravat at the high neck. A scarlet and silver sash was tied above his sword belt. His hat was embellished with tricolore plumes, and beneath it the lank "dog's ears" hair fell to his shoulders. As Napoleon raised his hand to salute Joséphine, his face stern with adoration, Marie was near enough to hear her whisper, "He's still wearing his hair in that old-fashioned way!"

The general was off his horse and up the steps. He bowed before his wife, who swept a graceful curtsey. He had no eyes for anyone else, and taking Joséphine's hand he led her down the hall like a man in a dream.

Then a voice shouted "Dis-*mount*!" and in the escort Marie saw her husband, unfamiliar in a heavy dark moustache, swinging out of the saddle and hurrying across the yard. In a matter of seconds a hard, sunburned cheek was pressed against her own and a man's hard arms were round her yielding body. What they said was incoherent and inaudible, for Charles Latour was only the first of the men crowding into the hall, with Junot, Marmont and Joseph Bonaparte close at his heels. The house servants offered glasses of chilled white wine to the thirsty men of the escort, and Marie was the centre of a storm of greetings, teasing and congratulations. After days in the cramped and isolated world of the carriage, she felt as if her head would turn with the crowding, the compliments and the flattery. She kept tight hold of her husband's hand, and could only nod acquiescence when he whispered, "I want to be alone with you, my darling love."

"My sweet, how beautiful you are!"

The first words Marie Latour heard as she emerged from the deep repose into which a tumult of love had plunged them made her believe it was their wedding day, and that she and Charles were back in the Quai Voltaire. He and she were lying in a nest of lace and tangled sheets, and his hand was tracing the outline of her breasts. This was how it had been in those wonderful beginning days, but . . . the illusion faded as Marie realised that there were slatted shutters on the windows, through which streaks of late sunlight fell on a green room where the furniture stood at unfamiliar angles, and the most familiar sight was the face bent above her own. When Charles said "Beautiful'" for the second time she kissed him and said with a languorous lack of interest, "What time is it?"

"Past six, if your little Bréguet watch is right." He glanced at the dressing table, where the watch was propped against a bowl of mignonette, which had replaced the roses.

"I've been asleep. Have you?"

"I think so. But now it's time to wake up, Marie. The general expects us to dine with them tonight."

"That's nice." Marie yawned and buried her head more deeply in the pillow. "It's so dark and warm," he heard her murmur, and he laughed.

"Don't go back to sleep, you lazy girl. I'll open the shutters." He raised himself on his elbow, and stifled a groan.

"What's the matter?"

"Nothing. Just a twinge from my souvenir of Lodi."

"Oh, Charles, you make so little of it!"

He was out of bed, pulling on shirt and breeches, and dragging the shutters apart. The first breeze of the evening came in through the open window. Marie, in a new silk negligée, came up behind him and pressed her lips to his arm. "What does the doctor say?" she asked.

"Nothing to say, now; but he did say I was a damned lucky fellow. So I was, and am." He stroked her silk sleeve. "This is a pretty thing. You had a velvet robe at the Quai Voltaire."

"Because it was so cold in Paris. Besides, I have a position to keep up here. I'm the *signora contessa*."

"And so you are." Charles sat down on the green sofa.

"Come here and tell me about your trip. Did Joséphine behave herself?"

"Of course she did." Marie stiffened slightly in the curve of his arm. ". . . Charles, do you think you're quite consistent? Before you went away you told me not to live with Joséphine again, and I didn't, but when I was asked to accompany her to Milan – all those days, all those miles – you didn't object at all. Why was that?"

He shifted slightly to gaze into her face. Charles Latour had a chronic fear of being laughed at, and he thought she might be mocking him. But when he saw Marie's innocent smile he decided she must be only teasing, and he said, "I jumped at the chance of getting you here at any price. But it must have been rough going, wasn't it?" He was going to add, "You were an angel to come," but she interrupted him.

"The trip was quite enjoyable except for one thing, but tell me about the war. Why has there been no major action since Borghetto? Junot told me General Bonaparte had been doing odd jobs for the Directory, but he wouldn't say what *kind* of jobs: do you know?"

"Junot seems to have been unusually discreet. It's no secret now that the Directors ordered Bonaparte to make huge requisitions on the north Italian states like Parma and Modena – money, provisions for our army and works of art – "

"But there was no fighting in Parma and Modena, was there?"

"No, but Bonaparte occupied Leghorn – Livorno – so the British lost their naval base. Serve them right, it was out of Leghorn that Admiral Nelson's squadron captured our transports carrying the siege artillery badly needed at Mantua. Next, the general occupied the legations of Ferrara and Bologna and threatened to march on Rome. The Pope paid him 20 million *livres* to stay away, and heaven knows what in art treasures too."

"The convoys!" said Marie. "All those wagon trains we passed in the mountains were full of Italian property!"

"Don't be sentimental, Marie. It's 'woe to the conquered' when Napoleon goes to war. I only wonder what the comrades of the men he hanged for looting in Milan thought when Napoleon started looting on the grand scale himself."

"You don't mean he took pictures and statues from all those places?"

"Hardly, he's not a connoisseur. A Research Commission was sent from Paris to select the stuff. Four art experts, and their mandate was 'to put mankind's masterpieces under the protection of the French Republic'." Charles laughed, he thought it was an excellent joke.

"But Napoleon will get the blame," said Marie. She was silent, thinking, while the colour of the sunset light dyed her cheek, and Charles stole a glance at his own watch. It was high time they began to dress for a dinner which was sure to begin with military punctuality. He said coaxingly, "Now, darling, I hope I've made you understand we haven't been wasting our time for the past two months. But you've told me nothing about your journey. Was it comfortable? Were you nervous? What was the one thing that went wrong?"

"Oh – nothing. We were terribly cooped up, but I expected that. Only, when we stopped in cities like Lyon and Turin, I wanted to go out by myself and see the streets and the shops and the people – "

"It wouldn't have been wise, Marie."

"You sound like Monsieur Joseph." She rubbed her cheek against his lips, said of his moustache "It tickles!" and went on, "But it'll be different in Milan. You'll show me the city. We'll visit the Duomo (if you don't mind going to church) and we'll hear Grassini sing at La Scala. Junot says she's marvellous. There'll be so many things to do! Oh, everything will be different now you've come!"

"You *do* love me, my sweet!" It was all he could say while she lay soft and supple in his arms. He had not the heart to tell her that he only had forty-eight hours' leave.

* * *

Charles Latour felt very proud of his wife as he ushered her into the state dining-room of the palace. The shot silk dress rippled against her long limbs with the changing blue and green of the sea, and she wore her grandmother's pearl parure. Napoleon smiled when she curtsied to him and kissed her hand.

"*Ma chère Marie*," he said, "welcome to Milan. My wife says you were a tower of strength on the journey." And when Marie went on to kiss Joséphine he tweaked Charles's ear – always a mark of favour – and said "*Eh bien, mon brave Latour*, are you happy now?"

It was obvious that Napoleon was a happy man as he introduced the young Latours to two older couples, the handsome blonde Signora Viviani and her husband, and "our latest bride, Madame Clouzot, and her husband, the colonel commanding the French garrison." The Clouzots were not young and romantic. The French officer was at least forty and his Italian bride nearer thirty than twenty, wearing a sober grey dress as if she had been a widow, her only bridal distinctions being a spray of orange blossom tucked into her sash, and the privilege of sitting on Napoleon's right. Lucia Clouzot was plain-faced and plain-spoken, but Marie liked her better than the statuesque Madame Viviani, who was observing Joséphine with a critical eye.

"What magnificent diamonds, *madame la générale!*"

"Family heirlooms from Martinique."

Marie, who knew that the diamonds were a gift from Paul Barras when he was Joséphine's lover, looked expressionlessly at the other guests, who all looked blankly back. The three men who had brought Joséphine to Milan were waiting to take their cue from the general, whose pride and joy in his wife were evident. Equally evident was General Berthier's infatuation with Madame Viviani, who distributed her smiles between him and Bonaparte.

It was the first time Marie had seen Napoleon as a gracious host, and she thought he played the part very well. He was still thin and haggard in appearance, but courtly in manner, determined – as he said when dinner was served – to ban all war talk for this one evening. "No talking of strategy in the presence of four such lovely ladies. Let us talk of literature instead."

Literature was a heavy subject for people intent on enjoying an unusually good dinner, and the duke's major domo, for his master's sake, had provided an elaborate meal. It was served by a butler and four footmen, whose service General Bonaparte seemed to appreciate. He was making an obvious effort to eat slowly, and dinner, which when alone with his Staff he finished in twenty minutes, was on this occasion extended to an hour and a half. Pauses in his eating gave more time for talk which soon became a monologue, his literary affinities being far above the heads of his guests. Rousseau was the first subject he proposed: Rousseau, whose pre-Revolutionary writings he said he had devoured as a boy in military school at Brienne, and he sought their opinions on Rousseau's books and theories. Silence. Charles Latour admitted to having "done" the *Social Contract* in school, and Marie murmured that Monsieur Guiart had lent her *La Nouvelle Heloïse*.

"And what did you think of it, Marie?"

"I'm afraid I didn't understand it very well."

Whereupon Napoleon waxed eloquent on Rousseau's theories of the return to nature and the noble savage, until his eloquence was punctured by a remark from Junot, who had not been following, that there had been enough of savagery for most victims of the Terror, ha! ha! The monologuist then turned to the poet Ossian, his great weakness in spite of revelations that Ossian's poems were fakes by a Scotsman called Macpherson.

"Do you really believe, *mon général*, that Ossian was a Gaelic bard living in the third century?" said Lucia Clouzot, over her husband's whispered remonstrance.

"Certainly I do."

"Amazing how his poems have survived for nearly fifteen hundred years."

"They are immortal," said Napoleon solemnly. "They show us a world of heroic simplicity set in a – a landscape of mountains and mist . . ."

"Do Ossian's poems remind you of Corsica?" said Marie unexpectedly.

"Corsica?" echoed Napoleon. "What do you know of Corsica, Marie?"

"You used to tell my uncle and me about the mountains, years ago, when we were talking in the old garden – "

"Among the lettuces and the pot-herbs – I remember," said Napoleon with a smile.

"And then Monsieur Guiart lent me a book a Scotsman wrote, a man called Boswell, about a tour in Corsica just before the Revolution . . . it's been translated into French."

"I bought a copy in Paris," said Joseph Bonaparte. "I remember our father talking about meeting this Boswell, just before the war of independence. He was a great admirer of our mountaineers."

"As I used to be," said Napoleon grimly. "Marie, you must see Corsica some day – the Corsica of our boyhood, not as it is today. When I have driven the British out."

"Come now, my dear Bonaparte," smiled Joséphine, "isn't that what you call war talk?"

Her husband took her left hand and kissed it. "Yes, my dear," he said, "and you recall me to my duty. Friends, I fear our little holiday is over. Berthier, you told the Staff I would meet them at nine o'clock?"

"Yes, sir." The party broke up very quickly after that, Madame Clouzot finding a moment to whisper to Marie, "Come and see me – I live with my parents – I'll send you a card."

When Marie took Charles back to her bedroom the bed had been freshly made up and the oil lamp lit above the statue.

"That's quite a woman," said Charles, surveying the

146

naked torso. "Do you know who she reminds me of? Madame Viviani. What do you think of Berthier's flame?"

"I didn't expect it of Berthier – a man who fought under Rochambeau on the Ohio."

"She made a dead set at Napoleon when we first came in, but he passed her on to the Chief of Staff."

"Napoleon enjoyed himself tonight," said Marie, going to the dressing table and untying the metallic blue fillet round her curls.

"He likes to hear himself talk. But you, Marie! You were brilliant. Rousseau first and then Ossian – "

"Actually I didn't find *La Nouvelle Heloïse* so difficult to understand, but I didn't want you to think I was what you used to call showing off," she said calmly.

"Of course I didn't," Charles said insincerely. "And then when you got on to Corsica, that really was a master stroke. You must have done a lot of reading lately?"

"It passes the time."

"I didn't know old Guiart was running a lending library."

"Charles!" she said, standing up very straight. "I must talk to you – I must tell you about Monsieur Guiart . . ."

Oh God, Charles Latour said to himself, not now. Not a scene about old Guiart and his infernal labo.

"That can wait until tomorrow," he said, and took Marie in his arms. "Darling, come to bed."

11

Charles and Marie left the Palazzo Serbelloni before nine next morning. Charles had urged haste: he wanted to get her away, all to himself before anybody – he thought of Joséphine – could come whimpering about the early departure from Milan ordered by Napoleon. Marie herself was eager to set out. There was only one slight delay as they were leaving, the appearance of a servant bearing a charming note from Madame Clouzot inviting Marie to luncheon the next day "if *monsieur le comte* can spare you. There will only be four of us," the note went on, "my mother, my aunt Julia, myself and you, but we shall all be delighted to have your company." She handed it to Charles with a smile. "Shall I accept?" she said, and with an effort he replied "Of course."

"I'll write to Madame Clouzot this afternoon, but do let's go now." She was laughing with pleasure as they crossed the courtyard and, the great gate being opened, stood in the street. They were in the heart of Milan, in the centre of such animation and energy as seemed wonderful to the girl from Paris, where the splendour of past centuries was shadowed by the sullen mood of the present day. She hardly realised that the handsome French officer and the pretty lady were objects of interest to a people constitutionally disposed to admire young lovers, but when the Italians smiled she returned their smiles, and Marie was happy.

They walked first to the great square called the Piazza

del Duomo, and there Marie stopped, lost in admiration of the cathedral's frozen magnificence, while Charles's admiration was all for her. So often, before he left Paris, he had seen her come home tired and jaded from that wretched labo, or sitting under the lamp and frowning over some musty tome of materia medica; now she was refreshed and beautiful again. He followed her into the Duomo and watched, while he could not share, her awe at the great church where men and women were free to practise the faith in which he and she had been baptised. They did not linger long in the cathedral.

In a different mood, he took her to a great gallery with a glass roof, where there were boutiques containing all the fripperies just beginning to be on sale in the Palais Royal. Marie loitered from one tempting window to another, until Charles, who had his eye on a certain jeweller's, told her to come and choose a belated birthday present. The selection took time, but presently Marie was the owner of a heavy gold bracelet and a pair of matching earrings, and could only whisper "Consider yourself kissed!" as Charles fastened the bracelet round her wrist.

"Some day you'll wear diamonds, darling," he said. "In the meantime, on a less exalted plane, shall we have ices? You used to enjoy them at Frascati's, and Milan ices are famous."

Marie was ready for anything, including ices, and the place where they were sold was little more than an alcove in the gallery, almost private, and ideal for what he had been putting off for too long, the breaking of his bad news. He had no idea of the flavour of the confection set before him, but when Marie had finished hers, pronounced it better than Frascati's, and was sipping the water which came with it, he began by saying, "I'm glad you're going to luncheon with Madame Clouzot tomorrow."

"Oh, I am too. I liked her very much last night." And with a sidelong glance at the nearest mirror to see how her new earrings became her, Marie added with a smile, "So *monsieur le comte* can spare me for a couple of hours?"

"Darling," he said desperately, "I won't be there. Napoleon and all the bodyguard leave Milan at six o'clock tomorrow morning."

The pretty coquetry died out of Marie's face. "Oh no!" she said, "you can't be *leaving*! You've only just come!"

"I know. My love, it kills me to tell you, but after the couriers left, the general made it clear to us that we would only go to Milan for forty-eight hours, and that only because of Joséphine."

"Do you suppose she knew last night – oh no, she would have been hysterical. Wretched woman! If she'd left Paris a month earlier, we'd have had that much longer time together. Oh Charles!" Marie's mouth quivered, and he dreaded an outburst of tears. He took both her hands in his.

"Darling, I'm so terribly, terribly sorry – "

"It isn't your fault," she said, biting her lips. "You're under orders, like Napoleon with the Research Commission. But where are you going? Back to Mantua?"

"No, Sérurier will have to do the best he can outside Mantua, even without a siege train. The truth is, Wurmser's on the move at last. We've had no reinforcement from our Rhine armies, but he's got 30,000 picked men from theirs, making his total strength over 70,000, and our vedettes report that he's begun to move them down both sides of Lake Garda. He wants a pitched battle and he's going to get it."

"Where?"

"*I* don't know where, but the general does, and I wager the Staff does too, after that long meeting he had with them last night. He knows the terrain so well, my guess is that he'll move nearer Lake Garda, perhaps not very far away."

"Then might you have a chance to come back to Milan again?"

"Not likely. I'll be back with my regiment, Marie. Being

in the bodyguard this time was a special favour for a special occasion."

Marie nodded. Her husband thought she had taken it very well, no tears and no reproaches – not that he would have minded if there had been a few quiet tears. He lifted her hands to his lips and said, "Forgive me, dear!" He was not prepared for her reply.

"This makes it easier for me to tell you about Monsieur Guiart."

"What about old Guiart? You promised to finish up with him in April and you stayed on till May, you naughty girl!"

"I stayed until early June, but I did finish then, it couldn't go on for ever. But now – there's something else."

"What else can there be?"

"Dr Claude Berthollet, a research chemist who was once a doctor, came to the labo one day while I was working, and we had a talk. He has a big laboratory of his own on the Rue de Seine, quite near the Quai Voltaire, where medicines are prepared for the retail trade, and now he's got a contract to supply the army medical service. He's increasing his staff and he wants me to join them."

Charles released her hands and sat back in his chair. He said in a kind of gasp, "You can't mean it!"

"I know it sounds absurd," she admitted. "An apprenticeship lasts three years, and I've only been six months with Guiart. But Dr Berthollet says I'm very quick, and speed is what he needs, and – it's for the army, Charles!"

"You don't mean you want to do it?"

"Yes I do."

How well he knew the obstinate set of her jaw, and the chill in her dark blue eyes. She was set on it, that was clear, and he rehearsed all the old arguments in vain. At last he almost lost his temper when she told him unblushingly that "the pay was very good."

"You mean you want to work for money?"

"Why not, if I can earn it?"

"If people knew you were doing that, they'd say I couldn't support you."

"Who cares what people say?"

'That's not what I was brought up to believe."

"You were brought up to a life of privilege, and you rejected it. When the Revolution came, you ran away from home and joined the National Guard rather than go to England with your family. Why should you be surprised if I want to be independent too?"

Charles Latour looked about him. A few more customers had come into the little place, but not enough to disturb their privacy. He said firmly to his wife, "Now you listen to me. You've told me exactly what you want and don't want. You don't want to stay on in Milan, dancing attendance on Joséphine – I sympathise with that. You want to go back to Paris with Joseph Bonaparte, whenever that may be, and then you want to trudge to the Rue de Seine every day, wet or shine, and prepare medicines for the army. You want my full approval of your plans, though you know already that I disapprove. Now listen to *my* plan, and tell me what you think of it.

"Go back to Paris if you can't be happy in Milan, though I don't know why you can't be contented in the Palazzo Serbelloni. But instead of wasting your time in a laboratory, start looking for a decent house to live in, one big enough for a nursery, with a garden for a child. Marie! we've talked so little about this, but – don't you want a child?"

She whispered without meeting his eyes, "Of course I do . . . I can't think why it's never happened . . . I'm sorry, Charles."

He smiled, feeling much more in command of her, although their holiday morning had turned into one of their frequent misunderstandings. "Never mind, darling," he said. "When I come home, we'll have our little Henri. My brother's first name was Henri," he explained, seeing her look of surprise, "it's the family name. He was Henri

Edouard Louis. The old king – I mean Louis Capet – was his godfather."

"I don't care what you call him," said Marie, "as long as he comes to us – some day. But darling, you said 'when I come home'. When will that be?"

"In a few months, I hope."

"You used to say the Italian campaign would be a long one."

"I don't think so now. A few more of his lightning victories and this campaign will be over by the end of the year."

"And then? Another campaign, in Austria? Or an attack on Corsica? You heard what he said last night about driving the British out. He won't be satisfied with victory in Italy. He's in the saddle now and he'll never stop until he's ridden down the world."

Her way of speaking as if she had a special knowledge of the mind of Bonaparte never failed to exasperate Charles Latour. He said, "I suppose when we go back for luncheon you'll run to the general and get his support in your Berthollet plan."

"I shall do no such thing."

"Why not? He was your sponsor with old Guiart, and I heard him tell you he expected you to do him credit."

"I haven't forgotten what he said."

The two women who stood on the threshold of the Palazzo Serbelloni to welcome their husbands were not there when the general and his men rode out. The Staff followed the bodyguard, a clear indication that Bonaparte meant to set up a new headquarters, and Joseph Bonaparte followed his brother, handling his mount so clumsily that Charles Latour was reminded of the inadequacy of Aunt Geltruda as a teacher of equitation. The farewells were said in private and the tears fell unchecked: in Marie's case they were bitter tears, not only because one of their two days had been spoiled by the old difference of opinion, but also because she had translated her husband's "when I come back" into the "*if* I come back" of a soldier returning to the firing line.

It was mid-morning before she felt composed enough to go in search of Joséphine. She found her composed also, though tear-stained, lying on a couch in the study Napoleon had used, where his relief maps, protractors and callipers were still lying on the desk. Joséphine was petting Fortuné, who was snarling and nipping her fingers between his sharp little teeth in token of his displeasure at spending the whole of his rival's visit securely tied up in the stables. His mistress was apathetic, she seemed more interested in stuffing Fortuné with bon-bons than in talking to Marie, and the greatest tragedy of her day appeared to be when the pug, as a result of the sweet stuff, was sick on the duke's oriental carpet.

It was a relief to get out of doors again, and to be driven in a ducal pony-chaise to a part of the city which had not been fashionable since the seventeenth century. There Madame Clouzot lived with her widowed mother and maiden aunt, her late father, Prince Colonna, having left her a great name, a decaying mansion called by courtesy a *palazzina* and no money at all. Marie guessed that this was why the Principessa Lucia, at twenty-seven, had been allowed to marry a French officer, once a soldier in the royal army, "with nothing but his cloak and his sword" – a reproach her own attorney had once addressed to her.

Colonel Clouzot, of course, was on garrison duty, and the simple luncheon of pasta, salad and ices from a pastry-cook's, was shared by the four ladies and served by two country girls. Princess Colonna and her sister were both hard of hearing, so that the conversation was carried on between the two young women, who used it to lay the foundation of a real friendship.

It was the first time Marie had found a friend of nearly her own age and very much her own tastes. For an Italian woman, Lucia Colonna had been unusually active in local affairs, especially charitable affairs, working through the organisations of her parish church. She envied Marie her opportunities for study. Her own enthusiasm was for literature, and perhaps their first point of contact was their shared amusement at Napoleon's belief in Ossian. She introduced Marie to the great feminists – Mary Wollstonecraft in translation, Olympe de Gouges, dead by the guillotine, and Madame de Staël, who was very much alive. For all her feminism, she was in love with her husband, and longing to have his child.

Colonel Clouzot was so tied by his garrison duties that he saw his wife at irregular hours of the day, and Marie never saw him at all until a week after the Bonaparte dinner. Then he arrived at the *palazzina* at ten in the morning, when Lucia and Marie were preparing to take a drive, and, after a brief greeting, asked the girl from Paris if she had any news from Major Latour.

"No, why? Is he all right? They haven't been in action, have they?" said Marie, instantly alarmed.

"No news of any kind has reached me," said the garrison commander. "I only asked because I didn't know if your husband would have any objection to your meeting Surgeon-Captain Legendre."

"The army doctor who cared for him after Lodi? I'm sure he wouldn't," said Marie. "I didn't know Dr Legendre was in Milan."

"He came to inspect the French military hospital," said Clouzot. "He's very anxious to meet you, madame."

"And I'd be glad of a chance to thank him," said Marie with a smile. "Would he like to call on me at the Palazzo Serbelloni? I'm always there in the afternoons."

"He leaves town tomorrow, might he call today?"

"Certainly."

The Serbelloni was like the palace of the Sleeping Beauty at three o'clock, when grooms and servants were deep in the siesta. Marie, not yet accustomed to daylight sleeping, was in one of the small salons when Dr Legendre was announced by the footman on duty, and nervously dropped his hat on his way across the room to greet her. Marie tried to set him at his ease, remembering

155

that Charles had said of him only that he was an alarmist and a scaremonger, and feeling that his red-rimmed eyes, blinking behind thick spectacles, did not inspire confidence. The topic of Charles's elbow was soon exhausted, and Marie advanced the subject of the French military hospital. She hoped he had found good conditions there?

"Very good, I thank you. The Italian doctors are very competent, the Sisters of Charity devoted, and the patients are fortunate."

"I'm very glad."

"Are you, madame?" The spectacles glinted. "Do you realise that there are just fifty wounded men in hospital, out of thousands left behind at Lodi Bridge?"

"Left behind? What do you mean, Dr Legendre?"

"I mean Lodi was a shambles of neglected men. I told the commanding general myself that three or four wagons, called ambulances, were no substitute for properly equipped field hospitals. A more experienced commander would have provided those – "

"Your commander was experienced enough to win a great victory at Lodi – "

"Victories are easy to win if a man has no regard for human life."

"That's a horrible thing to say."

Marie saw, as he took out his handkerchief to mop it, that the little man's forehead was unpleasantly moist. He said, "Forgive me, madame. I'm telling my story in the wrong way. Permit me to try again. To explain that I joined the Republican army because I believed in the Declaration of the Rights of Man. I felt that General Bonaparte did not respect those rights when I saw our walking wounded as bands of stragglers, begging food from the villagers – "

"My husband told me the army was particularly well fed."

"When we first came into Italy, yes. But as our lines of communication lengthen the rations arrive late or not at all, and the purveyors make a huge profit on bad food. I understand the Compagnie Bodin hopes to get the contract – I saw their representative in the Piazza del Duomo today – a fellow the men call 'Wide-awake Charlie' . . ." He paused suggestively.

"Well, what then?" said Marie. "Am I supposed to know a man with this extraordinary nickname?"

"You do know him, madame. He travelled in your company as far as Lyon, when you were on your way to Italy with Madame Bonaparte – his *intimate* friend."

"Captain Hippolyte Charles!"

"The same." And Legendre actually smiled to think he had caused embarrassment to this haughty young lady. But he had reckoned without Marie.

"May I ask if this is why you have imposed yourself on me," she said, "to add to your stock of gossip?"

"Madame, you quite misunderstand me. I came to you because Major Latour is known to have the ear of General Bonaparte. His appeals may succeed where mine have failed."

"My husband owed a great deal to the general's interest at one time. He has absolutely no influence now. He isn't on the Staff, he isn't even an ADC." She rose to her feet, and Legendre, still clutching his hat, scrambled up too. "You will never influence Napoleon Bonaparte by backstairs intrigues, citizen. The commissariat department is responsible for the rations: your own *Service de Santé* for the field hospitals. You should write to Director Carnot, from whom the general *takes his orders*, and lay your complaints before him – if you dare."

In spite of her bold words of dismissal, Dr Legendre had made an impression on Marie Latour, although not the impression he had hoped to make. His description of the walking wounded, straggling and starving through Lombardy, had filled her with fears for Charles, so happy, so lively, so short a time before. In the great battle now preparing, so all the news received in Milan seemed to say, would he be wounded, neglected, lost? She vividly remembered the sufferings of the men wounded on the day of the "whiff of grapeshot", men whom for a few hours she had been permitted to tend. She remembered, too, how Napoleon had visited them after the battle, and how devotedly they looked at him as he stood beside their beds. It was impossible that he could be so callous, so hard-hearted as that little man made out!

She passed a lonely, anxious hour, and as soon as the renewed hum of activity in the great house indicated that siesta time was over, went to her room to dress. She and Joséphine had been invited to dinner at the Vivianis', for the Marchesa di Viviani was very attentive to the general's lady, and declared she was "quite cross" with dear General Berthier for the lack of real news in his letters from the new headquarters at Castiglione, the infatuated Chief of Staff being not quite such a fool as to include troop movements in his frequent and flowery epistles.

Joséphine was in a tantrum. An Italian maid was sent out of the room when Marie appeared and was obliged to listen to an account of her French maid's latest impertinence. It was a confused narrative, of the "she said – and then I said – and then she answered back" kind and leading to the climax of "I'm through, Marie, I'm absolutely done with her. I mean to dismiss her, give her two weeks' wages and send her back to Paris with the next convoy . . . Or with Joseph Bonaparte, and let's see if she behaves as badly with him as she did with Junot on the way here!"

"Junot was quite as much to blame as she was," said Marie. "But Joséphine, that's ancient history. Tell me, had you a letter from the general this morning?"

"No, dear . . . Oh yes, I did, all about Wurmser's advance and covering me with kisses, the usual rigmarole. But that wretched Louise, after all I've done for her – "

"Was she trying to blackmail you?" asked Marie casually.

"Blackmail me?" Joséphine laughed uneasily. "What ever put that into your head?"

"Because I've just been told that Captain Hippolyte Charles is in Milan. You didn't tell me he was expected."

"I told *Bonaparte* he was expected," said Joséphine in triumph. "It was too bad they missed each other, because my husband is *so* anxious to meet Hippolyte."

Marie managed to articulate the one word "Why?"

"I told him how I met Hippolyte shortly after our marriage, and what a good friend he'd been to me this spring. Escorting me to parties, doing errands for me – that sort of thing. What appealed to Bonaparte was Hippolyte's wish to be returned to the Hussars, and of course he can help in that – "

"Who better?" agreed Marie. "So your good friend Hippolyte has had enough of the Purchasing Commission."

"Apparently."

"But not of the Bodin Company?"

"What do you know about the Bodin Company, Marie?"

"Not very much," said Marie. "But I'm learning." She came close to Joséphine's armchair and Fortuné sat up in his basket, growling. "I know they're army contractors and Captain Charles is one of their representatives, or salesmen, or whatever they call themselves. I remember that the very day I met him first in the Rue Chantereine you became hysterical and sobbed that 'it would all end in trouble.' I thought you meant it was just a silly flirtation, which was bad enough, but now I think you're playing with fire. What's *your* connection with the Bodin Company?"

"What a tirade!" said Joséphine. "I shan't answer any of your impertinent questions – you're as bad as Louise. You're so self-righteous, Marie, so censorious – you've changed from the girl you used to be."

Major Latour had been wrong in predicting one detail of Napoleon's battle plan. General Sérurier, who had thought he might leave the army rather than serve under "a boy", had changed his mind after the boy's first brilliant series of victories and had been sent to conduct the siege of Mantua. On Wurmser's approach he was ordered to raise the siege and proceed with all his troops to join Bonaparte, who had established his headquarters near Castiglione. From a commandeered farmhouse the Frenchmen watched the clumsy and classic approach of the Austrians. When least expected the French attacked on the enemy's flanks, fighting two pitched battles before the final attack on 5 August. Wurmser's army was annihilated, and the aged marshal, bewildered by what he called a *Blitzkrieg*, fled into the now open fortress of Mantua.

The Staff celebrated the victory of Castiglione uproariously, though without much encouragement from Napoleon. He brought his brother with him when he joined them, Monsieur Joseph, always tactless, having chosen the very hour of conquest to ask for a serious talk with the conqueror. Napoleon was in a heavy mood. They all saw he was exhausted, and Berthier put a stop to the toasts and the singing, so that the general might snatch a few hours of troubled sleep. When he awoke he wrote one of the most revealing letters he ever sent to Joséphine.

I am told that you have known for a long time and know *well* this gentleman whom you recommend to me for a business contract. If this were true you would be a monster. What are you doing at this hour? Are you asleep?

And then the mere thought of Joséphine asleep beside him, sated with his caresses, roused all the old erotic impulses, so that the letter begun in rage ended in rhapsody.

Adieu, my fair beloved, my incomparable, my divine one! A thousand loving kisses, everywhere, everywhere, *everywhere*!

He feared and longed to set out for Milan, but the need to develop a new plan of campaign kept him at Castiglione for several days. There was time to receive a reply from Joséphine, and one promptly arrived by special messenger. Characteristically, she made no allusion to the disagreeable part of his letter, but congratulated him on his victory, and said she hoped he would be in Milan to celebrate his birthday (the twenty-seventh) on 15 August. She signed herself "Your loving MONSTER."

Joséphine had been clever enough to get her story in first. She had told him about Hippolyte Charles before his brother could do so, and she was sure of her power over Bonaparte. When he rode into Milan at the head of a long column of infantry she was waiting for him, not on the steps of a palace, but seated in a barouche drawn up near the Porta Romana, and when she saw the light in his eyes she knew she had nothing to fear. He pulled his horse alongside and took the salute as his men marched past. The captured Austrian flags were dipped to Joséphine, and the veterans cheered the lady smiling under her tilted parasol. "There she is!" "That's the one!" "She's his Lady Luck!" were among their uninhibited comments.

Marie Latour was not at the Porta Romana, but with Lucia Clouzot in the crowd gathered in the cathedral square. She had been a guest in the Colonna *palazzina* since her quarrel with Joséphine. In spite of everything she had enjoyed her visit, and it was with regret that she said, when the last French troops had passed, "I'd better go back to the Serbelloni today. That's where Charles will expect to find me." "Oh no!" said Lucia. "My husband says the 21st Chasseurs won't be here till the day after tomorrow. You've heard from your Charles, you know he's all right, so why don't you stay with us for one more day?"

So Marie stayed, and next day saw French wounded from Castiglione brought into Milan in covered army wagons and straw-filled country carts, scores and scores of them, a ghastly company. Colonel Clouzot said the

Spedale Santa Caterina was crowded out. There were pallet beds in the corridors and Church property had been commandeered for the walking wounded, but in or out of hospital these survivors were suffering from a great shortage of drugs and medicines. And these were what Legendre had called "the fortunate ones"!

Marie went back next day to the Serbelloni *palazzo*, where the spacious rooms were certainly not overcrowded, and lunched alone with Joseph Bonaparte. Joseph was full of himself. The general, he said, wished him to be appointed French ambassador to Rome, and he was eager to be back in Paris to see his Julie and get his embassy confirmed by the Directory. Marie did not interrupt him, but she managed to interject one or two ideas of her own. She had no intention of "running to the general" in her husband's sarcastic phrase, but after the siesta she was not at all surprised, knowing Joseph's turn for gossip, to receive a message from General Bonaparte, requesting her presence in his study.

That study, which was the duke's library, had been kept locked during the general's absence by the footman Marco, who had sensibly decided that otherwise it would become an extra boudoir for the general's lady and stuffed with all sorts of feminine fripperies. So the room into which he showed Marie was still completely masculine, with the addition of two blackboards, one covered with chalked calculations, the other with an ordnance map of Lombardy. As well as the standish and the fresh supply of writing paper, the desk was piled high with files and folders. Napoleon was seated behind it, making notes. He got up as soon as Marie entered and bade her welcome.

"Let's sit over here, shall we?" he said, pulling two armchairs into the window bay. The glass was covered by an outer awning, through which the sun was filtered in a golden glow. It was very becoming to Marie. Hours of outdoor life had given her a warm colour, matched by her simple dress of rosy cotton.

"You're looking very pretty, Marie," said her old friend. "Very *contadina!*"

"Too countrified, general?" said Marie with a smile. She was thinking it was the first time, except for accidental meetings, that they had met to talk alone since his visits to the old garden "among the lettuces and the pot-herbs" with the sound of her uncle's occupations in the shop behind them. She congratulated him on another great victory, and almost in the same breath asked if the casualties had been heavy.

"Heavier for the enemy than for us," said Napoleon with a shrug. "He's left us with a lot of prisoners on our hands in what they call a *lager*; feeding them will be a problem . . . You've heard from Charles?"

"Yes, it was a great relief. He's coming in today?"

"Tonight rather, not before ten o'clock. Would you like to have dinner upstairs with us, or wait to have supper with your husband?"

"I had better wait, but thank you. How is Joséphine?"

"Still asleep, I think." Joséphine had been whimpering, last night, that Marie was a naughty girl, she'd gone tearing off on a visit to these Colonna women, but he hadn't paid much attention. Bonaparte thought no sensible man should pay attention to women's tiffs, which were usually due to jealousy.

"Marie," he said in his abrupt way, "my brother tells me you want to go back to Paris, to work at pharmacy."

"Yes I do," said Marie – abruptly too.

"What's the matter? Don't you like being in Milan?"

"I'd like it better if I had work to do."

"Work for Monsieur Guiart?"

"Not exactly. I didn't tell Monsieur Joseph all the details, but the work I've been offered – daily work, for thirty francs a décade – is in the laboratory of a chemist called Dr Berthollet."

"I know Claude Berthollet," Napoleon said. "A clever man, and a brave one too. Did you know he saved the life of Gaspard Monge, in the bad old days? Where did you meet *him*, Marie?"

"Monsieur Guiart brought him in one day when I was working."

"Which means he thinks you're very good."

"Oh, no," she said honestly, "not really. Not even if I served a full apprenticeship. I know now that I could never be an innovative pharmacist, a real researcher. I'm imitative, not creative. But they say I'm very quick, and speed is what Dr Berthollet wants. He's just got a contract to supply the army with drugs and medicines. Colonel Clouzot says these are badly needed here."

Napoleon agreed. "You said Berthollet had an army contract. Did he specify which French army, or all of them together?"

"Not while he was talking to me," said Marie, crestfallen.

"If I were in Paris now," said Bonaparte, obviously talking to himself, "I could make sure that the northern armies don't get more than their fair share. The Rhine Army, the Sambre et Meuse are Carnot's favourites, but they don't send me reinforcements . . . Marie! when you join Berthollet's team, will you keep reminding them of the needs of the Army of Italy?"

Marie's face was radiant. "You said 'when I join', *mon général*," she said. "Does that really mean you think I should do it?"

"Why not, if the scientists think you can," said Bonaparte. "Joséphine will be disappointed, she counts on you, but you'll be better employed in Paris than idling in Milan, going to card parties and the Opéra. But what does Charles say?"

"Charles disapproves. He thinks it's unwomanly."

"He'd prefer to keep you dangling here on the chance of seeing him for forty-eight hours every few weeks or so? Would it do any good if I had a word with him?"

"Quite the reverse, I'm afraid . . . Someone is at the door."

"Yes, who is it?" Bonaparte raised his voice.

The door was opened by the merest crack. "Le Marois, sir," came the voice of the junior ADC. "General Berthier is here."

"Ask him to wait five minutes."

"Yes, sir."

"Well, Marie," said the general as she rose to her feet, "what you want to do is unusual, but then you're an unusual girl."

He looked up at her appraisingly. He had always thought Marie Fontaine "unusual", "pretty", "amiable", but at that moment, when the first seed of doubt of Joséphine had been sowed in his mind, he felt the pull of her attraction.

He stood up and asked if she meant to take his advice.

"Of course. Don't I always?"

It was a moment of intimacy. As the man who had been her hero looked at the slender figure in the pink *contadina* dress he thought how the charming exterior belied the inner resolution.

"And you'll make sure the Army of Italy is properly supplied with drugs?"

The dark blue eyes were steady on his own. "You can rely on me," she said.

12

That brief talk with Napoleon was the real beginning of
Marie's return to Paris, although the actual journey did
not begin until the first week in September. She rode in a
closed vehicle with the pompous Joseph Bonaparte and
the sullen Louise Compoint in the middle of a convoy
taking seventy-five paintings by Rubens, others by Cor-
reggio and drawings by Michelangelo into the protective
care of the French Republic, and under the nominal care
of the Research Commission they were much less comfortable than when Marmont was in charge. There was a
great deal of scrambling over rocky uphill paths, punctuated by bad meals, and Marie's system was thoroughly
out of order. Ten days out of Milan a reason for an
unusual irregularity occurred to her, and she paid less
attention to Joseph's wordy speculations on the latest
campaign in northern Italy and more to what the future
might hold for herself and Charles.

When they entered Paris the newsboys were shouting
another victory for Bonaparte. Marshal Wurmser had
ventured out of Mantua only to be soundly beaten at
Bassano. The news was followed by a cryptic telegraphic
message from Major Latour: "All well here and now he is
talking about his Star." Marie smiled. Napoleon was not
the only human being to claim a star. Surely one was
shining for Marie Latour among the myriad stars shining
above the Seine? One that held the promise of a baby, the
Henri her husband wanted, an heir for the La Tours!

166

Henri Charles it would have to be. No, Henri Charles Prosper, because her uncle deserved remembrance as well as any émigré *aristos*. With such fancies Marie filled her days, now hoping the Vicomte Henri de la Tour would look like his father, now wishing he might become a leader among men in a happier France.

Dr Berthollet did not expect to see her until the end of the month, and nobody knew she was in Paris except the two Bélards and Armande, whose only interest was the steady rise in the price of food, so for over a week Marie was alone in the Quai Voltaire. She was not close enough to any of her women friends to discuss her hopes of motherhood with them or ask their opinion of the one positive symptom and the absence of any other. She did not miss such confidences, for there was such peace in the shabby, familiar apartment that her bright dream flourished and grew more compelling every day. Until the day when the fantasy was shattered, and became only what Teresa Tallien, in her ribald way, would have called a false alarm.

The Marie Latour who reported at Dr Berthollet's laboratory was a good deal quieter than the young woman who had responded so eagerly to his offer of work, but he put that down to the novelty of her position, alone among a score of male assistants. He had already given his staff, porters included, strict injunctions on civil behaviour to Citizeness Latour, and the pharmacists, responsible men, were civil enough to Prosper Fontaine's niece. That was a title which counted for more than the *signora contessa* of Milan.

Dr Berthollet's entirely modern laboratory had been constructed round three sides of the ground floor of an ancient mansion on the Rue de Seine, and what had been the stables was now occupied by the packers and drivers. These men whistled and catcalled when "the little woman" walked through the yard where the pharmaceuticals were packed in crates and then into wagons for delivery to the army depots, but Marie reacted so pleas-

167

antly, with a smile and a wave, that they soon took her for granted. She was too glad to be at work again to take offence. Soon her practised hands were busy preparing the febrifuges, demulcents and vulneraries required by every army of the Republic.

As for her domestic solitude, that was broken – as she might have known it would be – by the gossiping tongue of Joseph Bonaparte, who was often at the Luxembourg while wooing the Directory for an embassy, and found it quite natural to mention that he had escorted Madame Latour back to Paris. That brought an indignant letter from Teresa Tallien, accusing Marie of neglecting her best friends, and inviting her forthwith to an evening party in honour of Citizen Talleyrand, who had just returned to France after a long exile in Philadelphia.

Marie had seen Talleyrand when she was a girl of sixteen and he the Bishop of Autun, conducting Mass before a great company on the Champ de Mars on the first anniversary of the storming of the Bastille. King Louis XVI had been there, prepared to take the oath as a constitutional monarch, with Queen Marie Antoinette, radiant in beauty. Within three years they had both been guillotined. General de La Fayette had been there in command of the National Guard, and if he was still alive he was immured in an Austrian dungeon. All that had happened to Talleyrand was his exile and his excommunication by the Pope. Marie was curious to see this remarkable survivor. She put on her pearls and her pretty shot silk dress and had herself driven in style to the party.

There were already so many demands on Talleyrand's time that he had sent apologies for his late arrival. The full attention of the company was thus given to Marie Latour, once a *merveilleuse* and later known for good works, who had taken an immense journey to Milan with Madame Bonaparte, stayed there for only two months and then came home alone. Marie had known most of the other guests well. She felt the insincerity of their enquiries for her husband – never a popular figure – felt their disbelief in her tale of work in the new labo – guessed that the Latour marriage would be written off as a failure. But there was another incipient scandal, more to their taste: the gossip seeping northward from Milan about the *affaire* of Joséphine and Wide-awake Charlie. What had Marie to say about that?

"I saw him once at the Palazzo Serbelloni," said Marie demurely. "When he came to be presented to General Bonaparte." There was a stifled laugh, and someone called out, "Walking on his feet or his hands?"

"Right side up when I saw him," said Marie, "and Joséphine told me the meeting was a great success. The general would have been delighted to reinstate Captain Charles in the Hussars, only there are no Hussar regiments under his immediate command!"

"Why don't he get rid of the little jackanapes – ship him out to the Rhine front or the Vendée?" said another voice.

"You must ask Director Barras about that," Marie was inspired to say. The Director smiled and shook his head. He was standing quite near her, with two of his colleagues – not Carnot – all in their red robes of state, and now, perhaps with a view to changing the subject, he slid one hand under her elbow and led her to a sofa "to have a glass of champagne," he said. "God knows how long Talleyrand means to keep us waiting."

"Marie, my dear," he began confidentially when the wine was served, "we're old friends, you know, so don't take amiss what I'm going to ask you. Is everything all right between you and Charles? No disagreements, no little frictions, that made you come home so soon?"

To be truthful Marie could have said there had been plenty of both, but choosing another form of the truth she replied that she had been invited to accompany Joséphine to Milan, not to spend the summer with her there, and as to seeing her husband Charles had had forty-eight hours leave at the beginning of her visit and twenty-four hours after Castiglione. The general himself had taken no more time from his command.

"I know," said Barras. "He's driving himself to death. Do you think his health is really good?"

"He looked very tired and – *wasted*, after the battle of Castiglione."

"There's not very much of him to waste. I wish he had a good doctor on his staff."

"Better than Surgeon-Captain Legendre?"

"Ah! You've met Legendre?"

"Once. May I ask if you've heard from him?"

"I have, also once, and Carnot has had two letters, very unbalanced in tone, about the shortage of field hospitals and the lack of care for the wounded – that sort of thing. Bonaparte has said nothing about it, and until he complains officially, what can we do?"

"I'll tell you what you could do," said Marie boldly. "I saw myself how bad the conditions were in the Spedale Santa Caterina in Milan, where the French wounded were nursed. What I thought was . . . I know the Directory is always ready to appoint commissions. There's the Purchasing Commission, for army supplies, and the Research Commission for – for the art works. Why shouldn't the Directory appoint a Sanitary Commission, of doctors and pharmacists as well as commissioners of the Republic, to arrange for regular field hospitals, and medical corpsmen in combat, and liaison with foreign municipalities – " Her eloquence, or perhaps her bravado, was cut short by Paul Barras's easy laugh.

"Come now, my child," he said, "you're getting into deep water. We Directors are always blamed for inflation and accused of extravagance: I don't know what the voters would say if we set up a huge expensive complex like your Sanitary Commission! Besides, you ladies aren't supposed to bother your pretty little heads with field hospitals and suchlike. Leave that to us mere males. Come along!" he said, rising and offering Marie his arm, "let's take a turn through the rooms before they get too crowded. Monsieur de Talleyrand can't be much longer now . . . Tell me, have you seen the Beauharnais children since you came back?"

"No, because they couldn't get a holiday from school, but Agathe Rible is bringing them both to see me tomorrow. General Bonaparte entrusted me with gifts – I'm ashamed they've had to wait two weeks for them."

"Do you know the gift the boy wants most?"

"He makes no secret of it – a lieutenant's commission."

"He'll get it too, when he's sixteen."

"Sixteen!" said Marie. "A whole year away. But then he'll be a man and a soldier. His opinion will be worth having."

It was the only sarcasm, and a mild one at that, which she threw back at the Director's banal remarks about deep water and ladies not bothering their pretty heads about commissions, and judging by the man's awkward laugh she doubted if he understood her. But she had asked for the snub, as Charles warned her she would do if she tackled any of the Directors about what was their business and not hers. "You're so conceited, Marie!" Charles had said. "You always think you're the one to set everything right!"

Her husband called her conceited, her friend said she was self-righteous and censorious, and perhaps they were both right. Marie moved about the splendid, familiar Luxembourg rooms with a heavy heart. She stood smiling in the throng which gathered round the guest of honour, a lame man dressed in the style of the old régime, with a broad cat's face which masked an innate secrecy, and wondered what Charles Maurice de Talleyrand, excommunicated bishop and revolutionary émigré, had in store for France.

Happily there was always work. Marie enjoyed the morning walk, straight down the *quais* to the Rue de Seine, passing the Institute where the Académie Française had met before it was closed in the Revolutionary hatred of intellectualism. Then the labo, where Dr Berthollet was conducting an experiment on producing a decoction made from willow leaves, said to be good for rheumatism, which was later to be the basis of salicylate acid. After the "Sanitary Commission" fiasco Marie thought twice about tackling the chemist on the supply of drugs for the Army of Italy, but he opened the subject himself when news was received in Paris that an expeditionary force sent from Italy had chased Admiral Nelson and the British Viceroy out of Corsica.

"I hope the British left their pharmaceuticals behind them. I'd hate to have to send supplies to Corsica," said Berthollet. He was bending over Marie's work bench and speaking in a lowered voice, since he discouraged talking in working hours.

"I think General Bonaparte is more concerned about the situation on the mainland," Marie ventured. "I know there's a serious shortage of drugs in Milan."

"He'll get his fair share, never fear," said Berthollet, straightening up. "I'm no admirer of Napoleon Bonaparte – you are, aren't you?" And Marie's tell-tale blush came back. "I think he's a great soldier," she said.

"He's more than a great soldier, he's a military genius," said Berthollet. "We don't know yet if he's a political genius too. If he is – and with all that Corsican spirit thrown in – we may be in for trouble. He may be the French fortune – or he may turn out to be the ruin of France . . . But don't you worry, citizeness," he said, recollecting himself, "he'll get his drugs from me."

That was in October, and on 17 November Napoleon proved his military genius by winning one of his most spectacular victories at Arcola, a village not far from Verona. This time his Austrian adversary was General Alvinczy, who advanced with the fourth Austrian army deployed against Bonaparte. "The terrain," reported the *Moniteur*, "was peculiarly unfavourable for combat, two causeways and extensive swampy ground protecting the vital bridge. The commanding general's favourite offensive by flank attack once again proved successful."

This lifeless account was fleshed out, for Marie, by an

unusually long letter from her husband. There must have been a top page missing, for it seemed to begin in the middle of a sentence.

. . . of us had our clothes off for five days. You know how often I've heard *him* say a vital faculty of generalship is the power of grasping instantly the picture of the ground and the situation? This time I saw him do it. Honestly, Marie, I think he has an ordnance map for a brain. He laid an ambush for the Austrians in every wood, every side road on their advance, and when he was ready he took them on the flank. I saw him often, and I understood finally what he once told me about his Aunt Geltruda's teaching him to ride, because he was riding like a fishwife, sawing at the poor brute's mouth – a farrier-sergeant told me five horses foundered under him from the start of the action. Well, we were coming pretty near the end, but we still had to cross the Alpon river. It was like Lodi Bridge all over again, except that there wasn't any bridge. We've never had any pontoons, and Bonaparte had ordered a boat bridge to be built, like a series of rafts, not very efficient. I saw him riding up to it to lead the charge. He was on the causeway bordering the swamp when all of a sudden his horse threw him with a great splash into the waterweeds. I got up to him as fast as I could, dismounted, and Marie I tell you I thought he was done for. I picked him up by his sword belt like a dead cat, and he was covered in mud from head to foot, hair, nostrils, ears and all, choking in mud and hardly able to breathe. I gave a hollo to one of our troopers (very good fellow, name of Balthasar, comes from the High Pyrenees) and told him to give me a hand with the general, for he was a dead weight in my arms. "My God, is he dead?" cries Balthasar. (Mind you, death was close enough, for the Austrian cannon had found the range across the Alpon.) At that Bonaparte seemed to quiver, he said something in Italian, spat the mud

173

out of his mouth and wiped his face with his cuff. "Are you all right, sir?" cries I. "*Si, grazie,*" he said, and then to the trooper, "Give me that flag!" – for a poor devil of a regimental standard-bearer was lying shot dead beside us, with his banner in his hand. Then Bonaparte, mud and all, slid away from me and on to Balthasar's horse, a wild brute far too heavy for him, and he shouted "*En avant!*" and led the charge across that flimsy bridge with the flag in his right hand. The rest of us went pelting after him, and the Austrian cannoneers turned and fled.

Marie laid down the stained pages. It might have been emotional susceptibility, but she felt as if she too were "choking in mud and hardly able to breathe", so vivid was the image of war which Charles had drawn for her. At last she took up the final page, which was written in a steadier hand.

I didn't see him again until this morning. Junot came to fetch me and said the general wanted to see me. I was in the horse-lines and not very presentable, but Junot said "Bonaparte won't care about that for once" and when we got to the little tent where he sees the Staff *he* was immaculate in a clean shirt and breeches, with his boots shined until you could see your face in them. I saluted, and Napoleon said, "I am greatly in your debt, *Colonel* Latour. Put on the sash." Then I saw the red and white sash of an ADC lying on his work table. I could only stammer "*Merci, mon général,*" and good old Junot knotted the sash round my left arm, for I couldn't have tied a decent bow to save my life. Later I found it was Junot's own sash, for a general doesn't carry spare decorations into battle does he? Napoleon said, "Alvinczy will try again, but give me another day like yesterday and the campaign in Italy will be won." Then he gave me a purse. "That's for the trooper whose horse I borrowed," he said, and we were dismissed.

Oh Marie, next to our wedding day, this is the

happiest day of my life! I love you and I wish you were here.

Your husband,

Ch. Latour,
Colonel, ADC.

She knew he was utterly sincere. She knew how he had longed to be one of Napoleon's ADCs, not in the nominal office of 1795 but in reality, as one of his personal staff on campaign, and in her joy Marie kissed his letter once, and twice on the pompous, laughable, lovable signature. Thank God he's safe! Thank God it was given to him to save Napoleon's life! Thank God above all that I never told him about my foolish fancy and raised his hopes for nothing.

Then she saw that there was writing on the reverse of the last page, which like all the others looked as if it had been torn from her husband's field service notebook. The single paragraph was undated, but headed "Somewhere in Lombardy." It began:

I open this to say I spent exactly two hours in Milan. N. couldn't wait to see his precious Joséphine, so we broke all the riding records to get here, and lo! the dear creature had gone off on a jaunt to Genoa with a party of friends, including of course *the* friend, Wide-awake Charlie. Isn't that a story? I don't know how it ended because Murat and I were ordered to set up the new forward headquarters, and we're on our way. In haste, your C.

But I know how it ended, thought Marie grimly. She wheedled Napoleon into believing her everything pure and loving, and turning a blind eye on her folly. Is she really in love with that silly little Hippolyte, or has he got some hold on her? One answer to Marie's question came in a single line in the *Moniteur*, saying Captain Hippolyte

Charles had been ordered to Paris for a further posting, the second in a charming letter from Joséphine, with her New Year wishes and thanks for Marie's kindness to her children.

I still wish you hadn't gone away, [the letter continued]. You would have enjoyed the pleasant trip some friends and I made to Genoa last month. The Doge and his Council gave me a civic welcome and presented me with a necklace and headband of coral and pearls. Rather handsomer, I must say, than the cameo set I had from the Pope! I also met a clever young painter, Baron Antoine Gros, and invited him to Milan to paint Bonaparte and myself. My portrait isn't very flattering – something wrong with the mouth, but Bonaparte says he'll keep it in his room always. His is splendid, though it was very difficult to get him to sit still for it. He is wearing his black uniform with the scarlet sash and holding up a flag. Gros means to call it "The Victor of Arcola."

Dress uniform and scarlet sash – how different from the mud-bespattered figure Charles Latour had dragged from the swamp! Not a subject for a court painter! But that man had had the cold nerve to spit out the mud and lead the charge across the bridge; to Marie Latour, the mudlark was the victor of Arcola.

On 12 January 1797 Napoleon won the last of his Italian victories, and the one destined to be the best known, since it was commemorated in the name of a magnificent street to be built in Paris.

Rivoli was not his most brilliant success, since at one point he risked being caught in a pincer movement initiated by Alvinczy and a fresh army. It was two o'clock in the morning when Bonaparte came up with the Austrians on the plateau of Rivoli, which rises on the right bank of the Adige river, and General Joubert, one of his best men, charged the enemy in vain. The battle had been raging for eight hours when Masséna came up in support, and with another cavalry charge led by General Leclerc Alvinczy was brought to an unconditional surrender.

Twenty-one days later, when Bonaparte appeared before Mantua, Marshal Wurmser followed his example, and when the French entered that stubborn fortress the campaign in Italy was indeed at an end. But, as had been predicted by many, the campaign in Austria had only begun, and, sickened by the repeated defeats of the old men, the Emperor Francis II sent his last hope against Napoleon. His own brother, the Archduke Charles, who had won victories against the French on the Rhine, was a year younger than the Corsican. He harassed the French rear and threatened their lines of communication so successfully that Bonaparte halted his advance 150 kilometres short of Vienna, and prepared to conclude an armistice at Leoben.

"So now we know," said Dr Berthollet when this was announced in the *Moniteur*. "Clever Bonaparte, to get himself inside Austrian territory and out of reach of his employers before he begins to demonstrate his political genius."

"What do you mean exactly?" asked Marie.

"I mean you won't see your husband for a long time yet. Political *pourparlers* drag on endlessly. First the terms of the armistice must be settled, then there's the signing of the document, then comes the actual treaty of peace, all giving General Bonaparte a chance to shine as a statesman. He'll need all his aides-de-camp around him as he moves from one conference to another."

"I suppose so," said Marie. She was disappointed. Ever since the Arcola letter she had been hoping to see her husband soon. The verve of that letter – headlong and unpunctuated like his lovemaking – had roused her from the depression of September and excited her to hope for a new beginning. When Berthollet told her bracingly that they must all regard April, the month of Leoben, as the real New Year of 1797, she reminded him that the Republican year began in September, but she thought he was probably right. Certainly the armistice with Austria ushered in nearly twelve months which were to be the most solitary and studious of her life.

The life of the labo, which she had chosen for herself, was taking her out of touch with her closest friends. Teresa Tallien was preoccupied. Her brief fling with Barras was over, and indeed had only been begun for the pleasure of taking him away from Joséphine, and Gabriel Ouvrard, the millionaire banker, was established as the man in possession. He wanted to buy a house for her in the Rue de Babylone, and she thought (after a few "false alarms") that she might be with child by him.

Joséphine kept up an intermittent correspondence with Marie, but it was essentially a recital of triumphs. She had been fêted in half a dozen Italian cities, acquiring new necklaces and earrings in each one. The French troops always cheered her when she appeared with Bonaparte. His family had arrived *en masse* and were thoroughly disagreeable, treating her as an old woman who had seduced their dear Napoleon, but her own Eugène had arrived from Paris to take her part. Then tragedy struck, and the letters rose to a perfect shriek of despair. Fortuné was dead. The cook's dog, a great bully who ought to be put down, had set upon the dear little pet and killed him.

Marie wondered if the master strategist of the age had entered into a secret treaty with the cook.

Teresa might have her millionaire and Joséphine her delusions of grandeur, but a quarrel with her old friend Marie-Josèphe Beauchet was really upsetting to Marie. It came about when General Bonaparte failed to secure the release of the La Fayette family from their Austrian prison, which the Directory proposed as part of the armistice terms. The fault was La Fayette's own. He said he could not agree to promise never to return to Austria, a promise which his duty to his own country might one day cause him to break. It was a matter of principle.

"Damn his principles!" Bonaparte was reported to have said, before leaving the negotiations in other hands. La Fayette and his ailing wife and daughters had to endure five more months of dungeon captivity before they emerged to go into exile in Holland, broken in health but never in stupidity.

Madame Beauchet, whose loyalty to the Marquise de La Fayette had never wavered, came to Marie crying with rage. "It's all the fault of that Corsican upstart," she sobbed. "He abandoned that poor helpless family – "

"Oh, don't be so silly," snapped Marie. "He couldn't help them if they wouldn't help themselves – "

"General de La Fayette is a man of principle. How could Bonaparte understand a gentleman's code of honour?"

"The code of honour of the court of Versailles?"

"From what the papers tell us your friend Bonaparte is leading a Versailles kind of life in that summer palace he's commandeered at Montebello. A levée every day, and a guard of honour all the way from Poland – "

"Charles says he's hardly ever there. He's on the move all over Italy, planning the future – "

"I'll bet he's feathered his nest pretty well in the past year."

The angry altercation finished when Madame Beauchet flounced out of the apartment on the Quai Voltaire. The two women did not meet again until mid-August, and then it was with tears and whispered apologies, for they met in church. Against all belief St Roch, which had been the parish church for both of them and locked for years, was allowed to open its doors for a parish feast celebrated with great pomp. It was wonderful to see Father Carrichon and Father Vincent again, joined in the celebration of the Mass, and it seemed to the crowded congregation that better times were on their way. The Directory, so often reviled for its ruinous financial policies and the terrible inflation, worse than before the Revolution, seemed at last to be turning back to Christianity.

But France still put military glory ahead of Christian

worship, and of course they had the man for glory in Napoleon Bonaparte. He had fought the Austrians to a finish, and was now remaking the map of Italy. Without any reference to the Directory he created the Cisalpine Republic with Milan as its capital. Genoa became the capital of the Ligurian Republic, while the Pope, if he continued to misbehave, might find the Papal States transformed into the Roman Republic. These new states, like the federation of the Rhine, were not independent, but satellites of France.

Napoleon's doings were sometimes discussed in the noon break at the labo. It was short, for as the autumn advanced the assistants came to work earlier and left earlier rather than use candle light or oil lamps. Dr Berthollet was a good master, who increased the wages to match the cost of living, and paid a nearby eating-house to send in vegetable soup and bread at noon. On the day when the chief assistant, Citizen Thomas, called out to Marie, sitting on a stool at her work-bench with her soup bowl, "Come along, Madame Marie! Come and sit by the fire with the rest of us and don't be so exclusive!" she knew that her bonding with the labo had begun.

Dr Berthollet's staff preferred to talk shop. They were interested in Edward Jenner's theories of vaccination, and the German Martin Klapworth's production of uranium oxide from pitchblende. Marie was interested in another German, Friedrich Seturner, who was working on the isolation of a narcotic derivative of opium. It was the same research as had occupied her tenant, Louis Rocroi, for over three years. She was beginning to realise that her uncle, who had bequeathed all his property to her, had left her a better legacy in the spirit of scientific enquiry. Her nights were lonely, but not her days, for in them she found rest from years of strain in the Terror, in the prison, in the conflicting jealousies and the unavowed loyalties of her life.

13

This season of rest and reflection came to an end when the Treaty of Campo Formio was signed on 17 October 1797. Napoleon Bonaparte was the sole representative of France, and his signature alone appeared on the document. When the announcement appeared in the *Moniteur* Marie lingered behind the others at the end of the work day, and said to Dr Berthollet,

"My husband will soon be coming home."

"And you're glad?"

"Very glad. But it probably means I shall have to leave the labo."

"Don't be in too great a hurry," the chemist told her kindly. "Colonel Latour's an aide-de-camp, he'll certainly have to be in attendance on the great man at this peace congress they mean to hold at Rastatt. And who knows how peaceful it'll be? . . . You knew Bonaparte when he was a lieutenant, didn't you?"

"When he was nothing at all. When he'd been cashiered from the army for taking too many 'sick leaves' in Corsica."

"And he talked to you a lot. You knew who his heroes were?"

"Alexander the Great first, and then Julius Caesar."

"Did he tell you what Alexander did when he'd defeated all his enemies?"

"He wept because there were no more worlds left to conquer."

"But there *are* worlds waiting for Bonaparte, as we'll

very soon find out . . . Think it over, Marie! You shall have leave, generous leave, from the labo, when it's needed. But I won't let you go for good. You've become one of my best assistants, do you know that?"

She made him a little curtsey and went out.

The Treaty of Campo Formio represented tremendous gains for France. The Austrian Netherland, the Cisalpine Republic, the Ionian Islands which closed the Adriatic Sea, the Rhine frontier and the capital fortress of Mainz, for failure to take which both General Custine and Joséphine's first husband had been guillotined – all had been won for France by Bonaparte's sword. The Austrians received Venice and Venetia in exchange, although Joséphine had taken a bribe of a diamond ring to "say a few words" on behalf of Venetian independence at one of the innumerable banquets. Paris was preparing a hero's welcome for the conqueror, and Charles Latour wrote to say that he would be at the Quai Voltaire on 5 December.

Everything was in readiness. Armande, the *femme de ménage*, who to suit Marie's working hours now did the shopping in the late afternoons and prepared supper (for the rest of the day she found employment in the building) came in specially to give the apartment a thorough cleaning and to supervise the artisans who hung new curtains of indigo velvet in the living room. Marie bought a new dress of Charles's favourite blue. The style was more ample, requiring more material than in the early days of post-Thermidor, but the shoulders and bust were still revealed above the high waist, or else veiled in net.

Without summoning an army of beauticians, like Joséphine on her first day in Milan, Marie treated herself to intensive beauty care. In her gloomy kitchen she prepared the cosmetics of the Pharmacie Fontaine: witch hazel for a skin tonic, cucumber cream for night nourishing and a blend of glycerine and rosewater for her hands. She had her hair cut and curled by the hairdresser who had attended herself and Joséphine in the old apartment, and who had now opened a small salon of his own. Her mirror told her that at the advanced age of twenty-three she was the same Marie Fontaine whom Sergeant Vautour had fallen in love with when she was nineteen.

When the fifth of December came Marie was on the watch early, half expecting to see some sort of military parade outside the Tuileries, but all she saw was a convoy of army wagons delivering more "art treasures" to the tender care of the Republic. She wondered that there was any art left in Italy. The Horses of St Mark had been taken away from the Venetians (whose ancestors had stolen them from Constantinople in 1204) and had joined the Apollo Belvedere, the Medici Venus, the Laocoön and other famous statues in the new Louvre organised by Hubert Robert, but obviously there was more to come. Marie's nervous tension grew as she watched the empty *quais*. After all, it was fifteen months since she and her husband had seen one another, like so many other soldiers and their stay-at-home wives. Would he find her changed? Would Charles be changed himself?

It was nearly four o'clock before the familiar step was heard on the landing, the familiar rat-tat on the door knocker, and in another moment Marie was in her husband's arms, half hidden in the folds of his military cloak. "Darling, my darling!" she heard him whisper between kisses. "We've been apart too long . . ." and she whispered in reply, "I've missed you so much!"

When Charles hung up his accoutrements on the pegs in the little hall and followed her into the salon, he said how much he had hoped to be with her earlier. "But we were waylaid," he explained, "by three of the new Directors, not very impressive, and by Citizen Talleyrand, very impressive indeed." He turned one of the shabby armchairs towards the fire for Marie, and pushed up another for himself. "Oh, and," he continued, "the man you've been working for, Citizen Berthollet, he was there too."

"That was a mixed group!"

"Talleyrand made a little speech when we arrived. He said they had wanted to welcome General Bonaparte on the very day he returned to Paris, before the public rejoicings began."

"Talleyrand is the minister for foreign affairs now," said Marie. She was more interested in Dr Berthollet, she hadn't thought he was so much of a Bonapartist. She asked Charles if he had spoken to the chemist.

"Didn't have a chance, the bigwigs lunched in a private room. The rest of us ate in the officers' mess."

"What did Joséphine do?"

"Joséphine? She wasn't there."

"Not *there*? Didn't she travel with him?"

"Not she. Bonaparte and his Staff and the ADCs took the short cut through Switzerland, and she came on with Pauline Bonaparte through Turin and Lyon."

"I thought she couldn't abide Pauline Bonaparte."

"She could put up with Pauline's company to receive a queen's homage and a sackful of presents from the towns on their route." Charles smiled a smile which was no longer sullen but bland, and said, "Don't let's talk about boring old Joséphine, tell me about yourself. You're looking wonderfully well."

"So are you," she said. "The sash suits you to perfection."

He stroked the scarlet and white silk complacently. "The poor old flat's looking nice too," he said. "What have you been doing to it? Oh, I know, you've got new drapes. Very handsome. Much better than Ovize's tattered damask."

"They keep the salon warm too."

"Has it snowed in Paris yet? There was early snow in Switzerland as we came through."

Now they were talking about the weather. Marie had expected to be in his arms on the daybed, whispering the familiar words of love. She tried to bring the conversation back to his promotion, to his rescue of Bonaparte at Arcola, but that was too old a story for a man who lived in the present, and Charles Latour interrupted her abruptly.

"Marie, when did you see Maître Vial last?"

"About three months ago, when we made up that list of vacant property he was going to send on to you. Did you get it?"

"Oh yes, I got it, but I'm not interested in buying house property at present. I suppose he told you I'm paying the rent here from my army pay?"

"Well yes, he had to, darling. He told me the money your father left with him had all been spent. And of course he can't get any more from England."

"Does he even hear from my parents?"

"I'm afraid not."

Charles sighed, and muttered "Lucky I got my promotion." Then, with an effort, he asked Marie about the letting of her house and pharmacy. This was so completely out of character that she hardly knew how to tell him that the Rocrois' lease had expired in October and had been renewed for a second term of three years, of course at an increased rent. She felt as if they were two brokers discussing a bill of exchange.

"You manage very well, Marie." Charles sighed again and closed his eyes. In the gathering dusk the leaping firelight threw his face into sharp relief, and Marie saw that he was very tired.

"Charles, would you like a glass of wine? Would you like dinner early – or late, after your luncheon at Grenelle? Just say which you would prefer . . ."

"Why don't we go out to dinner?" he said, wide awake. "Murat and some other fellows are going to Véry's, and I half promised we would join them."

"Oh, but . . . Certainly, if that's what you would like."

The querulous voice of the concierge at the front door announced a trooper with the colonel's valise, and their awkward reunion ended in unpacking. As she sorted out the scanty piles of clothing Marie thought there was a bitter truth in the words Charles had spoken so tenderly when he came in:

They had been too long apart.

* * *

When the saluting and the presenting arms were over and the Grenelle barracks left behind, General Bonaparte sat back in the closed carriage and shut his eyes. The reception committee he had met at luncheon had been a surprise, and he needed to evaluate its members before he gave himself up to the luxury of going home. The two young ADCs sitting at rigid attention with their backs to the horses would not disturb him by one word.

The three new Directors, appointed by the system of rotation, were negligible. Carnot was out of the Directory now, and of all men General Schérer, whom he had superseded at Nice, was Minister for War. Schérer would be easy to handle. Berthollet too, an excellent fellow, was concerned with nothing but army medicine. But Talleyrand – ah, there was the enigma, the question mark! A brilliant talker, but how much substance was behind the talk? He would have to discuss Talleyrand with Berthier as soon as the gigantic public ovation in the courtyard of the Luxembourg was over. Meantime – home!

Bonaparte opened his eyes and bestowed on the two youngsters the brilliant smile which transformed his haggard face. "Well, Eugène," he said to his stepson, "glad to be back? And you, Le Marois, how do you think Paris is looking now?"

Le Marois was not twenty yet, Eugène de Beauharnais sixteen, and the commanding general was all of twenty-eight. Le Marois, who had been a witness at his wedding, took it upon himself to answer.

"I think Paris needs a big clean-up, sir."

"I agree. Broken pavements, broken cobbles, weeds and rubbish everywhere – it's worse than when I came back in '95. I hope the Rue Chantereine is tidier than the Champs Elysées."

"We heard in the officers' mess, sir," said Eugène diffidently, "that it's to be renamed the Rue de la Victoire in your honour."

"So they tell me." Napoleon smiled again. "What with

that and the redecorations your mother says she's ordered, we shan't know ourselves, shall we, my boy?"

Going home. Going back to the villa where he first was Joséphine's lover, where as her husband he had been the master of the house for just two nights, and half of one of them spent in doctoring a bite by Fortuné! Well, Fortuné would bark and bite no more. But – Joséphine! If only she could be there on the steps of the villa to bid him welcome home!

As it was, the welcome came from Agathe Rible, who was expecting them, and who was the perfect house-keeper in a black silk dress with a white frilled apron and mob cap. She overwhelmed the general with congratulations, she curtsied to the boy she had helped to bring up and was hugged in return, and she somehow contrived to spirit him and Captain Le Marois up the back stairs and away from General Bonaparte, who was standing stupe-fied in the front hall.

"Were these the decorations ordered by madame?" he asked in a strangled voice.

"I don't know, sir. Citizen Vautier, the architect, said she wanted everything to be the last word in elegance, and gave him *carte blanche*."

The last word in elegance appeared to be Roman, and the austere draperies were caught back by bronze fasces, the ancient Roman symbol of authority.

"Is it all like this, Agathe?"

"Come this way, sir."

The salons were decorated in a variety of styles, with painted friezes, mahogany furniture created by the Jacob brothers, the leading cabinet makers of the day, marble-topped console tables, huge mirrors and ornamental vases of porphyry and malachite. A collection of the gifts from Italian cities was waiting to be installed.

"What about upstairs?" asked the strangled voice.

"Madame did the design for the principal bedroom herself."

Agathe expected an explosion when Napoleon saw the

187

bedroom he was to share with Joséphine. She thought it was dreadful, and she saw by his face that he did too, but as any member of his Staff could have told her, Bonaparte's silent anger was more terrifying than his rage. Joséphine had had the fatal idea of remodelling the pretty feminine bedroom on a military theme. The tented ceiling imitated an armed camp. The bedside tables resembled drums, the oil lamps on each one having tricolore shades. Instead of the vast fourposter there were narrow twin beds, camp style, and Agathe mutely showed how a switch could be pulled to bring the beds together. To a man accustomed to wrap himself in his old grey coat and bivouac beneath a gun it was luxury, to a man in love it was a hideous reminder of what, in his wife's arms, he wanted to forget.

Agathe finally broke the silence by saying there was a letter for the general from madame's banker in Dunkirk. She had locked it away for safety, should she fetch it now?

"Please do," he said like an automaton. When the woman was gone he looked round for a comfortable chair, and finding none sank into a kind of camp stool, from which he had a good view of the crossed swords hanging behind the beds. Did she intend them to fight a duel?

In his too-vivid imagination Joséphine's room had been a kind of shrine to Napoleon. The flowers, the firelight, the scents, the cosmetics, the silks no smoother than her flesh, had made of the place an altar to love. And she, in her complete failure to understand him, had made of it a memorial to war.

He tried to remember the banker in Dunkirk. Of course! Mr Emmery was the man who handled her occasional remittances from Martinique. And his letter, when Agathe handed it to him, was short and to the point. He dismissed the woman before he broke the seals.

Citizen General!
Many congratulations on your victories. I hope you are satisfied with the work Citizen Vautier has carried out at the villa. Madame Bonaparte directed that no

188

expense was to be spared, as she intended it to be a present for yourself. Unfortunately there are no funds in her account with our house, so I shall forward the bills to your good self as they come in. The estimated total will be 300,000 francs, errors and omissions excepted.

Fraternally yours, Emmery.

Three hundred thousand francs!

Bonaparte's army pay had been generous, and supplemented by presents for each of his victories. He was now sufficiently well off to have planned on buying the lease of the villa from Barras, and paying off that entanglement for good and all. The villa was worth 50,000 francs at the most. But *three hundred thousand . . .!*

He was ruined.

14

Only five months after that homecoming, which in two homes had been no great success, Colonel and Madame Latour stood in a reserved section of the docks at Toulon, viewing the greatest French fleet assembled there since the Crusades.

Their places were reserved behind the picket fence, patrolled by gendarmes, which kept in check the crowd of hundreds assembled to watch General Bonaparte's departure for the goal of his boyhood's dreams, the invasion of the East. Their movement orders, which they knew by heart, directed them to embark on the flagship, L'Orient, in less than two hours' time.

Latour's movement orders were military, stamped with the insignia of the Republic and the words "Liberty, Equality, Fraternity" and signed by General Berthier. Marie's were headed "Scientific Commission", signed in Dr Berthollet's copperplate hand writing, and countersigned "Bonaparte" in an indecipherable scrawl.

When she thought how this had come about she still felt as if she were dreaming, although it was some weeks since she had known what the two signatories had in mind for her.

Her husband thought only that Marie was looking very well. She could trace her ancestry only as far back as a Breton farmer, her great-grandfather, while he could trace his to Hugh Capet, King of France, but the Breton stock was sturdy, and Marie had stood up as well as he had to the hardships of a journey in an army convoy from Paris to Toulon. She wore a linen sheath and a short tailored jacket in grey and white striped linen, "Just the thing for shipboard," he said approvingly, "but too cold for the weather if it turns stormy." For the wind had risen and he saw Marie shiver.

"I've got a good thick shawl in my portmanteau," she said. "Charles, do you think it will? Turn stormy, I mean?"

"You needn't be afraid of storms aboard the largest warship in the world!'

"I'm afraid of being seasick, and disgracing you!"

Charles laughed, and drew her arm through his own. Now he could feel her trembling. She really was nervous, and he said hastily what he had said more than once before.

"Darling, if you think it'll be too much for you, tell me now. There's still time for you to change your mind about going on to Egypt – personally I don't think they had any right to ask you – "

"I'm very glad they did," said Marie in her decisive way, "and you know I want to go to Egypt. Don't you want us to be together, dear?"

"Of course I do." He kissed her quickly. It was a trifle public, but there was a lot of kissing going on in the crowd on the other side of the picket fence as the hour grew nearer for the French fleet to put to sea. There were musicians and singers, strollers with performing monkeys, hawkers selling neckerchiefs with two faces painted on them in crude colours intended to represent General Bonaparte and Admiral Brueys, with a sketch of the flagship *L'Orient* on the other side. It was a *jour de fête* for Toulon: the biggest *fête* the city had celebrated since the day, not five years ago, when the young Captain Bonaparte had delivered Toulon from the English occupants.

"Here comes Eugène de Beauharnais," said Charles, as Bonaparte's youngest ADC pushed his way through the crowd and reached the fence, where a gendarme saluted the red and white sash. "I'm looking for Colonel Latour," they heard the boy say. " – Oh, there you are!"

"Marie," he went on without a break, as he hurried up to them, "Marie, how nice you look, aren't you excited? I'm very, very sorry, but I just missed the Clouzots. When I tracked them down to their *pension* they'd left an hour before, to go aboard the *Tonnant*."

"Oh, Eugène! Oh, I *am* disappointed!" cried Marie. "Now I shan't see poor Lucia until we reach Alexandria. How I wish they were sailing in *L'Orient*!"

"Well, they aren't," said Charles, yielding to sarcasm, "but since there'll be two thousand other people aboard, you're sure to find another bosom friend before we land."

"Not one like Lucia," said Marie sadly, and Eugène, saying again how sorry he was, added "I must be off to the Hôtel de la Marine. I don't want to intrude on my mother and the general, but the ladies are assembling outside the balcony, and *he* ought to be going aboard. So must you!" and the dutiful messenger waved his hand and was gone.

Both Latours had been keeping their eyes on a wooden balcony specially erected above the dock, just opposite the flagship, which was dressed overall, and every deck was black with the shakos of the élite troops embarked earlier in the day. A cheer arose from the men when a dozen ladies, dressed overall in their own way, began to file on to the flower-decked balcony. It rose to a storm of cheering when Madame Bonaparte appeared. She wore the white which became her so well, and in her left hand she carried a white silk handkerchief which she constantly touched to her wet eyes. With her right she blew kisses to her husband's men, who replied with shouts of "Long live Lady Luck!"

"Listen to them!" said Charles Latour. "Astonishing how the troops believe in her!"

"I wonder if she'll be cheered at Plombières," said

Marie, for Joséphine, while her husband was in Egypt, was to take the cure at the Vosges spa with a great reputation for putting an end to infertility. She was now as eager to give Bonaparte a child as she had been reluctant at the start of their marriage.

"She'd find an audience anywhere . . . Hush now," said Charles. "He's coming."

The crowd on the dockside parted, and a small man came through. He walked rapidly to the gangway of *L'Orient*, which was decorated with miniature flags and swags of flowers. He was followed by a group of tall men, who stopped when he stopped, and came to attention on the steps beneath him.

Napoleon Bonaparte, who had a fine sense of the dramatic, was not wearing the black uniform of the Arcola portrait. He was in the old familiar army blue, with the familiar cockade in his hat, the sabre which always seemed too big for his meagre body dragging at his belt. He acknowledged the cheers from land and shipboard with a grave salute, while the Tricolore was broken from the mast high above his head and the bands played the *Marseillaise*. Then he turned and ran up the last steps of the gangway, followed by his generals.

Charles Latour named them as they followed him. "There goes Berthier, you know him of course, . . . and Kléber, wildly jealous of Napoleon . . . and Menou, who backed down before the rebels on the day before the whiff of grapeshot . . ."

"He can't be much of an asset," said Marie. "And who's that huge man, very dark?"

"Dark? He's a mulatto, that's what! He's General Dumas, did very well in the Tirol. Then Duroc, Lannes, and Desaix, one of the best. You'll meet them all tomorrow, if not tonight. Come along!"

Marie hung back. "But Charles – only seven generals? Where are the others?"

Charles laughed at her. "Embarked with their men, of

course. All aboard for Alexandria – where we should be, and it'll take some time to get through the crowd." He took her arm. "Don't worry about the generals. There are twenty-seven or thirty-seven, I'm not sure which. But I *have* heard Bonaparte say all his generals are expendable."

The young Latours knew nothing of the horror which had overwhelmed Napoleon when he first saw his wife's foolish redecorations and the bills which accompanied them. Not a man to give way to despair, he handled the matter so promptly that it never became a topic for gossip, or for anything but the admiring comments of the guests invited to the villa on the renamed Rue de la Victoire. Napoleon applied to the financier Gabriel Ouvrard, arms supplier to the navy, whose personal fortune was said to be over 15 million francs. It was easy for him to lend Napoleon 300,000 francs at – under strict conditions of secrecy – the very favourable interest of two per cent per annum. When Joséphine came home and learned what her husband thought of her transactions, she was sufficiently punished by hearing his opinion of her military decorations, and when she hysterically offered to sell the jewels she had acquired, so as to pay at least part of the bills, he merely laughed at her.

Napoleon adored her. After their long separation he would have lain with her on the floor, let alone the imitation camp beds (with the machinery which always sprang apart at the wrong moment) but he did not respect her. She was a woman, whose function was to be the warrior's rest; apart from his mother . . . and perhaps one other, there was no woman whom Napoleon Bonaparte did respect. But he admired the grace and charm which she displayed in public as well as in private. The banquet at which they were entertained by the Directory soon after her return was much more successful than the public ovation in the courtyard of the Luxembourg at which he appeared alone. He never spoke well to a civilian audience.

"What are they going to do with him?" Marie asked her husband, when the rejoicings were over and the conqueror was once again an unemployed general, back in his old office in the Pavillon de Flore, and talking to no larger an audience than his faithful ADCs.

"If somebody, say Junot, dares to ask him a direct question he gets snubbed, but my guess is the Directors want him to invade England," said Charles.

"Even after Hoche's terrible fiasco a year ago?"

"That was an attempt to invade Ireland, when our ships were scattered in Bantry Bay, but – yes, I suppose it comes to the same thing. And poor Hoche is dead now – Joséphine's prison sweetheart! I wonder how she feels about that?"

"We may find out tonight."

They had been invited to the first really grand party General and Madame Bonaparte had given in the Rue de la Victoire, and certainly the lady, resplendent in a golden gown, showed no sign of grief for her former lover, dead at thirty of lung trouble. What she did demonstrate in many ways was a pretty deference to the husband she had previously treated with amusement bordering on contempt. The guests, too, were different, being intellectuals rather than politicians, for one of the honours done to Napoleon was membership (Mathematical Section) of the new Institute. It was natural that among the important guests should be the mathematician Monge, now the principal of the Ecole Polytechnique, and Monge's friend Dr Berthollet, to whom Marie was glad to introduce her husband. Poetry was represented by Arnault and Joseph Chénier, with whom Napoleon had a lively discussion about Ossian, and art by David, who had painted a frieze round one of the salons. He had idealised an evil man in his painting called *The Death of Marat* and now appeared to be ready to idealise Bonaparte.

Marie turned from one salon into another to avoid a meeting with Citizen David.

"What's the matter with you?" Charles whispered, and she whispered back, "I hate that man."

"I didn't know you knew him."

"I don't, and I don't want to, but I was as near to him as I am to you now when we stood on the steps of St Roch's church, on the day of Queen Marie Antoinette's execution, and he was sketching the poor woman sitting in the tumbril – it was horrible."

"You're morbid, to let your mind dwell on the past."

"That was the day you and I first met, remember?"

Charles laughed indulgently and said of course he remembered. He pinched the inside of her bare arm. They were lovers again, but since Charles returned the loving had become routine and the shared confidence had ceased to exist. They had been too long apart.

Colonel Latour was more confidential with his wife when he was ordered to accompany General Bonaparte on a tour of the Channel ports to study the possibility of an invasion of England.

"Dunkirk, Calais and Boulogne?" hazarded Marie.

"And further south than Boulogne, to Dieppe and St Valéry-en-Caux. He means to do the thing thoroughly if he has to do it at all."

"And who's going with him besides yourself?"

"Le Marois and young Beauharnais and perhaps Napoleon's brother Lucien."

"Lucien? Not Joseph? And not Junot?"

Charles smiled grimly. "We're hand-picked, my dear. We're the aides who know how to avoid painful subjects. Joseph Bonaparte and Junot insist on telling him things he doesn't want to hear . . . about Captain Hippolyte Charles."

"Wide-awake Charlie? You don't mean . . . It was announced months ago that he was coming back to Paris for reposting . . ."

"He's been posted out of the army, certainly, but he

only arrived in Paris when *she* did. My innocent Marie, the wretched fellow never left Italy, and she kept seeing him on the sly."

"I hope she behaves herself while the General's away," said Marie. "How long shall you be gone on the Channel trip?"

"About three weeks. I'm afraid you'll be lonely," said Charles glibly. "Why don't you go back to the labo for company?"

She did go back to the Rue de Seine, and found that Dr Berthollet, gone to the Tuileries, had left instructions for a rush order for an ophthalmia remedy. Returning, he found Marie in her old place, intent on the preparation of one part of water to one third of a part of rosewater and two pinches of zinc sulphate. Beyond a word of approval and welcome he said very little, but a few nights later he asked her to remain behind, and began without preamble:

"Marie, would you be willing to continue this sort of work in the army, in a foreign land?"

"As your assistant?" she said, amazed.

"Not precisely mine, but I would be there."

"I don't know what my husband would say. Not in England?"

"There will be no invasion of England. General Bonaparte knows England has a sure shield in the Channel. He has another idea, which he shares with Talleyrand and some of the Directory, and he means to discuss it with your husband and yourself. May I tell him you are willing to listen?"

That was all Dr Berthollet was prepared to say. Marie stammered "Of course," and "Whenever you wish," and went home walking on air. Could it be true? Would she really be given the opportunity for which long training had fitted her, to join the *Service de Santé* (she could think of nothing else but that) in an army led by a great soldier into a foreign land which, remembering his youthful dreams, could only be Egypt or India?

When Charles came home ten days later, he very soon accused her of being *distraite* and inattentive to his account of the miseries of trailing round the Channel ports in wintry weather. Of course there was to be no invasion of England – but one thing he would say for Bonaparte, he had made so much parade of the whole thing, had kept himself so much in evidence, as to convince the English spies with whom the coast was honeycombed that the French intended to attack England.

Within a week his real purpose was revealed. He intended to invade Egypt, rid the country of the Mameluke oligarchy which was draining the country dry, earn the gratitude of the Ottoman Empire, and appoint Monsieur de Talleyrand ambassador to Constantinople. He would cut off the access of the English to India and regain the lost French possessions in the sub-continent.

Talleyrand, less ambitious but whole-heartedly in support, saw the occupation of Egypt as an outlet for French trade and commerce.

Further, Napoleon intended to create a Scientific and Artistic Commission of over a hundred *savants*, or scholars, who would form a French Institute in Cairo, to promote learning and to achieve a better understanding of the ancient Egyptian civilisation.

"So Egypt was the foreign land you meant," said Marie to Dr Berthollet, when all Paris was discussing the latest development.

"Does it scare you?"

"What scares me is telling Charles about your offer. I don't know how to begin, and every day I put it off makes it worse."

"Leave it to the general. You've had an invitation to their *soirée* on Friday?"

"Just a printed card saying 'General and Madame Bonaparte at home. Music.'"

"That's when we'll get it settled." Berthollet's tone was final and Marie said no more. She knew the chemist had been given the task of recruiting the whole of the Scientific

Commission, compared to which her own problems were unimportant. She waited for Friday, thankful that Charles was in attendance at the Pavillon de Flore, discussing the Egyptian expedition with other men.

It was of course the chief subject of conversation at the musical *soirée*, in itself a departure for the inhabitants of the villa on the Rue de la Victoire. It might as well have been called a family evening, for the hired performers on the piano, violin and harp were kept in the background, providing background music in what had been the dining-room. The Bonapartes were out in force. The only one absent was the youngest son, Jérôme, a naval cadet, but Joseph, Lucien and Louis were there with their three sisters. The mother of the clever and ambitious brood, Madame Letizia, shared a loveseat with her daughter-in-law. Joséphine, to Marie's eyes, seemed diminished by the three handsome sisters – one an authentic beauty – all of whom were twenty years her junior, and allowed their dislike of her to be seen. Nearer in age to Madame Letizia, who was always kind to her, Joséphine divided her attention between little tender murmurings to the Corsican lady and anxious backward glances at the Corsican gentleman who stood behind them. Napoleon was giving a polished performance of a buck in attendance on two belles at the court of Versailles, and while he was silent not even his favourite sister, Pauline the beauty, dared to approach.

Presently he advanced into the centre of the room, and taking Charles and Marie each by a hand bowed with exaggerated courtesy to his wife.

"Will you excuse us, madame?" he said. "I want to have a few words with our young friends, if you can spare them?"

"Certainly," she said, looking so uncomfortable that Marie thought, "Why, she's afraid of him. What can have gone wrong now?"

They went through the room where the musicians were playing to an audience of half a dozen people, and entered the salon where, among the redecorations, Joséphine's dainty escritoire had been replaced by a masculine writing table. Dr Berthollet got up at their entry. He had slipped away from the grand salon earlier. He had had only the most fleeting encounter with Colonel Latour, and his impression of the general's "young friend", who was two years his master's junior, was the conventional one of a handsome youngster with the cavalryman's swagger and the cavalryman's moustache.

"He's a good soldier – saved my life at Arcola, and a first rate ADC," Napoleon had said, "but he's infernally jealous of his wife."

"Really?" said Berthollet. "I shouldn't have thought Marie Latour was the woman to give her husband cause for jealousy. I didn't know she ever looked at another man."

"I don't mean he's jealous of other men. He's jealous because he's not as clever as she is, and he doesn't approve of cleverness in women. He's jealous because she's purposeful and independent. He's still an *aristo* at heart."

"I see," said Berthollet, and the subject was changed. But he looked at Napoleon with a speculative eye.

As an experienced man of fifty, who unlike his colleague Lavoisier had dodged the guillotine, Berthollet was interested in studying Marie's husband. He had heard the Arcola story, and privately believed that Napoleon, having the nine lives of a cat, could have wriggled out of that swamp by himself, but then – he hadn't been there! Dr Berthollet waited until they were all seated comfortably and Napoleon began:

"Charles, I want to tell you about a little plan Citizen Berthollet and I have been hatching, which we hope will make you and Marie very happy."

"A plan for us, sir?" said Charles Latour.

"Briefly, we want Marie to accompany the Egyptian expeditionary force."

"You can't mean it," said Charles.

"I'm absolutely serious," Napoleon said.

"But what would she do – what would she be, in Egypt?"

"She'd be assistant to the Chief Pharmacist, Citizen Royer. Paid at the same rate as the other junior assistants of the Scientific Commission."

"Marie in the Scientific Commission?" said Charles, reddening. "It's preposterous."

"I don't think you appreciate your wife's talent, colonel," said Berthollet.

"I know she's clever," said Charles. "But have you no man in your laboratory who would be just as good an assistant to this Royer?"

"Not as – " Berthollet began, but Bonaparte interrupted.

"Charles, this is disappointing. I thought you would leap at the chance of having Marie with you."

"Sir, with the greatest respect, I've heard you say the battlefield was no place for a woman. Does Madame Bonaparte accompany you?"

"Madame Bonaparte will join me later, after she has taken the cure at Plombières. And who said anything about a battlefield? Your wife will be in a place of absolute safety and comfort, like all the scholars who are eager to visit Egypt – "

"An enemy country?" Irresolute, Charles looked from one man to the other, and Berthollet thought how insecure that shifting glance made him appear. Then he turned on his wife, whose pretty face showed no sign of emotion as she looked at the hands quietly folded in her lap.

"You knew about this!" he challenged her. "Why didn't you tell me?"

"Because I wasn't sure," she said. "I had to wait until it was official."

Oh, the minx was *deep*, Berthollet silently applauded. Twice as deep as her husband, worth two of him at least . . . and he knows it.

"Marie, tell me this is just a joke," her husband begged. "You don't really want to go to Egypt – do you?"

Marie looked at Napoleon. He was smiling, the rare smile which gave his face a rare beauty. She returned the smile.

"Oh yes I do," she said, and in a voice little more than a whisper, "because I want to be with you."

15

So there they were, leaning side by side on the rail of a crowded deck on the flagship *L'Orient* as she was towed out of the harbour of Toulon at the head of thirteen ships of the line and four hundred transports carrying 35,000 troops to the Near East. Her complement of sailors had been drastically reduced to make room for land officers and civilians and the gun crews manning one hundred and thirty guns. With 2000 persons aboard, the largest warship in the world was a floating city.

"We've given Admiral Nelson the slip, sure enough," said Charles Latour with satisfaction. "Our *avisos* – that's what they call the little courier ships, Marie – report that his squadron is making for Gibraltar."

"No wonder the people are cheering on shore," said Marie.

"Let's hope they'll cheer when we come back. Well, we can't wait to see the last of France, I've got to be on duty at the reception. Are you coming back to the cabin to get dressed?"

"Me? I'm not dressing. Oh, I see what you mean. I'm not invited to the reception."

"I thought all the Scholars were invited to meet the flag officers in the admiral's great cabin!"

"The Scholars, yes, but not the junior assistants," smiled Marie. "I'll come back to our cabin presently, when you've had time to put on your dress uniform."

"Time *and* room," said Charles. "You couldn't swing a cat in that place!"

The cheers on shore had died away and the hills behind Toulon were growing dim when Marie returned to the cramped little cabin and began to unpack her portmanteau, which with Charles's valise was supplemented by two folding canvas stools and some articles of chinaware. At least the place was airy, for Charles had left the port open, and an increasingly stiff breeze was blowing. She took her dress off and crept under the covers of an uninviting berth. When Charles came back she was half asleep, clutching a damp handkerchief in her hand.

"Succumbed already, have you?" he said cheerfully. "She *is* rolling a bit, and the reception was a fiasco. Half the Scholars sent apologies, and Napoleon left it to Admiral Brueys to do the introductions. He went off to his own cabin – I think he's made up his mind to be seasick too."

A faraway voice said "Poor man."

"I think he's going to read himself out of it. I saw Eugène staggering under a load of books for his cabin." Charles was untying his cherished sash with care. "Do you feel equal to some supper, dear? A sip of brandy out of my flask?"

"No – thank you. I'm going to go to bed properly and try to sleep."

"You do that, and you'll be all right in the morning."

She was not all right, and the chinaware was put to various humiliating uses. The Mediterranean, a tideless sea, boiled and frothed in a May storm, and the passengers in the largest warship in the world suffered as much as the veterans of the Italian war in the transports, who had never left the land before. By afternoon Charles was alarmed enough to ask Dr Berthollet's advice, and the chemist brought a medical man to prescribe a sedative for Marie. Dr Desgenettes, an irascible man from Montpellier, did more: he recruited a woman from the bowels of

L'Orient to give Marie a blanket bath and make the cabin clean and tidy.

The newcomer, who announced herself as Jeanette Tête-de-Bois, was a woman of forty, as tall as Marie and twice as heavy; she was one of nearly two hundred women accompanying the army as authorised military personnel. She was a *cantinière*, carrying liquor for the troops, and not a laundress, but after the bath she washed Marie's pillow case and found clean sheets, while telling Colonel Latour to be off with him and leave his good lady to her. She sang Marie to sleep, so that when the patient awoke at sunset and found the woman gone and Charles in the cabin the first thing she asked was "Why do they call her Jeanette Wooden-head? She isn't stupid!"

'She's Head of Wood because she can drink any man in her company under the table, I've been told. Do you want her to come back tomorrow?"

"I mean to get up tomorrow. Charles, I'm so sorry – I feel such a mess, and such a fool . . ."

"Better take it easy for another day."

She did, and found Jeanette's humming, gossiping presence oddly comforting. Marie had hoped to be re-united with Lucia Clouzot, her friend of Milan, and now "poor Lucia" because her baby girl, so much desired, had lived just two sickly months before she died. Joséphine's unsympathetic comment had been that there was a lot of bad blood in those old Italian families, "the Colonnas and the Borgias and all that crowd, you know!" Marie's sympathy would have to wait till Alexandria – how many days away? All the ships of the expeditionary force were mortally slow.

On the fourth morning after sailing, the storm had blown itself out, the seasick passengers had all recovered, and Marie was installed in a sheltered corner of the deck under an awning which, before saying "Goodbye and good luck, *ma petite dame!*" Jeanette Tête-de-Bois had made two sailors put up for her. Here she had a stream of visitors: the two doctors, Chief Pharmacist Royer, and even the eminent Professor Monge, who as well as being a brilliant mathematician had been a member of the Research Commission, and had sent no fewer than three hundred crates of art treasures from Italy to the tender care of the French Republic. General Bonaparte did not appear at once. He had been reading *The Marriage of Figaro* for its political significance and was intent on finishing the Acts of the Apostles – not from religious conviction but because St Paul, the apostle of action and quick wits, was a man after his own heart.

When Bonaparte came along the deck, attended by the devoted Eugène, Marie was chatting with a merry little urchin in uniform, who snapped to attention and gave the commanding general a smart salute. When the latter had made all the correct enquiries for Marie's health, he tweaked the child's ear and asked his name.

"Midshipman Casabianca, to serve you, *mon général*."

"And your age?"

"I'm nine years old, sir."

"Well, Casabianca, be off with you, and see you do your duty."

When the boy scurried away Bonaparte said softly, "Nine! The same age as I was when I left Corsica for Autun to learn French. But it's young to be a midshipman."

"He was telling me his father's an officer in this ship," said Marie. "So he isn't quite alone."

"That's good," said the general. "Marie, I'm glad to see the roses back in your cheeks. The sea air is doing you good too. Rest, eat lightly, sleep well, and in a few days you shall have some entertainment. Have you anything to read?"

"Our orders were to travel lightly, so we didn't bring any books with us."

"Never mind. I'll lend you a copy of the *Arabian Nights*; it'll put you in the mood for Egypt."

* * *

The entertainment Napoleon had in mind was the capture of Malta, then in the hands of the Knights Hospitallers of St John of Jerusalem. But it took more than a few days for the drama – well prepared in advance – to be staged, for the great fleet was mortally slow. Having sailed from Toulon on 19 May, it came within sight of Malta only on 10 June, and the three intervening weeks were increasingly tedious for the Scholars and the Staff. They were required to meet with Napoleon every evening in the great cabin, where he led them in literary and philosophical debates or tested, by question and answer, their knowledge of Egypt. A band played between decks, and the evening ended with Napoleon's favourite piece, *The March of the Tartars*.

"Those damned Tartars were a noisy lot," said Charles Latour, arriving back in the cramped cabin after one of those intellectual evenings. "I've got a splitting headache. Don't laugh! Junot fell asleep and snored as usual, and your Scholars had much the best of it."

But the Staff had the best of it at Malta, where the garrison made a token sortie from Valetta which was easily repulsed by the French. The Knights promptly surrendered, and Bonaparte spent forty-eight hours in turning the island into a French possession and removing all the treasures of the Hospitallers into the hold of *L'Orient*. When she set sail again the Tricolore was flying from the fortress of Valetta, and one of General Bonaparte's easiest victories was toasted in champagne.

Admiral Brueys and his officers joined in the rejoicings, and said nothing about their anxiety for that day at least. They had received information that an English fleet had been seen steering for Malta. Was Admiral Nelson, beguiled into sailing westward, on the right scent now and turning east? *Sir* Horatio Nelson, as he now was, had lost an eye in the fighting at Calvi in Corsica and an arm at Santa Cruz. His health was shattered but his spirit was as high as ever, and Brueys, with his slow-moving armada, dreaded an encounter with him before Egypt could be reached. But Nelson was short of frigates, "the eyes of the fleet", and once off Malta and again off Alexandria he lost the French in fog and heavy weather.

On 22 June Napoleon informed his soldiers that they were going to fight the Mamelukes, former slaves who had made themselves masters of Egypt, a part of the Ottoman Empire. They would conquer because the Destinies were in their favour. They must respect the Mahommedans and their Islamic faith. They would soon arrive at Alexandria, a city built by Alexander the Great, and with every step they took would meet with objects capable of exciting emulation.

"I hope he's right," said Charles Latour. "The French consul at Alexandria said nothing about emulation when he came on board this morning. Seemed to think the natives might want to emulate *us*."

"Charles – I *saw* him coming on board this morning."

"Who – Citizen Magagallon?"

"Is that his name? He *climbed* up the side of the ship."

"No gangways here, my dear, and no tugs. *L'Orient* can't put in to Les Bequières, she's going to anchor in Marabout Bay while we disembark."

"Then we'll have to climb down on those rope-ladder things? Into the water?"

"No, no, into small boats. Don't be nervous, darling. I'll be right beside you. I won't let you fall."

Marie was nervous, but too proud to admit it. She stared resolutely at the unfriendly landscape which had appeared to starboard. Hillocks and dunes of sand rolled away to a grey horizon, punctuated by a narrow neck of land where mud huts indicated the fishing village of Les Bequières, the French corruption of the Arab name of Al-Bukir, or Aboukir.

"Why can't we go in directly to Alexandria?"

"Magagallon says the mole's in ruins . . . What are they shouting now?"

The debarcation officers were shouting orders for a general assembly on deck, and sailors were collecting baggage outside the cabin doors. Marie knotted her big shawl firmly at her waist. Charles was looking at her with the quizzical smile which meant, she knew, *I told you not to come.*

She said, in as matter of fact a voice as possible, "If we do get separated, we'll meet in Alexandria."

The debarcation officers were shouting, "Women first! Women this way!" She heard a woman she knew, Madame Tempié, the wife of a naval officer, shrieking as she was lifted over the side and held firmly until her feet found the rungs of the rope ladder.

"That's my brave girl. Oh, Marie!" He strained her in his arms and whispered "Come now!" Then other, stranger arms were round her, and a rough voice was shouting, "No, colonel, you can't go with her! The women have to go first and you're needed here!" Then she was lifted bodily over the rail and Charles was shouting too, "Just let me hold her hands, damn you!" She felt his warm hands round her wrists and heard him gasp "Hold tight to the rope!" as her feet in their buckled leather shoes slid into the rungs.

She was crawling like a human fly down the wooden walls of *L'Orient*, her hands scratched and her skirts torn, and what was worst of all her body was so light that the rope ladder swayed with it like the pendulum of a clock. For a time all was darkness, and then by torchlight she saw a small boat manned by sailors calling her to jump. There were weeping women in the boat, and as she fell, wrenched and terrified, beside them she heard one of the oarsmen say,

"My God, it's Marie Fontaine."

It was several minutes before Marie recognised the man who had spoken, and who was holding her up out of the bilge water at the bottom of the boat. Torchlight showed her sailors in tattered shirts and trousers, as villainous in appearance as the *sans-culottes* of the Terror, but the man who held her on his shoulder wore what had been a dark suit and a uniform cap on his red hair streaked with grey.

He said, "Marie, are you all right?" and she knew him. He was Teresa Tallien's discarded husband.

"Jean, what are you doing here?"

"I might say the same to you."

"I'm with the Scientific Commission."

"So am I. I'm going to edit their paper."

"But – are you a sailor too?"

"Temporary. The cox'n of this boat was injured and I took his place. Used to do a lot of rowing when I was a boy. – Hold steady, lads! Here come two more."

Two more women, shrieking like peahens, were climbing down the perilous ladder. When there were six females huddled in the boat, Tallien ordered the crew to pull for the beach. Marie listened in amazement. This was a different Jean Tallien from the nail-biting lout who stumbled on Teresa's heels as they entered a salon. This was the man who had been a ruthless commissioner of the Republic, who had connived with Barras to drag Robespierre to the guillotine – a man with authority.

While the place at the foot of the ladder was taken by another ship's boat, the sailors helped their passengers (not without sly pinches and rough jokes) to wade through the surf and up the sandy slopes of Marabout beach. Tallien bent over Marie.

"Where's your husband?"

"I don't know. They wouldn't let him come with me."

"I suppose not." Without a change of tone Tallien added, "You knew Teresa left me?"

"I'm very sorry, Jean . . ."

"A grace-and-favour apartment in the Luxembourg was nothing compared to that palace Ouvrard bought for her in the Rue de Babylone."

"What's become of your little girl?"

"Gone with her mother, of course. I hardly ever saw her, poor little Terri." Marie remembered that the Talliens had called their daughter by the absurd name of Thermidor, after the great time of their lives.

"This is the second time you've helped me, Jean. Thank you."

"When was the other time?"

"When you got me out of the Carmes prison. But what do we do now?" With her gesture Marie indicated all the women shivering on the wet sand.

"Wait, I suppose. There's a road of sorts along the shore, but it's six miles to Alexandria, you can't possibly walk it."

"The men are calling for you, Jean."

"Yes, I must go. Good luck, Marie."

Some of the other women were standing up, stretching, clambering up the shifting sand to see if any help was coming. There was a great deal of noise from the direction of the ships, and among the noise was the sound of horses' hooves and whinnies, for six hundred animals had been taken aboard the transports: there was even the encouraging sound of wheels. Then a company of soldiers appeared, with torch lights carried ahead and in the centre, marching in close order. They called out encouragement to the trembling women. "Won't be long now, girls. Help's on its way!"

An hour passed before help came in the shape of two of the "flying ambulances" new in this campaign, and the carriage in which Napoleon, the new Alexander, had meant to make his triumphal entry to the city of Alexander the Great. In these assorted vehicles the women were driven in relays to the house of the French consul. As they went, women and children threw stones at them while men fired ancient flintlocks, and from the desert the French cannon began to boom.

The debarcation in darkness had been bad enough, but the French had to fight their way into what they had expected to be a welcoming city before daylight. They succeeded by sheer weight of numbers, for as regiment after regiment emerged from the ships in the bay the townsfolk lost heart, and at noon the mayor, in his caftan and turban, sullenly handed over the keys of the city to

General Bonaparte. It was not quite as good as a triumphal entry, but it had to do, and Napoleon wasted no time in regrets. He had raged at Admiral Brueys – one of the rages which were nearly always calculated – over the difficulties of the debarcation, and ordered him to have the harbourage at Alexandria repaired at once, so that the ships of the line could anchor there. Aboukir Bay, and still less Marabout Bay, were no places for warships.

His first tour of the city was a huge disappointment, though he showed nothing of that to the Staff and the ADCs who accompanied him through the dirty narrow streets lined with houses with flat roofs and holes for windows through which peered not the houris of the Arabian Nights, but women whose veils were dirty linen with slits for their eyes. He looked in vain for the traces of ancient grandeur. The Library, once one of the largest in the known world, had entirely disappeared, and so had the Lighthouse, one of the world's Seven Wonders. Some of the obelisks of Cleopatra were lying on their sides, mere piles of stone, but Pompey's Pillar was still standing, and there Bonaparte decided to set up his headquarters. On the way there they passed the French consulate, and the general, who had not been impressed by the consul, gave the man credit for giving shelter to some thirty French and Italian ladies who, with one exception, ought never to have been there at all. He was minded to say to his ADC, Colonel Latour, "You had better go to the consulate, Latour, and see after your wife. Give her my compliments and join us in ten minutes."

The consulate was fairly large, but almost as ramshackle as the houses of the Arabs, though built of wood and stone. He could hear the women chattering like a cageful of parrots as he stood on the verandah parleying with a manservant who spoke some French. On the verandah Marie rushed into his arms, and in their kisses all the perils and dangers of the night were forgotten.

"And oh, Charles, Jean Tallien was in the boat!" That Paris talk with Tallien on the wild seashore still seemed to

Marie the most extraordinary part of the adventure. "He says he's going to be an *editor!*"

"What does he know about editing?" said Charles. ". . . Tell me later, dear, I haven't time for Tallien now. Got to get along to the new HQ at Pompey's Pillar. Oh, and" – reluctantly – "the general sent you his compliments."

"Do thank him, and ask when we're going to get our baggage."

"Ask *him?*" said the shocked ADC. "The quartermasters are in charge of that. I saw your stuff in a pile to be delivered in Alexandria before we start the march to Cairo."

"You're not starting tomorrow, are you?"

"Day after, maybe. Don't worry, dear; I'll try to get to see you tonight."

And with that Marie had to be content.

General Bonaparte had appointed Kléber, the jealous Alsatian who thought he should have been the commander-in-chief, to be the governor of Alexandria, and Menou to be governor of Rosetta, at the mouth of the Nile Delta. Menou was to commandeer boats to take the women and the Scholars to Cairo by the great river, starting after he himself had left. General Desaix was to command the first corps bound for Al-Quahira, Cairo the Victorious, the largest city in the world.

Roads across the desert there were none, only the tracks made by the caravans coming from Mecca and even from India, and these were drawn by camels. Bonaparte and Desaix agreed that a reconnaissance of these tracks and of the neighbouring wells should be done before the corps set out, and four groups set out in the cool morning of the next day.

One man alone came back to Pompey's Pillar before sunset, and he was bleeding and limping, with his tongue swollen in his mouth from thirst. Trembling and ashamed, he told the ring of generals that he and his comrades had been set on by a band of mounted gipsies – at least he thought they were gipsies, who appeared from the sandhills screaming and howling, and shot them down. The gipsies had cut off ears and noses, had hamstrung them, and – and – asking your pardon, citizens – had sodomised them all.

"You were outnumbered, I suppose?" The cold voice of Bonaparte cut through the silence.

"Fifty to one, I reckon."

"But you had your firearms, hadn't you?"

"They were on us so fast we hadn't time to fire, citizen general."

"H'm. And you had no idea who those gipsies might be?"

"Not Mamelukes, not from what the sergeant told us about the Mamelukes. Cruel desert devils I call them, sir."

"Quite so," said Napoleon. "Now, my man, what you need is to have those cuts dressed and then some food and wine and sleep. Remember," he added, as the man saluted, and was about to be led away by the corporal who had brought him in, "Remember, those men may have outraged your body, but you won't die of an outrage like that. You're still alive."

When the door closed he turned to the French consul who was standing by and looking alarmed.

"Well, *monsieur le consul*, and who do *you* think those mysterious gipsies were?'

"Er – probably some of the Bedouin, sir – a tribe of desert nomads who travel with their own flocks of sheep or goats, and prey, when they can, on the Arab caravans . . ."

"And on the soldiers of France, it seems. *Imbécile!*" cried the general, "why was there no mention of the Bedouin in your reports to the Directory? You were meant to give us every word of information – "

"The Bedouin give us no trouble in Alexandria."

"And that was enough for you, was it? Oh, get out of my sight, you fool. Go back and look after the women from the ships. Brush their hair, be their lady's maid, it's all you're fit for."

214

After this stinging rebuke from the General in Chief, the consul performed miracles of organisation for the women in his care. He sent his own servants to carry jars of water to his house, and a retinue of Arabs chosen by the mayor and escorted by French troops was sent off to bring up the baggage under guard on Marabout beach. The Scholars, or, as the soldiers called them, the Donkeys, sorted out the bags and boxes and took them to the consulate or to the one transport which had been able to anchor in the Alexandria dock, aboard which they were to sleep. By the time Charles Latour arrived to say another farewell to his wife, Marie had had a bath, washed and combed her hair and was dressed in the pink cotton which Napoleon had called *contadina* in Milan. He left her happy, too, in the presence of her Milan friend, for Lucia Clouzot had been brought to the consulate by none other than Jean Tallien, who had been her fellow passenger in the *Tonnant*.

The women were sleeping eight to a room at the consulate, which Marie told her friend was "a great improvement on the Carmes prison; we were seventeen in my cell there". They had tossed for who should sleep in the two European beds, and Marie was one of the losers who had to sleep on the floor. She thought about the prison while she tried to sleep in the strange, crowded room. Here, at least, morning would bring no jailer with the list of victims of the guillotine! Otherwise there was a strange resemblance in the two groups of women. The Duchesse d'Aiguillon had been the tyrant of the Carmes, and here she was again in an officer's wife who complained of everything and called the landing an insult to womanhood. Lucia Clouzot, who had cried herself to sleep after telling Marie every detail of her baby's brief life, was Anne de Beaupré, pathetic and kind, and Joséphine . . . was there a Joséphine among them?

If so, thought Marie, it was the youngest of them all, the wife of a lieutenant in the *chasseurs à cheval*. "I'm Pauline Fourès," she had announced. "My maiden name

215

was Bellisle, so you can call me Bellilotte." She had stowed away with her husband, wearing his old uniform now bedraggled and torn. In Joséphine's best style she soon wheedled a length of white linen out of the consul and, having worked for a dressmaker in Carcassonne, made herself a pretty dress. She was a pert little thing, with a high bust like the statue in that green room in Milan, and ready to flirt with any man in sight.

None of the European women was awake when the French corps led by Desaix left Alexandria on the long march south-west across the desert to the left branch of the Nile delta and then south along the river to Cairo. They left before first light, so as to get as far on their way as possible before the great heat of the day began, but no sooner did the sun rise than the Bedouin were seen lurking among the sandhills. Desaix was ready for them: he had posted sharpshooters in his outer ranks of infantry, and their quick accurate firing soon taught the Bedouin to keep their distance. Desaix kept his men in close order. He realised that any stragglers could meet the same fate as the reconnaissance groups of yesterday.

On that first day there were no stragglers. The men were keen, and eager to reach Cairo. There was food in the wagons and their bottles were full of water from the sweetest and freshest well in Alexandria, but the water bottles were empty by noon and the desert was empty of wells: it was not until evening that the bottles could be refilled. They bivouacked, and the sudden chill after the sun went down pierced their sweating bodies. They preferred to lie round the fires kindled to warn off the Bedouin. The khamsin wind arose and blew sand into their faces, so that they began to rub their smarting eyes and made them worse.

Before long they had lost their brisk marching step and were shuffling or stumbling through the desert sand. A midday meal of pita bread and beans was not satisfying, and the regimental troublemakers complained that they weren't Arabs, to subsist on a handful of dates. "Thank

God the horses aren't along," said another. "They'd have jibbed at this stuff for fodder!"

The cavalry horses had been stabled in Alexandria (where there was very little difference between shelter for horses and humans) but the cavalry general was marching with Desaix and complaining louder than any of the men. The huge mulatto, the natural son of a French marquis and a black girl of Santo Domingo, had risen through the ranks while fighting in the Pyrenees, the Vendée and the Tirol, and nowhere (said General Dumas) had he encountered such vile conditions. General Bonaparte should be informed of their sufferings. Would General Desaix consider sending couriers back to Alexandria?

"No, sir, I will not," said Desaix shortly. "To send two men, or three, back through the country of the Bedouin is sending them to certain death. General Bonaparte is joining us with the second contingent at Damanhur."

"We're still twelve leagues from Damanhur. What if the Mamelukes attack us on the march?"

"We stand and fight, that's all."

Desaix had other and more subtle enemies than the Mamelukes. There was hunger: the only food now available was dry biscuits. There was thirst, the terrible, searing thirst of the desert and its awful accompaniment, the mirage, that vision of lakes filled with limpid water which changed to the reality of sand when the thirsty reached it, so that some raved in their despair and some, unbalanced, blew their brains out. And above the gasping, groaning columns there hovered all day long death's reminder, the vultures waiting to pick their bones.

Most of Desaix's corps were veterans of the Army of Italy, whose disillusion was the more profound because they could remember the promise, made before that campaign began, and kept. "I will lead you into the most fertile plains in the world," Napoleon had said, and sometimes they had the spirit to repeat these words to each other, and compare the desert with the lush green meadows and orchards of Lombardy. When the second contingent arrived in the same wretched state they kept a lookout for the General in Chief, and when the carriage to which his rank entitled him arrived at Damanhur, he was greeted with an ironical cheer.

Desaix had tried to get General Dumas to hold his tongue, but the big man was excitable and determined to be heard. Dumas had been rather a favourite of Napoleon, who had nicknames for him: General Hercules for his great strength, General Horatius for his feat in "keeping the bridge" of Clausen in the Tirol, and sometimes even *der schwarz Teufel*, as the Austrians did. There were no nicknames and no jokes as Dumas poured out his grievances. The men had suffered terribly and should be compensated, the whole impossible expedition should be abandoned, and he, Alexandre Dumas, wanted to go home to his wife and baby girl.

Dumas towered above the little general, but there was something that froze his blood in the icy voice that said, "We haven't so much as seen the Mamelukes yet. I never expected *you* to retreat in face of the enemy! You may withdraw, General Dumas."

The average age of the Scholars bound for Cairo was fifty. They were quite willing to wait until it was safe to travel, but their junior assistants asked leave to cross the desert with Napoleon and the second contingent. One junior assistant in particular was anxious to start out for the new laboratory which the chief pharmacist told her he meant to open in Cairo. Marie Latour was tired of the overheated female society of the French consulate which, if the consul had had his way, he would have turned into a fairly good imitation of a Paris prison. He had been so badly scared by the Arab resistance of the first day that he would have kept them behind the locked gates of his courtyard in the interests of their own safety. Happily General Kléber thought there was nothing to fear from the torpid population of Alexandria, where the men sat all day in the dingy coffee-houses open to the street, and gave permission for the ladies to take an evening stroll along the sea front as far as Ras-el-Tin, provided they had male companions, and went veiled.

Sometimes they walked west to look at the shipping. Most of the transports were on the way back to France to bring out reinforcements, but the capital ships were still in Aboukir Bay, where the admiral was having *L'Orient* repainted from stem to stern. But in whatever direction they walked they came up against the same invisible prohibition: no departure from Alexandria until the French were in Cairo. And the days dragged by.

The French made their first contact with the Mamelukes on 13 July at a place called Shubra Knit, not far from the Nile. It was not so much a battle as a rehearsal in which each side tried to take the measure of the other, for the fierce horsemen of the desert had a fixed way of fighting: to charge, and if the charge were not immediately successful to run away. This they did at Shubra Knit, and Napoleon was sure that they would attack again when he was nearer Cairo. He marched on doggedly at the head of his men, wondering if there would be messages for him at Cairo from the ruler of the Ottoman Empire, no longer as powerful as when it had extended to the gates of Vienna, but still representing Islam in the Near East. He had sent his own messages from Paris to the Sultan Selim III, promising the sultan to deliver his land of Egypt from the tyranny of the Mamelukes, and had not received a word of thanks as yet. He had asked the Directory to appoint Talleyrand ambassador to Constantinople, but where was Talleyrand now? Those anxieties, discussed with nobody, occupied the General in Chief until the day came when he saw in the dim distance the shapes of the Pyramids and the minarets of Cairo, and against the skyline the horsemen of the enemy.

It was no time for the flank attacks of Italy. Heavily outnumbered, Napoleon stood on the defensive, as he had done at Shubra Knit. He had made the desert a drill ground in the days that followed, and put his men relentlessly through the formation of the hollow square. Baggage carts and wagons were piled in the centre of a series of squares in which ten ranks of riflemen stood waiting while the Mamelukes came on.

"Soldiers!" cried their general in the voice they trusted to bring them victory, "from the height of these Pyramids forty centuries are looking down on you!" It was an implicit challenge: what were these Egyptian relics to look down on the French? Or what indeed were the Mamelukes of today? They were known to go into battle wearing or carrying all their valuables in gold or jewels, and each rider was a moving arsenal carrying a carbine at his stirrup, two pistols at his belt, with the weapons they relied on most. Every man had a *djerid*, a javelin made from a palm branch, stripped and sharpened, and carried two scimitars, which he swung while holding his reins in his teeth.

"Savages!" muttered Bonaparte to Charles Latour, who was by his side, and the yells of the enemy were drowned in the grand climax of the *Marseillaise*. "Fire!"

The leader of the Mamelukes was Murad Bey, called the Emir-al-Hadj because he had once been to Mecca. He was a forward-looking man, who was preparing to launch a Mameluke flotilla on the Nile and had already founded an arsenal at Cairo, but the medieval weapons of his men were no match for the fire power of 1798. The French troops had been marching for seventeen days on nothing more nourishing than hard tack and occasional spoonsful of brackish water, but they stood rock steady while the horsemen raved around them, trying in vain to break through each corner of the hollow squares. The front rank fired at the word of command, then dropped to one knee and fired again. The second rank fired above their heads while on the bloody sand the enemy horsemen, dead or alive, blocked the retreat of their comrades. When Napoleon shouted "*En avant!*" his men broke ranks and rushed forward in the *furia francese* known for centuries on the continent of Europe, and as recently as Lodi Bridge and

Arcola. A treasure of gold coins and golden jewels was captured in the next hour, while the minarets of Cairo gleamed temptingly on the horizon; and the battle fought at Embaba passed into history as the Battle of the Pyramids.

16

Marie Latour's journey up the Nile was sheer delight. To be away from stuffy Alexandria and the fussy consul, to be out on the broad river, to have another victory to celebrate with Charles – all that was much in the abstract, but there was also the interest of new scenes. The palm-fringed banks of the Nile were succeeded by fields of sugar cane and plantations where camels were tethered, and other fields where the *fellaheen*, the peasants in tattered blue shirts instead of *galabeyahs*, were working like dumb animals, hardly looking up to see the foreigners sail past.

In the same felucca as Marie was her friend Lucia Clouzot, looking much better and stronger than when they met at Alexandria. Lucia's husband had volunteered for Egypt to get her away from Milan and the memories of their dead child, and ever since they landed Lucia had tormented herself with the thought that she had led him to his death. Since the victory of the Pyramids her mind had been at rest, and now she sat happily chatting with Marie about the joy of seeing their husbands again.

La Bellilotte had very little to say about meeting Lieutenant Fourès. She was sharing a plank seat with Jean Tallien and flirting with him, while his gratified laughter showed that Citizen Tallien had learned nothing from his experiences with Teresa. Marie heard them planning to "meet at the Tivoli" which had a homesick sound of Paris about it, but the houses of Cairo were beginning to appear around them, and the only time to think of was the present.

These three women were holding veils folded in their laps, beautiful chiffon veils which Bellilotte had wheedled out of General Menou when they met that warrior in Rosetta. More fortunate in love than war, Menou had already established a nubile Arab girl as his "housekeeper" and it was she or one of her innumerable family hangers-on who had bought the veils in the market of Rosetta. Marie quietly cut off the row of gilt sequins which jangled on the veil just below eye level and irritated the bridge of her nose.

She was glad she had done so when she saw the company assembled to meet her at the landing stage over which the French and Turkish flags were flying side by side. Behind Napoleon, wearing gilt epaulettes on his dress uniform and a gilt handled sword, stood a ring of men with turbans, caftans and long white beards, who might have got the wrong impression from ornamental veils, although some of them seemed to be eyeing Madame Fourès appreciatively. These were the Arab elders of the city (the Mamelukes were of mixed Circassian, Georgian and Albanian stock) and the leaders of Islam. It was they whom Bonaparte told, when he entered the city, that he came in the name of the Sultan Selim III, and had been gratified by the title of Sultan Kebir – the great sultan – though when asked if he would accept the faith of Islam he replied that he would on no account accept circumcision.

Bonaparte was smiling that day, for he counted it a triumph. His entry into Cairo, which the populace greeted with sullen looks and silence, had been triumphal only in the noise made by his own fifes and drums. This was a triumph of another kind, and the distinguished Arab scholar at his right hand, who was Sheikh Al Charkawi, the rector of the famous university contained in the mosque of Al Azhar, was obviously impressed by the arrival of Europeans so distinguished in their own fields of science and art. Through an interpreter he bade them welcome to Cairo.

The foreign women standing under awnings in the background were not presented to the Arab dignitaries. The latter had left the tented landing stage before the waiting husbands joined their wives, for the affectionate greetings and public embraces would have seemed shameless to the Arabs. Napoleon himself came first to Marie Latour and bade her welcome to Cairo. He smiled when she dropped her pretty curtsey and congratulated him on yet another victory.

"Now here's Charles," he said. "He'll escort you to the Institute, where you'll live and work. I was out there yesterday, and I think they've done wonders in a very short time. I hope you'll be impressed by it."

"I know I will be," said Marie. "I'm thrilled to be going to work there."

"You'll be one of its ornaments," said Napoleon. "My carriage is waiting for you just outside the gate. Charles, look after her."

At the gate Marie turned to look back; General Bonaparte was talking to Colonel Clouzot and Lucia. It was the last time she was ever to see him as she remembered him first – the thin keen face, the brilliant eyes and the black hair falling to his shoulders. It was a fleeting impression but a profound one. She turned away with Charles and realised with a sinking heart that Charles was in a bad mood.

He showed his temper as soon as he had handed her into the carriage.

"What it is to be married to a member of the Scientific Commission," said Charles in the cutting tone she knew so well. "See, I've earned a ride in the great man's carriage."

"I think we're very lucky not to have to walk," said Marie, looking out at the narrow *souk* where the booths of the traders hardly left room for a carriage to pass through the crowd of men and donkey riders.

"And how the compliments were flying," pursued Charles Latour. "You praised Napoleon and he praised you, it was pretty to hear. But don't you think, Madame Ornament, that he might have invited you to the platform with the Scholars, to make your curtsey to the city fathers?"

"Oh, don't be silly, dear. I wouldn't have known what to say to them," said Marie, with a warning glance at the back of the French soldier-driver. "Tell me about the battle of Embaba. Were there heavy losses?"

"You mean the Battle of the Pyramids," corrected Charles. "The losses were far heavier on Murad's side than on ours. God, I'll never forget the sight of our fellows tearing the clothes off Murad's dead to get at the gold and jewels in their clothing . . ."

"That must have been quite a sight for Sergeant Vulture," was Marie's retort to the man who had used "Vautour" as his alias in the National Guard. "But Murad got away himself?"

"Yes, and so did his lieutenant, Ibrahim, who didn't bring up the reinforcements, luckily. They're both in Upper Egypt by this time; we'll have to go after them before they rally the blacks in the Sudan and have another go at us . . . Don't worry! They won't get anywhere near Nasriya, where you're going to 'live and work'. Live and work! I like that!" Charles repeated, his annoyance rising to the surface again.

"Why are you so angry, Charles? I have to live somewhere."

"I thought the whole idea was that you were coming out to Egypt to live with me. I thought we'd have a little house in Cairo all to ourselves. That's what the Clouzots are going to have, Colonel Clouzot told me himself. And he's only an old *embusqué* from Milan."

"So where *do* you live?"

"All the ADCs are with the General in Chief in the house he commandeered. The palace of Elfi Bey in Esbekya Square."

"Well there, you see, we both have to live with our work."

"Your work, indeed! What a farce the whole thing is!"

Cairo was called the largest city in the world by virtue of its 300,000 inhabitants. Most of them lived in poverty, but the houses of the Mamelukes were handsome, and these had been commandeered by the French as barracks and hospitals. The French Institute, as it was called, was housed in the pleasant suburb of Nasriya, in the palace of one Qassim Bey, who had fled with Murad and Ibrahim into Upper Egypt, and the sessions of the joint Scientific and Artistic Commissions were to be held in the drawing-room of what had been the bey's *haremlik*. Another room was to be the library, and books in French, Italian and Turkish were being arranged on shelves made to fit the walls.

Built of stone and with high ceilings, the huge rooms were cool even in the great heat of July, but the chief attraction to the new French tenants was the vast garden with its shade trees and ornamental fountains. The botanists gloated over the raised terraces, ideal for the cultivation of rare specimens of flowers and plants; the zoologists claimed a space of land for the rudiments of a zoo. As for the archaeologists, when they were able to visit Karnak and Luxor they brought back artifacts which were to be the nucleus of the great Cairo Museum of future years.

The former home of Qassim Bey was the focus of similar dwellings in Nasriya, all used for one purpose or another by the Institute. The Chief Pharmacist, Royer, was installed in the house of another absentee, Zulficar Kalkhoda. He lived there and he worked there, not one but two laboratories having been fitted up, complete with furnaces, by the skill of the Chief Mechanic, Nicholas Conté.

"You'll meet Citizen Conté tomorrow," Dr Berthollet told Marie Latour. "He's one of the brightest men we have. His chief interest is in aerostatics, but he can turn his hand to anything from furnaces to library shelves. The two printing presses were slightly damaged in transit, but Conté soon had them in working order, and the first number of *La Décade Egyptienne* will appear next week."

"I know Citizen Tallien, who's going to be the editor," said Marie, and Berthollet remarked drily that it was quite a new departure for Tallien.

"But I didn't know we were to have two presses," said Marie.

"One with French type and one with Arabic. The Arabic was General Bonaparte's idea. He caused Italy to be ransacked until Arabic type was found in Rome."

"He thinks of everything," said Marie.

Dr Berthollet showed her the laboratory on the ground floor of the Kalkhoda mansion. "Citizen Royer has just gone upstairs," he said. "I know he wants to see you. But first you must see your own rooms." As they walked up the polished steps he continued conversationally, "I was sorry Colonel Latour couldn't wait until we all got back from that little ceremony. I want to know him better. Perhaps he will join us for luncheon tomorrow?"

Marie turned on the landing to face him.

"Today he had to go back on duty," she said. "About tomorrow I don't know."

"Of course his time is not his own – "

"That's the problem. Dr Berthollet, I'm sure you remember that night at the villa when you and General Bonaparte talked to Charles and me and said your plan was for me to come to Egypt so that we could be together?"

"Of course I do."

"I'm afraid Charles took that to mean we would *live* together – be given a house or some other sort of married quarters, and not be separated, one in Nasriya and the other in Esbekya Square."

"I don't recall that there was any absolute promise of a house," said Dr Berthollet, "and I don't really know who's responsible for housing, but I do think you'll find your rooms here very attractive. General Bonaparte has eight

227

ADCs now, on duty in rotation, so when your husband is free he could come to you here. Married life without the problems of housekeeping, eh? When things settle down it'll all work out, I feel sure. Come this way."

He ushered Marie into a large salon, sparsely furnished and decorated in the Oriental style, where a young girl was sitting with folded hands upon a cowhide stool. She snatched up her veil as Dr Berthollet came in.

"This is your little maid," the chemist said, "the daughter of one of the gardeners. As far as we can make out her name is Leila."

"*Bonjour*, Leila," said Marie with a smile. At the sound of her own name the girl touched her hand to heart, lips and brow, while over the edge of the veil her great brown eyes studied Marie curiously. Then she slid rather than walked to a door in the further wall, which opened on a bedroom furnished in the European style, in the middle of which stood Marie's battered portmanteau.

"Oh good, your bag has come," said Berthollet. "Give Leila your keys and she'll look after it."

In sign language he indicated to the Arab girl that she was to start unpacking, and without asking Marie what she thought of her apartment he whisked her across the landing and into the upstairs laboratory, where the Chief Pharmacist was berating a sallow youth in a dingy *galabeyah* and a red tarbush, in which the tricolore cockade looked out of place.

"Get out of my sight, you clumsy hound," Citizen Royer was saying, "that's the third measuring glass you've broken this afternoon. Ha, Berthollet" (without a change of tone) "brought me Madame Latour, have you? Thank God for an assistant who speaks a civilised language! Welcome to the Institute, madame. You'll soon learn to cope with the descendants of the men who built the Pyramids, and now have no idea how to use a wheelbarrow . . . Take off your hat and gloves."

"I'll leave you to it," said Berthollet, and took his

departure. The Arab youth, who had understood not one word, slipped out behind him.

"Now then, Marie," said the Chief Pharmacist, "(I can't go on calling you Madame Latour). You've had a drive through the city today. Did you see anything that gave you an idea of what we should start work on first?"

"I did," said Marie promptly. "I also saw why Dr Berthollet started me on preparing a remedy for ophthalmia. Every second man I saw today had diseased eyes."

"Ophthalmia and conjunctivitis," said Royer. "If they spread among our troops we're in for trouble. But something else has started which is fearfully debilitating – I mean dysentery. The men suffered so much from thirst crossing the desert that when they arrived in water melon country they went wild and ate all they could lay their hands on until their bowels collapsed. Of course they reject a diet of boiled rice, so we must get after them with – what?"

"A decoction of rhubarb with laudanum and quinine," said Marie, and over Royer's grunt of approval she asked if the dysentery cases were serious enough for hospital treatment.

"Some may be, but they're not admitted to hospital," the man said. "Our two emergency hospitals are for the wounded from Embaba. When we entered Cairo we found the Arabs had *one* hospital for the whole city, with seventy-five beds, fifty made of stone, and chains for twenty lunatics. Not a good beginning, was it?"

"A challenge for our *Service de Santé*," said Marie.

"That's an optimist's answer – a challenge. What if the challenge fails? You young people think 'we are the conquerors, we are the enlightened Europeans, our general claims to act in the sultan's name, therefore to us everything is possible.' I tell you we are prisoners in Egypt. We can take ship and go back to France, but as long as we remain here we are the prisoners of disease, the prisoners of a hostile population . . . and the prisoners of history."

It was next morning before Marie had recovered from Citizen Royer's rhetoric (a form of speech to which she soon discovered him to be addicted) and morning brought the disappointing news that Charles had been ordered into the desert with the cavalry general, Dumas, Colonel Murat and three farrier sergeants to examine the kind of horse-shoeing and exercise which should make French horses as good on sand as the Mameluke mounts. "We're going as far as Giza," Charles's letter read, "won't be back for two or three days, depends on the horses, stay well, love, C." But the man who came to see her two days later was not her husband. It was Napoleon Bonaparte.

She was working steadily on the rhubarb, laudanum and quinine decoction, and Royer was in the middle of one of his tirades against Ahmed, the breaker of glass, when a messenger came in to say the General in Chief was at the Qassim house and asking for her. Then Marie was glad to have a maid, as Leila helped her out of her stained overall and into a fresh blue cotton, and brought scented water for her hands. She was cool, outwardly at least, when she crossed into the garden of the Qassim palace and found Napoleon standing with another man near the entrance gate.

"Good day, Marie," he greeted her. "I don't believe you know my ADC, Captain Lavalette."

"*Bonjour, mon capitaine*" – the man bowed. She had heard of him from Charles – an ADC whose florid face and bulbous nose suggested heavy drinking, but who seldom tasted wine. Napoleon had recently arranged his marriage to Joséphine's niece Emilie de Beauharnais, left behind in Paris.

"Won't you come indoors, citizen general?" Marie asked.

"I'd be waylaid by a dozen people in five minutes," said Napoleon. "Lavalette, make sure that nobody disturbs us. I'm going to sit under the trees with Madame Latour."

"*A vos ordres, mon général!*" Lavalette saluted, and Marie remarked conventionally, as they walked across the lawn, that there were many pleasant places to sit in the Qassim gardens. She was puzzled by Napoleon's manner and by his appearance. There was something different about him, and she realised what it was when he laid his cocked hat on one of the chairs grouped under a clump of palms. The long "dog's ears" had gone. Napoleon's hair was cropped, with a few locks brushed forward on his brow in the "Titus" cut of the day.

"Are you admiring my new *coiffure*, Marie?" He was very conscious of her gaze.

"It's very – fashionable."

"It takes some getting accustomed to, but – it's too hot for long hair in Egypt. Have you heard from Charles?"

"Yes, he's gone to Giza with General Dumas."

"To see about the horses."

"He may come back tomorrow."

"More likely today." Then, abandoning all pretence of an ordinary conversation, Napoleon asked, "Marie, how long have you and I known each other?"

"About six years, I think."

"I think so too. So if I ask you some questions, and tell you some secrets, you'll treat it as absolutely confidential?"

"Of course."

"Well, then! You knew my wife was – seeing a great deal – of Captain Hippolyte Charles?"

"He travelled with us as far as Lyon on our journey to Milan. Your brother could tell you about that."

"You never saw him at our house in Paris?"

"Yes, once, at tea. Monsieur Joseph was there too."

"And then, after the coach trip, he turned up in Milan, representing the Bodin Company?"

"Yes, he did."

"Was that why you went back to Paris?"

"I had to go to work for Dr Berthollet. You approved of that."

"Come now, Marie, don't equivocate. Tell me the truth.

You and Joséphine had a quarrel. Was it about Captain Charles?"

"About that little whipper-snapper? Certainly not!" exclaimed Marie, stung. "It began when I told Joséphine I didn't understand her connection with the Bodin Company."

"Nor did I – then," said Napoleon, with a sigh. "She wanted me 'to help a friend', and give him a contract for supplies to the troops. To please her I did, but for three months only. In that time complaints came in from all sides. The food was rotten, the shoes were made of carton, the uniforms were shoddy. Bodin was the worst of all the army contractors, which is saying something. I cancelled the contract and ordered Charles out of that theatre of war."

"And that ended it?"

"So I thought."

"But look here!" said Marie. "That was more than a year ago. All last year you and Joséphine were together in Italy, a happy couple, and people admired her, she did you credit wherever she went – "

"I didn't know then that she was taking money from Bodin."

"Oh *no!*"

"You can't believe it, can you, Marie? That's what we told her, Joseph and I, when my brother had put together the evidence of her guilt. She wept and wailed, but she didn't deny it. I told her it was inconceivable that the wife of the commanding general should stoop to share in the profits of fraudulent dealings with his troops."

In spite of herself Marie spared a mite of pity for the pretty, heedless woman being badgered by two Bona-partes at once.

"When did all this come out?" she asked.

"One day last March."

"Then that was why – "

"What was why?"

"That night at the villa, when you and Dr Berthollet

232

talked to Charles and me, I thought Joséphine looked very nervous and scared."

"Well she might," said Napoleon grimly.

"Yes, but – that was in March, and in May I saw you together at Toulon – and she was weeping when you went on board *L'Orient* – "

"I didn't know Junot had her letters on him when we sailed."

"What letters?"

Napoleon put his hand in his breast pocket and withdrew a few closely written sheets. "That's Joséphine's handwriting, isn't it?"

"So much of it's crossed out, but – yes, I think it is."

"And superscribed to Captain Hippolyte Charles at the Compagnie Bodin?"

"Where did Junot get these letters?"

"From my brother Joseph."

"And where did *he* get them? Not from that man?"

"From an anonymous friend, he says. You're not reading them. Go on."

Marie unfolded the top sheet. "Junot would enjoy being the courier," she said. "He never forgave Captain Charles for a silly prank he played on the way to Milan."

"What did the fellow do?"

"Filled Junot's scabbard with glue." Marie began to skim through the letters. The damning words leaped out at her from every page.

Hippolyte, I shall kill myself – yes, I wish to end a life that henceforth would be only a burden if it could not be devoted to you.

And again:

Life is a continued torture. You alone make me happy.

And yet again:

You alone can make me happy. Tell me that you love me, and only me. I shall be the happiest of women. Send me 50,000 livres from the notes in your possession.

While her head was bent over the miserable pages, Marie's brain was working rapidly. She saw Joséphine's little salon, her unlocked escritoire; she saw a disgraced servant fumbling in a drawer. She heard Napoleon, with a hand shading his eyes, saying "She never wrote love letters like that to me!"

"But how do you know those letters were ever sent?"

"What the devil do you mean? – I beg your pardon, Marie."

"Look at the scribbling. Look at the crossings out. Look at the language, copied from a cheap romantic novel. See, there's no date; you don't know when they were written. But I'm pretty sure they were never meant to be read, either by your brother or his anonymous friend."

"Then why were they written?"

Marie actually laughed. "You don't know much about women, General Bonaparte," she said. "Joséphine was acting a part – being a girl again, lonely and misunderstood and dreaming of a fairy prince. That's why she scribbled such rubbish – to pass the time."

"Joseph says these letters are grounds for divorce. As soon as I hear from the Sultan, I have a mind to go back to France and divorce her."

"She's probably on her way to Egypt by this time, and when you see her again, you'll forgive her – you always do. Now, why don't you go back to headquarters and put all this out of your mind until tomorrow? We'll talk about it again whenever you like – but only if you agree to be sensible."

She stood up, hoping the man wouldn't see how her limbs were trembling, and Bonaparte stood up too. "You're a faithful friend, Marie Fontaine," he said. "I doubt if Joséphine deserves it."

"I can never forget that Joséphine gave me a home when I was homeless," she said, and bit her lips to keep the tears back as he took both her hands in his, and kissed them.

Much the better for having unburdened himself to the girl he still thought of as Marie Fontaine, Bonaparte needed no advice to put the problem of Joséphine out of his mind until the next day. He had the capacity, which in him amounted to genius, to concentrate on one thing at a time, and back at headquarters he found many things to occupy his mind completely. In less than an hour after he left the Institute, General Dumas and Colonel Latour arrived to present their report on horse-drawn transport. They were not optimistic about his own plan to establish a regular *diligence* service between Cairo and Alexandria; in fact they were downright miserable. Dumas, he knew, had been disaffected since Damanhur, and Latour, usually so keen, was sulking and surly. He dismissed them, and sent for two young scientists from the Institute, who had been investigating the possibility of getting running water into the Cairo citadel and the digging of additional wells in the desert.

Marie, too, tried to give her mind to her work, and was rewarded next morning when Dr Berthollet told her Charles was coming to luncheon at noon. He appeared punctually, rather cool and offhand at first, and out of his element among so many scholars. To be on the safe side he called all the older men Professor.

There was another guest, whom he called General, and who was the life and soul of a party which to Marie's pleasure included Lucia Clouzot and her husband. This was General Louis Desaix, who had led the march into Cairo and was preparing to pursue the Mamelukes into Upper Egypt. Desaix was a wit and a born raconteur, with a chameleon-like gift of changing his expression, so that, as another guest jokingly complained, it was impossible to draw him twice alike. One thing was constant, however: he was the untidiest officer in the Army of Egypt, and with his "dog's ears" hair – no Titus cuts for him – and the broken-backed feathers in his hat, he looked for all the world like a street musician.

The artist who complained about the difficulty of drawing Desaix was called Vivant Denon, and he was to join the expedition to Upper Egypt as a soldier in the 21st Demi-Brigade to record the antiquities in his sketches. Meantime he sketched at the luncheon table, recording Marie's pretty face and Lucia's grave good looks for the pleasure of their husbands, and there was a great deal of joking and fun.

"Isn't it lovely to be with so many clever people?" whispered Marie when the party broke up at the hour of the siesta, and Charles replied reluctantly that he supposed it was. "But now I want to see what they've done with you," he said. "Can't we go to your apartment now?"

"Of course we can. But we'll have to cross the garden for that."

"Do you often walk in the garden?"

"Whenever I can."

The silence of the siesta already lay over the Qassim palace, and Lucia Clouzot, supine in a deep armchair, sketched a sleepy farewell as they went out. "Lucia's lucky," said Marie. "Even in Alexandria, she always fell fast asleep at siesta time."

"Didn't you?"

"Not always. I couldn't get used to it somehow, and there were always so many queer noises in Alexandria."

"It's quiet enough here," said Charles, as they entered the silent hall of the Kalkhoda house.

"It's like *la Belle au Bois Dormant*," said Marie softly.

"And here's *la Belle*," said Charles, as they entered the little salon. The "sleeping beauty" was Leila, lying on the divan with one flushed cheek pillowed on her hands.

"Leila!"

The girl sprang up with a quick cry of apology, wound

her veil over her face, and being veiled made obeisance to the member of the omnipotent male sex.

"Can she speak French?" asked Charles.

"A few words, as many as I speak Arabic. But she's a good little maid for all that . . . Come and see our room."

Charles expressed approval of the big cool room, and especially of the European bed.

"Where does that child sleep?" he asked.

"Leila? In her father's house, I suppose. He's one of the gardeners here. They're Georgians, not Arabs, so Leila's really in a place of safety here. The Mamelukes take girls as well as boys, you know."

"Savages," said Charles, imitating Napoleon. "I wish I could be sure you're in a place of safety, darling. Couldn't that girl sleep in the outer room? The divan's quite big enough."

"Perhaps she could. But you'll be here quite often, won't you?"

"I'll try. But listen, Marie, there's one thing I don't like. There aren't any locks on these doors."

"I don't believe they had locks in the harem. The eunuchs guarded the doors with scimitars, didn't they?"

"*Please*, Marie! Can't these great *savants* have locks or bolts made? On this door too," he said, going back to the salon. Leila was still standing submissively by the divan.

"In Citizen Conté's workshop they can make anything," said Marie, following him. "I'll speak to them about it."

"Thank you, my dear," he said, and kissed her. With his lips close to her ear he whispered "Send her away!"

Charles Latour felt, rather than saw, the quick movement of the head with which Marie dismissed the Georgian girl, and heard the quiet closing of the door. He folded his arms about his wife.

"I want to make sure you sleep in this siesta," he said.

"Presently."

After Charles Latour's first visit to the Institute, no more was heard of his worry that Marie would be insulted or molested or worse when she was alone in a laboratory full of men. The gentlemen whom he met at luncheon were all in their fifties – to him ancient – and, as Napoleon said, they lived "at the centre of a flaming core of reason", a long way from flirtation. Colonel Latour had his own ideas about a possible rival, who was not a member of the French Institute.

He did not meet Dr Dominique Larrey, Principal Medical Officer of the Army in Egypt, who was an attractive man of only thirty-three. More than five years earlier, as a young surgeon-major, Larrey had invented the "flying ambulances", the lack of which for transporting the wounded had been severely felt in Italy. In Egypt he called them "moving ambulances" and improved upon them by adding a supply of drugs and bandages for the benefit of Desaix's foray into Upper Egypt. Marie, in the upstairs laboratory of the Kalkhoda house, prepared most of the drugs single-handed, while an Arab youth made the bandages. Marie supervised him with the aid of a few phrases from *Exercises in Literary Arabic*, the first book to come off the printing press for which Bonaparte had found the Arabic type.

At the request of Dr Desgenettes, the Chief Physician, she added a preparation of ammoniac and silver nitrate, a cure for scorpion bites, to the ambulance supplies, and also a decoction of soap dissolved in spirits of wine for ophthalmia sufferers to rub on their eyelids in the morning – eyelids too often stuck together by the prevalent malady. It was also necessary to provide *sirop de cusenier* or *eau de Lisbonne* against venereal disease, for syphilis was on the increase among soldiers turned loose in Cairo after three months' deprivation of sex. The very word *harem* had a fascination for the men, and raids were made on the homes of the remaining beys or pashas reported to contain the exciting *haremlik*. These raids were quelled by officers, using the flat of their swords, who defended their men by saying a tourist trip to see the Sphinx was no substitute for living female flesh. What the poor devils needed was more fighting in the desert.

When the fighting came, it came by sea, and was a complete disaster.

On 13 August Napoleon and his Staff had gone outside the city walls of Cairo to inspect the caravan track to Suez. He hoped it would be viable by carriage, for he intended to visit Suez after he had celebrated the approaching anniversary of Mahomet's birth. This year, it was to take precedence of his own twenty-ninth birthday, and the city fathers were hoping to hear of his conversion to Islam.

They were all in good spirits, talking and joking, pleased that the General in Chief, who had been in a heavy mood, was in a jesting humour too, when they saw one of the *fellaheen*, who appeared to be exhausted, come staggering towards their group with a sheet of paper in his hand.

"Probably a petition," said Bonaparte. "See what the fellow wants, Lavalette."

Captain Lavalette, who with Charles Latour was one of the two ADCs on duty, took the paper from the man, who sank down on the ground, clutching his tattered shirt around him.

"I think you should read this, sir," said Lavalette. "A despatch from General Kléber."

A despatch from the governor of Alexandria, and by such a bearer! The laughter died away as Bonaparte took the paper and read it at a few paces' distance with his back towards them.

"They always say the English pride themselves on 'keeping a stiff upper lip', don't they?" said Charles Latour when he told the story to Marie later that day. "Our Corsican's face was stiff, let alone his lips. Stiff and set, but deathly pale. 'Well, gentlemen,' he said, 'I'm glad you've been amused this morning. We may have to stay in Egypt longer than we thought. We have now no fleet.'"

Admiral Nelson, who had twice "lost" the French fleet in June, had found them on the last day of July, anchored

239

not in Alexandria but in Aboukir Bay. He had engaged them at sunset and fought them until three o'clock next morning, emerging victorious without the loss of a single British ship, but having destroyed eleven of thirteen French sail of the line, including the flagship *L'Orient*. Only two of the French warships, and two frigates had escaped to the open sea.

This was the substance of Kléber's first message. In the days to come it was to be supplemented by many details furnished by the French wounded being cared for, under cartel, in Alexandria and the village of Aboukir, but the bare facts were sufficiently terrible. The French in Egypt were cut off from France; they had lost a battle fleet, and they had lost five thousand men.

The icy calm with which General Bonaparte received the news lasted until he returned to headquarters, when alone with Berthier he gave way to his rage and despair at the loss of the flagship. The death in battle of Admiral Brueys was of secondary importance. "*Briccone*!" he called the admiral. "*Scelerato*! Why did he not go into Alexandria, as I told him to do? He would have been safe enough there with our shore batteries to protect him – "

"He had twelve ships of the line to protect him," said Berthier grimly. "Nelson destroyed them, all but two."

"And the money! *Corpo di Bacco*, the money! How are we going to pay the troops? Why didn't we bring the bullion with us? Why did I leave it in the strong room of *L'Orient*?"

"You wouldn't risk its falling into the hands of the Mamelukes."

"Bah! I took care of the Mamelukes when we met at the Pyramids. I was a fool to entrust the French fortune to a man like Brueys. Call in the secretaries: it's time to make new plans."

The orders came thick and fast after that. Mourning scarves were to be worn by the Staff and every man above the rank of field officer for the space of one month, and the ADCs were to wear black sashes instead of the scarlet and white. There was to be no public discussion of the tragedy at "Les Béquières" and all letters home were to be suspended for the time being. The troops were to be paid as usual from the money in hand. Nothing was to interfere with the celebrations in honour of the Prophet, due to begin within the next few days. And so on, and on, while the Chief of Staff sat in his private room and grappled with his own instructions: to find the money for the French troops by taxing the impoverished Egyptian people.

It was a secret which only the highest-ranking Staff officers knew, and kept at the time, that the treasure in *L'Orient*'s strong room consisted not only in the priceless relics taken from the Knights of Malta, but in bullion and diamonds contributed by (in other words extorted from) Switzerland and the Papal States, and worth about three million francs. Charles Latour did not know the secret, nor did any of the Scholars whom he met when he went to see Marie at the Institute.

They irritated him, and Marie most of all, by what seemed to be their calm assumption that their work took precedence of any military defeat by land or sea, and that while regretting the dreadful death roll of their country-men their first duty was the care of the living. Doctors Berthollet, Royer and Desgenettes, who took wine with him, and Marie, who drank sherbet, lamented the break down in communications with the Institute of Egypt in Paris, which Napoleon had established before he left, as if that were more important than being out of touch with the government, the source of pay, supplies and reinforce-ments. Desgenettes did say he had ordered *vésicatoires* and *synapismes* from Paris (whatever these might be) and probably would never see them now.

"General Bonaparte wrote home for a troupe of actors and a hundred dancing girls for the Tivoli," Charles retorted flippantly. "I don't suppose we'll see any of them either."

"Oh, Charles, don't make fun of serious things," said

Marie impatiently. "Dr Desgenettes requires all these supplies for the School of Medicine and Pharmacy he's planning."

"What, here in Cairo?"

"I'd like to start a primary school in French first," said the doctor. "I know I could recruit at least ten teachers from the Institute."

"I doubt if you'll enrol many pupils after today's news gets around," said Charles. Conceited asses! Planning classes in French and medicine when the whole problem was one of survival! And there was Marie listening to all their nonsense with the kind of attention she never gave to him! He had meant to spend the night with her, in the apartment which Conté's workshop had now provided with two locks and two keys, but he wasn't in the mood for love-making and he was sure she wasn't either. Colonel Latour took his leave of the self-absorbed Scholars with the excuse of reporting for night duty.

The news of the catastrophe at "Les Béquières" filtered down from the beys and pashas of Cairo to the shop-keepers of the *souks* and the *fellaheen* tending sugar cane in the Delta. It reached Upper Egypt, where the Mameluke bands rejoiced that the French were no longer to be feared. It was known before Admiral Nelson left Aboukir Bay. His Commander-in-Chief, Earl St Vincent, wanted him to proceed to action against Minorca, but having received a head wound at what was now officially called the Battle of the Nile he pleaded ill health and sailed for Naples, where he had a lady love. He left three warships keeping station between Alexandria and Damietta to maintain the blockade on the French, and continue the pleasant task of fishing from the deep the letters, private and official, which revealed the French situation in Egypt.

These were published in England, where the whole nation rejoiced in what was called "the downfall of Boney" – for the Corsican had a nickname now – and where on government buildings the Royal Standard was flying above the defeated Tricolore.

Bonaparte was less concerned with the rejoicing of his enemies than with outwitting them, and now it was known that Rear-Admiral Villeneuve was the man who had escaped with two warships from the Battle of the Nile, he and the Staff spent much time in discussing the possibility of an officer of flag rank, commanding *Le Généreux* and *Le Guillaume Tell*, plus two frigates, returning to Egyptian waters and challenging HMS *Zealous*, *Swiftsure* and *Goliath*, three British 74s.

"Where is Villeneuve now, sir?" Berthier ventured to ask.

"How the devil should I know? But since we have the Ionian Islands to fall back on, our best hope is that he reached some harbour in Crete."

That was the wretched truth – they didn't *know*, and strategy had to be planned by guesswork. On the day when something he had long dreaded became a fact, Napoleon rode out to the Institute for a talk with Madame Latour.

Colonel Marmont and Colonel Latour were the ADCs in attendance, Marmont very wretched because his bride could not now be expected to arrive from France, and Latour watching with jealous eyes while his own wife walked slowly up and down the garden walks with his general.

They had never talked about Joséphine again, and it was clear that she, like Madame Marmont and many other wives, could no longer join her husband in Egypt. But he had told Marie himself about the end of *L'Orient*: the pots of paint and oil cans on the decks which had caught fire from the British shells, fire which climbed up the masts and down the newly painted sides until it reached the powder magazine and the ship blew up in an explosion heard ten miles away. Wounded men, and men like living torches, jumped into the flaming waters of the bay, and Marie wept when she learned that her little friend, Midshipman Casabianca, had died, not "standing on the burning deck" as a foolish poem was to aver, but in his father's arms as they clutched drowning at a spar.

On this later visit he told her that he had news of the Sultan. "*Of*, not from, Marie," he emphasised. "The Grand Signior has not seen fit to write to me."

"News from Constantinople?"

"No, from Aleppo. You know that Turkish merchants from Aleppo and Latakia often visit Cairo?"

"Yes, I do."

"They speak the *lingua franca* of the Mediterranean, which I understand. I had no difficulty in understanding the two men who waited on me yesterday, with news which they had pleasure in telling me. Which was, that the victorious admiral is now Lord Nelson of the Nile, and he has been loaded with gifts from the Sultan Selim III."

"Oh, but – "

"The Sultan is not grateful to me for ridding Lower Egypt of the Mamelukes. He has declared war on the French Republic, represented by my expeditionary force."

"Is this generally known?"

"In Paris, I presume, but not here, as yet."

"Did he return Monsieur Talleyrand's passports? Don't you have to do that to an ambassador when you declare war on his country?"

"If Talleyrand left France, which I doubt, he never arrived in Constantinople."

"I see. It's an awkward situation, isn't it?"

"Very awkward. Hemmed in on all sides, and with a quite insufficient force to tackle the entire Ottoman Empire."

"You had an insufficient force when you tackled the Holy Roman Empire, and yet you won. And the last time the Sultan declared war, on Russia, he lost the whole of the Crimea."

Napoleon smiled for the first time. "You have a good memory, Marie. Thank you. It helps to have a talk with you. Now you must come and cheer up Charles and the lovelorn Marmont. I'm going to have a word with Tallien."

An hour later, riding back to the palace of Elfi Bey, Napoleon was still glad of his talk with Marie. It had helped to crystallise a thought at the back of his own mind – that he might do well to attack the Sultan before the obsolescent war machine of the Ottoman Empire could be brought into action. The contact with another mind, keen but absolutely discreet, had stimulated his own. Even a woman's mind! How curious it would be if the real "warrior's rest" should prove to be his old friend Marie Fontaine . . .

General Bonaparte could have told, to a day, when the news brought by the Turkish merchants from Aleppo reached Sheik al Charkawi, the rector of Al Azhar university. Whatever his anxieties, he had never missed his daily hour with the rector, when through an interpreter they studied the Koran together. A shade less deference in the rector's manner, a shade of doubt if the general's interest in the doctrines of Islam were really genuine caused Bonaparte to decide on a bold stroke. On 4 October he invited the city fathers to a general council, called a Divan, admitted to money difficulties following the naval defeat, and asked them to accept a system of taxation to cover the deficit.

To the grey-bearded Arabs it must have seemed like a return to the methods of the Mamelukes, but they bent with dignified resignation to the Sultan Kebir's will, and it was agreed that the tax gatherers should be appointed from among the Coptic Christians, a Cairene sect with special gifts for business and finance. One Moallem Jacob, of such distinction that he was always known simply as *The Copt*, was to be brought back from Upper Egypt where he was campaigning with Desaix to be the chief executive officer of the whole scheme.

The approval of the Divan was one thing, but even the most limp and listless inhabitants of Cairo rebelled against the imposition of taxation by a foreign army. Opposition became vocal among the students of Al Azhar, and the name of Saladin, its founder, and his feats against the Crusaders, were invoked by the youths who incited each other to revolt. The *muftis* and the *ulemas* who thronged the arcades of Al Azhar added religious fuel to the flame, and from all the minarets of the city the *muezzins* called the House of Islam to rise against the infidel in a *jehad*, or holy war.

For three days the city was in an uproar. The French commander of the garrison was murdered, so were two army doctors who died defending their patients, so, sporadically and pointlessly, were soldiers in the streets. Napoleon issued pitiless orders. All prisoners taken inside the citadel were to be beheaded. The mosque of Al Azhar was bombarded into surrender and six student ringleaders also suffered the death penalty. But it was the heavy guns, mounted in the squares and sweeping the main streets, which ended the Cairo insurrection in three days.

The Sultan Kebir was magnanimous. He absolved the Divan from all complicity, and – although he declined to continue studying the Koran with the rector of Al Azhar – he bestowed a General Pardon on the rebels. To prove his affability he ordered his ADCs to accompany him to an evening entertainment at the Tivoli, that dingy pleasure garden where coloured lights and scraping catgut were supposed to convey exotic and erotic charm.

Some of the women who frequented the Tivoli were the rejects of similar pleasure grounds or theatres in Europe, cast up on the shores of Africa. Some few were officers' wives, eager like their husbands for a little change from that city of the sickly and the blind, where pariah dogs scavenged the streets like the beggars. Among them was one very pretty girl whose wheedling manner reminded Napoleon of his faithless Joséphine, although she was half Joséphine's age and half as graceful. She was with her husband, Lieutenant Fourès, and he was calling her Pauline, though she was already known to a wide circle of admirers as Bellilotte.

17

Nasriya was so far distant from the centre of Cairo that the French Institute was not in any danger during the October insurrection. Charles Latour laughed sarcastically when he heard that forty muskets and thirty rounds of ammunition had been issued to the Scholars. "Forty muskets among a hundred able-bodied men!" he jeered. "You won't put up much of a defence with that!"

"We took what we were given," said Marie. "Fortunately the muskets weren't needed."

"And you? What did you do?" Charles asked. "Barricade yourself and your maid into your rooms behind Monsieur Conté's excellent locks?"

"I turned the keys in the locks, I admit," said Marie, "but I was alone. Leila was terrified and ran off to her father's home. She only came back yesterday, and Professor Royer's Arab boys haven't turned up at all. It's too bad – just when he was depending on them to keep the furnaces going."

"What for?"

"To distil water for drinking here, and for the emergency hospitals. He says Nile water is contaminated – I hope you don't drink it, Charles!"

"Not when I can get a glass of wine instead. But wine's in short supply these days. That doesn't suit the troops. They want meat and bread and wine, and they're getting bean mash and sour milk."

"Fermented milk – *kefir*. We prepare it for the hospitals."

"Seems to me you're talking a lot about the hospitals. You're not planning to repeat your Tuileries performance here, are you?"

"I don't think the general would allow it, and I know Dr Larrey wouldn't."

"I'm very glad to hear it."

"Oh, Charles, you just don't understand."

There was no longer any mutual comprehension between them. Marie began to feel the truth of Royer's assertion that they were all the prisoners of history, doubly true since the British blockade cut them off from Europe and the students' uprising cut them off from any bonding with Egypt. She began to chafe at her own confinement to the rooms and grounds of the French Institute. Even to organise a visit to Lucia Clouzot in her little house near Esbekya Square demanded more planning, involved more people and bodyguards than made it worthwhile to undertake. Even a chat with Jean Tallien would have been a change, but she never saw Tallien any more. Napoleon had not been to see her since the insurrection. She was a *femme savante*, a bluestocking, and that was all.

A visit to the French Institute was not on General Bonaparte's agenda for the last week of October 1798. He saw either the Principal Medical Officer or the Chief Physician daily at his own headquarters, and regularly visited the military hospitals which the Egyptian students, running amok, had been unable to destroy. He knew the doctors feared an outbreak of cholera from contaminated water, and gave every support to the precautions they were taking, but how to avoid some sort of epidemic in this pestilence ridden city was more than any soldier could tell.

His plans for Egypt had gone badly awry. The country was barbaric, and it would take years to develop its natural resources, even if that development were not interrupted by the war on which its suzerain the Sultan appeared to be bent. His plans for India would have to be shelved indefinitely. He could write letters to Indian princes in conflict with Britain, promising the support of his "invincible army", but he could no more cross the Red Sea and go charging to their support than he could fly.

His only hope lay in massive naval reinforcements from France, but would the Directory order Admiral Bruix's squadron out of Brest to tackle Commodore Hood in Alexandria Bay, sailing blithely past Lord Nelson on the way? Bonaparte damned Lord Nelson, now engaged in dalliance at a foreign court, but he had a certain sympathy with Nelson – he was indulging in some very agreeable dalliance himself. When he had time.

He had stepped out of character that night at the Tivoli, when he invited Lieutenant and Madame Fourès to join his party, or rather he had stepped down from the pedestal on which his general officers had placed him. Well – most of them, not "agitators" like General Dumas, who had been behaving as if Napoleon had positively invited the British to destroy his fleet. He had acted like a subaltern, paying outrageous compliments to the prettiest girl in the Tivoli, plying her with champagne and laughing at her pert replies. The husband – a decent fellow – was as abashed as a lieutenant of the 22nd *Chasseurs à Cheval* could be at finding himself drinking toasts with the General in Chief; his wife was not abashed at all. She was as forward as the streetwalker in the Palais Royal with whom Lieutenant Buonaparte had his first sex experience – and *she* had said he talked too much.

The young woman was not so forward when she came to him in the Elfi Bey palace about a week later. Her husband had been sent to Giza for a couple of days, and she was so nervous, wasting time in chatter about his splendid apartment, that he almost believed her when she murmured that this was the first time – ever – that she had – had –

"So why now?"

"Because you're so *wonderful* . . ."

"Stop talking and come to bed."

She was quiet under his caresses, more subtle and more satisfying than in the past because of all he had learned from Joséphine, but in the lassitude which followed she had regained confidence enough to tease him about his silence and ask him what he was thinking about.

"You, of course, Pauline."

"I'm usually called Bellilotte."

"Why?"

"My mother's name's Bellisle . . . She isn't married."

"That's not your fault." He searched for the right words to say. "You're very pretty, Bellilotte, and very sweet – and I'm afraid you must go home now."

"So soon! Why?"

"My child, I have work to do. Will you come back tomorrow?"

She was clever enough to say nothing. Instead, slender young arms drew him close to her, firm young breasts were pressed against him, and in a kiss from lips as fresh as summer fruit he had his answer. When Bellilotte was gone and he was back in his study, Napoleon remembered that the first time Joséphine admitted him to her bed, he had knelt and kissed her feet in adoration when he took his leave. Today he had given that girl a playful slap on her firm little rump when he said "*au revoir*." And inevitably his thoughts went back yet again to Joséphine. What was she doing while he took possession of his new love? Amusing herself in Paris with her popinjay of a *cavaliere servente*? Demanding more money from her accomplices (it wasn't too strong a word) in the Compagnie Bodin? Or preparing to pledge his own, Bonaparte's, credit in the purchase of the country house, La Malmaison, she had dragged him to see last spring?

For nearly three years General Bonaparte had been absolutely faithful to his wife. His passion for Joséphine was known to the whole army, the sentimental soldiers regarding her partly as a surrogate for the girls they left behind them, and partly as the source of their general's luck. For him to take a mistress was bound to create a storm of gossip and speculation, from which Eugène de Beauharnais was the principal sufferer. But Eugène, trying to warn his mother while completely loyal to his step-father, was not old enough, or as far as the knowledge of that day went informed enough, to perceive that Joséphine had dealt her husband a psychic wound from which he would never recover.

Lieutenant Fourès was promoted to captain and ordered to remain at Giza while a new mounted corps was formed, but even with the husband absent the concealment of an adulterous affair in the palace of Elfi Bey was impossible. Napoleon behaved like an autocrat with nothing to hide. He showed off his young mistress at the Tivoli and took her out for drives in his carriage as if he were repudiating Joséphine before the world.

None of the gossip reached the French Institute, where the workers led such busy and secluded lives, and Charles Latour, whose visits were more and more erratic, repeated none of it. It was not until the middle of November, when Lucia Clouzot prevailed upon her husband to take her out to Nasriya, that Marie Latour heard the story of the general and the pretty girl who had shared their room in the consulate at Alexandria. Lucia was not a scandalmonger, and she had been in Marie's apartment for an hour before the topic was broached.

Colonel Clouzot had lunch in the Scholars' mess, and Leila brought Marie and her guest a tray laden with bowls of lentil soup, *basbousa* pastries, *aduwa* dates from Upper Egypt, and sweetmeats.

"You are lucky, Marie," said Lucia enviously. "Lovely rooms, and your own maid, and no problems with those thieving Arab servants who cheat us all the time in the bazaars. Do you do this every day?"

"Mostly I eat lunch in the mess. But I do like having a little salon. Charles wanted me to have Leila sleep in here on the divan, but I didn't fancy having my sitting room turned into a bedroom, so she goes home at night. I don't think that child would be much protection if we had a riot."

Lucia shuddered. "It's easy to see you weren't in the city when we had the real riots. All that yelling and la-la-la-ing for a *jehad*! I was scared out of my senses. Oh, when are we ever going to get away?"

"I don't know, Lucia. I think all we can do is live one day at a time . . . Tell me, has Colonel Clouzot been to visit any of the military hospitals? He was very interested in the Spedale Santa Caterina in Milan, I remember."

Lucia looked surprised. "Yes, but that was different. He was the garrison commander at Milan; here, he has nothing to do with the hospitals."

"I see," said Marie. "Well, Dr Larrey has been talking to me about them. He's been trying to recruit Egyptian women as nurses, but they're so clumsy because of their heavy robes and veils. They send little girls of twelve who don't have to wear the veil yet, and those poor children are trying to nurse grown Frenchmen, wounded at the Pyramids, or diseased, or suffering from dysentery, and – it isn't right, Lucia!"

"I know it isn't, but what can we do about it?"

"I've been thinking – you had so many charitable interests in Milan and you know a lot about sick people already – if you and I got one of the doctors to help us, we could take some of these women in hand and teach them how to handle the veil problem in practical nursing, like the Sisters of Charity do, and teach them to keep the patients clean and be clean themselves – Dr Larrey thinks it would make a big difference in the hospitals – why do you shake your head?"

"Dr Larrey might approve, but I don't think any of the other doctors I've met would want two European women interfering in their hospital management. And all my charitable work was done through the Church, my dear."

"If I spoke to General Bonaparte and got *his* approval, the doctors would have to accept our help . . ."

"You could try, but I doubt if the general wants to be disturbed about hospital matters in the middle of his love affair with Bellilotte."

"With *Bellilotte*? You mean that Fourès girl who turned up at Alexandria in her husband's uniform? *That* girl?"

"Yes, isn't it terrible? It's the talk of the town. He picked her up at the Tivoli, they say, and he shows her off everywhere. I thought you'd be sure to know. I saw your husband riding beside their carriage, only last week. Aren't you shocked?"

"Not about Charles," said Marie, trying to speak evenly, "but about the two of them. After all, he's got a wife in Paris and she's got a husband here. Is Fourès a *mari complaisant*?"

"*Captain* Fourès has been sent to Giza. And if you ask me he's well rid of her, except that it's so bad for the general's prestige to have all his officers laughing behind his back. Well, we know what men are, don't we dear? As I said to my husband, it only proves that the great Bonaparte is a man like other men."

"No," said Marie. "No, I won't accept that. A soldier with a soldier's faults, maybe; but you'll never get me to believe that Napoleon Bonaparte is a man like other men."

She went back to the labo as soon as Madame Clouzot had left and helped Professor Royer to set up his latest experiment, an investigation into the properties of Nile water, which kept at bay the thoughts of Napoleon's caresses given to Bellilotte. She was fresh and smiling in a pretty dress when Charles arrived about six o'clock, and she favoured him with a detailed account of the experiment, complete with Latin terms. He listened with courteous boredom and then sent Leila for a bottle of wine. He was getting very familiar with Leila, who was picking up French like a little parrot. He explained that he couldn't stay for dinner – had to go on duty – but would like a glass of wine.

"I had Lucia Clouzot here for luncheon today," said Marie.

"Nice woman – I haven't seen her for some time," said Charles, sipping Vouvray.

"She saw you only the other day," said Marie, looking at him over her glass. "She said you were riding equerry for the general and Madame Fourès."

"Oh, to the devil with her gossip!" said Latour, furious. "You know an ADC has to ride alongside the *calèche* when the general drives out. I was taking the place of poor de Beauharnais. He's very upset about their silly affair."

"Yes, I'm sorry for Eugène," said Marie. "But do you know, I'm inclined to be sorry for Bellilotte. She was born too late. She should have been one of the *merveilleuses* of four years ago, just after Thermidor, when we were all dancing mad. Remember those nights at Frascati's?"

"I thought you'd forgotten them," said Charles Latour. "Don't waste your sympathies on Pauline Fourès, darling. Fourès made a damned bad bargain when he picked up that little shopgirl from behind her counter in Carcassonne."

"I was a little shopgirl behind a counter in Paris when you knew me first."

"Yes, and now you're the Comtesse de la Tour de Vesle, my dear."

"I don't suppose poor Fourès will ever be a count. What's he doing at Giza?"

Charles grinned. "Napoleon noticed how keen the fellows are on riding camels and dromedaries when they have leave. He's decided to mount a Dromedary Regiment, to cope with the great sand problem. That's what Fourès is working on at Giza."

"The dromedaries are the ones with two humps, aren't they? Or are they the Bactrian camels?"

"Correct. Junot says two horns would be more suitable for *le mari cocu*."

She had been laughing and joking with him, without allowing herself to cry out that Napoleon had only begun this affair to get even with Joséphine for Hippolyte Charles. Now she said gravely, "Charles, why did I have to hear about all this from Lucia? You must have known about it from the beginning. Why didn't *you* tell me?"

"Because I didn't know how you would react when you knew your idol had feet of clay."

18

The French in Egypt were not so entirely cut off from Europe as some of them believed. It was true that Rear-Admiral Villeneuve, safe in port in Crete, had not yet challenged the British blockade squadron, far less Lord Nelson – that had to wait until Trafalgar; but the little courier boats, the *avisos*, which had scattered on the arrival of the British, regrouped at Alexandria, and gamely ran the blockade whenever it seemed possible to do so. They carried mail, for Napoleon had relaxed his ruling on home letters, and his own mail was voluminous. He appealed to the Directory again and again for help, for reinforcements, for the despatch of Talleyrand to Constantinople – there, with all his well-known diplomatic skill, to bring the Sultan back to "reality". But Talleyrand remained in Paris, and Napoleon described him to his Staff as "*de la merde dans un bas de soie*".

All captains carrying mail had strict orders to throw the letter packets overboard attached to lead weights, but Perfidious Albion was equal to the challenge, and British divers brought up weights, letters and all. When Napoleon's vile scrawl was deciphered by experts and printed, his letters – particularly those to his brother, describing his love life – made breakfast time entertaining for readers of the *Morning Chronicle*.

News came into Cairo from the outer world, chiefly through that phenomenon better known in later wars than Napoleon's as "the neutral traveller just arrived from overseas". Some of them came from Greece, some from the ports of the Adriatic, and the news they brought was for Napoleon's eyes alone. From General Kléber and General Menou came reports of a new arrival in the British squadron. A genuine English eccentric, the "Sir Sidney" of Levantine legend, otherwise a naval officer by the name of Sir William Sidney Smith, appeared to believe that he had superseded Commodore Hood in command of the squadron. His was a Swedish knighthood, which he had been allowed to keep by King George III in one of his madder moments, and he was a thorn in the flesh of Lord Nelson, still courting Lady Hamilton at Naples. Thanks to Nelson's intervention, Hood remained in command, but "Sir Sidney" proved very effective in transporting food supplies to the small Turkish garrisons in Syria.

Since the Ottoman Empire had declared war on France the Sultan was automatically the ally of Britain, and the only way General Bonaparte could fight them both was by attacking through Syria, which at that time included the Holy Land. The Staff were dubious. The Army of Egypt was now dispersed, a large part being with Desaix in Upper Egypt, and three considerable detachments on garrison duty at Alexandria, Rosetta and Damietta.

"We must decide how many of these effectives to recall," said Napoleon. "I can't attack with less than fifteen thousand men."

"A recall will take some time, general," said Lannes, one of his best men.

"And weaken Desaix in his attack on Murad," said Bessières.

"Murad's lieutenant, Ibrahim, is in Syria now," said Napoleon. "By striking north we'll strike at him . . . Gentlemen, let me have your own proposals for recall on a single sheet of paper. Regiments, location, transportation and time-table, first thing tomorrow morning. That's all for the present."

He was followed out of the room by General Dumas, whom he now considered as an "agitator" and who repeated his request to be relieved of his command and sent back to France.

"How do you propose to cross the sea?" said Bonaparte brusquely. "Walking on the water?" He shut himself in with the Chief of Staff, and said, "I suppose you want to be sent back to Paris too, Berthier?" For Berthier's mistress was in Paris now, her husband, the Marchese Viviani, having been appointed ambassador from the new Cisalpine Republic.

"I'll never leave you, *mon général.*"

"I know you won't. But doesn't it strike you as ironical that exactly two years ago we were going through Italy like a flame from Lodi Bridge to Rivoli, and now we're stuck in a mud city between a river and a desert? Exactly one year ago we were hailed as heroes in Paris, and now our engineers have had to work overtime to save our one and only drill ground from inundation by the Nile! What went wrong, Berthier? Was it my calculations?"

Berthier was too tactful to reply, and his master went back alone to the palace of Elfi Bey. He sent for Madame Fourès. He had a new name for her. Not the "warrior's rest" which he held to be the prime function of womanhood, but *"le délassement du guerrier"*, the warrior's relaxation. She amused him, and she kept telling him he was a wonderful lover.

The little shopgirl from Carcassonne had a wisdom – or a cunning – beyond her years, and she was exactly half as old as Joséphine. She came and went at his command. She never presumed, never called the General in Chief Napoleon, or anything but *mon trésor* or *mon amour* – he drew the line at *chou-chou*. She never asked for presents, and unlike Joséphine who, after the gifts began to flow in from the satellite states, would accept nothing less valuable than diamonds, she was happy with the gewgaws her lover bought for her in the Mouski bazaar.

When their affair had lasted for two months she began to coax him to give a party.

"Those lovely big rooms, all those rugs and things – it

258

would be perfect for a grand reception like they have at the Luxembourg."

"What do you know about the Luxembourg?"

"What I've read. Do say yes, *trésor*."

"Why don't you propose a ball, like they had at Versailles?"

"Don't you think dancing might be difficult, with so few ladies? But a grand *soirée*, now, that would cheer everybody up, and really, *mon amour*, you don't receive enough."

"I don't receive at all because I have no hostess."

He saw her pretty teeth close on her pouting lower lip as if to stifle the words, "You have me." Napoleon said, to tease her, "If I do give a party, I'll have to bring Fourès up from Giza to escort you."

"Oh surely not!"

"Oh surely yes. Don't you know that the essence of Paris society is the unfaithful husband and the unfaithful wife billing and cooing like turtledoves in public?"

"But what if there's a scene?"

"It'll make the party go."

When Charles Latour took their written invitation to Marie at Nasriya, she frowned and shook her head.

"A *soirée* at Elfi Bey! Must we go? I don't think I want to watch Bellilotte queening it over the ADCs."

"Poor Marie," said Charles. "You'll never forgive Napoleon for his Bellilotte, will you?"

At his tone Marie recovered herself.

"Forgiveness doesn't come into it," she said. "I was just being silly. Of course I'd love to go to the party. Do you realise I haven't even been to the Tivoli?"

She looked out the one piece of finery in her possession, a dress made by Madame Cécile for great occasions in Egypt, of which there had been none. Although it had been hanging up, it still showed the creases of the voyage, but steamed and pressed the dress regained its Paris chic, and Marie was satisfied. It was made of dark blue India muslin, extremely decolletée, with a sash of fuchsia-pink satin tied beneath her breasts, and a sequinned scarf of the same muslin laid round her shoulders. Marie wore no ornaments or head dress, having left her pearls in Paris, but her complexion, she was pleased to see, had not suffered in Egypt, although her fair hair seemed to have grown darker. She refused Leila's offer to put in henna highlights.

When Madame Latour entered the great hall at Elfi Bey on her husband's arm there was a buzz of appreciative comment, and Napoleon broke away from the group of Copts with whom he was trying to converse and came towards them with outstretched hands.

"Marie, you look magnificent," Napoleon said as she curtsied, "how d'you do it? Charles, doesn't she bring the very breath of Paris into this dull place?" Charles bowed and smiled.

"I want to talk to you, Marie," Napoleon went on, "but I'm having problems with the supper, and I must make sure everyone is comfortable. Some of my guests are not accustomed to western ways, and some have dietary problems . . ."

The anxious host hurried away to supervise the waiters in their white robes and red tarbushes, who were handing round cups of the green leaf soup called *meloxhia*, and portions of *hadam bel ferik*, pigeons stuffed with hulled wheat, raisins and pine nuts. There were pastries, veritable towers of dates held together with marzipan, and sweetmeats covered with gold leaf. Marie thought that if this was a sample of the fare at Elfi Bey it was no wonder that Napoleon was beginning to put on weight. The clear olive of his skin was sallow, and his jowl was flabby.

With Charles at her elbow she made the round of their friends. Captain Fourès, on forty-eight hours' leave from Giza, and his lady were a conspicuous couple, he because of his obvious popularity with officers who had never paid any attention to him before, and who now overwhelmed him with jokes he failed to understand. His wife did not shine. The Tivoli, not a palace, was the right background for Bellilotte. She wore too many of Bona-parte's tawdry gifts: an amber necklace, an onyx bracelet, a cameo brooch, and her very pretty face was over-shadowed by an immense aigrette in her headband. Marie's greeting to her was a cold bow, and a "Good evening, Madame Fourès, I hope I see you well."

Then Napoleon claimed Marie, and carried her off to a Turkish "sopha" where a waiter brought them wine, and for the general a narghilé which under the eyes of several members of the Divan he smoked for a few minutes. Then he laid down the mouthpiece and opened fire.

"Marie, what have you been doing? I had Colonel Clouzot here last week, asking me to put my foot down on some scheme of yours for instructing Arab nurses. I told him it reminded me of a girl who came to help me at a hospital in the Tuileries over three years ago."

"I noticed Colonel Clouzot wasn't here with Lucia," said Marie composedly. "I wish Dr Larrey was. He could have told you, better than I, what plan he and I had in mind."

"He has told me, and a very good plan it was. But, my dear Marie, it would simply never do. It would get us into more trouble with the Divan. You've no idea how touchy the Arabs are about their women. To have them in contact with a western woman might start another *jehad*. So it's no, I'm afraid, but what I want to know is, what made you listen to Larrey? Haven't you enough to do at the Institute?"

"Not really."

"But I thought you were devoted to your work. Berthol-let and Royer speak very highly of you."

"Thank you. It's turned into routine now; dysentery and ophthalmia and syphilis. It's not military pharmacy at all."

"I see," said the General in Chief. "Perhaps we shall gratify your bloodthirsty instincts before long . . . And it's only fair to tell you there is one circumstance, when adult women nurses are needed by the score, that would make me say Yes to you and Dr Larrey, only we must hope it never happens – "

"Oh, what's that?"

"The outbreak of a serious epidemic."

Two days passed and Captain Fourès was back at Giza before his wife returned to the stage of Elfi Bey, this time in a more intimate rôle. For the first time in her relationship with the general she permitted herself to be out of temper, sulking and pouting until he looked at the clock and snapped.

"What's the matter, didn't you enjoy your party?"

"*My* party, I like that! You hardly spoke to me."

"You were wearing too much rouge. Having a party means you have to talk to all the guests."

"You did most of your talking to that Madame Latour."

"She's a very old friend."

"I didn't like her at Alexandria, and the other night she had the impudence to patronise me. Doesn't she know who I am?"

"She was probably remembering that *she*'s the Comtesse de la Tour de Vesle."

"Is she indeed! I thought titles were abolished in the Revolution."

"Titles may be on their way back, who knows? Come on, Bellilotte, stop being so silly. Marie Latour is a brilliant woman, a Scholar in her own right, and you're my play girl, aren't you? Let's go to bed."

Napoleon's lovemaking had never been clumsier or shorter than it was in the next half hour. Bellilotte was surprised when he fell asleep, for he was a man who fought sleep, believing it to be the waste of precious time in a working day. This doze might last for only ten or fifteen minutes, but it allowed her to plan on how she might repair the damage done by her bad temper. Intuition told her that he was ready to end the affair, which she could not afford, and he would not end it if she kept her head. She had done that on the day not so long ago when he woke smiling from a happy dream and called her Joséphine; she could keep her head again. She had only lost it because of Marie Latour. Joséphine was an old woman, far away in Paris. Marie was here and had wounded her pride, and damn her she was beautiful. Bellilotte willed her tense, unsatisfied body to calm, she willed the tears to come into her eyes. She wound her limbs round his, matching the rhythm of his breathing to her own, and then with her lips on his she sobbed.

"What's the matter, Bellilotte?"

She put her arms round his neck and whispered, "I want to have a child of yours, Napoleon."

When he was alone again, staring with unseeing eyes at the papers on his desk, he could almost feel the chord she had struck vibrating in his heart. That his marriage to Joséphine was childless had been his one great grief, at least until the Hippolyte Charles affair erupted, and it was an uncomprehended grief. Joséphine was not sterile, for she had borne two children to de Beauharnais. She was thirty-two when they married (twenty-eight on their marriage lines) but the thirties were not too old for maternity. His own mother had borne three children between thirty and thirty-four. Yet he and Joséphine had lived for over a year in Italy and for months in Paris in the closest possible union without the slightest hint that a child was on the way. He had begun to fear, though never to admit, that the fault lay in himself.

Since this young girl, so pliant and so jealous, had admitted with tears that she wanted to have his child, to accomplish his manhood . . . it was surely worth some sacrifices.

The first sacrifice was Captain Fourès. When he was called from dromedary drill to talk to an ADC from Cairo, Captain Lavalette, he obeyed with relief, the dromedaries having the habit of settling down in the desert sand at will, while the troopers who fell out sideways over the hump shrieked with laughter. Relief turned to elation when Captain Fourès learned that he had been specially selected to carry "this packet of important despatches" to Paris.

"I'm honoured, *mon colonel*, but – I'm surprised. I mean, why me?"

"The general was impressed by you in Cairo last week. He thinks you're the right man for the job."

"And I shan't have time to say goodbye to my wife?"

"I'm afraid not, captain. But she's proud of your mission and she sends you her love. You are to proceed with all speed to Rosetta, where General Menou has been informed, and take ship on the *aviso* in readiness. Your further instructions are in the covering letter. Good luck to you!"

Over the desert sands sped Captain Fourès and his cavalry escort, making a gratifyingly important arrival at General Menou's headquarters. His sea voyage lasted twenty-four hours, the little *aviso* having surrendered to the guns of HMS *Zealous* and her crew and passenger being made prisoners of war.

Perfidious Albion had learned something of the Belli-lotte affair from previously captured letters, and it was considered a good joke in the wardroom of the *Zealous* to set the Frenchman ashore and allow him to return under parole to Cairo, where he found his wife installed in a neat villa close to Elfi Bey palace and under the protection of the General in Chief.

The noisy row which followed was a revelation to the Arabs, whose punishment for a guilty wife was strangulation. According to the woman's new servants the French officer had stamped and sworn and shouted, but he only gave her a few slaps, after which both parties began clamouring for divorce, he for infidelity and she for his alleged "brutality".

If Fourès had been a Moslem the thing was simple: he only had to say "I divorce you" three times and he was free. But how two of the infidel expected to sue for a civil divorce in a country where French civil law did not prevail was a problem which intrigued the Divan. With grave faces they asked the opinion of the Sultan Kebir, who replied that he was a soldier, not a jurist, and in any event was about to leave Cairo for Suez. They approved his attitude. He was above the law.

Captain Fourès put in for a new posting and disappeared from Cairo. Some said he had gone back to his dromedaries, others that he was in Upper Egypt; it was not important either way. He was an uninteresting young man, and like the male spider he had fulfilled his function, which was to take a dressmaker's assistant away from a little shop in Carcassonne and into the larger world, after which he was due to be devoured.

The Bellilotte episode, and especially the trip to Suez, cost Bonaparte some prestige among his officers, who refused to believe that he had gone on a reconnaissance for the invasion of Syria. The way to Syria lay north to El Arish, not west to Suez, said men who didn't know that for all his poor opinion of female intelligence Napoleon could never bear to see a woman cry.

Bellilotte wept a great deal before she left for Suez on 24 December, and the best he could say to her was "Don't worry, I'll look after you." She was quite content with that. She had seen how the land lay, and believed that if she gave him a child Napoleon would divorce Joséphine and marry her. Unlike Joséphine she was too honest to pretend to be pregnant when she was not.

Colonel Latour, not included among the ADCs for Suez, was faced like all the ADCs remaining in Cairo with extra duty in housing the reinforcements now arriving in a tent city stretching from the citadel to the Mokattam Hills. Latour, by consequence, was mildly critical of Napoleon, mildly supportive of General Dumas and the "agitators", and he lost his temper with Marie when, as often before, she claimed a special knowledge of Napoleon's motives.

"You're all so silly," she said in the tone of one instructing a backward child, "not to see he's gone to Suez to find out if there's any chance of carrying out his old plan of building a canal from the Red Sea to the Mediterranean."

"Forgive my ignorance," said Charles, "but I never heard of any such plan."

"He used to talk about it to Uncle Prosper and me, but perhaps I was wrong to call it a plan. His old dream, I should have said."

"Dream is right. Marie, what a fool you are to believe in all that nonsense! His dream of Eastern conquest is costing us all too dear."

The trip to Suez was unproductive, except for a reconnaissance of Arab caravan routes, and General Bonaparte returned to Cairo on 6 January. The public appearances with Bellilotte began again. Somewhere in the bazaars she had found a Levantine dressmaker who could copy French models from a tattered fashion book, and Bellilotte now had no reason to be jealous of Marie's indigo muslin. She had pretty dresses galore, with matching parasols, and scarves ornamented with dangling copper coins, iridescent sequins and motifs of mirror glass. It was a sight to see the couple driving round Esbekya Square, Bellilotte bowing graciously to her acquaintance, and her general absorbed in making notes in his table-book.

One afternoon in early February Professor Royer asked Marie if she would take a message from him to the editor of *La Dépêche Egyptienne*, which was about to go to press. Marie agreed with pleasure. She was always glad to have a chat with Jean Tallien, whom she liked much better than when he was tagging at Teresa's heels. He was a link with the old Paris days, and Marie was more homesick for Paris with every month of their Egyptian captivity.

Also she was glad to oblige Citizen Royer, even in so simple a matter as running an errand, for she had regretted complaining to Bonaparte about the repetition and routine of her work in his laboratory. He made it easy for her, as on this afternoon when he told her not to come back to the labo after she had been at the newspaper office. "Have a stroll in the gardens," he urged her. "Get some fresh air. Join Dr Berthollet and me for supper if you like. We have some fresh orders from Dr Larrey that you should know about."

"*Merci, monsieur le professeur.*" The French Institute was reverting more and more to the *ancien régime* style of address! Marie crossed the landing to her own apartment and told Leila to prepare her bedroom for the night and then go home. "I shall be late," she said, "I'm having supper in the mess. Good-night, Leila, see you in the morning."

"*Bonsoir, madame. A demain.*" Really her French was quite passable! Marie took her shawl, for the February evenings were chilly, and ran into the scented garden, where the south wind was ruffling the spring flowers. She stopped for a glimpse of the zoo, where the solitary camel had just had a young one "to keep her company", said the proud curator, and then hurried on to the building where the clatter and stamp of the press was heard.

Tallien came out to greet her, and observed professionally that she was "just in time to catch the edition" with Professor Royer's message in its sealed envelope. His face changed as he read it, and his voice was stern as he asked, "Have you seen this?"

"No, I haven't."

"I'd have stopped the press for this one."

The words blazed up at her from the single sheet of paper:

There is an outbreak of plague at Alexandria. All Institute personnel are advised to observe scrupulous cleanliness, take baths and change their linen daily.

"Oh Jean! Plague! How awful!"

"It's pretty bad," he admitted. "Still, Alexandria's a long way from Cairo, and a slight outbreak could soon be controlled – Marie, this has been a shock to you. Would you like a glass of brandy?"

"No thank you, Jean. Hadn't you better get Royer's

message into type?" She spoke mechanically. She was remembering what Napoleon had said about the outbreak of a serious epidemic. Was this what he had meant – the plague?

As if he read her thoughts, Tallien said, with his eyes on the paper in his hand, "Royer's message – Royer's handwriting. But dictated by General Bonaparte."

"What makes you think so?"

"The line about the daily baths. I wonder if he makes La Bellilotte take a daily bath? She uses too much perfume to care much for soap and water."

"I thought you were one of her admirers. It certainly looked like that at one time."

"Bah! She was hunting bigger game than me. Marie, wait! Don't go yet! Let me give this to the printers, it'll have to go in a box on page one, and then I'll see you back across the gardens."

"No, no, Jean, I must go. Professor Royer wants to see me, so – good-night."

She was outside, leaning against the wall for a moment to try to collect her thoughts, then hurrying again as she had come. The khamsin wind was blowing stronger, and the particles of reddish dust which it brought even to sheltered Nasriya were gritty against her face. Marie saw lamps already lighted in the Qassim palace, while the Kalkhoda house was all in darkness. Professor Royer must have closed the laboratory and gone away. Suddenly she knew that she wanted to be part of that darkness, to leave until morning her confrontation with Royer and Berthollet, to bury her sore heart and her fearful mind in the cool pillows of a darkened room. She found the Kalkhoda door and ran upstairs.

The handle of her own door refused to turn.

She rattled it impatiently. "Leila! Are you there? What's the matter? Open the door!"

There was nothing but thick silence on the landing. But a faint light, as from a single candle, appeared at the foot of the door as Marie fumbled in her reticule for the key.

The door opened, and the candlelight shone on the half-naked bodies of Leila and Charles Latour.

Marie stepped inside the room. "I'm sorry," she said. "I'm afraid I've come back too soon," and Leila started to sob.

Without looking at her Marie told Leila to put on her dress and get out.

"She said you weren't coming back," said Charles stupidly.

"Hadn't you better get dressed too?" said Marie. "You look ridiculous with your shirt tail flapping."

He picked up his breeches and boots and went into the bedroom. Marie took off her shawl and lit three more candles mechanically. By their light she surveyed the disordered divan and the brandy flask from her husband's kit, lying on the floor with some brown drops oozing out. She felt a deadly chill and weakness; nothing more.

When Charles came back she said at once, "I suppose I should thank you for not using our own bed." But he ignored this and picked up on her last words.

"I looked ridiculous, did I? I know that's how I appear to you. A ridiculous little man, not fit to hold a candle to that great Scholar, Marie Fontaine."

"A contemptible man, to take advantage of a child. That girl is only thirteen."

"She's no innocent. She gave me comfort when I needed it."

She touched the brandy flask with the toe of her slipper. "Couldn't you find comfort in this?" His slurred speech and flushed face suggested that he had emptied the flask.

"Not woman comfort. Not the comfort a man needs who has a wife like you."

"Charles!"

"Ridiculous and contemptible, that's how you think of me. I've known for a long time that you despise me; now you've made it plain."

"I don't despise you. I've tried to be a good wife to you —"

"How? You went on working at your silly chemistry, or whatever you call it, when you knew I didn't approve. You ran away from Italy when we had a chance to be together. You never protested when we were separated here, and when I did come to you I had to listen to endless stories about experiments I didn't understand and don't want to understand – "

"Like your noble ancestors and their *droit du seigneur* you prefer to seduce a poor little servant girl."

"Much you care about my ancestors – you, who haven't even given me an heir to their name!"

"That's not my fault," she said.

"How do I know that?"

Marie thought of the brief dream of motherhood which had gilded a few weeks in the Quai Voltaire. She tried to speak but could not, and the hectoring voice went on.

"Admit it, Marie – all you care for is yourself and hearing yourself called brilliant. That and the admiration of General Bonaparte."

She said icily, "General Bonaparte's admiration is amply engaged elsewhere."

"That's the way you talk, as if all the rest of us were peasants! You came to Egypt to be near him, didn't you? Because you wanted more than his admiration . . ."

Since he came back to the salon, Charles Latour had stood, swaying slightly beside the bedroom door. Now he took three strides forward and seized Marie's shoulders in his strong grasp.

"Can you deny that you were utterly in love with him?"

She was not in the least afraid of him. She gasped, "Don't touch me!" and then, "I was in love with you."

"For a few weeks, maybe. But that ended the night I saw you kiss his hand outside the Tuileries – the night of the whiff of grapeshot."

"That was my homage to the future."

"A fine future! How about the day soon after we came to this accursed country, when I rode up to the gates of the Qassim palace and saw you sitting with him on the lawn, lost in talk?"

"About Joséphine! We were talking about Joséphine – "

"It was Napoleon's turn then, to bow his head and slobber over *your* hands. Was that his homage to the future? Or a lover's gratitude?"

Marie wrenched herself free.

"You're mad," she said between clenched teeth. "Say what you like to me, but don't insult General Bonaparte. Go away now, Charles. Go away, and don't come back."

19

The news of an outbreak of plague at Alexandria was received coolly enough at the French Institute. The nature of the "plague" was not revealed; it might be nothing worse than chickenpox, and the military were not affected. In the Qassim palace there were even some smiles about the daily change of linen recommendation, and comments that it was lucky the Institute was well supplied with laundresses.

Some members of the Artistic Commission were not so light-hearted. They were about to leave for Giza, to make a study of the Pyramids, and there was a steady coming and going between Giza and Alexandria. Might not infection be carried by the desert travellers? The doctors assured them they were safe enough – all except Dr Larrey, who was taking the plague report very seriously indeed.

When he arrived from headquarters with an order for medicines to be stowed away in his "moving ambulances", an order which meant the pharmacists had to work round the clock for three days, he made an opportunity to take Marie Latour aside and tell her General Bonaparte had categorically refused to allow their scheme for the training of Arab nurses to proceed. "Madame Latour must not be exposed to infection," Napoleon had said, "and who knows what type of infection may not appear in our hospitals in the very near future?"

"He's thinking about the plague, you see, though we don't know the nature of the disease as yet," said Larrey.

"What do *you* think, Dr Larrey?"

"General Kléber has drawn a *cordon sanitaire* round the barracks in Alexandria," said Dr Larrey evasively, "and the men are forbidden to go into the town. But they must march in a few days when they come to join us at Damietta for the attack on Syria, and God knows what they may bring with them. An epidemic in the army is what I'm frightened of."

"When do you leave?" The doctor thought Marie was pale and heavy-eyed, as if she had not slept. He told her the expedition to Syria would start in two days.

On the first of those days Napoleon had two visitors, who between them took up most of his afternoon. The first, whom he saw in the room in the Elfi Bey palace which was his military headquarters, was General Dumas, Colonel Latour being the ADC in attendance.

"General Dumas," said Napoleon, when the big man was standing in front of the little man, "I have your letter before me, officially stating that you wish to be relieved of your command and given facilities to return to France."

"Yes, sir."

"You are the general in command of cavalry, and the cavalry will be going into action in Syria. If this were a court-martial and I the prosecutor, I would accuse you on the capital charge of desertion in the face of the enemy."

"Sir, I protest . . ."

"But considering that the enemy is several hundreds of kilometres away, and that you first asked to be relieved when we were at Damanhur last July, the court-martial might uphold your defence. So I shall grant you your discharge. Oh, General Hercules, General Horatius, you've come a long way since the days of your great exploits!"

In the embarrassed silence which followed he scribbled hastily on two sheets of paper.

"Here is your discharge and here are your movement

orders," said Napoleon. "You will leave in seventy-two hours for Rosetta and report to General Menou, in charge of shipping. There is a naval officer of flag rank at Rosetta now, Admiral Ganteaume, who will be responsible for your transportation. Colonel Latour will see you to the door."

When Charles returned the general uttered the one word "Well?"

"He was in tears, sir, when he said goodbye. Very emotional. Very disturbed."

"Well he might be," said Napoleon. "I saw he was going to blubber while I was talking to him, so I cut the whole thing short. Well, now we shall have to rely on veterans like Murat and yourself when the cavalry goes into action . . . Was there something else?"

"Yes, *mon général*. Colonel Clouzot is in the anteroom and requests the favour of a word with you."

"He'll have to wait until tomorrow morning, say at seven o'clock. It's probably only about El Arish – he's to be the garrison commander there – and the facilities for Madame Clouzot to go with him."

"Is Madame Clouzot going to El Arish too?"

"Yes, I agreed to that – unwillingly. Marie will be jealous, she likes to be in the forefront of the battle. Tell her about Signora Lucia when you say goodbye. And now I'm going back to the residence, to see this Citizen Hamelin. You might interrupt us at five o'clock."

Citizen Hamelin, as a civilian, was received in the great hall where Bonaparte's reception had been given. He was a merchant from Trieste, a square, solid bourgeois who was not impressed by his host or the grandeur of his surroundings, nor likely to be given to invention or exaggeration. Over tiny cups of Turkish coffee the two men talked for a long time, and the tale Citizen Hamelin had to tell was more horrifying to Napoleon than the reports of plague. Hamelin did not pretend to have any news of Paris or the position of the Directory. He did know, and gave many circumstantial details of, the situation in the heart of Europe.

Briefly, all Napoleon's victories in Italy had gone for nothing. The Austrians had invaded the country and were carrying all before them. The Russians, now their allies, had invaded Switzerland and were actually in Zürich. The satellites recognised by the Treaty of Campo Formio had been swept aside, and unless General Bonaparte returned to resume command Europe would return to its pre-Revolutionary shape. And he was locked into Egypt by the British.

The general and his visitor were still talking when Charles Latour opened the door and was motioned away, and it was nearer six than five o'clock when he was sent for to escort Citizen Hamelin to the house of his Coptic banker. When he returned Napoleon was pacing up and down the hall with his hands clasped behind his back, a posture which always indicated concentrated thought. He was thinking, in fact, that he might need Admiral Ganteaume's services himself before very long.

"Ah, Charles!" said Napoleon, when the young man appeared, "would you send one of the servants to Madame Bellilotte's villa with my compliments and apologies? She was expecting me at five. Say I'll certainly see her tomorrow before we leave . . . No, I shan't need you again this evening. Good night."

Charles Latour carried out his commission and went to his own little room. Too bad for Bellilotte, he thought. No *cinq à sept* tonight! He had been given a message to a girl who liked to be in the forefront of the battle, but if he went to Nasriya she would probably refuse to see him. It would have to be a letter, and so Charles wrote to Marie without salutation or endearment:

You were right. I was mad. Mad in my impulsive action, and mad in all I said to you. We go on campaign tomorrow. If I fall, please send for Maître Vial as soon as you return to Paris and ask him to inform my parents.

He has my Will. Everything I have is yours. I love you. Remember me. – Charles.

They started the long march to Damietta, the port at the eastern mouth of the Nile delta, and reached their destination undisturbed by either Bedouin or Mameluke. Napoleon and Berthier rode in the general's carriage, Berthier morose at leaving the Cairo tent in which he had arranged a little shrine to Madame Viviani, with her portrait on a cashmere-covered field table. He had the portrait in his valise, of course, but on campaign it might be difficult to arrange the shrine.

The two generals had to go over the plans made for Damietta. They were to be met there by General Kléber, too good a soldier to be left behind in Alexandria, with all his command, while Marmont with 5,000 men would take his place at the principal port. That meant Damietta would be turned into an armed camp for a week before they moved to cross the Syrian frontier at El Arish.

While the commissariat struggled with the problems of feeding the multitude (and they were so near Palestine now that the Bible metaphor was appropriate) sea bathing was ordered for the troops. The occasional Arab, riding past on his donkey, stared to see regiment after regiment marched down to the beaches and running mother-naked into the water with the whoops and hollos of school boys. The salt water was a great refreshment after the heat and dust of Cairo, and bathing was an important health measure. Napoleon had no medical knowledge, but out of his lifelong habit of taking baths he had hit on the one remedy – personal cleanliness – for what this new ailment turned out to be. No medicine had yet been discovered to cure bubonic plague.

For that was what it was. Not smallpox, not cholera, nor any other scourge, but the Black Death which first appeared in China, and moving west across the kingdom of Tartary into Europe had cost the lives of seventy-five million people in the fourteenth century.

General Kléber was proud of bringing his men up from Alexandria in good health, not a case of plague among them. Had he ever seen a case, Dr Larrey wanted to know. No, but an Arab *hakim* had described the cases to him: the onset of mounting fever and vomiting, then the appearance of ugly swellings in the armpits and groin, then delirium and death. Sometimes recovery was possible if the swellings were lanced, not otherwise.

"Yes," sighed Dr Larrey, "the swellings are called buboes, hence the name bubonic plague. The infection is spread by flea-infested rats. We don't know how to cure it but we know that much."

"There were no rats in my camps or barracks, doctor," said Kléber hotly.

"So we must hope for the best," said Larrey. "You brought a fine body of men to General Bonaparte."

"General Bonaparte would use a dividend of ten thousand men a day if he could get them," said Kléber.

Napoleon had only fifteen thousand men at his back, along with eight hundred cavalry, when they started along the coast road, or track, towards the two massive pillars called the Gates of Syria, and on to El Arish. It was a very different march from that blind stumble across the burning sands to Embaba, and the regiments were fallen out one after another to bathe in the Mediterranean Sea. Nor was El Arish, a walled town, able to resist for long. A breach in the walls, a battering ram against the gates, a cavalry charge with Eugène de Beauharnais riding knee to knee with Charles Latour, and the Syrian commandant was signing the articles of surrender, agreeing to march his men on parole to Damascus. His place and his house were taken by Colonel Clouzot, and the French marched in.

The veterans of Italy told each other that it was like the good old days. El Arish was at the centre of a green and fertile valley, with the sea beyond, and a profusion of orange trees. It was in reality a huge oasis, with several wells, and the soldiers sauntered about sucking oranges and smoking and eyeing the Syrian girls. Here too in an off-duty hour Charles Latour met old acquaintances he would rather have avoided, for they all wanted to talk about Marie.

The first of these hailed him with a cheery cry of "*Holà, mon colonel, comment ça va? Et comment va la petite dame?*" It was Jeanette Tête de Bois, the *cantinière* who had come to Marie's help when she was seasick on board *L'Orient*, and she wanted to hear all the news of "the little lady". Where was she living? What was she doing? No sign of a baby yet?

After he escaped from the good-hearted, vulgar, noisy woman (she was attached to the 2nd Light Brigade, she told him, and had come up with them from Damietta) Charles fell in with Lucia Clouzot and another Italian married to a French officer, Madame Verdier. They had travelled from Cairo in one of the "moving ambulances", and were in high spirits. El Arish was wonderful, so fresh and flowery, and they were already planning to open a small first aid post for the very minor French casualties of the assault.

"We can't do much," confessed Madame Verdier, "but Dr Larrey says we can renew the dressings, and issue fresh bandages to men who haven't been too badly hurt."

"How I wish Marie had been able to come with us," said Lucia. "She'd have told us exactly what to do, wouldn't she, Colonel Latour?"

"She ran a first aid post in Paris, madame."

"Still, what she's doing at the Institute is far more important. Wonderful person."

Wonderful person – whose last words to him had been "Go away and don't come back!" They rang in Charles Latour's ears as the cavalry picked its way along the stony uphill track, now, as March advanced, beginning to be spangled with the wild flowers of Palestine. Napoleon had left his carriage and horses at El Arish and marched with the infantry. The next garrison, Gaza, surrendered without a shot fired on either side, but the next day's march was somehow ominous, because for the first time they saw other riders on the skyline. They might have been some of Ibrahim Bey's Mamelukes, but they made no attempt at the usual Mameluke charge, or they might have been Syrians, holding their fire, but they certainly were spies from Jaffa, the next strong place on the way north.

The townsfolk and garrison of Jaffa put up a fierce resistance. After three days of preparation and demands for surrender, Napoleon ordered the town to be taken "by assault", which had the implication, "Show no mercy." The French, after all the setbacks of Egypt, were in the mood to be ruthless. The infantry went in first, and their attack soon turned into a massacre. When the cavalry followed, their horses slipped in the blood pouring down the steep and narrow streets.

If I fall, Charles had written to Marie, not believing it. He had come through so many battles that he believed he bore a charmed life. When he saw the piled bodies of women and old men, and his own countrymen mad with lust for blood, swinging their sabres and rifle butts to beat out the lives of little children, he was filled with horror, and shouted curses to stop the slaughter. Then his horse stumbled at a sharp corner, and as he gathered up the reins Charles Latour found himself looking into the muzzle of a brass-bound fowling-piece of antique design, held in the trembling hand of an old mountaineer. The bullet sang home, and as Charles fell out of the saddle he felt a searing pain go through his head. He heard the clatter of hoofs and the sound of familiar voices as some of his own men rode up to the rescue – heard but not saw, for sight was gone. Then he felt but not saw that he was being lifted, and the only words he whispered before he lost consciousness, perfectly inaudible to his men, revealed what he feared more than death:

"Am I blind?"

* * *

For the first few days after the scene with Charles, Marie nursed the same cold rage as when she told him "Go away and don't come back." She was realist enough to suppose there had been episodes, politely called romantic, during their long separation, but she had never heard of them and so could blot them out of her mind. But to find him *in flagrante*, in her own room, with her own maid, was too disgusting.

Had she been in Paris then she would have gone to her attorney, Maître Favart (he was married now, and they were on friendly terms) and asked him to arrange a divorce. Then all she had to do was wait until the Rocrois' lease expired, go back to her own house in the Rue St Honoré, and reopen the Pharmacie Fontaine on her own account. She wondered if her reluctance to sell the pharmacy outright had been due to hidden ambition or hidden fear.

When his letter came she analysed it word by word, and the half-hearted apology, like the reference to his Will, fell flat. The two phrases which touched Marie in spite of herself were *If I should fall* and *Remember me*. With them, the softening process had insensibly begun.

Professor Royer, who knew more about Marie Latour than she thought he did, helped it to develop by suggesting that as the Kalkhoda house was now almost empty she should change her living quarters to the more companionable Qassim palace. "You'll only have one room there," he said, "but then you won't need a maid. One of the French laundresses will look after you."

"It'll be nice to have someone who speaks French."

All so cosy, all so discreet. Dr Berthollet, who had been a medical man before he turned to chemistry, was keeping a close watch on the health of the Institute. It was unwise to cough or sneeze, and nobody dared complain of a headache. They were all living under the shadow of the plague. Marmont reported more cases in Alexandria, and a woman in Damietta, smitten with plague, confessed to having sex with a soldier of the 2nd Light Brigade before he left for Jaffa. It was spreading along the Mediterranean shore.

General Bonaparte was much missed at Cairo headquarters (as well as the fact that he had taken all the senior doctors with him) and so, in a different way, was General Dumas. The other "agitators" resented his discharge and return to France, which they envied, and hoped he would be returned ignominiously by the British, like Captain Fourès. But Admiral Ganteaume did his work well, and the vessel on which "General Hercules" sailed slipped safely through the British blockade. A storm forced it into the port of Tarentum, and the big mulatto spent the next three years enduring all the horrors of a Neapolitan prison. He did not live long after he was set free, but before he died his wife gave birth to his son, who became a writer. The second Alexandre Dumas could hardly remember his father, but in *The Three Musketeers* and *The Count of Monte Cristo* there is something of the adventures of General Hercules.

On the very day Dumas left Egypt Napoleon began the siege of Acre, against a citadel that broke the hearts of the Crusaders, and where he was to suffer one of the few defeats of his life. The Cairo establishment, which had heard nothing of the Syrian expedition since it left Damietta, was quite without news of Acre, but ugly rumours about Jaffa began to spread across the desert.

The plague was at Jaffa, carried by a soldier of the 2nd Light Brigade, and that was much. Napoleon had visited a pest-house where the victims were dying, and had soothed them, and that was to his credit. Then, said rumour, he had ordered them all to be poisoned. At the same time the Syrian prisoners of war, taken when Jaffa surrendered, were shot dead on the sea shore.

These horrible rumours, the one as likely to be true as the other, met with disbelief in Cairo. At the Institute, for so long above politics and interested only in the arts and science, they were discussed feverishly. Marie Latour, that ardent Bonapartist, took no part in the discussion. She had received a letter from El Arish.

> My dear Marie [Lucia Clouzot wrote] I must at least try to let you know that your dear husband is out of danger. He suffered a head wound at the storming of Jaffa. Dr Larrey, who treated him, sent him back to Army Rear at El Arish, where you may be sure Madame Verdier and I will give him our best care. How I wish you were here! He misses you.
>
> Ever your friend, Lucia Clouzot.
>
> P.S. There may be some damage to the optic nerve.

This message, which explained so little and implied so much, left Marie in a turmoil of feeling. She could only guess that Lucia was holding something back: she could not know that the plague in Jaffa, because of which Dr Larrey was sending patients he hoped to save back to Army Rear, had outpaced him and was in El Arish before them, and that Lucia, one of its first victims, was dead before Marie read her letter.

Bonaparte faced two formidable enemies at Acre: Djezzar Pasha and the redoubtable Sir Sidney Smith. Against immensely strong fortifications and two hundred and fifty guns, and with no large-calibre guns of his own, he led a force decimated by plague in forty assaults over a period of two months, and in the end had to withdraw. Once and once only he fought a battle on his own terms, when he broke away from Acre on 16 April to rescue Kléber from a Mameluke attack in the Plains of Esdraelon. It was called the victory of Mont Thabor, and it was Napoleon's compensation as he trod the valley of humiliation, littered with the bodies of the plague-stricken and the wounded, with the vultures waiting to pick their bones.

When the survivors were back in Egypt, Napoleon had two problems to consider: the news from Europe brought by Citizen Hamelin, which he had imparted to no one, and a report that a Turkish army was on its way by sea from Constantinople to Alexandria. He had the feeling of fighting on all fronts. He had only one ADC left, Colonel Lavalette, but with Lavalette's help he compiled a list of the wounded ADCs and Staff who would be returning to Cairo. All had been certified clear of plague by Dr Desgenettes who, contentious as ever, had argued with Dr Larrey that the malady was not bubonic plague but some unspecified kind.

The list began:

Beauharnais	Head wound at Acre
Duroc	Thigh wound at Acre
Latour	Lost eye at Jaffa

and so on. Dr Berthollet, who had been Marie's mainstay all along, obtained a copy of the list at headquarters and took it back to Nasriya.

"Now don't begin to cry, my poor Marie," he said kindly. "One eye isn't so bad. He might have been killed outright."

"I thought – from what Lucia said – that he'd been blinded."

"I know you did. Now, listen to me. He's got *pratique* as regards plague, and he mustn't go into a military hospital here. We can find room for him at the Institute – can't we?"

"In my room – yes."

The fourteenth of June was the date fixed for the return of units of the Syrian expedition to Cairo, and Dr Berthollet commandeered the *calèche* reserved for the Institute to take himself and Marie into the city. He had learned that all the wounded, walking or travelling in vehicles, were to be taken straight to the citadel.

"But why?" asked Marie.

"I suppose because they wouldn't look too well in a triumphal procession."

"This is a *triumph*?"

An effort had been made to stage one. When Marie, standing in Esbekya Square, heard a band strike up out of sight she prayed silently, "Don't let them play the *Marseillaise* – not today!" and sighed with relief when she heard *The March of the Tartars*, so often listened to outside the great cabin of *L'Orient*. Bonaparte, of course, led the parade on horseback, his face impassive, his eyes not once lifted to the window of the villa where Bellilotte was watching. He wore a hat with tall tricolore plumes and looked thinner in his worn uniform. It was the first time Marie had ever watched him without a quickening of the heart.

The plague had not reached Cairo, but the Egyptians, watching as the ranks went past, carrying palm branches and the Ottoman flags captured at El Arish, Gaza and Jaffa, looked as miserable as they did a year before. There was no applause.

When Bonaparte dismounted in front of Elfi Bey, where members of the Divan were waiting to congratulate him on the victory of Mont Thabor, Marie and Berthollet pushed their way out of the Square and drove to the citadel. There all was confusion. Street sellers had been allowed to enter, and beggars demanding *baksheesh*, and the soldiers were buying sweetmeats, with much bargaining.

"Where is Colonel Latour? Has anybody seen Colonel Latour?" As Berthollet's authoritative voice cut through the din they saw him, sitting on a stone seat with his head against the wall. There was a bandage round his eyes, but his hearing was unimpaired, for when he heard his own name he said, "Who is that? Who's there?" and gasped when the voice he had loved once said "It's your wife, Charles. I've come to take you home."

They took him home in the *calèche*, swaying slightly between the two of them, and almost silent until they reached Nasriya. There he recognised the voice of Jean Tallien, who organised men to take him up to the big airy bedroom in the Qassim palace and help him to undress, while servants brought hot water and cool drinks. Then Tallien told Marie to go to him. "Dr Berthollet wants you to change the bandage," he said. "What Charles needs is a good night's sleep, he says, and he's mixing a sleeping draught that'll make Charles sleep till morning. But I think what Charles needs is you."

"Thank you, Jean. You've been very kind."

When Marie entered the bedroom carrying the fresh dressing she thought he was already asleep. Charles lay very still, with both hands relaxed on the sheet. His moustache had been shaved off, and in spite of the hospital pallor he looked very like the Sergeant Vautour of long ago. Then his quick ears caught the rustle of her skirts, and he said, "Is that you, Marie?"

"Yes, dear. I want to change your bandage."

He lifted his hand and fumbled at his forehead. The old bandage slipped off. "There you are!"

She hadn't known what to expect, but not this. The lid of his left eye was closed, and the whole socket, instead of being empty, was puckered up to half its normal size. An angry red welt ran from the outer corner of the eye to where the dark hair had been shaved above his ear. The right eye, brown and bloodshot, met her own.

"Not pretty, is it?"

"Hush, Charles, you mustn't talk now. Dr Berthollet wants you to have a long sleep."

"If I'm not too disgusting, will you kiss me?"

Marie bent down and laid her lips on his.

When she went into the room next morning he was still asleep, sprawled across the wide bed, and there was even a little colour in his face. Youth and strength had come to the aid of Charles Latour, and he soon recovered from the terrible journey by ambulance from El Arish. He was hungry and he wanted to get up. He wanted to talk!

Talk he did, for the whole of the next afternoon. He knew nothing about the defeat at Acre, beyond what other men had told him; his talk was all of Jaffa and El Arish, and above all of the plague. Marie listened with horror to his dispassionate tale of death. Poor Jeanette Tête-de-Bois, who had nursed him after his wound, was dead – she was a *cantinière* in the regiment that brought the plague to Jaffa. Lucia Clouzot and her husband had both died, and half of El Arish with them. The Verdiers had escaped and were on their way to Rosetta (where that old fool Menou had embraced Islam) with his discharge and a movement order to go back to France – if they could. At Jaffa Larrey had been wonderful, and Desgenettes had inoculated himself with the pus from a plague victim's buboes. He was quite well.

"Oh don't!" said Marie. She had let him talk, knowing it was a purge of his emotion, but now she had to interrupt.

"Charles, is it true Napoleon had all the plague patients at Jaffa poisoned before he left?"

"Certainly not! Whoever told you such a horrible lie?"

"It's a story that's been going about Cairo. Then is it another lie that he had the prisoners of war at Jaffa shot?"

She saw her husband's face twitch below the bandage. "Yes," he said reluctantly. "I'm afraid there is some truth in that. They say there wasn't enough food for our own men, let alone the prisoners – and so, fortunes of war, my dear! Marie, I hate talking to you when I can't see your face. How long do I have to wear this damned bandage?"

"I don't know, but I do know you've been talking for nearly two hours. Shall I get you some lemonade?"

"Please." He heard her rise from her chair and caught hold of her dress. "Darling, wait, there's something I must say. I should have said it yesterday, but my head was going round. Marie, have you forgiven me? I know I was a swine, but truly I'm sorry, and I love you . . ."

"You're my husband," she said with her hand in his. "I forgive you."

Marie tended him gently, bathing his good eye with a solution of water, lemon juice and vinegar. She rubbed a salve of white beeswax and sweet oil into the welt behind his left ear and the mark of bruises on his cheek. In a few days Colonel Latour was able to go downstairs, and in a few more he was fitted for a new uniform, and was strolling in the garden. Jean Tallien was always ready to lend the arm he needed, for the loss of an eye at first affected his balance and made him stumble. The deft hands of Nicholas Conté made him a black eyeshade, "just like Lord Nelson's," as the maker breezily said, and Charles declared he was twice the man when he could see who he was talking to. There were many people at the Institute eager to talk to a man from Jaffa, until the interest shifted to a man from Upper Egypt, who had brought his portfolio with him.

This was Citizen Vivant Denon, who had joined General Desaix in order to draw antiquities, and had drawn them with such passion that the officer assigned to keep him out of danger was all too often in danger himself. "Hurry up, for God's sake, citizen, the Mamelukes are upon us!" The soldiers fought well against Murad Bey, but they too became enthusiasts for antiquity, and, as Denon loved to recall, when they reached the site of ancient Thebes and saw the ruins of Luxor and Karnak, the French troops were so impressed that they formed ranks of their own accord while their bands played, and presented arms in honour of the majestic spectacle.

Denon was received by General Bonaparte, who remarked that he envied Desaix, who had no plague to contend with, and later came out to the Institute to admire the beautiful portfolio of drawings from antiquity. The sketches led to the great *Description de l'Egypte* which appeared in ten volumes, and were to earn for Denon the curatorship of the Louvre. Meantime, Bonaparte suggested, the artist should come with him to the Pyramids of Giza, and draw the Great Pyramid and the Sphinx.

"Are you really going to Giza, *mon général*?" said Marie. They were all sitting round a garden table, Napoleon, Denon, Tallien (making notes for his paper), Charles and herself, and she had been very quiet while the Arab servants served coffee, leaving the talk to the men.

"Yes!" said Napoleon. "I intend to leave about the middle of July."

"With Lavalette as your ADC, sir?" hinted Charles Latour.

"No, I'm taking de Beauharnais."

"But I thought Eugène was wounded?" said Marie.

"Not so badly as poor Charles, and he made a good recovery. I'll tell him you're concerned about him. Denon, you'd better come back and have dinner with me at Elfi Bey. I want to discuss your coming to Giza."

"Always in a hurry," said Tallien when the two men had left. "Charles, shall I give you a hand to get up those stairs?"

"Marie lets me lean on her." And lean on her Charles did after he had bumped against the newel post at the foot of the staircase, as he was in the middle of saying that he used to be jealous of Eugène de Beauharnais. Perhaps Napoleon's slightly patronising "poor Charles" had pricked the memory of an older jealousy, for no sooner were they in what had been a sickroom than he was begging Marie to let him love her, and she, touched by his pleading for what he used to take without asking, went to bed with him again.

Vivant Denon begged leave to continue his studies of Upper Egypt and allow his colleagues of the Arts Commission to continue the work already begun at the Pyramids, and he was wise. Bonaparte did not stay long at Giza. He had been keeping in close touch with Marmont at Alexandria, who had been ordered to watch for the sails of the Turkish fleet reported to have sailed from Constantinople. Now an express from Marmont informed him that not only had the Turks been seen at sea, they had landed at Aboukir, captured the fort and massacred the garrison.

With the minimum of delay Bonaparte massed an army at that place of the ill-omened name. Les Béquières – Aboukir – where his huge armada had been unable to land, where it had been destroyed by Nelson, was now the site of a great attack by the Ottoman Empire, which he had come to save. Outnumbered by two to one, Napoleon struck one of the lightning blows which the Austrians knew so well. With a ferocious charge by Murat's cavalry, and an artillery attack on the English blockade ships waiting to support the Turks, the enemy was driven into the sea, and a brilliant tactical victory was won.

Napoleon did not immediately leave the scene of action. Two of his best leaders, Lannes and Murat, had been wounded in the fighting, and he wished to supervise the aftermath of battle himself. He had a new luxury, a campaign tent of green striped material equipped with a folding table and folding chairs, and inside the tent, sheltered from the damnable, eternal sun of Egypt, he saw his Staff, heard reports from the outposts, and settled the exchange of prisoners. So few of the Turks had survived the long swim to the British ships that they had no Gazi, nor Pasha, nor Bashi-Bazouk worth offering in exchange, but there were two or three Frenchmen, taken on the first day at Aboukir fort, that he wanted back. He told two majors – that was about the right rank – to row out to the British ships under a flag of truce and negotiate the exchange with Commodore Hood.

"Your pardon, citizen general, it is Sir Sidney Smith who is in temporary command of the squadron."

"What? Sir Smith? The Smith who was at Acre? The devil you say! But go ahead, what are you waiting for?"

The majors, who both had a smattering of English, were back in two hours. It was all right, the exchange was arranged, and Sir Sidney, with his compliments, thought General Bonaparte might like to have a look at the French newspapers.

Confound his impudence! But the roll of papers respectfully laid on the little table was too tempting: there had been no news from France for months.

Except, of course, the news brought by Monsieur Hamelin, merchant of Trieste. Napoleon sent for an oil lamp, sent for some food and wine, told Eugène they would not leave for Cairo until morning, and began to read.

It was all there, what Hamelin had said, but in detail far worse. There was a coalition against France. His old adversary the Archduke Charles had defeated Jourdan and the army of the Upper Rhine in March and Masséna in Switzerland in June. Old Schérer had been defeated (no surprise) commanding the army of Italy at Magnano in April. The Russian general Suvarov had entered Milan, dissolved the Cisalpine Republic and occupied Turin. It had all vanished, his French Europe, while Napoleon Bonaparte, of his own wilfulness, had been dreaming his eastern dream.

Eugène de Beauharnais, still weak from his wound, slept on the floor of the tent that night. When he woke the dawn was breaking, the oil lamp was guttering, and his stepfather, grey with exhaustion, was shaking his shoulder.

"Come on, Eugène," he said. "We've got to get back to Cairo as fast as we can travel."

It seemed to all of them as if there were some sort of crisis, but if so it didn't follow its usual course. No storming, no orders and counter-orders, just urgent messages sent to Nasriya for Denon – fortunately caught before he left to join Desaix, Monge and Berthollet, and then long separate conferences with the three of them. Hours spent alone with Berthier. Then hours spent in writing letters by hand. Not, as Bonaparte had been doing for some time past, dictating to two secretaries at a time, one relieving the other. Complete concentration on whatever the matter in hand might be. Lavalette, opening the door apologetically, realised that.

"Madame Bellilotte's compliments, *mon général*, and she expected you for luncheon at one o'clock."

"What of it?"

"Sir, it's half past two."

"Tell her I'm busy."

This burst of solitary activity lasted for three days, and on the fourth Napoleon began to clear away the newspapers the Englishman had sent, and which no one but his visitors had seen. There were two English rags among them, only fit for trash, he thought, until his eye caught, as he turned the pages over, a name he recognised.

Bonaparte rang for one of his acting ADCs.

"Get that translated . . . Into French, of course, you fool!"

There was a delay, because the interpreter said his job was to translate Arabic, not English, but when the translation lay on his desk Bonaparte read it quickly through and nodded.

"Send a vehicle to the Institute to bring Colonel and Madame Latour here at once."

Another delay, much longer, and then Marie came in alone, without a curtsey, twisting her gloves in one hand, her hair out of curl and wearing an old black dress as if she had come straight from her work-bench.

"Where's your husband?"

"I'm sorry, Dr Berthollet is keeping him in bed. He says Charles is suffering from delayed shock."

"M'm. He ought to be the one to hear this, but you can read it."

"What is it?" she asked, as he put the paper into her hand.

"It's the translation of a notice that appeared in a London paper called *The Times*, dated the eleventh of June. Read it aloud, I'd like to hear it again."

The Marquis de la Tour de Vesle, one of the leaders of the French émigré colony in Britain, died at his London residence yesterday, aged sixty-three. He is survived by his widow and one son.

Napoleon almost laughed at Marie's startled look.

"*Mes condoléances, madame la marquise,*" he said.

"Oh!" she said, "thank you. I can't pretend to be sorry,

because I never knew him, but this might mean a difference to Charles."

"What, to be called *monsieur le marquis*?"

"He'll like that too, but I meant – if his mother gets in touch with him now that she's alone. I know he's always hoping she will, and she never does."

"There was considerable property, wasn't there?"

"National Property, where it wasn't vandalised."

"You ought to go back to Paris, both of you, and see about it. Don't let those Commissioners of Emigré Property, or whatever they call themselves, cheat you out of it."

"Back to Paris! That's so very likely, isn't it?"

Napoleon dropped his abrupt tone and took her hand. "I'm going back to France myself," he said gently. "Come with me."

20

Marie Latour stood by the little bay of Bulaq, and though the night was cloudy and warm she shivered. The men were all busy about the little convoy that was to take them back to Europe, and they were as quiet as possible, for even though they were three miles from Alexandria someone might hear them and raise the alarm, discovering that the General in Chief, who had arrived in these waters at the head of an army, was leaving by stealth with only a few friends around him.

Nobody spoke to her, nobody seemed to feel that this was an ignominious departure. Charles had been helped aboard the frigate among the first, with the other invalids: Duroc, Lannes and Murat, the latter two wounded at the Battle of Aboukir. Eugène de Beauharnais should have been among them, but he was faithful in his attendance on his stepfather, who would go aboard among the last. The two men must have been quite near her, for she heard Napoleon's clear voice in the darkness:

"Eugène, you are going to see your mother again!"

She missed Eugène's reply, for at that moment her arm was seized and a rough voice said, "Now then, citizeness, it's time for you to go on board."

General Bonaparte had not been able to leave Cairo as soon as he would have liked. One of the private letters he wrote after he read the English papers received Admiral Ganteaume's answer that it was impossible to move at present with an Anglo-Turkish fleet blocking the way, but he had laid his hands on two frigates and two *avisos* as requested, and would move them into Bulaq cove as soon as he could.

The general turned back to routine matters, but first he went out to Nasriya to congratulate the Marquis de la Tour de Vesle. He found that *aristo* up and in an armchair, having recovered from his delayed shock as soon as he heard Marie's exciting news. He was thrilled to be going back to France, understood the need for secrecy, and was very willing to discuss his inheritance with Napoleon.

"You say your father's house at Versailles was destroyed in 1792, and your mother's estate in the Ile de France was declared National Property and sold to a speculator? You can get compensation for that, I know."

"Can I really?"

"Of course you can. Talk it over with Jean Tallien, he's an expert on National Property, he can tell you where to apply. Now, what about the Vesle estate?"

"The Prussians knocked it about pretty badly, and the estate agent was guillotined, so I just don't know . . ."

"Well, why the devil don't you go and find out? You're a landowner now – *monsieur le marquis.*"

"I'm a soldier, sir. Do you want me to retire from the army?"

"Because of your eye?"

Charles said yes.

"Well," smiled Napoleon, and tweaked his ear, "I don't see why having one eye should be a handicap. Milord Nelson seems to do quite well with one eye and one arm, doesn't he?"

Back in Cairo, the secretaries were called in to handle routine correspondence. The letters to the Directory which never reached them, the appeals for 6,000 reinforcements, the admission (putting it rather low) that the General in Chief had lost fifteen per cent of his effectives in Syria. Alone, Napoleon planned a letter to Kléber, who would succeed him in the command he had coveted so long.

With the Divan he planned the annual celebration of the Prophet's birth. On 15 August he gave a dinner to celebrate his own thirtieth birthday, which incidentally was the fourth anniversary of the Latours' wedding. They were there and so was Bellilotte, fawning on Napoleon and also on Marie.

Bellilotte's day was over, and she knew it. Napoleon had paid her one or two perfunctory visits since his return from Syria, but he was tired of her. She had been his mistress for three months without the slightest sign of breeding, and she was no longer his play girl, his relaxation, but a burden. He intended to leave her behind in Cairo, of course with a suitable provision for her future.

Marie Latour, now, was a different kind of woman. Because he sensed her criticism of what he was about to do – had she said, or had he dreamed it, that he was "deserting the army" – he was careful to explain the details of their trip to her.

"When I get the word from Ganteaume," he told her in the garden at Nasriya, "the Scholars, all three of them, will go on one day, the soldiers and you and I will go on another. Taking the minimum of baggage, and we'll all meet at Bulaq cove. The frigates waiting for us are called *La Muiron* and *La Carrère*, both armed. The *avisos* will be armed too. Yes?"

"Excuse me for interrupting, but are these the same frigates that escaped with Admiral Villeneuve?"

"No. They're two frigates Ganteaume bought from Cyprus, with French privateer captains and Cypriot crews. Venetian-built and very slow, and not by any means as comfortable as *L'Orient*."

"I hope I shan't be as sick as I was aboard *L'Orient*."

Napoleon laughed. "You won't be seasick in *La Muiron*. We'll stick close to the shore and avoid the storms."

"And what's our destination? Toulon?"

"No, not Toulon. Fréjus."

It was cramped and crowded in the frigate, so cramped that when she heard the rattle of chains and felt the movement, Marie crawled out of her bunk, pulled on a dress and went on deck. Above her head the sails were set, the sailors were moving about, and Napoleon was standing alone by the rail with his eyes fixed on the last star paling in the dawn. Already the ship was standing out in the bay where so many lives had been lost.

Napoleon turned at her approach and said,

"Good-morning! We're under way at last."

"Yes," she said. "General, I've a confession to make. I couldn't help hearing what you said to Eugène down at the cove last night."

"What was that?"

"You said, 'Eugène, you are going to see your mother again!'"

"That was to make the boy happy."

"Of course. But you? Are you going to see her again – Joséphine?"

There was a long pause. Then "I want to talk to you about Joséphine," Napoleon said. "But not here. Wait until our voyage is safely over. Wait till we're back on French soil again."

The little convoy proceeded slowly along the African shore, the look-outs constantly on the watch for British ships or Barbary pirates. The Scholars, Berthollet, Monge and Denon, were all in *La Carrère*, and in *La Muiron*. Bonaparte complained bitterly that there was nobody to give him a game of chess. "I wish your uncle Prosper were here," he told Marie, "we had some good games at the Régence, a thousand years ago." They took turns in playing his favourite card game, reversi, and Napoleon cheated them all for the sheer fun of cheating, and at the end of the game divided his winnings among the losers. They dared not show a light after darkness fell, when the Cypriot sailors were forbidden to sing.

Tediously, furtively, the little convoy flying a flag of convenience instead of the Tricolore passed Tripoli unchallenged and crept along the Algerian coast. Off

Algiers the captain spoke to a *tartane* running for Genoa, and what he heard made him change his course. Marie, who had not understood the *lingua franca* of the exchange, asked Napoleon if they were heading for Fréjus now.

"Not yet. That Genoese skipper says there are two British frigates hanging about, so we're going to dodge them and take refuge in Corsica – "

"Corsica! Oh, how wonderful!"

"You always wanted to see it. We're making for my birthplace, Ajaccio – if they allow us to land."

"I'll see them damned if they don't," said the captain belligerently. "We come from Alexandria, right, but we've no plague on board and we've been forty days at sea. We'll get *pratique*."

The scent of Corsica came out to meet *La Muiron*, that mingled odour of flowers, pines, lentisk and thyme, which Napoleon told them was the perfume of *la macchia*. He grew excited, Marie could see, as they neared Ajaccio, where a row of low white houses stood behind a white beach, and some fishermen working offshore recognised him and began to cheer. If the quarantine officers had attempted to prevent *La Muiron* from entering harbour there would have been a riot, for it seemed as if the whole population of Ajaccio was on the dock to greet Napoleon and accompany him to his old home. To the wild native music, to cheer upon cheer, he stepped on French soil again.

"*Vive Bonaparte! Viva il Liberatore!*"

An elderly woman struggled through the crowd on the quay, calling out "*Caro figlio!*" and Napoleon, crying "*Madre!*" swept her off her feet in a huge embrace.

"Marie," he explained, "this is Signora Caterina, my first nurse. Please shake her hand."

With Marie's hand in hers, and tears in her own eyes, the woman asked Napoleon:

"Is this your wife?"

"No, no, Mamma Caterina, this gentleman, the March-ese della Torre, is her husband, and you must take great care of the *signora marchesa* while she is the guest of Corsica. You men!" turning to the fascinated bystanders, "find a conveyance to take my friends to the Casa Bonaparte!"

Every vehicle in Ajaccio was placed at his disposal, and after some confusion a procession of mule carts started with General Bonaparte in the lead, and after him the Scholars, the soldiers, the captain of the frigate, the mayor, two priests and a man selling candy. Flutes and drums were heartily played, and a band of urchins let off firecrackers. It was a real *festa*, and Marie watched it enchanted. She and Charles were in the second mule cart to draw up in front of a three-storeyed, brownstone house in a narrow street, behind a small square shaded by acacia trees. Bonaparte was waiting at the door. "Be the welcome guests," he bade them formally, and Marie exclaimed,

"Oh, *mon général*, what a wonderful ovation you get!"

"Yes, it was very pleasant," agreed Napoleon. "I saw several faces in the crowd that I remembered from six years ago, when I had to hustle my mother and the young ones out of Corsica after I declared against Paoli, when he handed over the island to the British."

"That was in 1793," said Marie. "Perhaps it's time for an act of oblivion."

"Perhaps – in Corsica," agreed Napoleon. "Marie, you need rest more than any of us, and here come Mamma Caterina and her daughter to take you to your room. Rest well beneath this roof!"

He gave his arm to Charles Latour, and Marie went upstairs with the two women. Caterina's daughter spoke French, and told her she was to have "Madame Letizia's room" which the general's mother had refurnished on her last visit ("after the house was wrecked and looted in '93, *signora marchesa*"). A very modern room it was, with red and white striped wallpaper and yellow damask uphol-stery, and Marie fell asleep to the sound of the last firecrackers and masculine revelry from the floor below.

Next day Marie explored Ajaccio with her husband,

followed by an interested crowd, and the Casa Bonaparte with Mammuccia, as she had learned to call Napoleon's old nurse. It had once been divided into three apartments, all teeming with members of the family, but the children had gone away, and Madame Letizia lived in France. That night it was crowded again, when Napoleon gave a dinner for forty people in the banqueting gallery which his ambitious father had added to the tenement house.

Marie slept late after the banquet, and was awakened by Charles dropping his boots and saying something about shooting, after which she slept again and woke when her breakfast tray arrived. Against the coffee-pot was a little note, which when deciphered read:

"Will you have luncheon on the terrace with me at 12 noon today? – B."

Another movement order! She had not yet seen the terrace, another of the late Carlo Buonaparte's additions to his home. She found it overlooking the garden at the back of the house, with a little summer house at one end, and a row of pots holding geraniums and herbs. The scent of *la macchia*, which to the French girl was *le maquis*, rose up from the neglected garden, a wilderness of orange trees, roses, palms and a few unpruned vines.

Bonaparte appeared on the stroke of twelve, in uniform of course. She had only once seen him in civilian clothes.

"What have you done with all the men?" she asked him when the ceremonious greetings were over.

"Sent them off with a guide for a day's rough shooting in the mountains. Even Denon, who wanted to stay here and draw."

"I hope it won't be too much for Charles."

"Berthollet will keep an eye on him, and I wanted to have you all to myself. Ah! here comes our lunch."

There was a coarse, clean cloth on the summer house table, with two-pronged forks and bone-handled knives. Mammaccia's daughter set out plates of sliced *coppa* and salad, *bruccio* cream cheese with maize cakes, and a dessert of chestnuts and pomegranates. It was Napoleon's favourite meal as a child, and he offered Marie a glass of "our own wine". It was a delicate rosé.

"This didn't come from those vines down there!" said Marie.

"We own two vineyards," said Napoleon proudly. "And a cottage. My mother had this shelter built especially for me, and when I was a second lieutenant on leave I used to study fortification here." Marie nodded sympathetically, and Napoleon went on, "On this very spot, before there was a shelter here, I stood crying at my mother's knee. I was bidding her goodbye before I went to Autun to learn French. I remember so well that she didn't cry herself, or pet me. She only said '*Coraggio, Napoleone!*'"

"She must have been sorry to see her little boy go so far away," said Marie softly.

Napoleon smiled. "She was a Spartan mother . . . Come, my dear, if you're finished, shall we sit in the shade?"

They walked down the terrace to where a wide wooden seat stood in the shadow cast by a mimosa tree. Napoleon began:

"You asked me to tell you if I intended to see Joséphine again."

"It was an impertinent question, I'm afraid."

"Oh no, you deserve an answer. I told you all my troubles at Nasriya, remember? Besides, I can answer you more fully now."

"How? There's been no news from Paris that I know."

"That night, when *La Muiron* was still in Bulaq cove, Eugène told me he'd had a letter from Hortense. It arrived in Cairo just before he left, the first of many letters from the poor child ever to reach him, and he had no chance to tell me about it until we were alone in our cabin."

"Of course she wrote about their mother?"

"Yes, and very cleverly worded it was. Hortense said maman was well, but living very quietly. Not going out to parties, not entertaining. Which means, I suppose, that Captain Hippolyte Charles has had enough." He waited for Marie to speak, but she was silent.

"*But*," said Napoleon forcibly, "Hortense also said that maman had bought the little estate called La Malmaison, that she tried to wheedle me into buying before we left for Egypt. A manor house and forty-five acres, if you please! Well, that was the last straw. I knew she'd pledged my credit to pay for it, as she did with her silly decorations. I won't go back to her. I won't even see her, and our lawyers can work out the divorce . . . Well, are you dumb, Marie? Say something, can't you!"

She said, without meeting his eyes, "I suppose you know best."

"Of course I do." Napoleon said more calmly, "I'm sorry to inflict all that on you, my dear, but it had to be done. Now let's say no more about Joséphine, she belongs to the past . . . I want you to tell me what you think my chances are in France. The captain tells me we can sail to Fréjus in a couple of days."

Marie managed to laugh. "After your reception in Ajaccio, I should think they'll carry you shoulder high in Fréjus."

"Corsica isn't the mainland, Marie. Two years ago I came back victorious from Italy, now I've come back defeated from the east."

"But that's the French fortune, isn't it? We saw it all through the Revolution – up one year and down the next. And you weren't defeated in the east, except at Acre. You won three great victories at the Pyramids, at Mont Thabor and Aboukir, quite equal to Lodi Bridge and Arcola."

"Lodi Bridge," Napoleon mused. "Then I saw what I might become. I already saw the world beneath me, as if I were being carried through the air."

"Then if you know what you may become, go ahead! Fulfil your destiny! You won't do it by sitting in Corsica worrying about what they think of you in a French provincial town like Fréjus."

"But what about Paris?" said Napoleon. "Go on, Marie, you're a wise girl. Tell me frankly what the Directors are going to think of me."

"You won't like what I'm going to say . . . First of all, your enemies are going to say you left the Army in Egypt in the lurch, without warning and by night."

"I left a letter for Kléber – "

"And then you'll be blamed for shooting your prisoners at Jaffa."

"Marie, there wasn't food for my own men, let alone for Syrians. And half of those men were the troops from El Arish, who broke their parole to go to Damascus, and joined the garrison at Jaffa."

"People soon forget these details. They'll only remember that you shot your prisoners."

Napoleon stared at the girl he still thought of as Marie Fontaine. As pretty as ever in her old striped dress, with her dark blue eyes fixed so earnestly on his!

"Are you my conscience?" he said. "You speak to me as none of my Staff would dare to speak. They only want to flatter me upon my victories."

Marie had a sickening recollection of little Dr Legendre, at Milan, saying "Victories are easy for a man who has no regard for human life", and nerved herself for a final effort.

"You mustn't leave Joséphine," she said. "I know she's been a fool and worse, but it would do you too much harm to abandon her. Your troops call her your Lady Luck, and think of her as your inspiration – "

"Soldiers are sentimental fellows – "

"Can you afford to lose their faith in you?"

She thought, as he moved in his seat, that Napoleon was about to rise and walk away. Instead, he moved only to put his arm around her.

"Marie, there's no one like you," he said. "You are the girl I should have married long ago, when we were young."

"How many years is it, since we were young?"

"Seven. It was the summer of '92 when I first came to the Pharmacie Fontaine."

"And we were two innocents among the lettuces and the pot-herbs, as you used to say. We sat in the garden talking while Paris raged around us. The king was taken to prison and the priests were massacred while we talked."

"I think I was half in love with you that summer," said Napoleon Bonaparte. "Did you know that?"

He saw tears in her eyes. "I hoped, but I didn't know," she said. Then, with a sudden decision to show him her heart, she said, "But when you came back to Paris in '95, and we met again at the Victims' Ball – if you had told me that night what you've told me today – I would have followed you to the ends of the earth."

He said stupidly, "I never knew that before."

"But you didn't speak. I introduced you to Joséphine at the Victims' Ball, and from that moment you were infatuated with her, and never gave a thought to me." She was struggling with her sobs now, as Napoleon said sharply,

"You married Latour three months later. Why?"

"That was why."

He lifted her hands, and kissed them. "Oh, my dear, my very dear one," he said brokenly, "I've been a great fool. I saw you constantly, so brave in danger, so steadfast in your tasks, and I never realised you cared for me . . . Will you kiss me just once, my love?"

"I could never kiss you just once, Napoleon."

"Then, Marie, if this is true – will you leave Latour for me?"

"No."

"Why not? You don't love him. I know that, and I think he knows it too."

"Our love ended long ago, but I swore to keep faith with him when we were married, and I'll keep my word."

"You didn't take your vows in church. You entered into a civil contract, as I did myself. It can be set aside as easily as it was made."

"That doesn't matter. Charles needs me, Napoleon. How can I leave him, maimed and weakened as he is? He's going back to cares and problems which are bound to weary and worry him. He'll need me then."

Without begging for one kiss, the man she had always loved seized her in his arms and covered her lips, her cheeks, her eyes with kisses. "Do you know what you're doing?" he said. "You're sending me back to France like the poor child I once was, lonely among strangers – "

Marie smiled through her tears. "Not among strangers," she said. "The world will soon be at your feet. *Coraggio, Napoleone!*"